NIGHTS AT THE CIRCUS

Angela Carter was born in 1940. She read English at Bristol University, and from 1976–8 was fellow in Creative Writing at Sheffield University. She lived in Japan, the United States and Australia. Her first novel, *Shadow Dance*, was published in 1965, followed by *The Magic Toyshop* (1967, John Llewellyn Rhys Prize), *Several Perceptions* (1968, Somerset Maugham Award), *Heroes and Villains* (1969), *Love* (1971), *The Passion of New Eve* (1977), *Nights at the Circus* (1984, James Tait Black Memorial Prize) and *Wise Children* (1991). She published three previous collections of short stories, *Fireworks* (1974), *The Bloody Chamber* (1979, Cheltenham Festival of Literature Award) and *Black Venus* (1985). She was the author of *The Sadeian Woman: An Exercise in Cultural History* (1979), and two collections of journalism, *Nothing Sacred* (1982) and *Expletives Deleted* (1992). She died in February 1992.

D1464884

BY ANGELA CARTER

Fiction

Shadow Dance
The Magic Toyshop
Several Perceptions
Heroes And Villains
Love
The Infernal Desire Machines Of Dr Hoffman
Fireworks
The Passion Of New Eve
The Bloody Chamber
Nights At The Circus
Black Venus
Wise Children
American Ghosts And Old World Wonders

Non-Fiction

The Sadeian Woman: An Exercise In Cultural History
Nothing Sacred: Selected Writings
The Virago Book of Fairytales (editor)
Expletives Deleted

Angela Carter

NIGHTS AT
THE CIRCUS

This edition published 2003
by BCA
by arrangement with Vintage
The Random House Group Ltd

CN 124677

Printed and bound in Great Britain by
Mackays of Chatham plc, Chatham, Kent

LONDON

ONE

'Lor' love you, sir!' Fevvers sang out in a voice that clanged like dustbin lids. 'As to my place of birth, why, I first saw light of day right here in smoky old London, didn't I! Not billed the "Cockney Venus", for nothing, sir, though they could just as well 'ave called me "Helen of the High Wire", due to the unusual circumstances in which I come ashore – for I never docked via what you might call the *normal channels*, sir, oh, dear me, no; but, just like Helen of Troy, was *hatched*.

'Hatched out of a bloody great egg while Bow Bells rang, as ever is!'

The blonde guffawed uproariously, slapped the marbly thigh on which her wrap fell open and flashed a pair of vast, blue, indecorous eyes at the young reporter with his open notebook and his poised pencil, as if to dare him: 'Believe it or not!' Then she spun round on her swivelling dressing-stool – it was a plush-topped, backless piano stool, lifted from the rehearsal room – and confronted herself with a grin in the mirror as she ripped six inches of false lash from her left eyelid with an incisive gesture and a small, explosive, rasping sound.

Fevvers, the most famous *aerialiste* of the day; her slogan, 'Is she fact or is she fiction?' And she didn't let you forget it for a minute; this query, in the French language, in foot-high letters, blazed forth from a wall-size poster, souvenir of her Parisian triumphs, dominating her London dressing-room. Something hectic, something fittingly impetuous and dashing about that poster, the preposterous depiction of a young woman shooting up like a rocket, whee! in a burst of agitated sawdust towards an unseen trapeze somewhere above in the wooden heavens of the Cirque d'Hiver. The artist had chosen to depict her ascent from behind – bums aloft, you might say; up she goes, in a steatopygous perspective, shaking out about her those tremendous red and purple pinions, pinions large enough, powerful enough to bear up such a big girl as she. And she was a *big* girl.

Evidently this Helen took after her putative father, the swan, around the shoulder parts.

But these notorious and much-debated wings, the source of her fame, were stowed away for the night under the soiled quilting of her baby-blue satin dressing-gown, where they made an uncomfortable-looking pair of bulges, shuddering the surface of the taut fabric from time to time as if desirous of breaking loose. ('How does she do that?' pondered the reporter.)

'In Paris, they called me *l'Ange Anglaise,* the English Angel, "not English but an angel", as the old saint said,' she'd told him, jerking her head at that favourite poster which, she'd remarked off-handedly, had been scrawled on the stone by 'some Frog dwarf who asked me to piddle on his thingy before he'd get his crayons so much as out sparing your blushes.' Then – 'a touch of sham?' – she'd popped the cork of a chilled magnum of champagne between her teeth. A hissing flute of bubbly stood beside her own elbow on the dressing-table, the still-crepitating bottle lodged negligently in the toilet jug, packed in ice that must have come from a fishmonger's for a shiny scale or two stayed trapped within the chunks. And this twice-used ice must surely be the source of the marine aroma – something fishy about the Cockney Venus – that underlay the hot, solid composite of perfume, sweat, greasepaint and raw, leaking gas that made you feel you breathed the air in Fevvers' dressing-room in lumps.

One lash off, one lash on, Fevvers leaned back a little to scan the asymmetric splendour reflected in her mirror with impersonal gratification.

'And now,' she said, 'after my conquests on the continent' (which she pronounced, 'congtinong') 'here's the prodigal daughter home again to London, my lovely London that I love so much. London – as dear old Dan Leno calls it, "a little village on the Thames of which the principal industries are the music hall and the confidence trick".'

She tipped the young reporter a huge wink in the ambiguity of the mirror and briskly stripped the other set of false eyelashes.

Her native city welcomed her home with such delirium that the *Illustrated London News* dubbed the phenomenon, 'Fevvermania'. Everywhere you saw her picture; the shops were crammed with 'Fevvers' garters, stockings, fans, cigars, shaving soap . . . She even lent it to a brand of baking powder; if you added a spoonful of the stuff, up in the air went your sponge cake, just as she did. Heroine of the hour, object of learned discussion and profane surmise, this Helen launched a thousand quips, mostly on the lewd side. ('Have you heard the one about how Fevvers *got it up* for the travelling salesman . . .') Her name was on the lips of all, from duchess to costermonger: 'Have you seen

Fevvers?' And then: 'How does she do it?' And then: 'Do you think she's *real*?'

The young reporter wanted to keep his wits about him so he juggled' with glass, notebook and pencil, surreptitiously looking for a place to stow the glass where she could not keep filling it – perhaps on that black iron mantelpiece whose brutal corner, jutting out over his perch on the horsehair sofa, promised to brain him if he made a sudden movement. His quarry had him effectively trapped. His attempts to get rid of the damn' glass only succeeded in dislodging a noisy torrent of concealed *billets doux*, bringing with them from the mantelpiece a writhing snakes' nest of silk stockings, green, yellow, pink, scarlet, black, that introduced a powerful note of stale feet, final ingredient in the highly personal aroma, 'essence of Fevvers', that clogged the room. When she got round to it, she might well bottle the smell, and sell it. She never missed a chance.

Fevvers ignored his discomfiture.

Perhaps the stockings had descended in order to make common cause with the other elaborately intimate garments, wormy with ribbons, carious with lace, redolent of use, that she hurled round the room apparently at random during the course of the many dressings and undressings which her profession demanded. A large pair of frilly drawers, evidently fallen where they had light-heartedly been tossed, draped some object, clock or marble bust or funerary urn, anything was possible since it was obscured completely. A redoubtable corset of the kind called an Iron Maiden poked out of the empty coalscuttle like the pink husk of a giant prawn emerging from its den, trailing long laces like several sets of legs. The room, in all, was a mistresspiece of exquisitely feminine squalor, sufficient, in its homely way, to intimidate a young man who had led a less sheltered life than this one.

His name was Jack Walser. Himself, he hailed from California, from the other side of a world all of whose four corners he had knocked about for most of his five-and-twenty summers – a picaresque career which rubbed off his own rough edges; now he boasts the smoothest of manners and you would see in his appearance nothing of the scapegrace urchin who, long ago, stowed away on a steamer bound from 'Frisco to Shanghai. In the course of his adventuring, he discovered in himself a talent with words, and an even greater aptitude for finding himself in the right place at the right time. So he stumbled upon his profession, and, at this time in his life, he filed copy to a New York newspaper for a living, so he could travel wherever he pleased whilst retaining the privileged irresponsibility of the journalist, the professional necessity to see all and believe nothing which cheerfully combined, in Walser's personality, with a characteristically American generosity towards the brazen lie. His avocation suited him right down to the ground on which he took good care to keep his feet. Call him Ishmael; but Ishmael with an expense account, and, besides, a thatch of unruly flaxen hair, a ruddy, pleasant, square-jawed face and eyes the cool grey of scepticism.

Yet there remained something a little unfinished about him, still. He was like a handsome house that has been let, furnished. There were scarcely any of those little, what you might call *personal* touches to his personality, as if his habit of suspending belief extended even unto his own being. I say he had a propensity for 'finding himself in the right place at the right time'; yet it was almost as if he himself were an *objet trouvé*, for, subjectively, *himself* he never found, since it was not his *self* which he sought.

He would have called himself a 'man of action'. He subjected his life to a series of cataclysmic shocks because he loved to hear his bones rattle. That was how he knew he was alive.

So Walser survived the plague in Setzuan, the assegai in Africa, a sharp dose of buggery in a bedouin tent beside the Damascus road and much more, yet none of this had altered to any great degree the invisible child inside the man, who indeed remained the same dauntless lad who used to haunt Fisherman's Wharf hungrily eyeing the tangled sails upon the water until at last he, too, went off with the tide towards an endless promise. Walser had not experienced his experience *as* experience; sandpaper his outsides as experience might, his inwardness had been left untouched. In all his young life, he had not felt so much as one single quiver of introspection. If he was afraid of nothing, it was not because he was brave; like the boy in the fairy story who does not know how to shiver, Walser did not know *how* to be afraid. So his habitual disengagement was involuntary; it was not the result of judgment, since judgment involves the positives and negatives of belief.

He was a kaleidoscope equipped with consciousness. That was why he was a good reporter. And yet the kaleidoscope was growing a little weary with all the spinning; war and disaster had not quite succeeded in fulfilling that promise which the future once seemed to hold, and, for the moment, still shaky from a recent tussle with yellow fever, he was taking it a little easy, concentrating on those 'human interest' angles that, hitherto, had eluded him.

Since he was a good reporter, he was necessarily a connoisseur of the tall tale. So now he was in London he went to talk to Fevvers, for a series of interviews tentatively entitled: 'Great Humbugs of the World'.

Free and easy as his American manners were, they met their match in those of the *aerialiste*, who now shifted from one buttock to the other and – 'better out than in, sir' – let a ripping fart ring round the room. She peered across her shoulder, again, to see how he took *that*. Under the screen of her bonhomerie – bonnnefemmerie? – he noted she was wary. He cracked her a white grin. He relished *this* commission!

On that European tour of hers, Parisians shot themselves in droves for her sake; not just Lautrec but *all* the post-impressionists vied to paint her; Willy gave her supper and she gave Colette some good advice. Alfred Jarry proposed marriage. When she arrived at the railway station in Cologne, a cheering bevy of students unhitched her horses and pulled her carriage to the hotel themselves. In Berlin, her photograph was displayed everywhere in the newsagents' windows next to that of the Kaiser. In Vienna, she deformed the dreams of that entire generation who would immediately commit themselves whole-heartedly to psychoanalysis. Everywhere she went, rivers parted for her, wars were threatened, suns eclipsed, showers of frogs and foot-wear were reported in the press and the King of Portugal gave her a skipping rope of egg-shaped pearls, which she banked.

Now all London lies beneath her flying feet; and, the very morning of this self-same October's day, in this very dressing-room, here, in the Alhambra Music Hall, among her dirty underwear, has she not signed a *six-figure contract* for a Grand Imperial Tour, to Russia and then Japan, during which she will astonish a brace of emperors? And, from Yokohama, she will then ship to Seattle, for the start of a Grand Democratic Tour of the United States of America.

All across the Union, audiences clamour for her arrival, which will coincide with that of the new century.

For we are at the fag-end, the smouldering cigar-butt, of a nineteenth century which is just about to be ground out in the ashtray of history. It is the final, waning, season of the year of Our Lord, eighteen hundred and ninety nine. And Fevvers has all the *éclat* of a new era about to take off.

Walser is here, ostensibly, to 'puff' her; and, if it is humanly possible, to explode her, either as well as, or instead of. Though do not think the revelation she is a hoax will finish her on the halls; far from it. If she isn't suspect, where's the controversy? What's the news?

'Ready for another snifter?' She pulled the dripping bottle from the scaly ice.

At close quarters, it must be said that she looked more like a dray mare than an angel. At six feet two in her stockings, she would have to give Walser a couple of inches in order to match him and, though they said she was 'divinely tall', there was, off-stage, not much of the divine about her unless there were gin palaces in heaven where she might preside behind the bar. Her face, broad and oval as a meat dish, had been thrown on a common wheel out of coarse clay; nothing subtle about her appeal, which was just as well if she were to function as the democratically elected divinity of the imminent century of the Common Man.

She invitingly shook the bottle until it ejaculated afresh. 'Put hairs on your chest!' Walser, smiling, covered his glass up with his hand. 'I've hairs on my chest already, ma'am.'

She chuckled with appreciation and topped herself up with such a lavish hand that foam spilled into her pot of dry rouge, there to hiss and splutter in a bloody froth. It was impossible to imagine any gesture of hers that did not have that kind of grand, vulgar, careless generosity about it; there was enough of her to go round, and some to spare. You did not think of calculation when you saw her, so finely judged was her performance. You'd never think she dreamed, at nights, of bank accounts, or that, to her, the music of the spheres was the jingling of cash registers. Even Walser did not guess that.

'About your name . . . ' Walser hinted, pencil at the ready.

She fortified herself with a gulp of champagne.

'When I was a baby, you could have distinguished me in a crowd of foundlings only by just this little bit of down, of yellow fluff, on my back, on top of both my shoulderblades. Just like the fluff on a chick, it was. And she who found me on the steps at Wapping, me in the laundry basket in which *persons unknown* left me, a little babe most lovingly packed up in new straw sweetly sleeping among a litter of broken eggshells, she who stumbled over this poor, abandoned creature clasped me at that moment in her arms out of the abundant goodness of her heart and took me in.

'Where, indoors, unpacking me, unwrapping my shawl, witnessing the sleepy, milky, silky fledgling, all the girls said: "Looks like the little thing's going to sprout Fevvers!" Ain't that so, Lizzie,' she appealed to her dresser.

Hitherto, this woman had taken no part in the interview but stood stiffly beside the mirror holding a glass of wine like a weapon, eyeing Jack Walser as scrupulously as if she were attempting to assess to the last farthing just how much money he had in his wallet. Now Lizzie chimed in, in a dark brown voice and a curious accent, unfamiliar to Walser, that was, had he known it, that of London-born Italians, with its double-barrelled diphthongs and glottal stops.

'That is so, indeed, sir, for wasn't I myself the one that found her? "Fevvers", we named her, and so she will be till the end of the chapter, though when we took her down to Clement Dane's to have her christened, the vicar said he'd never heard of such a name as Fevvers, so Sophie suffices for her legal handle.

'Let's get your make-up off, love.'

Lizzie was a tiny, wizened, gnome-like apparition who might have been any age between thirty and fifty; snapping, black eyes, sallow skin, an incipient moustache on the upper lip and a close-cropped frizzle of tri-coloured hair – bright grey at the roots, stark grey in between, burnt with henna at the tips. The shoulders of her skimpy, decent, black dress were white with dandruff. She had a brisk air of bristle, like a terrier bitch. There was ex-whore written all over her. Excavating a glass jar from the rubble on the dressing-table, she dug out a handful of cold cream with her crooked claw and slapped it, splat! on Fevvers' face.

'You 'ave a spot more wine, ducky, while you're waiting,' she offered Walser, scouring away at her charge with a wad of cotton wool. 'It didn't cost *us* nothing. Some jook give it you, didn't 'e. *There,* darling . . . ' wiping off the cold cream, suddenly, disconcertingly, tenderly caressing the *aerialiste* with the endearment.

'It was that French jook,' said Fevvers, emerging beefsteak red and gleaming. 'Only the one crate, the mean bastard. Have a drop more, for Gawd's sake, young feller, we're leaving you behind! Can't have the ladies pissed on their lonesome, can we? What kind of a gent are you?'

Extraordinarily raucous and metallic voice; clanging of contralto or even baritone dustbins. She submerged beneath another fistful of cold cream and there was a lengthy pause.

Oddly enough, in spite of the mess, which resembled the aftermath of an explosion in a *corsetière*'s, Fevvers' dressing-room was notable for its anonymity. Only the huge poster with the scrawled message in charcoal: *Toujours, Toulouse,* and that was only self-advertisement, a reminder to the visitor of that part of herself which, off-stage, she kept concealed. Apart from that, not even a framed photograph propped amongst the unguents on her dressing-table, just a bunch of Parma violets stuck in a jam-jar, presumably floral overspill from the mantelpiece. No lucky mascots, no black china cats nor pots of white heather. Neither personal luxuries such as armchairs or rugs. Nothing to give her away. A star's dressing-room, mean as a kitchenmaid's attic. The only bits of herself she'd impressed on her surroundings were those few blonde hairs striating the cake of Pears transparent soap in the cracked saucer on the deal washstand.

The blunt end of an enamelled hip bath full of suds of earlier ablutions stuck out from behind a canvas screen, over which was thrown a dangling set of pink fleshings so that at first glance you might have thought Fevvers had just flayed herself. If her towering headdress of dyed ostrich plumes were unceremoniously shoved into the grate, Lizzie had treated the other garment in which her mistress made her first appearance before her audience with more respect, had shaken out the robe of red and purple feathers, put it on a wooden hanger and hung it from a nail at the back of the dressing-room door, where its ciliate fringes shivered continually in the draught from the ill-fitting windows.

On the stage of the Alhambra, when the curtain went up, there she was, prone in a feathery heap under this garment, behind tinsel bars, while the band in the pit sawed and brayed away at 'Only a bird in a gilded cage'. How kitsch, how apt the melody; it pointed up the element of the meretricious in the spectacle, reminded you the girl was rumoured to have started her career in freak shows. (Check, noted Walser.) While the band played on, slowly, slowly, she got to her knees, then to her feet, still muffled up in her voluminous cape, that crested helmet of red and purple plumes on her head; she began to twist the shiny strings of her frail cage in a perfunctory way, mewing faintly to be let out.

A breath of stale night air rippled the pile on the red plush banquettes of the Alhambra, stroked the cheeks of the plaster cherubs that upheld the monumental swags above the stage.

From aloft, they lowered her trapezes.

As if a glimpse of the things inspired her to a fresh access of energy, she seized hold of the bars in a firm grip and, to the accompaniment of a drum-roll, parted them. She stepped through the gap with elaborate and uncharacteristic daintiness. The gilded cage whisked up into the flies, tangling for a moment with the trapeze.

She flung off her mantle and cast it aside. There she was.

In her pink fleshings, her breastbone stuck out like the prow of a ship; the Iron Maiden cantilevered her bosom whilst paring down her waist to almost nothing, so she looked as if she might snap in two at any careless movement. The leotard was adorned with a spangle of sequins on her crotch and nipples, nothing else. Her hair was hidden away under the dyed plumes that added a good eighteen inches to her already immense height. On her back she bore an airy burden of furled plumage as gaudy as that of a Brazilian cockatoo. On her red mouth there was an artificial smile.

Look at me! With a grand, proud, ironic grace, she exhibited herself before the eyes of the audience as if she were a marvellous present too good to be played with. Look, not touch.

She was twice as large as life and as succinctly finite as any object that is intended to be seen, not handled. Look! Hands off!

LOOK AT ME!

She rose up on tiptoe and slowly twirled round, giving the spectators a comprehensive view of her back: seeing is believing. Then she spread out her superb, heavy arms in a backwards gesture of benediction and, as she did so, her wings spread, too, a polychromatic unfolding fully six feet across, spread of an eagle, a condor, an albatross fed to excess on the same diet that makes flamingoes pink.

Oooooooh! The gasps of the beholders sent a wind of wonder rippling through the theatre.

But Walser whimsically reasoned with himself, thus: now, the wings of the birds are nothing more than the forelegs, or, as we should say, the arms, and the skeleton of a wing does indeed show elbows, wrists and fingers, all complete. So, if this lovely lady is indeed, as her publicity alleges, a fabulous bird-woman, then she, by all the laws of evolution and human reason, ought to possess no arms at all, for it's her arms that ought to be her wings!

Put it another way: would you believe a lady with four arms, all perfect, like a Hindu goddess, hinged on either side of those shoulders of a voluptuous stevedore? Because, truly, *that* is the real nature of the physiological anomaly in which Miss Fevvers is asking us to suspend disbelief.

Now, wings without arms is *one* impossible thing; but wings *with* arms is the impossible made doubly unlikely – the impossible squared. Yes, sir!

In his red-plush press box, watching her through his opera-glasses, he thought of dancers he had seen in Bangkok, presenting with their plumed, gilded, mirrored surfaces and angular, hieratic movements, infinitely more persuasive illusions of the airy creation than this over-literal winged barmaid before him. 'She tries too damn' hard,' he scribbled on his pad.

He thought of the Indian rope trick, the child shinning up the rope in the Calcutta market and then vanishing clean away; only his forlorn cry floated down from the cloudless sky. How the white-robed crowd roared when the magician's basket started to rock and sway on the ground until the child jumped out of it, all smiles! 'Mass hysteria and the delusion of crowds . . . a little primitive technology and a big dose of the will to believe.' In Kathmandu, he saw the fakir on a bed of nails, all complete, soar up until he was level with the painted demons on the eaves of the wooden houses; what, said the old man, heavily bribed, would be the point of the illusion if it *looked* like an illusion? For, opined the old charlatan to Walser with po-faced solemnity, is not this whole world an illusion? And yet it fools everybody.

Now the pit band ground to a halt and rustled its scores. After a moment's disharmony comparable to the clearing of a throat, it began to saw away as best it could at — what else — 'The Ride of the Valkyries'. Oh, the scratch unhandiness of the musicians! the tuneless insensitivity of their playing! Walser sat back with a pleased smile on his lips; the greasy, inescapable whiff of stage magic which pervaded Fevvers' act manifested itself abundantly in her choice of music.

She gathered herself together, rose up on tiptoe and gave a mighty shrug, in order to raise her shoulders. Then she brought down her elbows, so that the tips of the pin feathers of each wing met in the air above her headdress. At the first crescendo, she jumped.

Yes, jumped. Jumped up to catch the dangling trapeze, jumped up some thirty feet in a single, heavy bound, transfixed the while upon the arching white sword of the limelight. The invisible wire that must have hauled her up remained invisible. She caught hold of the trapeze with one hand. Her wings throbbed, pulsed, then whirred, buzzed and at last began to beat steadily on the air they disturbed so much that the pages of Walser's notebook ruffled over and he temporarily lost his place, had to scramble to find it again, almost displaced his composure but managed to grab tight hold of his scepticism just as it was about to blow over the ledge of the press box.

First impression: physical ungainliness. Such a lump it seems! But soon, quite soon, an acquired grace asserts itself, probably the result of strenuous exercise. (Check if she trained as a dancer.)

My, how her bodice strains! You'd think her tits were going to pop right out. What a sensation *that* would cause; wonder she hasn't thought of incorporating it in her act. Physical ungainliness in flight caused, perhaps, by absence of *tail*, the rudder of the flying bird – I wonder why she doesn't tack a tail on the back of her cache-sexe; it would add verisimilitude and, perhaps, improve the performance.

What made her remarkable as an *aerialiste*, however, was the speed – or, rather the lack of it – with which she performed even the climactic triple somersault. When the hack *aerialiste*, the everyday, wingless variety, performs the triple somersault, he or she travels through the air at a cool sixty miles an hour; Fevvers, however, contrived a contemplative and leisurely twenty-five, so that the packed theatre could enjoy the spectacle, as in slow motion, of every tense muscle straining in her Rubenesque form. The music went much faster than she did; she dawdled. Indeed, she did defy the laws of projectiles, because a projectile cannot *mooch* along its trajectory; if it slackens its speed in mid-air, down it falls. But Fevvers, apparently, pottered along the invisible gangway between her trapezes with the portly dignity of a Trafalgar Square pigeon flapping from one proffered handful of corn to another, and then she turned head over heels three times, lazily enough to show off the crack in her bum.

(But surely, pondered Walser, a *real* bird would have too much sense to think of performing a triple somersault in the first place.)

Yet, apart from this disconcerting pact with gravity, which surely she made in the same way the Nepali fakir had made his, Walser observed that the girl went no further than any other trapeze artiste. She neither attempted nor achieved anything a wingless biped could not have performed, although she did it in a different way, and, as the valkyries at last approached Valhalla, he was astonished to discover that it was the limitations of her act in themselves that made him briefly contemplate the unimaginable – that is, the absolute suspension of disbelief.

For, in order to earn a living, might not a genuine bird-woman – in the implausible event that such a thing existed – have to pretend she was an artificial one?

He smiled to himself at the paradox: in a secular age, an authentic miracle must purport to be a hoax, in order to gain credit in the world. But – and Walser smiled to himself again, as he remembered his flutter of conviction that seeing was believing – what about her *belly button*? Hasn't she just this minute told me she was hatched from an *egg*, not gestated *in utero*? The oviparous species are not, by definition, nourished by the placenta; therefore they feel no need of the umbilical cord . . . and, therefore, don't bear the scar of its loss! Why isn't the whole of London asking: does Fevvers have a belly-button?

It was impossible to make out whether or not she had a navel during her act; Walser could recall, of her belly, only a pink, featureless expanse of stockinette fleshing. Whatever her wings were, her nakedness was certainly a stage illusion.

After she'd pulled off the triple somersault, the band performed the *coup de grâce* on Wagner, and stopped. Fevvers hung by one hand, waving and blowing kisses with the other, those famous wings of hers now drawn up behind her. Then she jumped right down to the ground, just dropped, just plummeted down, hitting the stage squarely on her enormous feet with an all too human thump only partially muffled by the roar of applause and cheers.

Bouquets pelt the stage. Since there is no second-hand market for flowers, she takes no notice of them. Her face, thickly coated with rouge and powder so that you can see how beautiful she is from the back row of the gallery, is wreathed in triumphant smiles; her white teeth are big and carnivorous as those of Red Riding Hood's grandmother.

She kisses her free hand to all. She folds up her quivering wings with a number of shivers, moues and grimaces as if she were putting away a naughty book. Some chorus boy or other trips on and hands her into her feather cloak that is as frail and vivid as those the natives of Florida used to make. Fevvers curtsies to the conductor with gigantic aplomb and goes on kissing her hand to the tumultuous applause as the curtain falls and the band strikes up 'God save the Queen'. God save the mother of the obese and bearded princeling who has taken his place in the royal box twice nightly since Fevvers' first night at the Alhambra, stroking his beard and meditating upon the erotic possibilities of her ability to hover and the problematic of his paunch vis-à-vis the missionary position.

The greasepaint floated off Fevvers' face as Lizzie wiped away cold cream with cotton wool, scattering the soiled balls carelessly on the floor. Fevvers reappeared, flushed, to peer at herself eagerly in the mirror as if pleased and surprised to find herself again so robustly rosy-cheeked and shiny-eyed. Walser was surprised at her wholesome look: like an Iowa cornfield.

Lizzie dipped a velour puff in a box of bright peach-coloured powder and shook it over the girl's face, to take off the shine. She picked up a hairbrush of yellow metal.

'Can't tell you who give 'er this,' she announced conspiratorially waving the brush so that the small stones with which it was encrusted (in the design of the Prince of Wales' feathers) scattered prisms of light. 'Palace protocol. Dark secret. Comb and mirror to go with it. Solid, it is. What a shock I got when I got it valued. Fool and his money is soon parted. Goes straight into the bank tomorrow morning. *She*'s no fool. All the same, she can't resist using it tonight.'

There was a hint of censure in Lizzie's voice, as if there was nothing that she herself would find irresistible, but Fevvers eyed her hairbrush with a complacent and proprietorial air. For just one moment, she looked less generous.

'Course,' said Fevvers, '*he* never got nowhere.'

Her inaccessability was also legendary, even if, as Walser had already noted on his pad, she was prepared to make certain exceptions for exigent French dwarves. The maid untied the blue ribbon that kept in check the simmering wake of the young woman's hair, which she laid over her left arm as if displaying a length of carpet and started to belabour vigorously. It was a sufficiently startling head of hair, yellow and inexhaustible as sand, thick as cream, sizzling and whispering under the brush. Fevvers' head went back, her eyes half closed, she sighed with pleasure. Lizzie might have been grooming a palomino; yet Fevvers was a hump-backed horse.

That grubby dressing-gown, horribly caked with greasepaint round the neck . . . when Lizzie lifted up the armful of hair, you could see, under the splitting, rancid silk, her humps, her lumps, big as if she bore a bosom fore and aft, her conspicuous deformity, the twin hills of the growth she had put away for those hours she must spend in daylight or lamplight, out of the spotlight. So, on the street, at the soirée, at lunch in expensive restaurants with dukes, princes, captains of industry and punters of like kidney, she was always the cripple, even if she always drew the eye and people stood on chairs to see.

'Who makes your frocks?' the reporter in Walser asked percipiently. Lizzie stopped in mid-stroke; her mistress's eyes burst open – whoosh! like blue umbrellas.

'Nobody. I meself,' said Fevvers sharply. 'Liz helps.'

'But 'er 'ats we purchase from the best modistes,' asserted Lizzie suavely. 'We got some lovely 'ats in Paris, didn't we, darling? That leghorn, with the moss roses . . .'

'I see his glass is empty.'

Walser allowed himself to be refilled before Lizzie stuffed her mouth with tortoiseshell pins and gave both hands to the task of erecting Fevvers' chignon. The sound of the music hall at closing time clanked and echoed round them, gurgle of water in a pipe, chorus girls calling their goodnights as they scampered downstairs to the waiting hansoms of the stage-door Johnnies, somewhere the rattle of an out-of-tune piano. The lightbulbs round Fevvers' mirror threw a naked and unkind light upon her face but could flush out no flaw in the classic cast of her features, unless their very size was a fault in itself, the flaw that made her vulgar.

It took a long time to pile up those two yards of golden hair. By the time the last pin went in, silence of night had fallen on the entire building.

Fevvers patted her bun with a satisfied air. Lizzie shook the champagne bottle, found it was empty, tossed it into a corner, took another from a crate stored behind the screen, popped it, refilled all glasses. Fevvers sipped and shuddered.

'Warm.'

Lizzie peered in the toilet jug and tipped the melted contents into the bath-water.

'No more ice,' she said to Walser accusingly, as if it were his fault.

Perhaps, perhaps . . . my brain is turning to bubbles already, thought Walser, but I could almost swear I saw a fish, a little one, a herring, a sprat, a minnow, but wriggling, alive-oh, go into the bath when she tipped the jug. But he had no time to think about how his eyes were deceiving him because Fevvers now solemnly took up the interview shortly before the point where she'd left off.

'Hatched,' she said.

TWO

'Hatched; by whom, I do not know. Who *laid* me is as much a mystery to me, sir, as the nature of my conception, my father and my mother both utterly unknown to me, and, some would say, unknown to nature, what's more. But hatch out I did, and put in that basket of broken shells and straw in Whitechapel at the door of a certain *house*, know what I mean?'

As she reached for her glass, the dirty satin sleeve fell away from an arm as finely turned as the leg of the sofa on which Walser sat. Her hand shook slightly, as if with suppressed emotion.

'And, as I told you, who was it but my Lizzie over there who stumbled over the mewing scrap of life that then I was whilst she's assisting some customer off the premises and she brings me indoors and there I was reared by these kind women as if I was the common daughter of half-a-dozen mothers. And that is the whole truth and nothing but, sir.

'And never have I told it to a living man before.'

As Walser scribbled away, Fevvers squinted at his notebook in the mirror, as if attempting to interpret his shorthand by some magic means. Her composure seemed a little ruffled by his silence.

'Come on, sir, now, will they let you print *that* in your newspapers? For these were women of the *worst class* and *defiled.*'

'Manners in the New World are considerably more elastic than they are in the old, as you'll be pleased to find, ma'am,' said Walser evenly. 'And I myself have known some pretty decent whores, some damn' fine women, indeed, whom any man might have been proud to marry.'

'Marriage? Pah!' snapped Lizzie in a pet. 'Out of the frying pan into the fire! What is marriage but prostitution to one man instead of many? No different! D'you think a decent whore'd be proud to marry *you*, young man? Eh?'

'Never mind, Lizzie, 'e means well. Here, is the boy still on? I'm starved to death, I'd pawn me gold hairbrush for some eel-pies and a saveloy.' She turned to Walser with gigantic coquetry. 'Could you fancy an eel pie and a bit of mash, sir?'

The call-boy was rung for, proved to be still on duty and instantly despatched to the pie shop in the Strand by a Lizzie still stiff with affront. But she was soon mollified by the spread that arrived in a covered basket ten minutes later – hot meat pies with a glutinous ladleful of eel gravy on each; a Fujiyama of mashed potatoes; a swamp of dried peas cooked up again and served swimming in greenish liquor. Fevvers paid off the call-boy, waited for her change and tipped him with a kiss on his peachy, beardless cheek that left it blushing and a little greasy. The women fell to with a clatter of rented cutlery but Walser himself opted for another glass of tepid champagne.

'English food . . . waaall, I find it's an acquired taste; I account your native cuisine to be the eighth wonder of the world, ma'am.'

She gave him a queer look, as if she suspected he were teasing and, sooner or later, she would remember to pay him back for it, but her mouth was too full for a ripost as she tucked into this earthiest, coarsest cabbies' fare with gargantuan enthusiasm. She gorged, she stuffed herself, she spilled gravy on herself, she sucked up peas from the knife; she had a gullet to match her size and table manners of the Elizabethan variety. Impressed, Walser waited with the stubborn docility of his profession until at last her enormous appetite was satisfied; she wiped her lips on her sleeve and belched. She gave him another queer look, as if she half hoped the spectacle of her gluttony would drive him away, but, since he remained, notebook on knee, pencil in hand, sitting on her sofa, she sighed, belched again, and continued:

'In a brothel bred, sir, and proud of it, if it comes to the point, for never a bad word nor an unkindness did I have from my mothers but I was given the best of everything and always tucked up in my little bed in the attic by eight o'clock of the evening before the big spenders who broke the glasses arrived.

'So there I was – '

' – there she was, the little innocent, with her yellow pigtails that I used to tie up with blue ribbons, to match her big blue eyes – '

' – there I was and so I grew, and the little downy buds on my shoulders grew with me, until, one day, when I was seven years old, Nelson – '

'Nelson?' queried Walser.

Fevvers and Lizzie raised their eyes reverently in unison to the ceiling.

'Nelson, rest her soul, yes. Wasn't she the madame! And always called Nelson, on account of her one eye, a sailor having put the other out with a broken bottle the year of the Great Exhibition, poor thing. Now Nelson ran a seemly, decent house and never thought of putting me to the trade while I was still in short petticoats, as others might have. But, one evening, when she and my Lizzie were giving me my bath in front of the fire, as she was soaping my little feathery buds very tenderly, she cries out: "Cupid! Why, here's our very own Cupid in the living flesh!" And that was how I first earned my crust, for my Lizzie made me a little wreath of pink cotton roses and put it on my head and gave me a toy bow and arrow – '

' – that I gilded up for her,' said Lizzie. 'Real gold leaf, it was. You put the leaf on the palm of your hand. Then you blow it ever so lightly onto the surface of whatever it is you want gilded. Gently does it. Blow it. Gawd, it was a bother.'

'So, with my wreath of roses, my baby bow of smouldering gilt and my arrows of unfledged desire, it was my job to sit in the alcove of the drawing-room in which the ladies introduced themselves to the gentlemen. Cupid, I was.'

'With her baby winglets. Reigning overall.'

The women exchanged a nostalgic smile. Lizzie reached behind the screen for another bottle.

'Let's drink to little Cupid.'

'I won't say no,' said Fevvers, proffering her glass.

'So there I was,' she went on, after an invigorating gulp. 'I was a *tableau vivant* from the age of seven on. There I sat above the company – '

' – as if she were the guardian cherub of the house – '

' – and for seven long years, sir, I was nought but the painted, gilded *sign* of love, and you might say, that so it was I served my apprenticeship in *being looked at* – at being the object of the eye of the beholder. Until the time came when my, pardon me, woman's bleeding started up along with the beginnings of great goings on in, as you might put it, the bosom department. But, though, like any young girl, I was much possessed with the marvellous blossoming of my until then reticent and undemanding flesh – '

' – flat as an ironing board on both sides till thirteen and a 'arf, sir – '

' – yet, startled as I was by *all that*, I was yet more moved and strangely puzzled by what, at first, manifested itself as no more than an infernal itching in my back.

'At first, but a small, indeed, an almost pleasurable irritation, a kind of physical buzzing, sir, so that I'd rub my back against the legs of the chairs, as cats do, or else I'd get my Lizzie or another of the girls to scrub my back with a pumice stone or a nail brush whilst I was in the tub, for the itch was situated in the most inconvenient location just between my shoulderblades and I couldn't get my fingers to it, no matter what.

'And the itch increased. If it started in small ways, soon it was as if my back was all on fire and they covered me with soothing lotions and cooling powders and I would lie down to sleep with an ice-bag on my back but still nothing could calm the fearful storm in my erupting skin.

'But all this was but the herald to the breaking out of my wings, you understand; although I did not know that, then.

'For, as my titties swelled before, so these feathered appendages of mine swelled behind until, one morning in my fourteenth year, rising from my truckle bed in the attic as the friendly sound of Bow Bells came in through the window while the winter sun shone coolly down on that great city outside, which, had I but known it, would one day be at my feet – '

'She spread,' said Lizzie.

'I spread,' said Fevvers. 'I had taken off my little white nightgown in order to perform my matutinal ablutions at my little dresser when there was a great ripping in the hind-quarters of my chemise and, all unwilled by me, uncalled for, involuntarily, suddenly there broke forth my peculiar inheritance – these wings of mine! Still adolescent, as yet, not half their adult size, and moist, sticky, like freshly unfurled foliage on an April tree. But, all the same, wings.

'No. There was no pain. Only bewilderment.'

'She lets out a great shriek,' said Lizzie, 'that brought me up out of a dream – for I shared the attic with her, sir – and there she stood, stark as a stone, her ripped chemise around her ankles, and I would have thought I was still dreaming or else have died and gone to heaven, among the blessed angels; or, that she was the Annunciation of my menopause.'

'What a shock!' said Fevvers modestly. She pulled a coil of hair out of her chignon and wrapped it round her finger, twisting it and biting it thoughtfully; then, suddenly, she whirled away from the mirror on her revolving stool and leaned confidentially towards Walser.

'Now, sir, I shall let you into a great secret, for your ears alone and not for publication, because I've taken a liking to your face, sir.' At that, she batted her eyelids like a flirt. She lowered her voice to a whisper, so that Walser needs must lean forward in turn to hear her; her breath, flavoured with champagne, warmed his cheek.

'I *dye*, sir!'

'What?'

'My feathers, sir! I dye them! Don't think I bore such gaudy colours from puberty! I commenced to dye my feathers at the start of my public career on the trapeze, in order to simulate more perfectly the tropic bird. In my white girlhood and earliest years, I kept my natural colour. Which is a kind of blonde, only a little darker than the hair on my head, more the colour of that on my private ahem parts.

'Now, that's my dreadful secret, Mr Walser, and, to tell the whole truth and nothing but, the only deception which I practice on the public!'

To emphasise the point, she brought her empty glass down with such a bang on the dressing table that the jars of fards and lotions jumped and rattled, expelling sharp gusts of cheap scent, and a cloud of powder rose up into the air from a jogged box, catching painfully in Walser's throat so that he broke out coughing. Lizzie thumped his back. Fevvers disregarded these proceedings.

'Lizzie, faced with this unexpected apparition, went shrieking downstairs in her shift –

'"Nelson, Ma Nelson, come quick; our little bird's about to fly away!" The good woman ran up two at a time and when she saw the way that things had gone with her pet chick, she laughed for pure pleasure.

'"To think we've entertained an angel unawares!" she says.

'"Oh, my little one, I think you must be the pure child of the century that just now is waiting in the wings, the New Age in which no women will be bound down to the ground." And then she wept. That night, we threw away the bow and arrow and I posed, for the first time, as the Winged Victory, for, as you can see, I am designed on the grand scale and, even at fourteen, you could have made two Lizzies out of me.

'Oh, sir, let me indulge my heart awhile and describe for you that beloved house which, although one of ill-fame, shielded me for so long from the tempests of misfortune and kept my youthful wings from dragging in the mud.

'It was one of those old, square, red-brick houses with a plain, sober façade and a graceful, scallop-shaped fanlight over the front door that you may still find in those parts of London so far from the tide of fashion that they were never swept away. You could not look at

Mother Nelson's house without the thought, how the Age of Reason built it; and then you almost cried, to think the Age of Reason was over before it properly begun, and this harmonious relic tucked away behind the howling of the Ratcliffe Highway, like the germ of sense left in a drunkard's mind.

'A little flight of steps ran up to the front door, steps that Lizzie, faithful as any housewife in London, scrubbed and whitened every morning. An air of rectitude and propriety surrounded the place, with its tall windows over which we always kept the white blinds pulled down, as if its eyes were closed, as if the house were dreaming its own dream, or as if, on entering between the plain and well-proportioned pediments of the doorway, you entered a place that, like its mistress, turned a blind eye to the horrors of the outside, for, inside, was a place of privilege in which those who visited might extend the boundaries of their experience for a not unreasonable sum. It was a place in which rational desires might be rationally gratified; it was an old-fashioned house, so much so that, in those years, it had a way of seeming almost too *modern* for its own good, as the past so often does when it outruns the present.

'As for the drawing-room, in which I played the living statue all my girlhood, it was on the first floor and you reached it by a mighty marble staircase that went up with a flourish like, pardon me, a whore's bum. This staircase had a marvellous banister of wrought iron, all garlands of fruit, flowers and the heads of satyrs, with a wonderfully slippery marble handrail down which, in my light-hearted childhood I was accustomed, pigtails whisking behind me, to slide. Only those games I played before opening time, because nothing put off respectable patrons like those whom Nelson preferred so much as the sight of a child in a whorehouse.

'The drawing-room was dominated by a handsome fireplace that must have been built by the same master in marble who put up the staircase. A brace of buxom, smiling goddesses supported this mantelpiece on the flats of their upraised palms, much as we women do uphold the whole world, when all is said and done. That fireplace might have served the Romans for an altar, or a tomb, and it was our very own domestic temple to Vesta for, every afternoon, Lizzie lit there a fire of sweet-scented woods whose natural aromatics she was accustomed to augment with burning perfumes of the best quality.'

'As for me,' interposed Lizzie, 'I'd never been any great shakes as a whore, due to an inconvenient habit I had of *praying*, which came to me from my family and which I never could shake off.'

This was patently incredible and Walser remained incredulous, although Lizzie's spitting black eyes dared disbelief.

'After I converted a score or two of regular customers to the Church of Rome, Ma Nelson called me into her office one afternoon and said:

'"Our Liz, all this will never do! You'll make our poor girls redundant if you go on so!" She took me off regular duties and set me to work as housekeeper, which suited me very well, for the girls saw to it I got my share of the gratuities. And, every evening, as dusk came on, I lit the fire and tended it, until, by eight or nine in the evening, the drawing-room was snug as a groin – '

' – and sweet as the room where burns the pyre of the Arabian bird, sweet and mauvish with smoke as hallucination itself, sir.

'Now, Mr Walser, the day I first spread found me, as you might expect, much perplexed as to my own nature. Ma Nelson wrapped me up in a cashmere shawl off her own back, since I'd busted me shift, and Lizzie must needs ply her needle now, to alter my dress to fit my altered figure. As I sat on my bed in the attic waiting for a garment to be ready, I fell to contemplating the mystery of these soft, feathery growths that were already pulling my shoulders backwards with the weight and urgency of an invisible lover. Outside my window, in the cool sunlight, I saw the skirling seagulls who follow the winding course of the mighty Thames riding upon the currents of the air like spirits of the wind and so it came to me: if I have wings, then I must fly!

'It was about the early afternoon and all quiet in the house, each woman in her own room busy with the various pastimes with which they occupied themselves before their labour began. I threw off that cashmere shawl and, spreading my new-fledged wings, I jumped into the air, hup.

'But nothing came of it, sir, not even a *hover*, for I'd not got the knack of it, by any means, knew nothing of the theory of flight nor of the launch nor of the descent. I jumped up – and came down. Thump. And that was that.

'So then I thought: there's that marble fireplace down below, with a mantel some six feet off the ground upheld on either side by straining marble caryatids! And down to the parlour I forthwith softly trotted, for I thought, if I jumped off the mantelpiece whilst in full spread, sir, the air I trapped in my feathers would itself sustain me off the ground.

'At first sight, you'd have thought this drawing-room was the smoking room of a gentlemen's club of the utmost exclusivity, for Nelson encouraged an almost lugubrious degree of masculine good behaviour amongst her clients. She went in for leather armchairs and tables with *The Times* on them that Liz ironed every morning and the walls, covered with wine-red, figured damask, were hung with oil paintings of mythological subjects so crusted with age that the painted scenes within the heavy golden frames seemed full of the honey of ancient sunlight and it had crystallised to form a sweet scab. All these pictures, some of the Venetian school and no doubt very choice, were long since destroyed, along with Ma Nelson's house itself, but there was one picture I shall always remember, for it is as if engraved upon my heart. It hung above the mantelpiece and I need hardly tell you that its subject was Leda and the Swan.

'All those who saw her picture gallery wondered, but Nelson would never have her pictures cleaned. She always said, didn't she, Liz, that Time himself, the father of transfigurations, was the greatest of artists, and his invisible hand must be respected at all costs, since it was in anonymous complicity with that of every human painter, so I always saw, as through a glass, darkly, what might have been my own primal scene, my own conception, the heavenly bird in a white majesty of feathers descending with imperious desire upon the half-stunned and yet herself impassioned girl.

'When I asked Ma Nelson what this picture meant, she told me it was a demonstration of the blinding access of the grace of flesh.'

With this remarkable statement, she gave Walser a sideways, cunning glance from under eyelashes a little darker than her hair.

Curiouser and curiouser, thought Walser; a one-eyed, metaphysical madame, in Whitechapel, in possession of a Titian? Shall I believe it? Shall I pretend to believe in it?

'Some bloke whose name I misremember give 'er the pictures,' said Lizzie. 'He liked her on account of how she shaved her pubes.'

Fevvers gave Lizzie a disapproving glance but spoiled the effect by giggling. Lizzie now crouched at Fevvers' feet using her own handbag as a footstool, her huge handbag, an affair of cracked leather with catches of discoloured brass. Her hooked chin rested on the knees she clasped with liver-spotted hands. She crackled quietly with her own static; she missed nothing. The watchdog. Or . . . might it be possible, could it be . . . And Walser found himself asking himself: are they, in reality mother and daughter?

Yet, if this were so, what Nordic giant feathered the one upon the swarthy, tiny other? And who or where in all this business was the Svengali who turned the girl into a piece of artifice, who had made of her a marvellous machine and equipped her with her story? Had the one-eyed whore, if she existed, been the first business manager of these weird accomplices?

He turned a page in his notebook.

'Imagine me, sir, tripping in nothing but Ma Nelson's shawl into that drawing-room where the shutters were bolted tight, the crimson velvet curtains drawn, all still simulating the dark night of pleasure although the candles were burnt out in the crystal sconces. Last night's fragrant fire was but charred sticks in the hearth and glasses in which remained only the flat dregs of dissipation lay where they had fallen on the Bokhara carpet. The flimsy light of the farthing dip I carried with me touched the majesty of the swan-god on the wall and made me dream, dream and dare.

'Well-grown though I was, yet I had to pull a chair to the mantelpiece in order to climb up and take down the French gilt clock that stood there in a glass case. This clock was, you might say, the sign, or signifier of Ma Nelson's little private realm. It was a figure of Father Time with a scythe in one hand and a skull in the other above a face on which the hands stood always at either midnight or noon, the minute hand and the hour hand folded perpetually together as if in prayer, for Ma Nelson said the clock in her reception room must show the dead centre of the day or night, the shadowless hour, the hour of vision and revelation, the still hour in the centre of the storm of time.

'She was a strange one, Ma Nelson.'

Walser could well believe it.

'I picked up the old clock to give me room to move and set it down with care by the disordered hearth. As I did so, the antique, defunct mechanism let out a faint, melodious twang, as if resounding with clockwork encouragement. Then I climbed up and stood where Father Time had stood and, like a man about to hang himself, I kicked away the chair so that I would not be tempted to jump down upon it.

'What a long way down the floor looked! It was only a few feet below, you understand, no great distance in itself – yet it yawned before me like a chasm, and, indeed, you might say that this gulf now before me represented the grand abyss, the poignant divide, that would henceforth separate me from common humanity.'

At that, she turned her immense eyes upon him, those eyes 'made for the stage' whose messages could be read from standing room in the gods. Night had darkened their colour; their irises were now purple, matching the Parma violets in front of her mirror, and the pupil's had grown so fat on darkness that the entire dressing-room and all those within it could have vanished without trace inside those compelling voids. Walser felt the strangest sensation, as if these eyes of the *aerialiste* were a pair of sets of Chinese boxes, as if each one opened into a world into a world into a world, an infinite plurality of worlds, and these unguessable depths exercised the strongest possible attraction, so that he felt himself trembling as if he, too, stood on an unknown threshold.

Surprised by his own confusion, he gave his mind a quick shake to refresh its pragmatism. She lowered her eyelids, as if she knew enough was enough, and took a sip of now flat champagne before she continued. Her eyes reverted once again to the simple condition of a pair of blue eyes.

'I stood upon the mantelpiece and I gave a little shiver, for it was perishing cold in there before Lizzie lit the fire and the carpet looked further away than ever. But then, thinks I, nothing ventured, nothing gained. And behind me, truly, sir, upon the wall, I could have sworn I heard, caught in time's cobweb but, all the same, audible, the strenuous beating of great, white wings. So I spread. And, closing my eyes, I precipitated myself forward, throwing myself entirely on the mercy of gravity.'

She fell silent for a moment and runnelled the dirty satin stretched over her knees with her fingernail.

'And, sir – I fell.

'Like Lucifer, I fell. Down, down, down I tumbled, bang with a bump on the Persian rug below me, flat on my face amongst those blooms and beasts that never graced no natural forest, those creatures of dream and abstraction not unlike myself, Mr Walser. And then I knew I was not yet ready to bear on my back the great burden of my unnaturalness.'

She paused for precisely three heartbeats.

'I fell . . . and give my poor nose such a whack on the brass fire-guard – '

' – and so I found her, when I come in to make up the fire, bum in the air and her little blonde wings still fluttering, poor duck, and though she'd taken such a tumble and near busted her nose in half and oh! how it was bleeding, not one cry did she utter, not one, brave little thing that she was; nor did she shed a single tear.'

'What did I care about my bloody nose, sir?' cried Fevvers passionately. 'For, for one brief moment – one lapse or stutter of time so fleeting that the old French clock, had it been in motion, could never have recorded it on its clumsy cogs and springs, for just the smallest instant no longer than the briefest flutter of a butterfly . . . I'd hovered.

'Yes. Hovered. Only for so short a while I could almost have thought I'd imagined it, for it was that sensation that comes to us, sometimes, on the edge of sleep . . . and yet, sir, for however short a while, the air had risen up beneath my adolescent wings and denied to me the downward pull of the great, round world, to which, hitherto, all human things had necessarily clung.'

'Since I was the housekeeper,' interjected Lizzie, 'happily I carried all the keys of the house in a ring on my belt and when I comes chinking into the parlour with my armful of sandalwood, I had the remedy for her bloody nose to hand, I slapped the front door key between her wings, it was a foot long and cold as hell. The flow stopped from shock. Then I mops her up with my apron and takes her down to the kitchen, in the warm, wraps her up in a blanket and anoints her abrasions with Germoline, slaps on a bit of sticking plaster here and there and, when she's as good as new, she tells her Lizzie all about the peculiar sensations she felt when she launched herself off the mantelpiece.

'And I was full of wonder, sir.'

'But, though now I knew I could mount on the air and it would hold me up, the method of the act of flight itself was unknown to me. As babies needs must learn to walk so must I needs learn to conquer the alien element and not only did I need to know the powers of the limitations of my feathery limbs but I must study, too, the airy medium that was henceforth to be my second home as he who would a mariner be needs to construe the mighty currents, the tides and whirlpools, all the whims and moods and conflicting temperaments of the watery parts of the world.

'I learnt, first, as the birds do, from the birds.

'All this took place in the first part of spring, towards the end of the month of February, when the birds were just waking from their winter lethargy. As spring brought out the buds on the daffodils in our window-boxes, so the London pigeons started up their courtships, the male puffing out his bosom and strutting after the female in his comic fashion. And it so happened that the pigeons built a nest upon the pediment outside our attic window and laid their eggs in it. When the wee pidgies hatched out, Lizzie and I watched them with more care than you can conceive of. We saw how the mother pigeon taught her babies to totter along the edge of the wall, observed in the minutest detail how she gave them mute instructions to use those *aerial arms* of theirs, their joints, their wrists, their elbows, to imitate those actions of her own which were, in fact, I realised, not dissimilar to those of a human swimmer. But do not think I carried out these studies on my own; although she was flightless herself, my Lizzie took it upon herself the role of bird-mother.

'In those quiet hours of the afternoon, while the friends and sisters that we lived with bent over their books, Lizzie constructed a graph on squared paper in order to account for the great difference in weight between a well-formed human female in her fourteenth year and a tiny pigeonlet, so that we should know to what height I might soar without tempting the fate of Icarus. All this while, as the months passed, I grew bigger and stronger, stronger and bigger, until Liz was forced to put aside her mathematics in order to make me an entire new set of dresses to accommodate the remarkable development of my upper body.'

'I'll say this for Ma Nelson, she paid up all expenses on the nail, out of pure love of our little kiddie and what's more, she thought up the scheme, how we should put it round she was a 'unchback. Yes.'

'Yes, indeed, sir. Every night, I mimicked the Winged Victory in the drawing-room niche and was the cynosure of all eyes but Nelson made it known that those shining golden wings of mine were stuck over a hump with a strong adhesive and did not belong to me at all so I was spared the indignity of curiosity. And though I now began to receive many, many offers for first bite at the cherry, offers running into four figures, sir, yet Nelson refused them all for fear of letting the cat out of the bag.'

'She was a proper lady,' said Lizzie. 'Nelson was a good 'un, she was.'

'She was,' concurred Fevvers. 'She had the one peculiarity, sir; due to her soubriquet, or nickname, she always dressed in the full dress uniform of an Admiral of the Fleet. Not that she ever missed a trick, her one eye sharp as a needle, and always used to say, "I keep a tight little ship." Her ship, her ship of battle though sometimes she'd laugh and say, "It was a pirate ship, and went under false colours," her barque of pleasure that was moored, of all unlikely places, in the sluggish Thames.'

Lizzie fixed Walser with her glittering eye and seized the narrative between her teeth.

'It was from the, as it were, top-sail or crows' nest of this barge that my girl made her first ascent. And this is how it came about: –

'Imagine my surprise, one bright June morning, as I watched my pigeon family with my customary diligence, to see, as one of the little creatures teetered on the brink of the pediment looking for all the world like a swimmer debating with himself as to whether the water was warm enough for him – why, as it dithered there, its loving mother came right up behind it and shoved it clean off the edge!

'First it dropped like a stone, so that my heart sank with it, and I let out a mournful cry, but, almost before that cry left my lips, all its lessons must have rushed back into its little head at once for suddenly it soared upwards towards the sun with a flash of white, unfurled wing, and was never seen no more.

'So I says to Fevvers: "Nothing to it, my dear, but your Liz must shove you off the roof."'

'To me,' said Fevvers, 'it seemed that Lizzie, by proposing thus to thrust me into the free embrace of the whirling air, was arranging my marriage to the wind itself.'

She swung round on her piano stool and presented Walser with a face of such bridal radiance that he blinked.

'Yes! I must be the bride of that wild, sightless, fleshless rover, or else could not exist, sir.

'Nelson's house was some five storeys high and there was a neat little garden at the back of it that went down to the river. There was a trapdoor leading to a loft in the ceiling of our attic, and another trapdoor in the ceiling of the loft that gave directly on the roof itself. So, one night in June, or, rather, early morning, about four or five, a night without a moon – for, like sorceresses, we required the dark and privacy for our doings – out on the tiles crawls Lizzie and her apprentice.'

'Midsummer,' said Lizzie. 'Either Midsummer's Night, or else very early on Midsummer Morning. Don't you remember, darling?'

'Midsummer, yes. The year's green hinge. Yes, Liz, I remember.'

Pause of a single heartbeat.

'The business of the house was over. The last cab had rolled away with the last customer too poor to stay the night and all behind the drawn curtains were at long last sleeping. Even those thieves, cut-throats and night-prowlers who stalked the mean streets about us had gone home to their beds, either pleased with their prey or not, depending on their luck.

'It seemed a hush of expectation filled the city, that all was waiting in an exquisite tension of silence for some unparalleled event.'

'She, although it was a chilly night, had not a stitch on her for we feared that any item of clothing might impede the lively movement of the body. Out on to the tiles we crawled and the little wind that lives in high places came and prowled around the chimneys; it was soft, cool weather and my pretty one came out in gooseflesh, didn't you, such shivering. The roof had only a gentle slope on it so we crawled down to the gutter, from which side of the house we could see Old Father Thames, shining like black oilcloth wherever the bobbing mooring lights of the watermen touched him.'

'Now it came to it, I was seized with a great fear, not only a fear that we might discover the hard way that my wings were as those of the hen, or as the vestigial appendages of the ostrich, that these wings were in themselves a kind of physical deceit, intended for show and not for use, like beauty in some women, sir. No; I was not afraid only because the morning light already poking up the skirt of the sky might find me, when its fingers tickled the house, lying only a bag of broken bone in Ma Nelson's garden. Mingled with the simple fear of physical harm, there was a strange terror in my bosom that made me cling, at the last gasp of time, to Lizzie's skirts and beg her to abandon our project – for I suffered the greatest conceivable terror of the irreparable *difference* with which success in the attempt would mark me.

'I feared a wound not of the body but the soul, sir, an irreconcilable division between myself and the rest of humankind.'

'I feared the proof of my own singularity.'

'Yet, if it could speak, would not any wise child cry out from the womb: "Keep me in the darkness here! keep me warm! keep me in contingency!" But nature will not be denied. So this young creature cried out to me, that she would not be what she must become, and, though her pleading moved me until tears blinded my own eyes, I knew that what will be, must be and so – I pushed.'

'The transparent arms of the wind received the virgin.

'As I hurtled past the windows of the attic in which I passed those precious white nights of girlhood, so the wind came up beneath my outspread wings and, with a jolt, I found myself hanging in mid-air and the garden lay beneath me like the board of a marvellous game and *stayed where it was*. The earth did *not* rise up to meet me. I was secure in the arms of my invisible lover!

'But the wind did not relish my wondering inactivity for long. Slowly, slowly, while I depended from him, numb with amazement, he, as if affronted by my passivity, started to let me slip through his fingers and I commenced once more upon the fearful fall . . . until my lessons came back to me! And I kicked up with my heels, that I had learned from the birds to keep tight together to form a rudder for this little boat, my body, this little boat that could cast anchor in the clouds.

'So I kicked up with my heels and then, as if I were a swimmer, brought the longest and most flexible of my wing-tip feathers together over my head; then, with long, increasingly confident strokes, I parted them and brought them back together – yes! that was the way to do it! Yes! I clapped my wing-tips together again, again, again, and the wind loved that and clasped me to his bosom once more so I found I could progress in tandem with him just as I pleased, and so cut a corridor through the invisible liquidity of the air.

'Is there another bottle left, Lizzie?'

Lizzie scraped off fresh foil and filled up all their glasses. Fevvers drank thirstily and poured herself another with a not altogether steady hand.

'Don't excite yourself, gel,' said Lizzie gently. Fevvers' chin jerked up at that, almost pettishly.

'Oh, Lizzie, the gentleman must know the truth!'

And she fixed Walser with a piercing, judging regard, as if to ascertain just how far she could go with him. Her face, in its Brobdingnagian symmetry, might have been hacked from wood and brightly painted up by those artists who build carnival ladies for fairgrounds or figureheads for sailing ships. It flickered through his mind: Is she really a man?

A creaking and wheezing outside the door heralded a bang upon it – the old nightwatchman in his leather cape.

'Wot, still 'ere, Miss Fevvers? 'Scuse me . . . saw the light under the crack, see . . .'

'We're entertaining the press,' said Fevvers. 'Won't be long, now, me old duck. Have a drop of bubbly.'

She overflowed her glass and shoved it across to him; he downed it at a gulp and smacked his lips.

'Just the job. You know where to find me if there's any trouble, miss –'

Fevvers darted Walser an ironic glance under her lashes and smiled at the departing nightwatchman as if to say: 'Don't you think I'd be a match for him?'

Lizzie continued:

'Imagine with what joy, pride and wonder I watched my darling, naked as a star, vanish round the corner of the house! And, to tell the truth, I was most heartily relieved, too, for, in our hearts, we both knew it was a do or die attempt.'

'But hadn't I dared and done, sir!' Fevvers broke in. 'For this first flight of mine, I did no more than circle the house at a level that just topped the cherry tree in Nelson's garden, which was some thirty feet high. And, in spite of the great perturbation of my senses and the excess of mental concentration the practice of my new-found skill required, I did not neglect to pick my Lizzie a handful of the fruit that had just reached perfect ripeness upon the topmost branches, fruit that customarily we were forced to leave as a little tribute for the thrushes. No person in the deserted street to see me or think I was some hallucination or waking dream or phantom of the gin-shop fumes. I successfully made the circumnavigation of the house and then, aglow with triumph, I soared upwards to the roof again to rejoin my friend.

'But, now, unused as they were to so much exercise, my wings began . . . oh, God! to *give out*! For going up involves an altogether different set of cogs and pulleys than coming *down*, sir, although I did not know that, then. Our studies in comparative physiology were yet to come.

'So I leaps up, much as a dolphin leaps – which I now know is *not* the way to do it – and have already misjudged how high I should leap, in the first place, my weary wings already folding up beneath me. My heart misses. I think my first flight will be my last and I shall pay with my life the price of my hubris.

'Scattering the cherries I had gathered in a soft, black hail over the garden, I grabbed at the guttering and – oh! and, ah! the guttering gave way beneath me! The old lead parted company with the eaves with a groaning sigh and there I dangled, all complete woman, again, my wings having seized up in perfect terror of a human fate – '

' – but I reached out and grips her by the arms. Only love, great love, could have given me such strength, sir, to permit me to haul her in onto the roof against the pull of gravity as you might haul in, against the tide, a drowning person.'

'And there we huddled on the roof in one another's arms, sobbing together with mingled joy and relief, as dawn rose over London and gilded the great dome of St Paul's until it looked like the divine pap of the city which, for want of any other, I needs must call my natural mother.

'London, with the one breast, the Amazon queen.'

She fell silent. Some object within the room, perhaps the hot-water pipes, gave out a metallic tinkle. Lizzie, on her creaking handbag, shifted from one buttock to the other and coughed. Fevvers remained sunk in introspection for a while and the wind blew Big Ben, striking midnight, so lost, so lonely a sound it seemed to Walser the clock might be striking in a deserted city and they the only inhabitants left alive. Although he was not an imaginative man, even he was sensitive to that aghast time of the night when the dark dwarfs us.

The final reverberation of the chimes died away. Fevvers heaved a sigh that rocked the surface of her satin bosom, and came out of her lapse of vivacity.

'Let me tell you a little more about my working life at this time – what it was I got up to when I was *not* flitting about the sky like a bat, sir! You will recall how I stood in for the Winged Victory each night in the parlour and may have wondered how this might have been, since I have arms – ' and she stretched them out, spanning half the dressing-room in the process – 'and the Winged Victory has none.

'Well, Ma Nelson put it out that I was the perfection of, the original of, the very model for that statue which, in its broken and incomplete state, has teased the imagination of a brace of millennia with its promise of perfect, active beauty that has been, as it were, mutilated by history. Ma Nelson, contemplating the existence of my two arms, all complete, now puts her mind to the question: what might the Winged Victory have been holding in 'em when the forgotten master first released her from the marble that had contained her inexhaustible spirit? And Ma Nelson soon came up with the answer: *a sword*.

'So she equipped me with the very gilt ceremonial sword that come with her Admiral's uniform, that she used to wear at her side, and sometimes use as a staff with which to conduct the revels – her wand, like Prospero's. And now I grasped that sword in my right hand, with the point downwards, to show I meant no harm unless provoked, whilst my left hand hung loosely at my side, the fist clenched.

'How was I costumed for my part? My hair was powdered white with chalk and tied up with a ribbon and my wings were powdered white, too, so I let out a puff if touched. My face and the top half of my body was spread with the *wet white* that clowns use in the circus and I had white drapes from my navel to my knee but my shins and feet were dipped in wet white, too.'

'And very lovely she looked,' cried loyal Lizzie. Fevvers modestly lowered her eyelashes.

'Lovely or not, Ma Nelson always expressed complete satisfaction with my turnout and soon took to calling me, not her "Winged Victory" but her "Victory with Wings", the spiritual flagship of her fleet, as if a virgin with a weapon was the fittest guardian angel for a houseful of whores. Yet it may be that a *large woman* with a *sword* is not the best advertisement for a brothel. For, slow but sure, trade fell off from my fourteenth birthday on.

'No so much that of our faithfullest clients, those old rakes who, perhaps, Ma Nelson had herself initiated in the far-off days of their beardless and precipitously ejaculatory youth, and others who might have formed such particular attachments to Annie or to Grace that you could speak of a kind of marriage, there. No. Such gentlemen could not shift the habits of a lifetime. Ma Nelson had addicted them to those shadowless hours of noon and midnight, the clarity of *bought pleasure*, the simplicity of contract as it was celebrated in her aromatic parlour.

'These were the kind old buffers who would extend a father's indulgence in the shape of the odd half-sovereign or string of seed pearls to the half-woman, half-statue they had known in those earliest days when she had played Cupid and, sometimes, out of childish fun, sprung off her toy arrows amongst them, hitting, in play, sometimes an ear, sometimes a buttock, sometimes a ballock.

'But with their sons and grandsons it was a different matter. When the time came for them to meet La Nelson and her girls, in they'd trot, timorous yet defiant, blushing to the tops of their Eton collars, aquiver with nervous anticipation and dread, and then their eyes would fall on the sword I held and Louisa or Emily would have the devil's own job with them, thereafter.

'I put it down to the influence of *Baudelaire*, sir.'

'What's this?' cried Walser, amazed enough to drop his professional imperturbability.

'The French poet, sir; a poor fellow who loved whores not for the pleasure of it but, as he perceived it, the *horror* of it, as if we was, not working women doing it for money but *damned souls* who did it solely to lure men to their dooms, as if we'd got nothing better to do . . . Yet we were all suffragists in that house; oh, Nelson was a one for "Votes for Women", I can tell you!'

'Does that seem strange to you? That the caged bird should want to see the end of cages, sir?' queried Lizzie, with an edge of steel in her voice.

'Let me tell you that it was a wholly female world within Ma Nelson's door. Even the dog who guarded it was a bitch and all the cats were females, one or the other of 'em always in kitten, or newly given birth, so that a sub-text of fertility underwrote the glittering sterility of the pleasure of the flesh available within the academy. Life within those walls was governed by a sweet and loving reason. I never saw a single blow exchanged between any of the sisterhood who reared me, nor heard a cross word or a voice raised in anger. Until the hour of eight, when work began and Lizzie stationed herself behind the peephole in the front door, the girls kept to their rooms and the benign silence might be interrupted only by the staccato rattle of the typewriter as Grace practised her stenography or the lyric ripple of the flute upon which Esmeralda was proving to be something of a virtuoso.

'But what followed after they put away their books was only poor girls earning a living, for, though some of the customers would swear that whores do it for pleasure, that is only to ease their own consciences, so that they will feel less foolish when they fork out hard cash for pleasure that has no real existence unless given freely – oh, indeed! we knew we only sold the *simulacra*. No woman would turn her belly to the trade unless pricked by economic necessity, sir.

'As for myself, I worked my passage on Ma Nelson's ship as living statue, and, during my blossoming years, from fourteen to seventeen, I existed only as an object in men's eyes after the night-time knocking on the door began. Such was my apprenticeship for life, since is it not to the mercies of the eyes of others that we commit ourselves on our voyage through the world? I was as if closed up in a shell, for the wet white would harden on my face and torso like a death mask that covered me all over, yet, inside this appearance of marble, nothing could have been more vibrant with potentiality than I! Sealed in this artificial egg, this sarcophagus of beauty, I waited, I waited . . . although I could not have told you for what it was I waited. Except, I assure you, I did *not* await the kiss of a magic prince, sir! With my two eyes, I nightly saw how such a kiss would seal me up in my *appearance* for ever!

'Yet I was possessed by the idea I had been feathered out for some special fate, though what it was I could not imagine. So I waited, with lithic patience, for that destiny to manifest itself.

'As I wait now, sir,' she said directly to Walser, swinging round to him, 'as the last cobwebs of the old century blow away.'

Then she swung back to the mirror and thoughtfully tucked away a straying curl.

'However, until Liz opened the door and let the men in, when all we girls needs must jump to attention and behave like women, you might say that, in our well-ordered habitation, all was "*luxe, calme et volupté*", though not quite as the poet imagined. We all engaged in our intellectual, artistic or political – '

Here Lizzie coughed.

' – pursuits and, as for myself, those long hours of leisure I devoted to the study of aerodynamics and the physiology of flight, in Ma Nelson's library, from among whose abundant store of books I gleaned whatever small store of knowledge I possess, sir.'

With that, she batted her eyelashes at Walser in the mirror. From the pale length of those eyelashes, a good three inches, he might have thought she had not taken her false ones off had he not been able to see them lolling, hairy as gooseberries, among the formidable refuse of the dressing-table. He continued to take notes in a mechanical fashion but, as the women unfolded the convolutions of their joint stories together, he felt more and more like a kitten tangling up in a ball of wool it had never intended to unravel in the first place; or a sultan faced with not one but two Scheherezades, both intent on impacting a thousand stories into the single night.

'Library?' he queried indefatigably, if a touch wearily.

''E left it to 'er,' said Lizzie.

'Who left what to whom?'

'This old geyser. Left Nelson 'is library. On account of she was the only woman in London who could get it up for him – '

'*Lizzie!* You know I abhor coarse language!'

' – and that in spite of, or, perhaps, because of, her black eye patch and her *travestie*. Oh, her little plump thighs like chicken cutlets in her doeskin britches! What a quaint figure she cut! He was a Scottish gentleman with a big beard. I remember him well. Never give 'is name, of course. Left her his library. Our Fevvers was always rooting about in it, nose in a book, nothing but a poke of humbugs for company.'

Humbugs, noted Walser with renewed enthusiasm. In England, a kind of candy; in America –

'As to my flight,' continued Fevvers inexorably, 'you must realise that my size, weight and general construction were not such as to make flying come easy to me, although there is ample room in my chest for lungs of the size required. But the bones of birds are filled with air and mine are filled with solid marrow and if the remarkable development of my thorax forms the same kind of windbreak as does that of a pigeon, the resemblance stops abruptly there and problems of balance and of elementary negotiations with the wind – who is a fickle lover – absorbed me for a long time.

'Have you observed my legs, sir?'

She thrust her right leg through the flap of her dressing-gown. Its foot wore a down-at-heel pink velvet slipper trimmed with grubby swansdown. The leg itself, perfectly bare, was admirably long and lean.

'My legs don't tally with the upper part of my body from the point of view of pure aesthetics, d'you see. Were I to be the true copy of Venus, one built on *my* scale ought to have legs like tree-trunks, sir; these flimsy little underpinnings of mine have more than once buckled up under the top-heavy distribution of weight upon my torso, have let me down with a bump and left me sprawling. I'm not tip-top where walking is concerned, sir, more *tip-up*. Any bird of my dimensions would have little short legs it could tuck up under itself and so make of itself a flying wedge to pierce the air, but old spindle-shanks here ain't fitted out like neither bird nor woman down below.

'Discussing this problem with Lizzie – '

' – I suggested a Sunday afternoon trip to the Zoological Gardens, where we saw the storks, the cranes and the flamingoes – '

' – and these long-stemmed creatures gave me the giddy promise of protracted flight, which I had thought was to be denied me. For the cranes cross continents, do they not; they winter in Africa and summer on the Baltic! I vowed I'd learn to swoop and soar, to emulate at last the albatross and glide with delighted glee on the Roaring Forties and Furious Fifties, those winds like the breath of hell that guard the white, southern pole! For, as my legs grew, so did my wing-span; and my ambition swelled to match both. I should never be content with short hops to Hackney Marshes. Cockney sparrow I might be by birth, but not by inclination. I saw my future as criss-crossing the globe for then I knew nothing of the constraints the world imposes; I only knew my body was the abode of limitless freedom.

'For starters, needs must be content with small beginnings, sir. To climb on to the roof on moonless nights, nobody there to see, and take off for secret flights above the slumbering city. Some early tests we found we could conduct in our own front room as the vertical take-off.'

Lizzie repeated, as if a lesson from a book: 'When the bird wishes to soar upwards suddenly, it lowers its elbows after it has produced the impetus – '

Fevvers pushed back her chair, rose up on tiptoe and lifted towards the ceiling a face which suddenly bore an expression of the most heavenly beatitude, face of an angel in a Sunday school picture-book, a remarkable transformation. She crossed her arms on her massive bust and the bulge in the back of her satin dressing-gown began to heave and bubble. Cracks appeared in the old satin. Everything appeared to be about to burst out and take off. But the loose curls quivering on top of her high-piled chignon already brushed a stray drifting cobweb from the smoke-discoloured ceiling and Lizzie warned:

'Not enough room in 'ere, love. You'll 'ave to leave it to 'is imagination. Nelson's drawing-room was twice as 'igh as this rotten attic and our girlie wasn't half as tall, then, as she is now; shot up like anything when you was seventeen, didn't you, darling.' Oh, the caress in her voice!

Fevvers reluctantly subsided on her stool and a brooding shadow crossed her brow.

'When I was seventeen, and then our bad years started, our years in the wilderness.' She heaved another volcanic sigh. 'Any of that fizz left, Liz?'

Lizzie peeked behind the screen.

'Would you believe, we've drunk the lot.'

Abandoned bottles rolling underfoot among the foetid lingerie gave the room a debauched look.

'Well, then, make us a cup of tea, there's a love.'

Lizzie ducked behind the screen and emerged with a tin kettle: 'I'll just trot off and fill it up at the tap in the corridor.'

Alone with the marvellous giantess, Walser saw the undercurrent of suspicion towards himself she had partially concealed during the interview now come to the surface. Her geniality evaporated; she squinted at him beneath her thick pale lashes with almost hostility, seemed ill-at-ease, reached out to toy with her bunch of violets in a bored fashion. Something, somewhere, perhaps the tin lid of the tin kettle, rattled and clanged. She cocked her head. Then the chimes of Big Ben came drifting towards them once again on the soundless night and all at once she was imbued with vivacity.

'Twelve o'clock already! How time does fly, when one is babbling on about oneself!'

For the first time that night, Walser was seriously discomposed.

'Hey, there! didn't that clock strike midnight just a while ago, after the night watchman came round?'

'Did it, sir? How could it have, sir? Oh, dear, no, sir! Didn't it go –

ten, eleven, twelve – just this very minute? Didn't we both sit here and hear it? Look at your own watch, sir, if you don't believe me.'

Walser obediently checked his fob; it clasped its hands at midnight. He put it to his ear, where it ticked away industriously in the usual fashion. Lizzie returned bearing a dripping kettle.

The dressing-room was fully equipped for making tea; there was a brass spirit stove in the cupboard beside the fireplace and a japanned tray on which lived a chubby brown teapot and thick, white, pot mugs. Lizzie set a match to the small flame and reached in the cupboard again for a blue bag of sugar and for milk.

'Off again,' she observed, peering within the jug.

'We'll have to have our tea black, then.'

'Waaall, maybe my ears deceived me,' Walser murmured as he slipped his fob back in his breast pocket.

'What's this?' pricked sharp-eared Lizzie.

''e thinks we put Big Ben back an hour,' said Fevvers with a straight face.

'Very likely,' said Lizzie contemptuously. 'Oh, very like.'

Fevvers had a powerfully sweet tooth. She dispensed with measures and tipped the sugar into her steaming mug directly from the bag, in a stream. Warming her hands on its side – for, whatever time it was, it was the chill of night – Fevvers began again.

Her voice. It was as if Walser had become a prisoner of her voice, her cavernous, sombre voice, a voice made for shouting about the tempest, her voice of a celestial fishwife. Musical as it strangely was, yet not a voice for singing with; it comprised discords, her scale contained twelve tones. Her voice, with its warped, homely, Cockney vowels and random aspirates. Her dark, rusty, dipping, swooping voice, imperious as a siren's.

Yet such a voice could almost have had its source, not within her throat but in some ingenious mechanism or other behind the canvas screen, voice of a fake medium at a seance.

'Ma Nelson met her end with terrible suddenness, for, slipping on some foreign matter, skin of a fruit or dog turd, as she was crossing Whitechapel High Street on her way to Blooms to treat us all to salt beef sandwiches, she fell beneath the oncoming hooves and wheels of a brewer's dray and was mangled to pulp in a trice.'

'Dead on arrival at hospital, poor old thing,' chimed in Lizzie like a cracked bell. 'No chance for even so much as a "Kiss me, Hardy", nor any tender final words like that. We give her a lovely funeral – black plumes and mutes with chiffoned toppers, sir; Whitechapel ain't never seen such a sight before or since! The cortège followed by droves of grieving whores.'

'But, as we were breaking a funeral baked meat or two amongst ourselves back in the parlour after our beloved old girl was laid to rest, comes a knocking at the door like Judgment Day.'

'And Judgment Day indeed it proved to be, sir; for who should I let in but a dissenting cleric, his dog-collar up to his ears, and he gnashing his teeth and crying: "Let the wages of sin pay for the Good Lord's work!"'

'Now, Nelson, being taken from us so sudden when she herself was in the prime of life – not much older than my Lizzie is now – had not thought to make a will, although she thought of us as her adopted daughters, and yet she could not bear to think of death, either. So, dying intestate as she did, all her estate went by due process of the law to this, her surviving kin. To – oh, the irony of fate! – that very stern and stony-hearted elder brother who cast her from his hearth when as a girl first she slipped, and so ensured her ruin, in one sense, although her fortune in another.

'Is there no justice in either earth or heaven? It would seem not. For this very same cruel, unnatural brother now arrived legally entitled to beggar her posthumously and, if we had not already paid for her gravestone out of the petty cash – '

' – we chose "Safe Harbour" for the epitaph – '

' – he'd have seen to it that good, kind, decent woman returned to the earth out of which she had been formed without so much as a *pebble* to mark her passage.

'He couldn't stand the sight of us sitting there, eating food he thought belonged to him. He overturned the pork pies and spilled on the carpets all Ma Nelson's vintage port that we had broken out. Announces he, our time is up; he gives us till nine o'clock next morning, such was the goodness of his heart, to pack ourselves up, bag and baggage, and make ourselves scarce. Leave the only home we knew and go out on the common. In this way, he planned to "cleanse the temple of the ungodly", although he was kind enough to hint that his God might smile at any of us who cared to repent and stay on, because, with a singular poetic justice, he intended to make of his inheritance a hostel for fallen girls and he thought a repentant harlot or two would come in handy about the place, poacher turned gamekeeper, you might say.'

'But not one of us would take up the wardress posts he offered. No, thank you!'

'After he'd departed in a growler back to his manse in Deptford, we held a council amongst ourselves as to our futures, which we foresaw would no longer be held in common. Though we grieved that this should be, yet the necessity that first united us must now drive us apart and so we bowed to necessity, as all of us must do, although the invisible bonds of affection would always knit us wherever we roamed.

'But the unexpected did not find our friends altogether unprepared. You will recall how Ma Nelson knew that the days of the grand old whorehouse were numbered and always urged the members of her academy to prepare themselves for a wider world.

'Louisa and Emily had formed that kind of close attachment to one another as often reconciles women of the profession to its rigours and, long before Ma Nelson passed away, had decided between them to retire early, after having saved sufficient to set themselves up in a little boarding-house in Brighton. They'd long cherished the plan and often whiled away the hours of toil, while some dirty bugger poked away at them with his incompetent instrument, by planning whether their pillowcases should be left plain or edged with lace and what wallpaper to put in the dining-rooms. Although the sudden termination of our contracts forced these resourceful girls to start out on their adventure with somewhat less capital than they could have wished, they forthwith consulted their bankbooks and vowed: nothing ventured, nothing gained, and went upstairs to pack their trunks immediately, to leave next day for the South Coast and start their search for a suitable modest property.

'Annie and Grace had also set by a little store between them and now elected to pool it in order to start up a small agency for typing and office work, for Grace could rattle away on those keys of hers like the best of castanets and Annie had such a head for figures she'd been keeping Ma Nelson's accounts straight for years. So they, too, packed up their things, and next day, would move out to lodgings and set about finding suitable premises. I'm glad to say those girls have prospered, too, sir, by dint of hard work and good management.'

'But, as for our Jenny, although she was the prettiest and best-hearted harlot as ever trod Piccadilly, she had no special talent to put to work for her and never saved a penny but give it all to beggars. Her sole capital was her skin alone and what with the funeral and the eviction notice and a drop too much of Ma Nelson's port, she fell a-weeping

"What will become of me?" For she'd no heart to go it alone, after the security and companionship of the Academy. As we were comforting her and drying her eyes, comes a rat-a-tat-tat on the doorknocker and, lo and behold, it's the telegraph boy.

'And what have the twanging wires brought her? Why, a husband! For the message reads: "One death brings on another, or so they say, and my wife just dropped anchor in the same port as the Admiral." (He always called Ma Nelson, the Admiral.) "Jennifer-gentle, be mine in sight of God and Man! Signed, Lord – "'

'Muck,' interpolated Lizzie, with a leaden and ironic discretion.

'Lord Muck,' agreed Fevvers reflectively. 'So let us call 'im, for you'd be very much surprised, sir, if I told you his name and you looked him up in *Burke's Peerage*. Now, as they say, no two deaths without a third follows. Well, married they were and a very refined affair it was, in St John's, Smith Square, she in off-white because he'd given out she is a provincial widow. And, afterwards, at the reception, which was held in the Savoy Hotel, nothing but the best – '

' – he chokes to death on the *bombe surprise*,' said Lizzie, and emitted a sudden, fierce cackle, for which Fevvers reproved her with a look.

'So she comes into thirty thousand a year, a place up in Yorkshire, another in Scotland, and a very nice house in Eaton Square, into the bargain. And our little duck would have been sitting pretty except she was a sentimental soul and grieved a good deal over the departed as, ever the optimist, she'd counted on a long and happy life with the old bugger.'

'Only a whore,' opined Lizzie with sudden force, 'could hope for so much from marriage.'

'Black did become our Jenny, as she is red-headed, and, in her mourning, she decided to take herself off to Monte Carlo, to have a bit of a flutter at the tables, it being November and bad weather at home and, if she'd a weakness, it was gambling. So she's sitting at the tables, in black by Worth, wearing only the most reticently widowed of her diamonds – '

' – when she catches the eye of a gentleman from Chicago who makes sewing-machines – '

' – you don't mean – ' interjected Walser.

'Indeed.'

Walser tapped his teeth with his pencil tip, faced with the dilemma of the first checkable fact they'd offered him and the impossibility of checking it. Cable Mrs — III and ask her if she'd ever worked in a brothel run by a one-eyed whore named Nelson? Contracts had been taken out for less!

Fevvers and Lizzie now sighed in unison.

'However, I understand this Husband Number Two ain't feeling any too chipper, these days. Poor girl, one wonders,' Lizzie intoned, poker-faced, 'whether all his millions will console her for her loss.'

Fevvers let her left eyelid droop briefly over her left eye.

'As for Esmeralda,' resumed Fevvers, 'she'd tootled away on her flute to such effect that one of Ma Nelson's regulars, a gentleman in the theatrical profession whom she knew well, chooses this aptest of moments to send a special messenger to say he'd fixed her up with an act in which she charms a snake out of a laundry basket, this snake, as it turns out, being a young man of handsome appearance and preternatural physical agility professionally known as the Human Eel. Esmeralda appearing clad in a tigerskin and Greek sandals for this number. So hers turned out to be a *magic flute* and this very artistic act has toured Britain and Europe to great applause.

'And the Human Eel soon contrives to wriggle his way into Esmeralda's affections to such an extent they've now a brace of little elvers of their own, bless their hearts, to which Liz and I stood godmothers, sir.'

'We two were not left homeless, either. Over the years, Fevvers and I had put all our earnings and our tips into my sister's business and there was a room ready and waiting for us with her. So there we decided to retreat, where we could "recoil in order to jump better", as the French say. My sister, Isotta. Best ice-cream in London, sir. Best cassata outside Sicily. Old family recipe. *Il mio papa* brought it with him. As for our *bombe surprise* – '

'Ooops!' interpolated Fevvers, who, at that moment, by some accident, had contrived to overturn her powder box. What a mess! It took a moment or two to dust the spilled powder off the things on the dressing-table and then it was she herself who continued.

'So all us girls was fixed up satisfactorily and none of us got a wink of sleep that night, as we was all busy with planning and packing. Once our things were stowed away at last, we foregathered in the parlour to crack the last bottle of Ma Nelson's port that Esmeralda thoughtfully hid behind the fireguard when that demented Minister bust in. How sad we were to say goodbye to one another and to that room, the repository of so many bittersweet memories and humiliation and camaraderie, of whoring and sisterhood. And, as for me, that room will be ever hallowed in my mind since it was there I first released myself from gravity. We each took a little souvenir to remind us forever of stout-hearted Nelson.'

'Myself,' said Lizzie, 'I took the French clock that always says, midnight, or noon – '

' – for ain't it living proof that time stands still, sir?'

And Fevvers opened her great eyes at him, again, with such a swish of lashes that the pages of his notebook rustled in the breeze even if, due to the lateness of the hour, the thick, shining whites of those eyes were now lightly streaked with red.

'That clock – you'll find it right there, on the mantelpiece, for we never move an inch without it. Why, I do declare! I must have tossed my knickers over it in my haste to dress for this evening's show, for it's quite hidden!'

She stretched one long arm across the room and twitched the voluminous drawers away from the very pretty, old-fashioned clock of her description, with Father Time on top and hands stuck at twelve for all eternity. Then dropped the drawers in a lacy heap on Walser's lap. The women chuckled a little as he removed them with tactful thumb and fingertips and laid them on the sofa behind him.

'But, as for me,' she said, 'I took my sword, Victory's sword, the sword that started out its life on Nelson's thigh.'

She thrust her hand into the bosom of her dressing-gown and brought forth a gilt sword, which then she flourished above her head. Although it was only the little toy sword of a full-dress Admiral, it flashed and glittered in the exhausted light so sharply that Walser jumped.

'My sword. I carry it about all the time, for reasons both of sentiment and self-protection.'

When she'd made sure he'd noticed what an edge it had, she replaced it in her bosom.

'At the end of the night, there we clustered like sad birds in that salon and sipped our port and nibbled a bit of fruitcake Lizzie had put up for Christmas but there was no point in keeping it. How sad, how chilly that room! We never bothered to light a fire, after the funeral, so there was only a few nostalgic ashes of yesterday's sandalwood in the hearth. It was: "Remember this?" and "Remember that?" until our Jenny says: "I say, why don't we open our curtains and let in a little light on the subject, since this is the last we shall see of this room?"

'And the curtains had never been opened in all my memory of the place, nor could a single one of the other girls recall when those curtains had last been opened, either, for with those drapes there had been made the artificial night of pleasure which was the perennial season of the salon. But now, with the Mistress of the Revels departed into darkness, it seemed only right and proper that we should give it all back to common day.

'So we threw open the curtains, and the shutters too, and then the tall window that opened above the melancholy river, from which came off a chill yet bracing wind.

'It was the cold light of early dawn and how sadly, how soberly it lit that room which deceitful candles made so gorgeous! We saw, now, what we had never seen before; how the moth had nibbled the upholstery, the mice had gnawed away the Persian carpets and dust caked all the cornices. The luxury of that place had been nothing but illusion, created by the candles of midnight, and, in the dawn, all was sere, worn-out decay. We saw the stains of damp and mould on ceilings and the damask walls; the gilding on the mirrors was all tarnished and a bloom of dust obscured the glass so that, when we looked within them, there we saw, not the fresh young women that we were, but the hags we would become, and knew that, we too, like pleasures, were mortal.

'Then we understood the house had served its turn for us, for the parlour itself began to waver and dissolve before our very eyes. Even the solidity of the sofas seemed called into question for they and the heavy leather armchairs now had the dubious air of furniture carved out of smoke.

'"Come, now!" cried Esmeralda, never one to mope. "What say we give the good old girl a funeral pyre like the pagan kings of old, and cheat the Reverend out of his inheritance, to boot!"

'Off she runs to the kitchen and comes back with a can of kerosene. We all make haste to shift our bits and bobs out on the lawn, clear of the conflagration, and then we ritually anoint the walls and portals of the old place with oil, sir. Thoroughly soak the cellars, drench the damned beds, douse the carpets.

'Lizzie, as she had been the housekeeper, sought for herself the last task of tidying up – she struck the match.'

'I wept,' said Lizzie.

'We girls stood on the lawn and the morning wind off the river whipped our skirts about us. We shivered, from the cold, from anxiety, from sorrow at the end of one part of our lives and the exhilaration of our new beginnings. When the fire had fairly taken hold, off we went, Indian file, clutching our bundles, up the towpath, until we got to the main road and found a rank of sleepy cabbies under the Tower only too pleased to see custom at that hour in the morning. We kissed and parted and went each our separate ways. And so the first chapter of my life went up in flames, sir.'

THREE

'What a long drive it was to Battersea! But such a welcome when we got there, the little nieces and nephews jumping up from the breakfast table to throw their arms around us, Isotta running to put fresh coffee on! A little, old-fashioned family life did not come amiss to either of us, after so long of the other kind, and we'd help out in the shop; I would turn the crank of the ice-cream machine in the mornings while Fevvers, discreetly shrouded in a shawl, would man the counter.'

'Hokey pokey penny a lump.

The more you eat the more you jump –

'I love to be among the little children sir! How I love to hear their prattle and their little voices lisping merry rhymes! Oh, sir! can you think of a more innocent way of earning a living, than to sell good ice-cream at modest prices to little children, after so many years of selling tricks to dirty old men. Why, each day in that white, well-scrubbed, shining ice-cream parlour was a positive purification! Don't you think, sir, that in heaven we shall *all* eat nothing but ice-cream?' Fevvers smiled beatifically, belched, and interrupted herself: 'Here, Liz . . . is there a bite left to eat in the place? I'm starved, again. All this talking about meself, sir; Gawd, it takes the strength out of you . . . '

Lizzie peered beneath the napkin in the basket, but found nothing except dirty crockery.

'Tell you, what, love,' she said, 'I'll just slip out to the all-night cab-stand in Piccadilly for a bacon sandwich, shall I? No, sir! put away your money. Our treat.'

Lizzie briskly slipped a jacket of grey, disturbingly anonymous fur over her dress and speared a queer little, still little round black hat to her cropped head with a savage pin. She was still fresh as a daisy. She tossed Walser a gratuitously ironic leer as she ducked out of the door.

Now Walser was alone with the giantess.

Who fell silent, as she had done the first time Lizzie left them alone together, and turned back to the inverted world of her mirror, in which she stroked an eyebrow as if it were imperative for her peace of mind that she set the hairs in perfect order. Then, perhaps hoping their scent would refresh her, she pulled her violets dripping from the jam-jar and buried her face in them. Perhaps she was tiring? After she'd imbibed whatever virtue she might obtain from her violets, she yawned.

But not as a tired girl yawns. Fevvers yawned with prodigious energy, opening up a crimson maw the size of that of a basking shark, taking in enough air to lift a Montgolfier, and then she stretched herself suddenly and hugely, extending every muscle as a cat does, until it seemed she intended to fill up all the mirror, all the room with her bulk. As she raised her arms, Walser, confronted by stubbled, thickly powdered armpits, felt faint; God! she could easily crush him to death in her huge arms, although he was a big man with the strength of Californian sunshine distilled in his limbs. A seismic erotic disturbance convulsed him – unless it was their damn' champagne. He scrambled to his feet, suddenly panicking, scattering underwear, grazing his scalp painfully on the mantelpiece.

'Ouch – excuse me, ma'am; the call of nature – '

If he got out of her room for just one moment, was allowed, however briefly, to stand by himself in the cold, grimy passage away from her presence, if he could fill his lungs just the one time with air that was not choking with 'essence of Fevvers', then he might recover his sense of proportion.

'Piss in the pot behind the screen, love. Go on. We don't stand on ceremony.'

'But – '

'GO ON.'

It seemed he must not leave the room until she and her familiar were done with him. So he humbly stepped behind the screen to direct the brown arc of the excess of her champagne, as bidden, into the white china pot. The act of engaging in this most human of activities brought him down to earth again, for there is no element of the metaphysical about pissing, not, at least, in *our* culture. As he buttoned his fly, earthiness reasserted itself all around him. The dressing-room suddenly sizzled with the salt, savoury smell of fried bacon and a hand holding the brown teapot appeared around the screen and upended the cold contents into Fevvers' dirty bathwater, on the scummed, grey surface of which the last deposit of tealeaves already floated. When he emerged from behind the screen the passage door stood open and a welcome draught freshened up the crusted air. The room echoed with the melody of running water and the chink of the plumbing as Lizzie refilled the kettle at the tap in the passage. Walser sighed with reassurance.

'Hark!' said Fevvers, raising her hand.

On the soundless air of night came the ripple of Big Ben. Lizzie slammed the door as she came back to put the kettle on the hissing stove; the mauve and orange flames dipped and swayed.

Big Ben concluded the run-up, struck – and went on striking.

Walser relapsed on the sofa, dislodging not only a slithering mass of silken underthings but also the concealed layer of pamphlets and newspapers that lay beneath them. Muttering apologies, he bundled together the musky garments, but Lizzie, chattering with rage, snatched the papers from him and stuffed them away in the corner cupboard. Odd, that – that she did not want him to examine her old newspaper.

But, odder still – Big Ben had once again struck midnight. The time outside still corresponded to that registered by the stopped gilt clock, inside. Inside and outside matched exactly, but both were badly wrong. H'm.

He rejected a bacon sandwich; the strips of rusty meat slapped between the doorsteps of white bread seemed to him for dire extremities of hunger only, but Fevvers tucked in with relish, a vigorous mastication of large teeth, a smacking of plump lips smeared with grease. Lizzie passed him a fresh mug of black tea for him to burn his gullet with. Everything aggressively normal about all this, except the hour.

The food put fresh heart into the *aerialiste*. Her backbone firmed up and she began to glow, again, quite brightly, as she wiped her mouth once more on her sleeve, leaving behind shining traces of bacon fat on the grubby satin.

'As I was saying,' she resumed, 'we lived for a while at Isotta's in Battersea amid all the joys of home. And, an especial joy – we were just a hop and a skip and a jump away from the good Old Vic at Waterloo where, at very reasonable prices, we perched up in the gods and wept at Romeo and Juliet, booed and hissed at Crookback Dick, laughed ourselves silly at Malvolio's yellow stockings – '

'We dearly love the Bard, sir,' said Lizzie briskly. 'What spiritual sustenance he offers!'

'And we'd take in a bit of opera, too – our favourites, sir? Why – '

'*Marriage of Figaro*, for the class analysis,' offered Lizzie, deadpan. Fevvers' hearty laughter did not quite conceal her irritation.

'Oh, Liz, you are a one! As for me, sir, I've a special fondness for Bizet's *Carmen*, due to the spirit of the heroine.'

She subjected Walser to a blue bombardment from her eyes, challenge and attack at once, before she took up the narrative again.

'So there we were, in Battersea; happy days! but a fearful cold winter came on with very little call for ice-cream and Gianni –'

'– Isotta's husband, my brother-in-law –'

'– Gianni's chest got very bad. They having the five little ones and another in the pot, with trade going so bad, we were hard put to manage, I can tell you. Then the baby fell sick and would take no nourishment and we was all crazed with worry.'

'One morning, the elder kiddies at school, Gianni out on business in the freezing November fog, poor soul, with his cough, Isotta upstairs grieving over the baby, myself in the kitchen chopping candied peel, Fevvers in the room behind the shop teaching the four-year-old her letters –'

'Though I know I should have no favourites among them, and truly, I love them all as if they was my own, well, my Violetta . . .'

She reached out to caress the bunch of Parma violets on her dressing-table with a smile that, for once, was not meant for Walser to see.

'My Violetta on my knee, we explore together the adventures of A and B and C when comes a jangle on the bell and there in the shop is the strangest old lady that ever I saw, dressed up in the clothes of her youth, that is to say, some fifty years behind the times, a dress of black chiffon that looked like rags hung over such a mass of taffeta petticoats you couldn't see at first how thin she was, that she was a lady all skin and bone. On her head she wore an old-fashioned poke bonnet of dull black satin with jet ornaments at either side and a black spotted veil hanging down in the front, so thick you could not see her face.

'"Let me through into the back room, Winged Victory," she said and she had a voice like the wind in telegraph wires.

'Violetta burst out crying at the sight of my visitor and I hustled her off into the kitchen to get a treat of nuts and citron off Lizzie but I was a good deal discomposed by this apparition, too, and set her by the fire on the best chair – for you could tell she was a perfect gentlewoman – with stammerings and nervous fussings, quite unlike myself. She stretched her hand towards the flames; she had those great-auntish black lace mittens on, that go no further than the first joint of the fingers and thumbs, so all you could see of her hands was bone and nail.

'"I reckon you've fallen on hard times since Nelson went," she says.

'"I won't say things are rosy," says I, although her very presence made me shudder and throughout our interview she never lifts her veil.

'"Well, Fevvers," she says, "I've a proposition for you." And with that names me a figure that takes my breath away.

'"And never any need to do the thing, oh, rest assured!" she tells me. "Not 'til you want to, that is." So I realise she has heard all about me, how I was Ma Nelson's flagship but always kept out of the battle, that Nelson never brought me to the block so I was known to all the netherside of London as the Virgin Whore.

'"I want you for my museum of woman monsters," she says. "Take your time about making up your mind." Rising, she leaves her card on the mantelpiece and departs, and, looking after her out of the shop door, I see her little, old-fashioned carriage, all closed in, drawn by a little black pony and, on the box, a black man with this mournful peculiarity, he had been born without a mouth. Then the sour, brown fog rising from the river swallowed them up but I heard the hooves trotting towards Chelsea Bridge, although the wheels I could not hear since they were solid rubber.'

'It was the famous Madame Schreck,' said Lizzie tonelessly, as if the mention of the name were sufficient bad news in itself.

Famous, indeed; Walser knew of her already, vague rumours in men's clubs, over brandy and cigars, the name never accompanied by guffaws, leers, nudges in the ribs, but by bare, hinted whispers of the profoundly strange, of curious revelations that greeted you behind Our Lady of Terror's triple-locked doors, doors that opened reluctantly, with a great rattling of bolts and chains, and then swung to with a long groan as of despair.

'Madame Schreck,' wrote Walser. The story was about to take a grisly turn.

'Oh, my poor girl!' exclaimed Lizzie on a sigh. 'If only . . . if only the baby had not taken a turn for the worse; oh, and if only Gianni's cough had not turned septic, so he had to take to his bed; if only Isotta never took such a tumble down the stairs that the doctor swore she must spend the last three months of her time flat on her back on the kitchen sofa . . . Oh, Mr Walser, the dolorous litany of the misfortunes of the poor is a string of "if onlys".'

'Had not the doctor's bills, that winter, swallowed up all our savings and as for the activities of the Special Branch – '

This time it was Lizzie who kicked furiously at Fevvers' ankle and the girl never missed a beat of her narrative but went smoothly on a different tack.

'And the little ones staring starvation in the face; oh! if our household had not been overwhelmed by an accumulation of those unpredictable catastrophes that precipitate poor folk such as we into the abyss of poverty through no fault of their own – '

'"Don't do it, Fevvers," our Gianni begged her, but then he coughed up blood.'

'So, rising early one morning, before the house was awake, when nobody could stop me, leaving Lizzie sleeping in our bed, I hastily packed a few things in a carpet bag, and not forgetting my pet talisman, Ma Nelson's toy sword, to give me courage, I left a scribbled message on the kitchen table and trudged over Chelsea Bridge just as the moon was setting. It was bitter, bitter cold and even at Nelson's funeral was my heart never so heavy. As I reached the last lamp-post on the bridge, out it blinked, and I lost sight of Battersea in the darkness before dawn.'

FOUR

'You've filled up your notebook,' observed Lizzie. Walser reversed it in
order to give himself a fresh set of blank pages. He sharpened his pencil
with the razor blade he always carried in an inner pocket for the
purpose. He flexed his aching wrist. Lizzie, as if rewarding him for
these activities, refilled his mug and Fevvers held out her mug for more
tea, too. 'Thirsty work, this autobiography,' she said. Her exuberant
hair was beginning to escape from Lizzie's hairpins and frolic here and
there along her bullish nape.

'Mr Walser,' she went on earnestly, spinning on her stool towards
him. 'You must understand this: Nelson's Academy accommodated
those who were perturbed in their bodies and wished to verify that,
however equivocal, however much they cost, the pleasures of the flesh
were, at bottom, splendid. But, as for Madame Schreck, she catered for
those who were troubled in their . . . souls.'

Darkly she turned her attention for a moment to her treacly tea.

'It was a gloomy pile in Kensington, in a square with a melancholy
garden in the middle full of worn grass and leafless trees. The façade of
her house was blackened by the London soot as if the very stucco were
in mourning. A louring portico over the front door, sir, and all the
inner shutters tightly barred. And the door knocker most ominously
bandaged up in crepe.

'That self-same fellow with no mouth, poor thing, opens the door to
me after a good deal of unbolting from the inside, and bids me come in
with eloquent gestures of his hands. I never saw eyes so full of sorrow
as his were, sorrow of exile and of abandonment; his eyes said, clear as
his lips could have, "Oh, girl! go home! save yourself while there is yet
time!" even while he takes away my hat and shawl, but I am the same
poor creature of necessity as he, and, as he must stay, then so needs I.

'Early as it was in the morning for a house of pleasure – it was not yet
seven – Madame Schreck, it seems, was wide awake but still in bed,
taking her chocolate. She had me sit meself down and have a cup with
her, which I did willingly enough, in spite of my trepidation, for that
long walk had worn me out and I was starving hungry. The shutters

were up, the blinds down, her heavy curtains drawn across and the only light in her bedroom a little nightlight or corpse light on the mantel so I was hard put to it to see what witches' broth there is in my cup and she's laid out in an old four-poster with the embroidered hangings pulled almost together so I can't make out the face or shape of her, and all cold as hell.

'"I'm glad to see *you*, Fevvers," she says, and her voice was like wind in graveyards. "Toussaint will show you to your quarters, presently, and you can take a rest until dinner-time, after which we shall measure you for your costume." From the way she said it, you'd think that costume was to be a winding sheet.

'As my eyes grew used to the penumbra, I saw the only furniture in the room, besides her bed and my chair, was a safe the size of a wardrobe with the biggest brass combination lock on it that I ever did see, and a desk with a roll-top all locked up.

'That was all she spoke to me. I made haste to finish my chocolate, I can tell you. Then the manservant, Toussaint, with the tenderest gesture, covers my eyes up with his hand, and, when he uncovers, Madame Schreck is up and dressed and stood there before me in her black dress and a thick veil such as a Spanish widow wears that comes down to her knees, and her mittens on, all complete.

'Now, Mr Walser, do not think I am a faint-hearted woman but although I knew very well it was all so much show, the black carriage, the mute, the prison chill, all the same she had some quality of the uncanny about her, over and above the illusion, so you did think that under those lugubrious garments of hers you might find nothing but some kind of wicked puppet that pulled its own strings.

'"Be off with you!" she says. But I thought of my little nephews and nieces who, that very minute, would be plaguing Lizzie for a bite of breakfast when we'd shared the last crust in the house at last night's supper, and I sang out: "How about a bit on account, Madame Schreck? Or else I fly straight up the chimney, you won't see me again." And I swept over to the fireplace, that ain't never seen a burned stock in its life, shoved aside the firescreen, ready to make good my promise.

'"Toussaint!" she says. "Get in a man to block up all the chimneys immediately!" But when I started to toss the fire-irons furiously this way and that way, she says reluctantly: "Oh, very well," feels under her pillow for a key, takes good care to put herself fair and square between me and the safe so I can't read the combination, and, in a trice, the door swings open. Aladdin's cave, inside! the contents shone with their own light, pile upon pile of golden sovereigns, a queen's ransom of diamond necklaces and pearls and rubies and emeralds piled hugger-mugger among bankers' draughts, bills of exchange, foreclosed mortgages etc. etc. etc. With a display of the greatest reluctance, she selects five sovereigns, counts 'em out again and, with as much painful hesitation as if they were drops of her dear heart's blood, she hands 'em over.

'What a shock I got when I felt the rasp of her finger-tips on my palm, for they were indeed hard, as if there were no flesh on 'em. Afterwards, when I was free again, Esmeralda's old man, the Human Eel, told me how this Madame Schreck, as she called herself, had indeed started out in life as a Living Skeleton, touring the sideshows, and always was a bony woman.

'As I goes out the bedroom, I glances over my shoulder, to see what the old hag's up to, now, and, bugger me, if she hasn't precipitated herself bodily into that safe, and is hugging the riches it contains to her skinny bosom with the most vehement display of passion, making faint, whinnying sounds the while.

'I trust Toussaint, to whom I have taken an immediate liking, to get these sovereigns straight to Battersea, lay my head on my hard, flat pillow, and take immediate refuge in sleep, to wake hours later, as night approaches. It was the barest, plainest chamber you ever saw, with a little iron bedstead, a deal washstand and iron bars across the window from which I can see the barren trees in the deserted garden and a few lights in the houses over the square. To see those lights in happy homes brought the tears to my eyes, sir, for I am in a house that shows no lights, no lights.

'Then it comes to me how I might never leave this place, now I have come here of my own free will; that I have voluntarily incarcerated myself among the damned, for the sake of money, even if from the best of motives; that my doom has come upon me.

'At this apocalyptic moment, the door opens, I see a shadow behind a kerosene lamp, I start up from the bed, crying out – and the shadow speaks, in broad Yorkshire: "It's nobbut old Fanny, luv, don't be afeared!"

'And I will find the companionship of the damned my only solace.

'Who worked for Madame Schreck, sir? Why, prodigies of nature, such as I. Dear old Fanny Four-Eyes; and the Sleeping Beauty; and the Wiltshire Wonder, who was not three foot high; and Albert/Albertina, who was bipartite, that is to say, half and half and neither of either; and the girl we called Cobwebs. During the time I stayed at Madame Schreck's, such was the full complement, and though she begged Toussaint to join in some of the *tableaux vivants,* he never would, being a man of great dignity. All he did was play the organ.

'And there was a drunk cook in the basement, but we never saw much of her.'

'This Toussaint,' said Walser, tapping his pencil against his teeth. 'How did he –'

'Eat, sir? Through a tube up his nose, sir. Liquids only but sufficient to sustain life. I'm happy to say that, since I began to prosper on the halls and started to frequent the company of men of science, I was able to interest Sir S—. J—. in Toussaint's case and he was successfully operated upon at St Bartholomew's Hospital two years ago last February. And now Toussaint has a mouth as good as yours or mine! You'll find a full account of the operation in *The Lancet* for June, 1898, sir.'

She gave him this scientific verification of Toussaint's existence with a dazzling smile.

It was true that Fevvers had won the friendship of many men of science. Walser recalled how the young woman had entertained the curiosity of the entire Royal College of Surgeons for three hours without so much as unbuttoning her bodice for them, and discussed navigation in birds with a full meeting of the Royal Society with such infernal assurance and so great a wealth of scientific terminology that not one single professor had dared be rude enough to question her on the extent of her personal experience.

'Oh, that Toussaint!' said Lizzie. 'How he can move a crowd! Such eloquence, the man has! Oh, if all those with such things to say had mouths! And yet it is the lot of those who toil and suffer to be dumb. But, consider the dialectic of it, sir,' she continued with freshly crackling vigour, 'how it was, as it were, the *white hand* of the *oppressor* who carved open the aperture of speech in the very throat you could say that it had, in the first place, rendered dumb, and –'

Fevvers shot Lizzie a look of such glazing fury that the witch hushed, suddenly as she'd started. Walser raised his mental eyebrows. More to the chaperone than met the eye! But Fevvers lassooed him with her narrative and dragged him along with her before he'd had a chance to ask Lizzie if –

'Before he met up with Madame Schreck, sir, Toussaint used to work the shows at fairs, what they call on your side of the herring-pond the

Ten-in-Ones, sir. So he was a connoisseur of degradation and always maintained it was those fine gentlemen who paid down their sovereigns to poke and pry at us who were the unnatural ones, not we. For what is "natural" and "unnatural", sir? The mould in which the human form is cast is exceedingly fragile. Give it the slightest tap with your fingers and it breaks. And God alone knows why, Mr Walser, but the men who came to Madame Schreck's were one and all quite remarkable for their ugliness; their faces suggested that he who cast the human form in the first place did not have his mind on the job.

'Toussaint could hear *us* perfectly well, of course, and often jotted down encouraging words and sometimes little maxims on the pad he always carried with him and he was as great a comfort and an inspiration to us in our confinement as now he will be to a greater world.'

Lizzie nodded emphatically. Fevvers went smoothly forward.

'Madame Schreck organised her museum, thus: downstairs, in what had used to be the wine cellar, she'd had a sort of vault or crypt constructed, with wormy beams overhead and nasty damp flagstones underfoot, and this place was known as "Down Below", or else, "The Abyss". The girls was all made to stand in stone niches cut out of the slimy walls, except for the Sleeping Beauty, who remained prone, since proneness was her speciality. And there were little curtains in front and, in front of the curtains, a little lamp burning. These were her "profane altars", as she used to call them.

'Some gent would knock at the front door, thumpety-thump, a soft, deathly thunder due to that crepe muffler on the knocker. Toussaint would unbolt and let him in, relieve him of his topcoat and topper and put him in the little receiving-room, where the punter would rummage among the clobber in the big wardrobe and rig himself out in a cassock, or a ballet-dancer's frock, or whatever he fancied. But the one I liked least was the executioner's hood; there was a judge who come regular who always fancied that. Yet all he ever wanted was a weeping girl to spit at him. And he'd pay a hundred guineas for the privilege! Except, on those days when he'd put on the black cap himself, then he'd take himself off upstairs, to what Madame Schreck called the "Black Theatre", and there, Albert/Albertina put a noose around his neck and give it a bit of a pull but not enough to hurt, whereupon he'd ejaculate and give him/her a fiver tip, but La Schreck always took charge of *that*.

'When the client had donned the garments of his choice, the lights dimmed. Toussaint would scurry down below and take his place at the harmonium, which was concealed behind a pierced Gothic fold-screen. He'd start pumping out some heartening tune such as a nice *Kyrie* from some requiem. That was our cue to off with the shawls and jackets we'd bundled ourselves in, to keep out the cold, and give over the games of bezique or backgammon with which we passed the time, climb up on our pedestals and pull the curtains shut. Then the old hag herself comes tottering down the cellar like Lady MacBeth, ushering the happy client. There'd be a lot of clanking of chains, there being several doors to open, and it was all dark but for her lantern, which was a penny candle in a skull.

'So, we all stood to attention at our posts and the last door opens and in she comes like Virgil in Hell, with her little Dante trotting after, whickering to himself with deliciously scarified anticipation, and the candle-lantern throwing all manner of shadows on the sweating walls.

'She'd stop at random in front of one niche or another and she'd say: "Shall I open the curtain? Who knows what spectacle of the freakish and unnatural lies behind it!" And they'd say, "yes", or, "no", depending on whether they'd been before, for if they'd been before, they'd got their fancies picked out. And if it was, "yes", she'd pull back the curtain while Toussaint wheezed out a shocking discord on the old harmonium.

'And there she'd be.

'It cost another hundred guineas to have the Wiltshire Wonder suck you off and a cool two fifty to take Albert/Albertina upstairs because s/he was one of each and then as much again, while the tariff soared by leaps and bounds if you wanted anything out of the ordinary. But, as for me and the Sleeping Beauty, it was: "look, don't touch", since Madame Schreck chose to dispose of us in a series of tableaux.

'After the door clanged shut again, I'd go and turn the light on, throw a blanket over the Sleeping Beauty, lift the Wonder off the perch from which it was too high for her to jump, and Toussaint would bring us a hot pot of coffee with a bit of brandy in it, or tea with rum, for it was perishing down there. Oh, it was easy work, all right, especially for me and the Beauty. But what I never could get used to was the sight of their eyes, for there was no terror in the house our customers did not bring with them.

'We were *supposed* to get a tenner a week each, basic, with bonuses per trick, those that turned 'em, but, out of that, she kept back a fiver each for our keep, which was scanty enough, boiled beef and carrots, spotted dog; and, as to the rest, which was riches beyond the dreams of most working girls, why, we never saw a penny of it. She "put it away for us in her safe", ha! ha! What a joke. Those five sovereigns I got out of her the first day I arrived in the house was the only cash I got in my hand all the time I worked there.

'For, the moment that her front door shut behind you, you were her prisoner; indeed, you were her slave.'

Lizzie, once again crouched at Fevvers' feet, tugged the hem of the *aerialiste*'s dressing-gown.

'Tell 'im about the Sleeping Beauty,' she prompted.

'Oh, what a tragic case, sir! She was a country curate's daughter and bright and merry as a grig, until, one morning in her fourteenth year, the very day her menses started, she never wakened, not until noon; and the day after, not until teatime; and the day after that, her grieving parents watching and praying beside her bed, she opened her eyes at suppertime and said: "I think I could fancy a little bowl of bread and milk."

'So they propped her up on her pillows and fed her with a spoon and when she'd eaten it all up, she says: "I couldn't keep my eyes open if I tried," and falls back asleep. And so it went on. After a week of it, then a month of it, then a year of it, Madame Schreck, chancing to hear of this great marvel, came to her village and let on she was a philanthropic gentlewoman who would take care of the poor girl and let the best doctors visit her, and Beauty's parents, getting on in years, could hardly believe their luck.

'She was loaded on a stretcher into the guard's van of the London train and so to Kensington, where her life went on as it had done before. She always woke at sunset, like night-scented stock; she ate, she filled a bedpan, and then she slept again. This difference, only: now, each night, at midnight, Toussaint gathered her dreaming body in his arms and took her to the crypt. She would have been about twenty-one when I first knew her, pretty as a picture, although a mite emaciated. Her female flow grew less and less the time she slept, until at last it scarcely stained the rag and then dried up altogether but her hair kept on growing, until it was as long as she was herself. Fanny it was who undertook the task of combing it and brushing it for old Four-eyes was a tender woman with a loving heart. The Beauty's fingernails and toenails kept on growing too, and it was the Wiltshire Wonder's task to trim them, owing to the marvellous dexterity of her tiny fingers.

'Because the Sleeping Beauty's face had grown so thin, her eyes were especially prominent, and her closed eyelids were dark as the under-skins of mushrooms and must have grown very heavy during those long, slumbering years, for, every evening, when she opened her little windows at the approach of the dark, it cost her a greater, even greater effort, as if it took all the feeble strength that remained to her to open up shop.

'And, every time, we who watched and waited with her supper were afraid that, this time, it might be the last time she would so valiantly strive to wake, that the vast, unknown ocean of sleep, on which she drifted like sea-wrack, had, that night, finally taken her so far from shore on its mysterious currents that she would not return. But, whilst I was at Madame Schreck's, the Sleeping Beauty always *did* wake up long enough to take a little minced chicken or a spoonful of junket, and she would evacuate a small, semi-liquid motion into the bed-pan Fanny held under her, and then, with a short sigh, she would sink down again under the soft weight of her dreams.

'For do not think she was a dreamless sleeper. Under those soft, veined webs, her eyeballs moved continually this way and that, as if she were watching shapes of antic ballets playing themselves out upon the insides of her eyelids. And sometimes her toes and fingers would convulse and twitch, as a dog's paws do when it dreams of rabbits. Or she might softly moan or cry out, and sometimes, very softly, laugh, which was most strange.

'And once, when Fanny and I were at backgammon one night when trade was slow, the Wonder, giving this dreamer a manicure, cries out of a sudden: "Oh, unendurable!"

'For, beneath those lashes, oozed out a few fat tears.

'"And I had thought," the Wonder said, "she was beyond all pain."

'Though so diminutive in stature, the Wonder was as perfectly formed as any of those avatars of hers, such as Good Queen Bess's pretty little confidante, Mrs Tomysen; or that Anne Gibson who married the little fellow who painted miniatures; or the beautiful Anastasia Borculaski, who was small enough to stand under her brother's arm, and her brother was a small man, himself. Besides, the Wonder was a most accomplished dancer and could do high kicks that was just like opening up a pair of embroidery scissors.

'So I says to her: "Wonder, why do you degrade yourself by working in this house, which is truly a house of shame, when you could earn a good living on the boards?" "Ah, Fevvers," she replies, "I'd rather show myself to one man at a time than to an entire theatre-full of the horrid, nasty, hairy things, and, here, I'm well protected from the dark, foul throng of the world, in which I suffered so much. Amongst the monsters, I am well hidden; who looks for a leaf in a forest?

'"Let me tell you that I was conceived in the following manner. My mother was a merry milkmaid who loved nothing better than a prank. There was, near our village, a hill, quite round, and, though overgrown with grass, it was well-nigh hollow, since it was burrowed through and through with tunnels like runs of generations of mice. Though I have heard it said this hill was no work of nature but a gigantic tomb, a place that those who lived in Wiltshire before us, before the Normans, before the Saxons, before even the Romans came, laid out their dead, the common people of the village called it the Fairy Mound and steered clear of it at nights for they believed it was, if not a place accursed, then certainly one in which we human beings might suffer curious fates and transformations.

'"But my madcap mother, egged on by the squire's son, who was a rogue, and bet her a silver sixpence she would not dare, once spent the whole of one midsummer's night inside this earthen castle. She took with her a snack of bread and honey and a farthing dip and penetrated to the chamber at its heart, where there was a long stone, much like an altar, but more likely, in all probability, to have been the coffin of some long dead King of Wessex.

'"On this tomb she sat to eat her supper and by and by the light went out, so she was in the dark. Just as she began to regret her foolhardiness, she heard the softest footfall. 'Who's there?' 'Why, Meg – who but the King of the Fairies?' And this invisible stranger forthwith laid her down on the stone slab and pleasured her, or so she said, as mightily as any man before or since. 'Indeed, I went to fairyland that night!' she said: and the proof of it was, nine months later, I made my infinitesimal appearance in the world. She cradled me in half a walnut shell, covered me with a rose petal, packed my layette in a hazel nut and carried me off to London town where she exhibited herself for a shilling a time as 'The Fairy's Nursemaid', while I clung to her bosom like a burr.

'"But all she got she spent on drink and men because she was a flighty piece. When I got too big to be passed off as a suckling, I said: 'Mother, this won't do! We must think of our security and our old age!' She laughed a good deal when she heard her daughter pipe up in that style for I was only seven years old and she herself not five-and-twenty and it was a black day for me when I took it into my head to turn that giddy creature's mind to the future because, at that, she sold me.

"'For fifty golden guineas cash in hand my own mother sold me to a French pastrycook with corkscrew moustaches, who served me for a couple of seasons in a cake. Chef's hat perched on his head at a rakish angle, he'd bear the silver salver out of the kitchen and set it down in front of the birthday boy, for the *patisseur* had this much sensibility, I was a treat for children only. The birthday child would blow out the candles and lift up the knife to cut its cake, but the pastrycook kept his own hand on the handle, to guide the blade in case it cut me by accident and blemished his property. Then up I'd pop through the hole, wearing a spangled dress, and dance round the table, distributing streamers, favours and bonbons.

"'But sometimes the greediest ones burst into tears and said it was a mean trick, and cake was what they wanted, not a visit from the fairies.

"'Possibly due to the circumstances of my conception, I had always suffered from claustrophobia. I found I could scarcely bear the close confinement of those hollowed cakes. I grew to dread the moment of my incarceration under the icing and I would beg and plead with my master to let me free but he would threaten me with the oven and say, if I did not do as he bid me, then, next time, he would not serve me in a cake but bake me in a *vol-au-vent*.

"'Came the day at last my phobia got the better of me. I clambered in my coffin, suffered the lid to close on me, endured the jolting cab-ride to the customer's address, was cursorily unloaded on to the salver in the kitchen and then came the trip to the table. Half-fainting, sweating, choking for lack of air in that round space no bigger than a hatbox, sickened by the stench of baked eggs and butter, sticky with sugar and raisins, I could tolerate no more. With the strength of the possessed, I thrust my bare shoulders up through the crust and so emerged before my time, crusted with frosting, blinking crumbs from my eyes. My eruption scattered candles and crystallised violets everywhere.

"'The tablecloth caught fire and all the little dears screamed blue murder as I ran down the length of the table with my hair and tulle skirt all in flames, pursued by the furious pastrycook wielding his cake knife and vowing he'd make a *bonne bouche* of me.

"'But one child kept her wits about her in this mêlée, sat gravely at the bottom of the table until I reached her plate, when she dropped her napkin over me and put out the flames. Then she picked me up and stowed me away in her pocket and said to the pastrycook: 'Go away, you horrid man! How dare you torture a human creature so!'

"'As it turned out, this little girl was the eldest daughter of the house. She carried me off to the nursery and her nanny put soothing ointment on my burns and dressed me up in a silk frock that the young lady's own doll sacrificed for me, although I was perfectly able to dress myself. But I was to find that rich women as well as dolls cannot put on their own clothes unaided. Later that night, when dinner was over, I was introduced to Mama and Papa, as they sat over their coffee, of which they gave me some, since it was served in cups of a size that just suited me. Papa seemed to me a mountain whose summit was concealed by the smoke from his cigar; but what a good, kind mountain it was! And after I had told my story as best I could, the mountain puffed a purple cloud, smiled at Mama, and spoke. 'Well, my little woman, it seems we have no course but to *adopt* you.' And Mama said, 'I am ashamed. I never thought that horrid trick with the cake might cause suffering to a living creature.'

'"They did not treat me like a pet or a toy, either, but as truly one of their own. I soon formed a profound attachment to the girl who'd been my saviour, and she for me, so that we became inseparable and, when my legs could not keep up with hers, she would carry me in the crook of her arm. We called each other 'sister'. She was just eight years old to my nine. My ship had come to rest in a happy harbour!

'"Time passed. We girls began to dream of putting up our hair and letting down our skirts and all the delicious mysteries of *growing up* that lay ahead ... although, as for me, I knew I'd never *grow up* in any worldly sense, which made me, sometimes, sad. One Christmas, came the question of the pantomime. Some sixth sense, perhaps, forewarned me that danger lay ahead. I told Mama that I'd put childish things away and preferred to stay at home that night, and read my book. But my sister was lagging a little behind me in the business of maturing, longed to see the bright lights and pretty tinsel and told me that if I was not one of the family party, then the treat would all be spoiled. I submitted to her tender bullying. As it turned out, the pantomime was *Snow White*.

'"I turned, first fire, then ice, in our box as the scenes unfolded before me, for, dearly as I loved my family, there was always that unalterable difference between us. Not so much the clumsiness of their limbs, their lumpish movements, oppressed me; nor even the thunder of their voices, as never in all my life had I gone to bed without a headache. No. I had known all these things from birth and grown accustomed to the monstrous ugliness of mankind. Indeed, my life in that kind house could almost have made me forgive some, at least, of the beasts for their beastliness. But, when I watched my natural kin on that stage, even as they frisked and capered and put on the show of comic dwarves, I had a kind of vision of a world in miniature, a small, perfect, heavenly place such as you might see reflected in the eye of a wise bird. And it seemed to me that place was my home and these little men were its inhabitants, who would love me, not as a 'little woman' but as – a woman.

'"And then, perhaps it was . . . perhaps the blood of my mother *did* flow in these scaled-down veins! Perhaps . . . I could not be content with mere contentment! Perhaps I always was a wicked girl and now my wickedness at last manifested itself in action.

'"It was easy for me to give my family the slip in the crush at the end of the show; easy to find the stage door and trot past its guardian as he took in a bouquet for Snow White. I soon found the door on which some cruel-comic hand had pasted seven tiny stars. I knocked. Inside, there sat the handsomest young man, on a safe just the right size for both of us, and he was busy mending a tiny pair of trousers with what, to your eyes, Fevvers, would have seemed an invisible needle and a length of invisible thread.

'"' 'What pint-sized planet did *you* spring from?' he cried out when he saw me.

'Then the Wonder covered her face with her hands and wept bitterly.

'"I shall spare you the sorry details of my fall, Fevvers," she said when she recovered herself. "Suffice to say I travelled with them seven long months, passed from one to another, for they were brothers and believed in share and share alike. I fear they did not treat me kindly, for, although they were little, they were men. How they abandoned me, penniless, in Berlin and how I came under the terrible protection of Madame Schreck are circumstances I relate to myself each night when I close my eyes. Over and over, I rehearse an eternity of fearful memories until the time comes to get up again and see for myself how those who come to slake their fantastic lust upon my small person are more degraded yet than I could ever be." '

Fevvers sighed.

'So you see how this lovely creature truly believed herself to have tumbled so far from grace that she could never climb out of the Abyss, and she regarded her pretty, spotless self with the utmost detestation. Nothing I could say would make her feel she was worth more than a farthing in the world's exchange. She would say: "How I envy that poor being – " pointing to the Sleeping Beauty " – except for one thing: she dreams."

'But Fanny was another kettle of fish, a big, raw-boned, plain-spoken hearty lass from Yorkshire whom you would have passed in the street without a second look but for the good cheer of roses in her cheeks and the spring of health in her step. When Madame Schreck pulled back the curtain on Fanny, there she'd stand, a bonny lump of a girl with nowt on but a shift, and a blindfold.

'And Schreck would say: "Look at him, Fanny." So Fanny would take off her blindfold and give him a beaming smile.

'Then Madame Schreck would say: "I said, *look* at him, Fanny." At which she'd pull up her shift.

'For, where she should have had nipples, she had eyes.

'Then Madame Schreck would say: "Look at him properly, Fanny." Then those two other eyes of hers would open.

'They were a shepherd's blue, same as the eyes in her head; not big, but very bright.

'I asked her once, what did she see with those mamillary eyes, and she says: "Why, same as with the top ones but lower down." Yet I do think, for all her free, open disposition, she saw too much of the world altogether and that is why she'd come to rest with all us other dispossessed creatures, for whom there was no earthly use, in this lumber room of femininity, this rag-and-bone shop of the heart.

'Seeing Fanny holding the Sleeping Beauty's head against her bosom to spoon coddled egg between those helpless lips, I said: "Why don't you marry, Fanny. For any man would be glad to have you, once he'd got over the shock. And bring into the world those children of your own you long for and deserve?" Placid as you please, she says: "How can you nourish a babby on salt tears?" Yet she was always cheerful, always a smile and a joke, but, as for Cobwebs, she never said much, she was a melancholy creature and sat by herself a good deal, playing patience. That was her life, she said. Patience.'

'Why did you call her Cobwebs?' asked Walser, out of his revulsion, out of his enchantment.

'Her face was covered with them, sir, from the eyebrows to the cheekbones. The things that Albert/Albertina would do to get to make her laugh! S/he was a droll one and always full of fun. But, no; Cobwebs would never so much as smile.

'These were the girls behind the curtains, sir, the denizens of "Down Below", all with hearts that beat, like yours, and souls that suffer, sir.'

'And what did *you* do?' asked Walser, chewing his pencil.

'Myself? The part I played in Madame Schreck's chamber of imaginary horrors? The Sleeping Beauty lay stark naked on a marble slab and I stood at her head, full spread. I am the tombstone angel, I am the Angel of Death.

'Now, if you wanted to sleep with the Sleeping Beauty, sleep in the passive and not the active sense it was, she being in such precarious health and Madame Schreck loth to kill the goose that laid the golden eggs. If you wished to lie down beside the living corpse and hold in your trembling arms the entire mystery of consciousness, that is and is not at the same time, why, that was available, cash down. Toussaint would put a bag over your head and lead you out of the Abyss upstairs to the Theatre and there you'd wait, hear nothing, see nothing . . . absolute darkness, absolute silence and you alone with your thoughts and those phantoms your imagination had distilled from the sight of the girls below. Then Toussaint would spirit the hood off you and there we'd be; he'd hauled us up from below on a well-oiled dumb waiter in the wall in the interim.

'Only a branched candlestick cast sombre light and shadow over Beauty sleeping on her bier and I stooping over, with my bent wings and my sword, Death the Protectress, you see. So if any of 'em does try to get up to anything not on the tariff, I can rap 'em over the knuckles there and then. As for Beauty, she sighed and murmured and all the time knew nothing, but I would watch the shivering wretch who had hired the use of the idea of us approach her as if she were the execution block and, like Hamlet, I would think: "What a wonderful piece of work is man!"

'By and by, there was a gent started to come marvellous regular, once a week, on Sundays. He always donned the most peculiar costume to venture Down Below, a sort of velvet frock that came down to his knees, plum-coloured and trimmed with grey fur and, on his feet, shiny red leather boots with little bells at the ankles that rang out very sweetly as he walked along. Round his neck, on a gold chain, hung a big medallion of solid gold most curiously figured that I often saw Madame Schreck cast her eye on enviously.

'The figure engraved on this medallion was that of a pardon my French *member*, sir, of the male variety; that is, a phallus, in the condition known in heraldry as *rampant*, and there were little wings attached to the ballocks thereof, which caught my eye immediately. Around the shaft of this virile member twined the stem of a rose whose bloom nestled somewhat coyly at the place where the foreskin folded back. Whether the thing was ancient or modern I could not tell, but it represented a heavy investment.

'He who sported this quaint jewel was in his later middle years, of long, lean, slightly stooping build, with a complexion veering towards the mauvish and mottled, as if he suffered from the cold, but fine, thin features with a high, crooked nose and very close-shaven cheeks. And a pair of wandering, watery, blue eyes, eyes of a man unhappy with his world. To finish off his outfit he always wore a big, round, beaver hat, like a drum, but with the brim turned up all round, and you could see no hair under it. The first time Madame Schreck lifted up the curtain on me, he jumps half out of his skin and calls out: "Azrael!" After that, he comes only to see me. He wants nothing of the Beauty but has me hauled up to the upper room by meself and walks round me, whickering to himself and playing with himself under his petticoat and Fanny, to tease me, calls him my "fancy boy".

'For six Sundays, he arrives to worship at my shrine, but, on the seventh, as we girls were sitting down to dinner, Madame Schreck sends a message by Toussaint for me to go and see her.

'We did very poorly for our dinners in that morbid sepulchre. The tippling old crone in the kitchen would have burned a boiled egg when she'd got a glass inside her so Fanny always put up the Beauty's invalid diet and I remember *that* Sunday especially because the cook passed out on the Saturday night and Fanny sent Toussaint out to pick up a bit of pork on tick, which he had done. So Fanny bustled about the pans and put a decent leg with crackling and a dollop of apple sauce on the table for us and just as we was tucking into it, I was summoned to Milady's bedroom and it was the last Sunday dinner I ever ate in that house.

'"There's a gentleman made an offer," says Madame Schreck. She's sitting at her desk with her back to me and only a gas mantle over her, hissing like a snake, to give light.

'"What gentleman and how much?" I asks, immediately suspicious.

'"He gives his name as 'Christian Rosencreutz' and very generous he is."

'"How generous is generous?"

'"Fifty guineas to you, less commission," she says, over her shoulder, keeping up her scribbling in her damned ledger the while, and all at once I lost my temper with her.

'"What, fifty rotten guineas for the only fully feathered intacta in the entire history of the world? Call yourself a procuress?"

'I grabs hold of her shoulder and picks her right up out of her chair and gives her a good shake. She is light as a bundle of sticks and gives out a faint rattle. How she squawks and: "Take your hands off me!" But I goes on shaking her until she gasps: "Well, very well, then – a hundred guineas."

'"Well, pull the other!" thinks I to myself for I don't believe *that* for one moment, but: "Madame Bloody Schreck," I insist, "you'll not take one penny commission, either, since you've paid me nothing since those five bright shiners six months ago and kept me here a prisoner since!"

'And I shook her again, until she squeals: "Very well, no commission! That makes two hundred guineas, you bloodsucker." Then I let her go.

'"Open the safe," I orders.

'She goes and roots under her pillow and fetches the key. Very reluctant she is to do it. She scuffles over the floor in her black rags and veil with a sideways, scurrying motion and her head turns from side to side as if she were looking for a rathole to slip down but I'm the avenging angel now, and she can't escape me. While her back is turned, I seize the opportunity to shed my blouse and shake out my plumage. She opens out the safe, stretches in her mittened hand, but just as her trembling fingers touch the gold, I catch hold of her shoulders again and – up we go! Up! Up! Up! Thank God for high ceilings! Up we go, until my head knocked against the plaster, and I hooked the old girl on the end of the curtain rail by her back collar and left her there, flapping and yapping and kicking her little arms and legs in the air and nothing she could do about it.

'"Now I can negotiate from a position of strength," I says. "How much did he *really* offer?"

'"A thousand! Let me down!" And she yips and yowls.

'"How much did he put down in advance?" I demanded, for I am an honest girl.

'"Half in advance! Let me down!" But I descend alone and plunge both hands in the safe, intending to take from it only what is mine by rights, plus her commission, but, while I sat on her bed counting out the shiners, comes a diabolical knocking at the door. Whoever knocks has ripped off the muffling crepe, to make his point, you never heard such a din,

'The gold it was that trapped me, for I could not bear to cast aside that glinting pile of treasure and flee, even when I heard furious footsteps on the stairs. Toussaint hurtles in, pale beneath his pigmentation, making the wildest gestures with his hands, and on his heels two great louts with gallows-meat all over them, rigged out in tunics, sandals and cloaks like a comic opera and they hold between them a fishing net.

'I spread my wings immediately but whither shall I fly? The windows is all boarded over . . . is it up to the ceiling, to hover there all night? Join my old Madame on the other end of the curtain rod, to lodge there with her like a pair of gargoyles? My wits deserted me and as I fluttered like the cornered bird I was, these bullies trawled me in a trice and hauled me off downstairs, banging my bum on each step as I went down, leaving behind us a gaping safe, a heap of money, a confounded manservant and the old bat hanging halfway to heaven, which is as far to it as she'll ever get, rot her soul.

'The front door slammed behind that thrashing bundle of fright and feathers that was myself, I am deposited in a four-wheeler and whirled off into the night.

'I demand of these fine gentlemen: where are you taking me? But each sits still as a statue with his arms folded on his chest, staring straight in front of him, and never says one word. The blinds pulled down, the horses galloping like blazes. And I resign myself to the hazard of events, sir, since I can do nothing else.'

FIVE

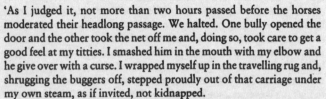

'As I judged it, not more than two hours passed before the horses moderated their headlong passage. We halted. One bully opened the door and the other took the net off me and, doing so, took care to get a good feel at my titties. I smashed him in the mouth with my elbow and he give over with a curse. I wrapped myself up in the travelling rug and, shrugging the buggers off, stepped proudly out of that carriage under my own steam, as if invited, not kidnapped.

'I saw before me a mansion in the Gothic style, all ivied over, and, above the turrets, floated a fingernail moon with a star in its arms. Somewhere, a dog, howling. Around us, a secrecy of wooded hills. Although this mansion was antique in design, in execution it was new; raw brick showed through the ivy and the front door of fumed oak had fresh brass plates hammered in to simulate studs. This door stood open and let out a great deal of bright light from the vestibule.

'The bullies grabbed hold one of each my arms, again, and would have frogmarched me up the front steps except I wrestled free but nowhere to go except that door, which shut behind me with a bang.

'Only the current copy of the London *Times* laying on an oak chest was proof I had not been somehow magically transported into an earlier age, in which all was new because it *was* new, not because it was repro. I stood in a square antechamber of large, square-hewn stones. The floor, flagged, the roof, fluted, and, in the central groin, aptly enough, the same figure of the winged, rosy phallus as Mr Rosencreutz wore round his neck. This was carved in some dark stone, perhaps marble. All brightly lit – as I judged by electricity, but the sources of illumination concealed here and there in folds of walls.

Through a stone portal was a small room, all panelled, and I could see a man sitting in one of a pair of carved oak chairs beside a low oak table with a lovely vase of white roses on it. His face was hidden because he was reading in a big book, like a Bible, with clasps.

'For one minute, I didn't recognise Mr Rosencreutz without his hat; bald as an egg he surely was, his head gleamed as if the maid had gone over it with the same cloth she used on the silver. He didn't have his plum-coloured frock on, either, but a sort of long, white nightshirt tied with a rope. But when I saw his pendant, I knew my man and bitterly regretted the thousand guineas I'd left behind at Madame Schreck's, I can tell you. Then I remembered how the deal had been, half on account, half on delivery, there was another pony owing, so, very politely, I gives him a: "Good evening, Mr Rosencreutz."

'Now he condescends to lower his book and look me over and I do not doubt I am a disappointment to him, bundled up in his old rug and all a mess. But he doesn't let on by a flicker of a muscle.

'"Welcome, Azrael," he says. "Azrael, Azrail, Ashriel, Azriel, Azaril, Gabriel; dark angel of many names. Welcome to me, from your home in the third heaven. See, I welcome you with roses no less paradoxically vernal that your presence, who, like Proserpine, comes from the Land of the Dead to herald new life!"

'Which is all very well, no doubt, but I thought, in that case, the least he could do was ask me to sit down and he never thinks of that, nor does he even offer me so much as a cup of tea after the very trying journey I've had of it, but he goes on smiling at me, his poor old rheumy eyes all a-swim.

'"And what a pretty angel it is!" he says, sentimentally. "Even if it *does* have a smut on its nose!"

'"Show us the bathroom and let's have a wash, then," I smartly ripostes, and he stops admiring his purchase sharpish, as if he hadn't bargained for it talking back. A mite crestfallen, he mumbles: "Through that door, up the staircase, first right on the landing," and goes back to his book which, as I pass, I see is written in the Latin language and goes by the name of *Mysterium Baphometis Revelatum*.

'What a bathroom! Dear God, talk about 'is 'alls were made of marble! And towels an inch thick! And bags of hot water steaming out of the taps! This is the life, I thought, and poured in half a bottle of Trumper's Essence of Lime before I immersed myself in the aromatic tub. But first of all I hung my petticoat over the keyhole so Mr Rosencreutz couldn't take a peek.

'Now, sir, you may wonder how I deal with my wings whilst I bathe. Well, as with all fowl, my feathers are reasonably waterproof but it's not "water off a duck's back" with me, alas. Best not get sodden, else I founders. I groom my wings a bit with my fingertips, as far as I can reach, and splash them a bit more, and give myself a good shake, and then I'm good as new. So I took care to keep my wings out of the bath, you see, but the rest of myself I washed perfectly normally and what with his lemon soap and all, I had a fine old time.

'As I was mopping up with the bathsheet, I heard, as I had known I would, a scrabbling at the door and I snap: "That's quite enough of that! And, what's more, I'm not coming out of this bathroom until you fetch me something decent to wear!"

'"Well, I assure you," said Mr Rosencreutz, "it would go the worse for you, Azrael, if you should come out of your lustrations in the rags in which you entered them, so I propose a little riddle with you. Are you fond of riddles, Azrael?"

'I said nothing.

'"If," he says, "you solve me this riddle, I will give you a hundred pounds gratuity, over and above what is owed already, and nothing to do with Madame Schreck."

'"Riddle away," says I at once and he snickers to himself with glee.

'"Beautiful lady who is neither one thing nor the other, nor flesh nor fowl, though fair is fowl and fowl is fair – tee hee! tee hee hee! in order to enact the ritual for which I have engaged you, you must come out of the water neither naked nor clothed."

'He wheezes away behind the door with delight at his own ingenuity.

'"And I won't let you out of the bathroom until you're ready!" he adds. Then the only sound through the keyhole is that of his heavy breathing.

'The thought of that hundred pounds concentrated my mind wonderfully and I sat down on the side of the bath until I had puzzled my way out of the conundrum. As you can see, sir, nature has blessed me with exceedingly long and abundant hair. So I combed it out and covered myself up with it in the same way that Lady Godiva insubstantially yet modestly clothed herself on her celebrated ride through Coventry. I had more than enough hair in which to hide myself, I'm happy to say, but how to make all secure? Well, I plaited one single lock and chopped it off with Nelson's swordlet, that I'd kept with me, as always, tucked in my stays. And I used that plait to girdle my waist and make all secure, not forgetting to strap my gilded mascot next my skin beneath it, I assure you.

'"Right you are!" I cried, unlocking the door, and burst out upon him in a cloud of citron steam, and he gobbles away to himself with a mixture of gratification and, perhaps, regret, for who can tell what he'd thought up for me if I *hadn't* come up with the answer.

'I'm happy to say a very substantial meal has arrived in the reception room below while I'm having my wash and brush up – salad, and cheese, and a cold bird. Which I'm that famished, I nibble a drumstick of, though, if there's the option, I won't touch a morsel of chicken, or duck, or guineafowl and so on, not wanting to play cannibal. But, this time, in my extremity, I whisper a prayer for forgiveness to my feathery forebears and tuck in. And there's a very decent bottle of claret, to wash it down, so I have some of that. Straightaway Mr Rosencreutz starts to ramble on.

'"Don't you run away with the idea there's anything fleshly, indecent or even remotely corporeal about our meeting this night of all nights, when the shining star lies in the moon's chaste embrace above this very house, signifying the divine post-diluvian Remission and Reconciliation of the Terrible, for there is a secret admonition of which the motto of pure courtesy is an obfuscation. For it is not: 'Honi soit qui mal y pense', but '*Yoni* soit qui mal y pense', yoni, of course, in the Hindu, the female part, or absence, or atrocious hole, or dreadful chasm, the Abyss, Down Below, the vortex that sucks everything dreadfully down, down, down where Terror rules . . . "

'So *that* was the signification of his gold medallion! The penis, represented by itself, aspires upwards, represented by the wings, but is dragged downwards, represented by the twining stem, by the female part, represented by the rose. H'm. This is some kind of heretical possibly Manichean version of neo-Platonic Rosicrucianism, thinks I to myself; tread carefully, girlie! I exort myself.

'He's so appalled himself at the notion of the orifice that the poor old sod mumbles and whimpers himself to a halt, though he's no stranger to the Abyss, himself, used to come every Sunday, just to convince himself it was as 'orrible as he'd always thought. I pour myself another glass of claret, to strengthen myself, and one for mine host, too, who seems to need it. He tosses it off absentmindedly and, after a few moments, recovers his equanimity sufficient to turn his mind to happier things.

'"Flora!" he cries. "Quick spirit of the awakening world! Winged, and aspiring upwards! Flora; Azrael; Venus Pandemos! These are but a few of the many names with which I might honour my goddess, but, tonight, I shall call you 'Flora', very often, for do you not know what night it is, Flora?"

'I try a dollop of his excellent Stilton, pondering as I savour it the baroque eclecticism of his mythology.

'"April thirtieth," I says, suspicious lest this turns out to be another riddle.

'"May eve, Flora, mia," he assures me. "In but a few moments, it will be *your* day, the green hinge of the year. The door of spring will open up to let summer through. It will be the merry morning of May!"

'I nervously fortify myself with another glass of wine.

'"Now the maypole is, self-evidently, nothing but the representation of a *phallos,* i.e. a lingam, i.e. a piercing and fructifying spear such as the lance of Longius – note that 'long'! The long lance of Longius . . ." but here he blinks and stutters, for he is about to lose his way in his own mythology and wax Arthurian, which will lead him up a blind alley in next to no time. He pours himself more claret with a shaking hand and lurches back to his fertility rites.

'"Maypole, phallus, lingam – ha! Up! heave ho and up he rises! up tomorrow on all the village greens of merrie England will spring the sacred phalloi of this blessed season and that is why, tonight of all nights, I chose to spirit you away from the dark house, the abyss, the erberus of perpetual winter ruled over by the old gnome of hell, Madame Schreck."

'Now, "old gnome of hell" fitted the said Mrs S to a 't', so I thought the fool may speak some sense in the midst of his folly and looked at him more kindly.

'Would you like to know his name, sir?' she interrupted herself, abruptly, giving Walser the touch of an eye like sudden blue steel. Her hairpins had all given away under the tumultuous impulses of her half hundredweight of hair, that now flowed and tumbled all around her, and she had become somewhat flushed, giving her a wild and maenad air. Walser wilted in the blast of her full attention.

'You don't half look done in, sir,' said Lizzie, with unexpected concern. And Walser did indeed feel himself at the point of prostration. The hand that followed their dictations across the page obediently as a little dog no longer felt as if it belonged to him. It flapped at the hinge of the wrist. All the same:

'No, no,' he lied. 'I'll be fine.'

'You must know this gentleman's name!' insisted Fevvers and, seizing his notebook, wrote it down. She had a fine, firm, flowing Italic hand. On reading it:

'Good God,' said Walser.

'I saw in the paper only yesterday how he gives the most impressive speech in the House on the subject of Votes for Women. Which he is against. On account of how women are of a different soul-substance from men, cut from a different bolt of spirit cloth, and altogether too pure and rarefied to be bothering their pretty little heads with things of *this* world, such as the Irish question and the Boer War.

'In the course of our interminable, if one-sided, conversation, he reveals to me how he is much afraid of growing old. And, indeed, who isn't! Who doesn't fear the relentless spinning of the celestial wheel off which, one day, all are doomed to topple. And after much hemming and hawing and mystical circumlocution, at last he gives it to me: that the sage, Artephius, invented a cabalistic magnet which secretly sucked out the bodies of young women their mysterious spirit of efflorescence – "efflorescence, Flora," he says, with a significant intonation. By applying a concentration of these spirits to himself by his magic arts, and continually rejuvenating himself, it was spring all year long with Artephius and so Mr Rosencreutz hopes it will be for him.

'Furthermore, opines Mr Rosencreutz, didn't King David, when he grew old, take Abishag the Shulamite to lie in his bosom and "thereby he got heat", and lived two, three hundred years more, and turned into one of the Nine Worthies? He went on, too, about a certain Signor Guardi whom Mr Rosencreutz himself had met in Venice, how this Signor Guardi possessed a portrait of himself as a young man *painted by Titian*. Proving this Signor Guardi was a cool three hundred years old, or so, and he told Mr Rosencreutz how he had himself rubbed all over by a baker's dozen young girls from the Apennines, their massage oil consisting of a distillation of spring flowers and chemical extracts known only to himself. But there came an exceedingly furtive expression over Mr Rosencreutz's face when he spoke of Signor Guardi's prescription, and I thought, there's something here he's keeping to himself.

'But this he *will* say. That, since he first grew versed in esoteric law and the magic arts, he has known of my existence, of the bright angel who will release him from the bonds of the material, the winged spirit of universal springtime – knew, too, I was locked away beneath the ground in Hell. H'm, I thinks, to that, and, h'm, again, when he starts rummaging away in his book and jabbing his stubby finger at the pages that tell him death and life are all the same. And then the book slipped off his lap, due to his trembling, and, at last, blushing and stumbling in his speech, lowering his voice, he tells me how he thinks that, by uniting his body with that of Azrael, the Angel of Death, on the threshold of the spring, he would cheat death itself and live forever while Flora herself will be forever free of winter's chill.

'This he has proved, in the seven weeks since he first saw me, by all manner of cabalistic geometry, of which he will gladly, he says, show me the proofs. But I poured out the last of the claret without offering him some, for I thought two thousand guineas was cheap at the price, and said so, but he was too far sunk in his own ecstatic reveries to hear me. I thought the least he could do was crack another bottle of claret, seeing as he was getting eternal life dirt cheap and I was obtaining only half the profit from this bizarre transaction but he was temporarily blind and deaf to the world, harkening only to the invisible angels shouting in his ears, so I rapped loudly with the book upon the table and that brought one of his bullies in, at the double – out of a door of a secret kind concealed in the panelling.

'"If the gentleman were not so exalted by the presence of his visitor, I'm sure he'd order up another bottle," I says. "Let's try the '88 vintage, this time, if the cellar will run to it."

('For I do like a nice glass of good wine, when I get the chance, Mr Walser.')

'" . . . in comparison with the hermetic adepts, monarchs are poor," mumbles Mr Rosencreutz, sunk in his dreams, and the bully tips me a wink as he piles up the dirty crocks on the tray, mutters: " 'e keeps 'is wallet in the top drawer of the bureau in the bedroom, you'll see it, remember me."

'Indeed I remember 'im, 'e's the one groped my right tit, and am almost sorry for my poor gull with his fancy-dress notions, fleeced by his servants, deluded by charlatans, until the rogue returns with the bottle. Mr Rosencreutz wakes up with a start, says: "What's this? Can't have your vital spirits dulled by base vapours!" And upends the claret into the jug of white roses, which blush. So I must sit on a horrid, hard chair, parched with thirst, and wait for dawn to get the business over with.

'For I plan to pick up the cash owing to me and so depart.

'Not – never! back to Madame Schreck, of course; but straight home to Battersea, for what Mr Rosencreutz is willing to pay for the privilege of busting a scrap of cartilege was quite sufficient to set my entire family up in comfort, I can tell you. And I passed the hours of that short summer night happily enough, fool that I was, for I was busy building castles in the air while Mr Rosencreutz repeats his cryptic orizens, for he seems so excited by the apotheosis he thinks is offered by my embraces as to appear half-crazed.

'Somewhere a clock tells the hours and when it gets to four or quarter past, he comes to his senses somewhat and tells me I must prepare myself.

'"Prepare myself how, master?" I asked craftily.

'"By pure thoughts," he says, and apostrophises me: "Queen of ambiguities, goddess of in-between states, being on the borderline of species, manifestation of Arioriph, Venus, Achamatoth, Sophia."

'I can't tell you what a turn it gave me, when he called me "Sophia". How did he stumble over my christened name? It was as if it put me in his power, that he should know my name, and, though I am not ordinarily superstitious, now I became strangely fearful.

'"Lady of the hub of the celestial wheel, creature half of earth and half of air, virgin and whore, reconciler of fundament and firmament, reconciler of opposing states through the mediation of your ambivalent body, reconciler of the grand opposites of death and life, you who come to me neither naked nor clothed, wait with me for the hour when it is neither dark nor light, that of dawn before daybreak, when you shall give yourself to me but I shall not possess you."

'Give yourself, that's rich! I thought, considering the amounts of money changing hands. But I outwardly adopted a submissive stance and asked in a humble voice: "How shall I do that, oh, great sage?"

'"The rest of the riddle you must answer at the appointed hour," he intones. So I had to make do with that.

'You may well wonder, sir, why I hadn't hopped straight out of the window and away long ago but all I knew of my location was that his house was somewhere in the Home Counties, and, further than that, I couldn't for the life of me think where it was. And wouldn't I be in a pickle, then, out in the middle of nowhere in me altogether, flapping for cover from tree to tree like a bloody dog all the way to Battersea!

'I must say, too, that I both hate and fear the open country. I do not like to be where Man is not, I tell you straight. I love the sight and stink and bustle of humanity as I love my life and a bit of landscape that has no people in it, no friendly smoke rising from the chimney of some human habitation, is as good as desert waste to me. Not that I ever spent much time in the woods and fields, I'm happy to say, but, sometimes, in Ma Nelson's day, on August Bank Holiday, she'd pack us all into a barouche and off we'd go to the New Forest for a picnic, and I was always heartily glad to get back to Wapping High Street, for there I breathed more easy – Cockney to the bone, sir!

'Besides, sir, I am an honest woman. And the poor old bugger had put his cash down on the nail, hadn't he, even if I'd pocketed none of it so far. But I'd high hopes of that thousand on delivery, plus the extra hundred he'd promised me. Why, I'd already bought one of those nice big houses off Lavender Hill, and fixed Gianni and Isotta and Violette and Lizzie and me and the rest of us up in it nice as you please.

'It was the promise of hard cash kept me there, and, well, I thought I'd not have too much trouble with the old fool when it came to the pinch, because he had the look of a Johnny-come-quickly, I can tell you. And, in my innocence, of a worse fate than that fate – why, I never thought!

'So time passed, as it sometimes does, he babbling to himself, until those leaded panes grow pale. At which he bursts into song.

'"Unite and unite! oh! let us all unite!

For summer is icumen today."

'And jumps up, switches off the electrics, flings open the casement. A little spring wind, still with a chill on it, blows into the room, and, silly, tender-hearted me, I fear for his middle-aged health.

'"You mind your bare head, or you'll catch your death!"

'That word, "death", had an electrifying effect upon him; he brayed and neighed, quivered and whinnied, clinging on to the casement frame as if, without its support, down he would flop, but, the spasm soon over, then he quavered:

'"Oh, my rejuvenatrix! the Fructifying disc is just now nudging his way up the backside of yonder hillock! Lie down on the altar!"

'Mr Walser, sir, though I blush to admit it to a man, *intacta* as I am, I knew enough to know if I got down on my back not only would it hold no joy for me, but the ensuing attempt at connection would cause a commotion similar to a bout of all-in wrestling in a pillow factory.

'"You may take me exclusively by the rear entry, oh, great sage, due to my feathers!" I warned him hastily, though I question in my mind his dislike of the orifice, and, even then, as in a flash of understanding, it comes to me that his idea of sex-magic and my own might not concur.

'"Never you mind that!" he cried in his frenzy. "Just you lie down!"

'Capering back to me, he clears off the table on which my supper had been served with one swipe of his scrawny arm, knocking book and roses to the floor. Yet, for all the sacred terror of his blue features, I spied in them something else, something that troubled me dreadfully, for it was just that look of anticipated naughtiness I've caught on the face of my goddaughter Violetta when she's just about to plunge her fingers into the forbidden glories of the chocolate ice. And then I think: this man is going to do me harm.

'Seeing the shadow of reluctance on my face, he recovers himself a little and, summoning to himself all the authority of a captain of industry, repeats:

'"Lie down upon the altar!"

'Wondering, I stretch out face down on the coffee table. He approaches with a purposeful stride. I'd have clenched my teeth and thought of England had not I glimpsed, peering over my shoulder, a shining something lying along his hairy old, gnarled old thigh as his robe swung loose. This something was a sight more aggressive than his other weapon, poor thing, that bobbed about uncharged, unprimed, unsharpened . . . in the cold, grey light of May morning, I saw this *something* was – a blade.

'Quick as a flash, out with my own! How I blessed my little gilded sword! He fell back, babbling, unfair, unfair . . . he'd not thought the angel would come armed. Yet, sir, strike I could not, nor harm another mortal even in self-defence . . . and, to tell the truth, even in the midst of my consternation, I was tickled pink to see the poor old booby struck all of a heap to see his plans awry and he was as much put out when I laughed in his face as he was to see old Nelson's plaything.

'Before he'd gathered his wits together, I was off and out of that open casement like greased lightning, I can tell you, although it was a tight squeeze and I left enough feathers to stuff a mattress caught on the frame. The mad bastard let out a shrill, high squeak to see his fleshy bottle of *elixum vitae* take off and only then came after me with what turned out to be an antique spear he'd found somewhere or other, and even succeeded in inflicting a flesh wound on the ball of my right foot, of which I still bear the scar – look!'

She withdrew one foot from its carpet slipper and thrust it on to Walser's knee, dislodging his notebook so that it fell to the floor. Across the sole there ran a pale, puckered seam of flesh.

'Oracular proof,' said Lizzie, smothering a yawn. 'Seeing is believing.'

Walser weakly retrieved his notebook.

'But for that upward leap earlier in the evening in Madame Schreck's bedroom, I hadn't tried my wings for a cool six months but fright lent me more than human powers. I soared up and away from that vile place, over the maypole on the front lawn towards which, even at that moment, a troupe of children he must have hired from the village came trotting, in flimsy gauze tunics, in spite of the drizzle, with daisy chains in their hair, ready to dance and sing for the hideously refreshed adept, who'd planned to make a May sacrifice of me, sir.

'They all scattered in fright, bawling for their mas, as I flew by.

'I took refuge in a nearby spinney, in the top branches of an elm, where I startled a sleepy congregation of rooks. When I got my breath back, I peered out to see what was afoot below and saw Mr Rosencreutz's bullies, now dressed as gamekeepers, beating the undergrowth for me, so I stayed put until night came on again. Then I went from covert to covert, always concealing myself, until I came to the railway line and borrowed a ride off a load of freight, climbed in amongst a truck of taters and pulled a tarpaulin over my head, because, at that time, I was not able to fly so high the clouds might hide me, and I can think of few things more conspicuous, even by night, than a naked woman dodging telegraph wires and hopping over signal boxes – for I needed the railway to guide me back to London. To my delight, the train soon steamed through Clapham Junction and I nipped out just by Battersea Park, to make my way with all speed through the empty dark up the Queenstown Road ducking behind the privet hedges as I went until I got at last happily home.

'Where who do I find in my own bed beside Lizzie but the Sleeping Beauty?

'I was so weary, so bedraggled, so hungry and my nerves so much on edge from my dreadful experience that I broke down and cried, that there was no room for me at the inn, so Lizzie woke up.'

'And wasn't I pleased to see her, I can tell you! For Toussaint had told all and we feared the worst. Our house was packed to the roof with the refugees from Madame Schreck's and, if Fevvers had a tale to tell, oh! we had a tale for her! I fixed her up a nice cup of coffee with milk and she had a couple of boiled eggs and some toast and soon was all smiles again. As for Toussaint's part in this scarcely credible narrative, sir, he wrote it down on a piece of paper which, happily, I have with me in my handbag.'

Lizzie thereupon excavated three impeccable sheets of manuscript, written on invoices for an ice-cream parlour, as follows:

After the man came and kidnapped Sophia, I was much distressed and would have followed them but the carriage vanished too quickly from my sight. I returned to the house and went to Madame Schreck's room. But, though the widow's weeds still hung from the curtain rod, now they were quite still. She did not move.

It came to me that there was *nothing left* inside the clothes and, perhaps, there never had been anything inside her clothes but a set of dry bones agitated only by the power of an infernal will and a voice that had been no more than the artificial exhalation of air from a bladder or a sac, that she was, or had become, a sort of scarecrow of desire. I climbed on a chair and lifted her down. She was weightless as an empty basket and her mittens fell to the floor with a soft plop. A little dust trickled out of the truncated fingers. I laid her weeds on the bed; they were stiff and dry as the shed carapace of an insect.

On her desk was a bill of sale. She had sold Fevvers to this Mr Rosencreutz for not two but five thousand pounds, half to be paid direct in cash to Madame Schreck when the bargain was struck, the rest to go to her . . . 'afterwards'. (All Fevvers had been told was lies.) I did not like the sound of that 'afterwards' in the least, but I was at my wits' end what to do next. I knew I had been the dumb witness to infamy but would the police believe that I, the last to have seen Madame Schreck living, had been the first to find her – not dead, for who can say, now, when she had died, or if she had ever lived, but . . . passed away? And who better than I to know what powerful friends the old procuress had in the force, since, every Friday since I entered her service, to me had fallen the task of taking by hand a *heavy envelope* to Kensington Police Station with orders to wait for no receipt?

Fanny was a pillar of strength. From Madame Schreck's open safe she took the money that was owed on Fevvers' account, and then, after some computations, a sufficient sum to recompense all the remaining five, including the Beauty, for the labour they had expended in that miserable place – not a penny more, not a penny less. Having dealt honestly with Madame Schreck's estate; 'now,' she said, 'let's be off, sharpish, or else we'll be accessories to the fact.'

'What fact?' I asked myself, gripped with fear. But we could do nothing except pray that Fevvers' wit and ingenuity would keep her from harm. As to a place of refuge for we friendless ones, all I could think of was the address Fevvers herself once gave me, where I took the first and only cash Madame Schreck ever gave her. We must be gone, and quickly – before the first clients of the night arrived.

I carried the Beauty out to Madame Schreck's carriage in the mews myself. I would take that carriage and the pony as the portion due to me; did not the slave deserve to inherit the means of escape? We arrived at Battersea just after midnight and those kind folk rose from their beds to give us a hospitable welcome, in spite of their distress at hearing of our beloved girl's disappearance, and Isotta found couches, mattresses and blankets for us all.

The next day seemed interminable as, in a state of agitation that increased hourly, we waited for news of our lovely friend. Only after a long night's watch had the house settled down for a few hours uneasy slumber when she miraculously returned.

Walser read this document, noted the scholarly handwriting, the firm signature, the all too checkable address. He handed it back to Lizzie humbly. She stowed it away again, with a pleased nod.

'That Toussaint!' she said. 'He's a lovely way with words.'

'What has become of them all, sir?' demanded Fevvers: and immediately answering herself, 'Why, gone their ways! Isotta and Gianni, most loving parents themselves, persuaded the Wonder that no child can fall so far a mother nor father will not stoop to lift it up, again, so she presented herself again to her adopteds, who wept with joy to have her restored to the bosom of the family after so many years, when all their other fledglings had long left the nest. Albert/Albertina got a post as ladies' maid with our Jenny and though s/he says s/he is much confined by female garments all the time, Jenny would not be without her treasure. Fanny returned to her native Yorkshire where, with the aid of her savings at Madame Schreck's, she established an orphanage in a mill-town for the children of operatives killed in accidents on the looms, so now she has twenty lovely babies to call her "mama". Happily, since, I came into my good fortune, I have been able to interest a good friend, the academician, Sir R—. F—. in Cobwebs. He perceived her unique quality of vision and trained her hand to match her sight. Now she had a fine reputation as a painter in chiaroscuro, so you could say that, though she had not come out of the shadows, all the same, she had made the shadows work for her. As for the Beauty – '

' – she is with us, still.'

Pause of three heartbeats.

'She sleeps. And now she wakes each day a little less. And, each day, takes less and less nourishment, as if grudging the least moment of wakefulness, for, from the movements under her eyelids, and the somnolent gestures of her hands and feet, it seems as if her dreams grow more urgent and intense, as if the life she leads in the closed world of dreams is now about to possess her utterly, as if her small, increasingly reluctant wakenings were an interruption of some more vital existence, so she is loath to spend even those few necessary moments of wakefulness with us, wakings strange as her sleepings. Her marvellous fate – a sleep more lifelike than the living, a dream which consumes the world.

'And, sir,' concluded Fevvers, in a voice that now took on the sombre, majestic tones of a great organ, 'we do believe . . . her dream will be the coming century.

'And, oh God . . . how frequently she weeps!'

Followed a profound silence, as the women clutched hands, as if for comfort, and Walser shivered, for the dressing-room had grown cold as death.

Then, on the soundless air of night, now drifted to them the sound of Big Ben once again, but the wind must have changed direction a little for the first chimes were faint with distance, as if they came from very far away, and, when she heard them, Fevvers froze and 'pointed', just like a huge golden retriever. She thrust up her muzzle as if snuffing the air and the muscles in her neck bunched and clenched. One, two, three, four, five . . . six . . .

During the less-than-a-blink of time it took the last chime to die there came a vertiginous sensation, as if Walser and his companions and the very dressing-room itself were all at once precipitated down a vast chute. It took his breath away. As if the room that had, in some way, without his knowledge, been plucked out of its everyday, temporal continuum, had been held for a while above the spinning world and was now – dropped back into place.

'Six o'clock! As late as that!' cried Lizzie, springing to her feet with refreshed energy. But Fevvers seemed as if utterly overcome, exhausted to the point of collapse, quite suddenly, as if by the relaxation of tremendous amounts of energy. Her breast fluttered as if her heart wanted to fly out. Her heavy head hung down like a bell that has ceased tolling. She even seemed to have diminished in size, to have shrunk to proportions only a little more colossal than human. She closed her eyes and let out a long exhalation of breath. The colour left her cheeks and she looked haggard and very much aged in the colourless light of morning that gave the mauve glow of the gas mantles a lifeless and unnatural look. It was left to Lizzie to conclude the story, which she did with despatch.

'After our joyful reunion,' stated Lizzie briskly, 'as we all sat lingering over breakfast, who should call in on us but Esmeralda and the Human Eel pushing an elver in a perambulator. "Tell you what, Fevvers," she says. "You ever thought of the high trapeze?"'

Then Lizzie bounded up and began to fold and tidy the lingerie on the sofa, tacitly dismissing Walser. But Fevvers stirred a little, eyed Walser in the glass, wearily added a coda.

'The rest is history. Esmeralda secured me that first engagement at the Cirque d'Hiver. No sooner did I venture on the high trapeze than I triumphed. Paris, Berlin, Rome, Vienna . . . and now my own, beloved London. The first night here, at the Alhambra, after I'd climbed off-stage over a Snowdon of Bouquets, when Lizzie was taking off my makeup just as we were when you found us, comes a knocking on the door. And there's a man in a billycock hat with a big paunch covered with a waistcoat made of Stars and Stripes, the jolly Old Glory itself, sir, and, right over his belly button, a bloody great dollar sign.

'"Hi there, my feathered friend," he says. "I've come to make your fortune."'

She yawned, not like a whale, not like a lioness, but like a girl who has stayed up too long.

'So I don't doubt I'll soon triumph in St Petersburg, in Tokyo, in Seattle, in San Francisco, Chicago, New York – wherever there's a roofbeam high enough for my trapeze, sir. Now, if you've quite finished – '

Walser snapped his notebook shut. There was no room in it for one more word.

'Yes, indeed. That's fine, Miss Sophie, just fine.'

'Fevvers,' she correctly sharply. 'Call me Fevvers. Now me and Liz must get home to bed.'

'Can I call you a cab?'

'Gracious, no! Waste good money on a cab? We always walks home after the show.'

But she tottered a little as she got up. The night had taken a heavy toll. She exchanged a last, inscrutable grimace with her warped reflection in the mirror.

'Excuse me, sir, while I get some clothes on.'

'I'll wait at the stage door, ma'am,' said Walser, stowing away his book. 'Perhaps you ladies will allow me to escort you?'

They looked at each other.

'Oh . . . he can come as far as the bridge, can't he?'

The stage doorkeeper in his creaking leather coat was brewing tea on his oil stove, stewing up tealeaves, milk and sugar all together, Indian style. Walser accepted a boiling jam jar full of the stuff. The October morning grew lighter every moment but no brighter; it was a grey day of low cloud. The discarded orts of pleasure littered the pavement outside.

'Spent all night with Fevvers, 'ave you?' said the stage doorkeeper with a wink and a nudge. 'Go on – don't take offence, guv'nor. That Lizzie guards her like a watchdog. Besides, she's a perfect lady, is our Fevvers.'

Yet, rolled up in a rusty black shawl, the big bones sticking through her face, dark stains under those blue eyes, her long hair roughly pinned up again, she looked like any street girl making her way home after an unsuccessful night, or even some girl rag-and-bone merchant, taking home a night's dolorous scavenging in a sack on her back – the enormous burden, jutting out between her shoulders, that seemed to weigh her down. She sparked into a semblance of theatrical vivacity for the sake of the stage doorkeeper: 'I'll see you later, me old cock!' but refused Walser's offered arm, and they walked through Piccadilly in silence, among early risers on their way to work. They skirted Nelson's

Column, went down Whitehall. The cold air was not freshened by morning; there was an oppressive odour of soot and horseshit.

At the end of Whitehall, along the wide road, past the Mother of Parliaments, there came at a brisk trot a coal cart pulled by clattering, jingling drays, and, behind, an impromptu procession of women of the poorest class, without coats or wraps, in cotton pinafores, in draggled underskirts, worn carpet slippers on their bare feet, and there were shoeless little children too, running, scrambling after the carts, the girls and women with their pinafores outstretched to catch every little fragment of coal that might bounce out.

'Oh, my lovely London!' said Fevvers. 'The shining city! The new Jerusalem!'

She spoke so flatly he could not tell whether she spoke ironically. She said nothing else. Walser was intrigued by such silence after such loquacity. It was as though she had taken him as far as she could go on the brazen trajectory of her voice, yarned him in knots, and then – stopped short. Dropped him.

Atop the sparkling tracery of the House, the gilt hands of Big Ben pointed to five minutes to seven. Both women looked up at the clock face and smiled a single, small smile of complicity of which Walser received the faded aftermath as she turned to shake his hand. A strong, firm, masculine grip. No gloves.

'It's been a pleasure, Mr Walser,' she said. 'I hope you've got enough to do your piece. If you have any further questions, you know where to find me. We can easily make our way home by ourselves from here.'

'It's been a pleasure,' agreed Lizzie with an odd little ducking bow, proffering a glacé kid glove.

'My pleasure, entirely,' said Walser.

The minute hand of the great clock above them inched over the face. The women set out for the smoky south over Westminster Bridge against the clattering traffic that now streamed into town. Because of the difference in their heights, they could not walk arm in arm, so they held hands and, from a distance, looked like a blonde, heroic mother taking her little daughter home from some ill-fated expedition up west, their ages obscured, their relationship inverted. Their feet dragged slow as poverty yet that, too, was an illusion; pelted with diamonds, assaulted by pearls, she was too mean to take a cab.

The clock coughed up the prolegomena to its chime and then rang out the prelude to the hour. When the wind suddenly seized hold of Fevvers' hair, tugged it from its pin and sent it flying over the sullen river in a wide, flaxen arc, he half expected her to unfurl too, all scarlet, crimson plumage, and clasping her tiny charge, her daughter, her mother, to her bosom, to whirl away up through the low ceiling of cloud, up and off. He shook his head, to clear away idle fancies.

Seven struck. Now the size of one big doll, one small doll, they reached the end of the bridge and looked back; he saw the pale wedges of their faces. Then traffic obscured them.

'Cab, sir?' The waiting horse blew a plume of oats over the top of the nosebag.

At his lodgings in Clerkenwell, Walser washed, shaved, changed his shirt and found, this morning, he preferred his landlady's ingratiating if inept attempt at American coffee to the tea he usually drank; Lizzie had marinated his insides in strong tea, that night, until his oesophagus must be the colour of mahogany . . . He flicked through his notes. What a performance! Such style! Such vigour! And just how had the two women pulled off that piece of sleight-of-hand, or ear, rather, with the clocks? When he took out his own pocket-watch, he found, to his unsurprise, it had stopped short precisely at midnight.

But how had she done – or known – that?

Curiouser and curiouser.

A war correspondent between wars and a passionate amateur of the tall tale, he dropped in at his London office later that morning to find his chief brooding behind a green eyeshadow over the latest from South Africa.

'How did you find the Cockney Venus?'

'It's the ambition,' said Walser, 'of every red-blooded American kid to run away with the circus.'

'So?' said his London chief.

'I don't think you realise just how much I'd like a break from hard news, chief. That last touch of yellow fever in Panama took more out of me than I thought. Keep me away from the battlefield for a while! I need to be refreshed. I need to have my sense of wonder polished up again. What would you say to a series of inside stories of the exotic, of the marvellous, of laughter and tears and thrills and all? What if, incognito, your correspondent follows the great confidence artiste in the history of the world to the world's most fabulous cities? Through the trackless wastes of Siberia and then . . . even unto the Land of the Rising Sun?

'Better still . . . why doesn't your correspondent, incognito, sign up with Fevvers on Captain Kearney's Grand Imperial Tour itself? The story straight from the Ringbark! Chief, let me invite you to spend a few nights at the circus!'

PETERSBURG

ONE

'There was a pig,' said the baboushka to Little Ivan, who perched, round-eyed, on a three-legged stool beside her in the kitchen as she blew on the charcoal underneath the samovar with a big pair of wooden bellows brightly painted with folk-art motifs of scrolls and flowers.

The toil-misshapen back of the baboushka humbly bowed before the bubbling urn in the impotently submissive obeisance of one who pleads for a respite or a mercy she knows in advance will not be forthcoming, and her hands, those worn, veiny hands that had involuntarily burnished the handles of the bellows over decades of use, those immemorial hands of hers slowly parted and came together again just as slowly, in a hypnotically reiterated gesture that was as if she were about to join her hands in prayer.

About to join her hands in prayer. But always, at the very last moment, as if it came to her there was something about the house that must be done first, she would start to part her hands again. Then Martha would turn back into Mary and protest to the Martha within her: what can be more important than praying? Nevertheless, when her hands were once more almost joined, that inner Martha recalled the Mary to the indeed perhaps more important thing, whatever it was ... And so on. Had the bellows been invisible, such would have been the drama of the constantly repeated interruption of the sequence, so that, when the old woman blew on the charcoal with the bellows, it could have been, if a wind had come and whipped away the bellows, a little paradigm of the tension between the flesh and the spirit, although 'tension' would have been altogether too energetic a word for it, since her weariness modified the pace of this imaginary indecision to such an extent that, if you did not know her, you would think that she was lazy.

And more than this, her work suggested a kind of *infinite* incompletion – that a woman's work is never done; how the work of all the Marthas, and all the Marys, too, all the work, both temporal and spiritual, in this world, and in preparation for the next, will never be over – always some conflicting demand will occur to postpone indefinitely any and every task. So . . . there was no need to hurry!

Which was just as well, because she was . . . almost . . . worn out.

All Russia was contained within the thwarted circumscription of her movements; and much of the essence of her abused and withered femaleness. Symbol and woman, or symbolic woman, she crouched before the samovar.

The charcoal grew red, grew black, blackened and reddened to the rhythm of wheezing sighs that might just as well have come from the worn-out lungs of the baboushka as from her bellows. Her slow, sombre movements, her sombre, slow speech, were filled with the dignity of the hopeless.

'There was . . . ' puff! . . . 'a pig . . . ' puff! . . . 'went to Petersburg . . . '

Petersburg! At that, the charcoal glowed and sizzled; Petersburg – the very name, enough to perk you up, even when you lived there; even the exhausted soul of Mother Russia stirred, a little.

St Petersburg, a beautiful city that does not exist any more. Today, another beautiful city of a different name bestrides the mighty Neva; on its site, St Petersburg once stood.

Russia is a sphinx. You grand immobility, antique, hieratic, one haunch squatting on Asia, the other on Europe, what exemplary destiny are you knitting out of the blood and sinew of history in your sleeping womb?

She does not answer. Riddles bounce off her sides, as gaily painted as those of a peasant troika.

Russia is a sphinx; St Petersburg, the beautiful smile of her face. Petersburg, loveliest of all hallucinations, the shimmering mirage in the Northern wilderness glimpsed for a breathless second between black forest and the frozen sea.

Within the city, the sweet geometry of every prospect; outside, limitless Russia and the approaching storm.

Walser paused to flex his chilly fingers and insert a fresh sheet of paper into his typewriter.

At the command of the Prince, the rocks of the wilderness trans-formed – turned into palaces! The Prince stretched out his lordly hand, pulled down the Northern Lights, used them for chandeliers . . . Yes! built as St Petersburg was at the whim of a tyrant who wanted his memory of Venice to take form again in stone on a marshy shore at the end of the world under the most inhospitable of skies, this city, put together brick by brick by poets, charlatans, adventurers and crazed priests, by slaves, by exiles, this city bears that Prince's name, which is the same name as the saint who holds the keys of heaven . . . St Petersburg, a city built of hubris, imagination and desire . . .

As we are, ourselves; or, as we ought to be.

The old woman and the child ignored the rattling of the typewriter behind them. They do not know what we know about their city. They lived on, without knowledge or surmise, in this city that is on the point of becoming legend but not yet, not quite yet; the city, this Sleeping Beauty of a city, stirs and murmurs, longing yet fearing the rough and bloody kiss that will awaken her, tugging at her moorings in the past, striving, yearning to burst through the present into the violence of that authentic history to which this narrative – as must by now be obvious! – does not belong.

. . . its boulevards of peach and vanilla stucco dissolve in mists of autumn . . .

. . . in the sugar syrup of nostalgia, acquiring the elaboration of artifice; I am inventing an imaginary city as I go along. Towards such a city, the baboushka's pig now trots.

'There was a pig went to Petersburg to pray,' said the weary baboushka, laying aside the bellows on which blossomed the only flowers in the barren garden of her life. She turned the spigot of the samovar on to a glass. How her old bones did ache! How bitterly she regretted having promised the child a story!

'What happened to the pig?' prompted Little Ivan, all eyes and spindleshanks, sucking a hot jam pie.

But it turns out the baboushka can't be bothered with the pig and its story. No Scheherezade, she.

'Wolf eat him. Take this tea to the gentleman and get out from under my feet. Get along out of doors with you. Go, play, boy.'

She fell to genuflecting in front of the icon. She might have prayed for the soul of her daughter, the murderess, had she not been so weary she could do no more than perform the physical rituals of faith.

In the shadowy recesses of the dour, soot-stained room, Walser, an indistinct yet vivid figure, sat at a crude wooden table banging out those first impressions of the city on a battered old Underwood portable, his faithful companion in war and insurrection. The child in felt boots inched reluctantly up and set down the glass of tea as far away from the typist as he was able.

'*Spasebo!*' Walser's flying fingers halted and he offered the boy one of his few words of Russian as if it were a gift. Little Ivan sneaked a single terrified look at Walser's face all covered with red and white make-up, gave a faint moan and was gone. In all his former life, Walser never frightened children; this child was very much afraid of the clowns, a nervous dread with the seeds of fascination in it.

Walser reread his copy. The city precipitated him towards hyperbole; never before had he bandied about so many adjectives. Walser-the-clown, it seemed, could juggle with the dictionary with a zest that would have abashed Walser-the-foreign-correspondent. He chuckled, thinking of his chief's brow wrinkling over the dispatch, and slid two gritty rectangles of grey sugar into his tumblerful of amber fluid – he respected his teeth too much to do as the baboushka did, suck the sugar lumps, precious as candy, while she sipped. No lemons, again. The clowns were lodged among the poorest.

He felt a draught on his forehead. His get-up was of the 'silly kid' type, with white shirt, baggy short pants, comedy suspenders, a schoolcap atop a fright wig and the wig was coming adrift. Hastily adjusting it, he returned to the keyboard. Dateline, St Petersburg, a city stuck with lice and pearls, impenetrably concealed behind a strange alphabet, a beautiful, rancid, illegible city. Outside, in the squalid yard, Little Ivan and his friend trapped a stray cat and walked it up and down the cobbles on its scrawny hind legs. They wanted to see the poor, starveling, piteously mewing creature dance, just as its cousins, the suave, mysterious tigers, danced in the circus of Colonel Kearney.

If one pig trotted off to St Petersburg to pray, another less pious porker travelled to Petersburg for fun and profit between silk sheets in a first class *wagon lit*. This lucky one, the very good friend of the great impresario, was particularly accomplished; she could spell out your fate and fortune with the aid of the alphabet written out on cards – yes, indeed! could truffle the future out of four-and-twenty Roman capitals if they were laid out in order before her and that wasn't the half of her talents. Her master called her 'Sybil' and took her everywhere with him. When Walser first presented himself at the Ritz Hotel in London begging for a job with the circus – feed the elephants, curry the horses, anything that would safeguard his anonymity – Colonel Kearney invited his pig to tell him whether to hire the young man or no.

'Ah'm ridin' high on the hawg's back, young man,' said Colonel Kearney in the inimitable lilt of Kentucky. 'Allow me to introduce you to the hawg in question.'

He cradled affectionately in the crook of his arm a lean, agile, inquisitive-looking young sow whose head sat, with as decapitated a look as that of John the Baptist's on a platter, on a wide, stiff, crisp, white taffeta frill. Her dainty little toe-dancer's trotters were neatly folded under her breast and her quick, small, bright, not unfriendly eyes twinkled away at Walser like pink fairy-lights. She was a delicious creamy yellow in colour and shone like a pig of gold because, every morning, the Colonel massaged her with the best olive oil from Lucca, to keep her delicate skin from cracking. The Colonel chucked her under the chin, making her dangling ears flap.

'Mr Walser, make the acquaintance of Sybil, my pardner in the Ludic Game.'

The Colonel lounged at his ease in a swivel chair, his varnished boots up on the desk in front of him among the makings of a mid-morning julep – the bottle of Old Grandad, the bucket of ice, a bunch of mint that turned the air a refreshing green. A little, fat man, with a sparse pepper-and-salt crop bristling on his round head to match the attempted goatee on his chin – he'd no great facility for growing hair. A snub nose, and mauvish jowls.

A gun-metal buckle, in the shape of a dollar sign, fastened the leather belt just below his pot belly, presumably the dollar-sign to which Fevvers had referred. Even in the relative privacy of his hotel suite, the Colonel sported his 'trademark' costume – a pair of tightly tailored trousers striped in red and white and a blue waistcoat ornamented with stars.

The Old Glory itself, topped with a gilt eagle, unfurled with grandiose negligence from a pole propped in the corner – born in Kentucky he might have been, but no Dixie patriot he! No profit margin to the bonny blue flag, these days; he was all for the stars and stripes. His shirtsleeves, rolled to the elbow, were secured with nickel bands. His full-tailed frock-coat of old-fashioned cut hung from the knob of his chair, on which was perched his billycock hat. He chewed as on the cud on a Havana the size of a baby's arm. Lilac, aromatic smoke lolled and swagged around his head.

His damask walls were layered over with an ill-secured frieze of showbills, on which Walser made his first acquaintance of those who would be his travelling companions – the lady with the big cat who called herself the Princess of Abyssinia; Buffo the Great and his troupe of white-face clowns; Monsieur Lamarck's Educated Apes ('clever as a barrel-load of monkeys'). High-wire walkers, earth-shaking elephants – no end to the marvels the Colonel intended to transport about the globe, joined together in amity at the sight of the dollar bill.

And there she was, again, Fevvers, the most marvellous, flourishing her coccyx at Walser as she took off for some empyrean or other out of the frame. So many showbills, it was as if the Colonel had rigged himself up a flimsy, impermanent, wonderful tent within the too-solid walls of the hotel; not only did the brightly coloured, loosely pinned posters jostle one another as if vying for attention as they rippled on the walls, but a mighty torrent of newspaper clippings, contracts, greenbacks, overflowed the enormous wastepaper basket he used as a filing cabinet, crisply rustling in the draught from the window open on to the cheerful bustle of Piccadilly outside. All within seemed in motion, eager to be up and off.

On the floor beside the Colonel was a blessedly static barrel of apples. From time to time, the Colonel reached down for a pippin, which Sybil would snap up.

'Yessir, we're old hands at the Ludic Game, Sybil and me,' he rasped, removing the cigar from between his gapped, discoloured teeth and squinting confidentially at the glowing tip. 'Years ago, years, down on my daddy's farm in Lexington, Kentucky, I was jest a kid, then, knee-high to a ham-hock, weren't I, Sybil, when I first made the acquaintance of the grandest little lady that ever drank pigswill, present company excepted. Yessir! that was Miss Sybil here's very own great-grandma, yessir! First in the great dynasty of my porcine assistants!

'I, being a young feller of an idle but perseverin' disposition, I'd spent my en-tire eleventh year perfectin' the technique of the bum-flute, know what I mean? used to get right up on the school-desk when my teacher's back was turned and let rip with a chorus of "My Old Kentucky Home!" on the good ol' bum flute whilst he was writin' up the principal rivers of Europe on the blackboard, that kind of young feller I was, could set my mind to anything provided it weren't of any use, soon as I clapped my eyes on Sybil's great-grandma, there, I says to myself: here's a challenge!

'Played hookey from school, took me three whole months un-tiring effort to get the old girl to stand on her hind legs and wave the flag. Didn't think nothing of it, at first, jest a way of passing the time, but after I charged my first nickel down at the bar-room for a sight of the Patriotic Pig, then, yessirree! we was on the road. Mighty oaks from little acorns grow, you know that, young man? My moveable feast, my opera of the eye, my peripatetic celebration of life and laughter – it all began one steamy southern mornin' all those years ago, when the great-grandma of Miss Sybil here got right up on her hind legs and taught me a lesson I never learned in school – know what it was, young man?'

Leering through the screen of cigar smoke, he paused, not for assent but for effect, before he gleefully sang out the motto of the Ludic Game: 'A fool and his money is soon parted!

'Ho! ho! ho!' he boomed, like Santa Claus. 'Care for another julep?' He kept a supply of glasses in the top right-hand drawer of his desk.

'So you hail from sunny California by way of the Horn, is it, young man? And, just like every red-blooded American kid, he wants to run away with the circus . . .'

His pale blue, pebbly, red-rimmed eyes went this way and that way; he never stopped looking at you just so long as it wasn't directly. He wasn't soothing company, there was something restless, something turbulent under his surface bonhomie, he was nobody's fool and did not suffer fools gladly. Walser had no special skills to offer, could not walk the high-wire, would have ridden a zebra like a sailor on horseback, yet all the Colonel's bountiful intuition told him the handsome young man might be hired cheaply, was strong, was versatile, was, perhaps, on the run, would be a bargain, but might be, not in spite of but because of all this, trouble. The Colonel shared his predicament with his partner.

'What's your opinion, Sybil? Hire or fire?'

She put her head on one side for a moment, scrutinising Walser's face; then she let out a curious, gruff little squeak – and nodded, ears jiggling.

'Reckon a handsome young man like yourself can charm a pretty lady the moment she sets eyes on him,' the Colonel remarked seductively, with another sidelong glance at Walser. He took the saliva-rimmed cigar butt from his mouth and knocked six inches off the end on to the carpet. Then he brought the famous pack of dog-eared, grease-stained alphabet cards from his waistcoat pocket, flicked through to make sure all were there, cleared the desk of its clutter with a single sweep of his arm. The empty bourbon bottle bounced harmlessly on a red-ribboned pile of court summonses. Breathing heavily, the Colonel set out the cards while Walser watched with bewildered amusement. The Colonel dropped the little pig squarely down on all fours in front of the capitals.

'Now, Sybil, tell me next, in what fashion might this bold caballero here delight us?'

Sybil studied the cards for a moment, squinnied again at Walser, appeared for a few moments sunk in thought, then, with her questing snout, she nudged out:

C-L-O-W-N.

And sat back on her haunches, gratified. The Colonel rewarded her with a round of applause, tossed her an apple, upset the wastepaper basket entirely and disclosed within its susurrating depths a cache of Old Grandad. Uncorking another bottle – 'let the ice and mint go hang' – he refreshed their drinks. The pig leapt back into his welcoming bosom where the Colonel nuzzled and cuddled her but his restless eyes, no pinker-rimmed than Sybil's own, kept on going over and over Walser: what's his game, what's his racket . . . is he the fool he looks or a bigger fool?

'So, young man,' he said, 'now you are a first-of-May. Don't ask me how the cognomen arose – it's what we allus calls the neophytes, the virgins in the ring, the green beginners in the art of playing. Just a coupla questions. First: is it squeamish about *bedbugs*?'

As Walser, laughing, shook his head: 'that's just dandy, on account of there ain't no place like a circus train for bedbugs. Why, a circus is just one big Pullman diner to *cimex lectularius*.'

Then he contrived to fix Walser with his twitching eye for as long as one entire second but he went on gnashing away at his cigar so the smoke bounced round him and his skinny fingers with the gnawed nails kept tweaking away at Sybil's ears; the pig herself cocked an intent head towards the young man, as if she, too, was anxious to hear Walser's answer to the second question the Colonel was about to pose:

'How does it stand humiliation?'

Startled, Walser coughed on his bourbon.

'I see you don't know the first thing about clowning,' said the Colonel in a melancholy voice. 'Very well. Okay by me. Some was born fools, some was made fools and some make fools of theirselves. Go right ahead. Make a fool of yourself. I'll take you on as apprentice august, young man; sign a contract for six months, we'll take you across Siberia. Siberia! Oh, the challenge of it! Old Glory across the tundra!'

At that, he flipped up Sybil's ear, dipped in, drew forth a stream of little silk handkerchiefs each printed with the stars and stripes and waved them round his head.

'Surely I can rely on a fellow Amurrican to see the glory of it! All nations united in the great Ludic Game under the banner of Liberty itself! D'you see the grand plan, young man? Old Glory across the tundra, crowned heads bow to the democratic extravaganza! Then, think of it, tuskers to the land of the Rising Sun, young man! Hannibal's tuskers stopped short after the Alps but mine, mine shall go round the en-tire world! Never before, in the en-tire history of thrills and laughter, has a free Amurrican circus circumnavigated the globe!'

What a visionary he was!

'And, after this unprecedented and epoch-making historical event, I'll land you safe and sound back home in the good old U.S. of A. Yessir!'

With that, he brought his fist (still grasping his streamer) down on the desk, rattling bottle and glasses, and cried out, with neither irony nor sarcasm but, evidently, from a full, buoyant and excited heart:

'Welcome to the Ludic Game!'

When Walser first put on his make-up, he looked in the mirror and did not recognise himself. As he contemplated the stranger peering interrogatively back at him out of the glass, he felt the beginnings of a vertiginous sense of freedom that, during all the time he spent with the Colonel, never quite evaporated; until that last moment when they parted company and Walser's very self, as he had known it, departed from him, he experienced the freedom that lies behind the mask, within dissimulation, the freedom to juggle with being, and, indeed, with the language which is vital to our being, that lies at the heart of burlesque.

Her orizens concluded, the baboushka lay down on top of the stove and soon began snoring. Walser typed: 'end' to his report for fear the rattle of his machine disturbed her ancient sleep. He did not want to draw attention to his reporting activities but he was doomed to his comic rig for his stay in the city because the clowns walked the streets in peripatetic advertisements for Colonel Kearney's circus. Therefore he went to the kitchen door and whistled Little Ivan away from his game. Even if the child found the presence of clowns inexpressibly sinister and troubling, he could be bribed with a few kopeks to take Walser's sealed envelope to the British Embassy, whence it returned to London in the discretion of the diplomatic bag. (Walser saw how the child hated to touch his hands.)

Unless he wanted to walk to work with the hooting, mocking company of half the rag, tag and bobtail of the city at his heels, he must skulk along the back ways, along stinking alleys hung with washing, past gloomy doors of stark tenements. Of this most beautiful of cities,

Walser, as it turns out, has, in reality, seen only the beastly backside – a yellow light in a chemist's window; two noseless women under a streetlamp; a drunk rolled under a doorway in a pool of vomit . . . In a scummed canal, ice in the pelt of the dead dog floating there. Mist, and winter coming on.

Fevvers, nestling under a Venetian chandelier in the Hotel de l'Europe, has seen nothing of the city in which Walser lodges. She has seen swans of ice with a thick encrustation of caviare between the wings; she has seen cut-glass and diamonds; she has seen all the luxurious, bright, transparent things, that make her blue eyes cross with greed.

Their paths converge only upon the brick barracks of the Imperial Circus.

TWO

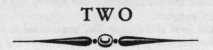

The Colonel coaxed, wheedled, insisted, demanded that the Old Glory should, during his visit, replace the Tsar's own flag on the pole that topped the Imperial Circus and there it slumped, as if succumbed to the lethargy of the alien air. The Circus itself, constructed to house permanent displays of the triumphs of man's will over gravity and over rationality, was a tall hexagon of red brick with a pompous flight of steps up to an entrance flanked on either side by ten-foot stone caryatids, splashed with pigeon droppings, in the shape of caparisoned elephants, squatting on their hind legs and holding their front legs up in the air. Such were the guardian spirits of the place, the elephants, the pillars of the circus itself who uphold the show upon the princely domes of their foreheads as they do the Hindu cosmos.

Once the paying customer successfully negotiated the ticket window, one left one's furs in a cloakroom that, during performance, became a treasury of skins of sable, fox and precious little rats, as though there one left behind the skin of one's own beastliness so as not to embarrass the beasts with it. Thus disencumbered, one entered an ample foyer with a mirrored champagne bar and climbed another, this time a marble and interior, staircase, to reach the arena.

Along the ringbank were red plush boxes trimmed with gilding, the plushest signed with the Imperial Eagle, in gold. Above the performers' entrance hung a gilded platform for the band. All was elegant, even sumptuous, finished with a heavy, rather queasy luxury that always seemed to have grime under its fingernails, the luxury peculiar to the country. But the aroma of horse dung and lion piss permeated every inch of the building's fabric, so that the titillating contradiction between the soft, white shoulders of the lovely ladies whom young army officers escorted there and the hairy pelts of the beasts in the ring resolved in the night-time intermingling of French perfume and the essence of steppe and jungle in which musk and civet revealed themselves as common elements.

Under the ring, in the cellarage, was housed the menagerie which the imperial beasts had temporarily vacated in favour of those of Colonel

Kearney. A tunnel led to a walled courtyard out at the back. Into this courtyard Walser now let himself by means of the modest wicket gate, the performers' entrance.

At this dead hour of the afternoon, under a sad sky tinted the lavender of half-mourning, the courtyard was empty but for a small bird with long legs who pecked with a gourmet air the fibres out of a mound of yellow elephant dung on the cobbles. A smashed bottle, a rusting can; a pump dripped water which froze as it hit the ground.

The only sounds drifting from the menagerie, the continuous murmuring purr of the great cats, like a distant sea, and the faint jingling of Colonel Kearney's elephants of flesh and blood as they rattled the chains on their legs as they did continually, all their waking hours, since in their millennial and long-lived patience they knew quite well how, in a hundred years, or a thousand years' time, or else, perhaps, tomorrow, in an hour's time, for it was all a gamble, a million to one chance, but all the same there *was* a chance that if they kept on shaking their chains, one day, some day, the clasps upon the shackles would part.

It was a forlorn place. The homeliest touch, a row of freshly washed white muslin frocks pegged out on a clothesline, and they were creaking already in a rigor mortis brought on by the first hints of frost.

The Princess of Abyssinia must have put *all* her frocks in the wash because, when she came out to collect her laundry, she had on just a petticoat, and a chemise with, over everything, a terrible apron stiff with blood from waitressing her carnivores. She unpegged each frost-starched garment and rapped it sharply at the waist so that it bent enough to hook on her arm. She was a slim thing with dreadlocks to her waist. In the ring, she looked like a child as she sat at the white Bechstein grand, big enough for two of her, and played for her roaring familiars, but, close to, her face, though neither lined nor wrinkled, was ancient as granite, with the blunt, introspective features of Gauguin's women, and a soft, matte, bitter brown in colour.

Crack! of her thin, musician's hand on her dresses of ice.

The gate into the lane outside opens. Enter Lizzie, in her jacket of the fur of, it might be, dog, her stiff boater of unseasonal straw, carrying a tray covered with a white cloth that does not quench the delicious smell of fresh pancakes. Lunchtime. She kicks the gate shut with her foot and trots up a clanging metal fire escape to an upper door she leaves a-swing behind her.

From this open door, drifting on the stagnant air, a raucous voice raised in not unmelodious if brassy song.

'Only a bird . . . in a gilded cage . . . '

Then that door, too, banged shut.

Walser wrenched his eyes from the closed door and ducked down the tunnel, on his way to the ring.

What a cheap, convenient, expressionist device, this sawdust ring, this little O! Round like an eye, with a still vortex in the centre; but give it a little rub as if it were Aladdin's wishing lamp and, instantly, the circus ring turns into that durably metaphoric, uroboric snake with its tail in its mouth, wheel that turns full circle, the wheel whose end is its beginning, the wheel of fortune, the potter's wheel on which our clay is formed, the wheel of life on which we all are broken. O! of wonder; O! of grief.

Walser thrilled, as always, to the shop-soiled yet polyvalent romance of the image.

The magic circle was now occupied by Lamarck's Educated Apes. A dozen chimpanzees, six of either sex, all in sailor suits, were seated in pairs at little wooden double desks, each with a slate and slate pencil clutched in their leathery hands. A chimp in a sober black suit with a watch-chain looped athwart his bosom, a mortarboard at a rakish angle on his head, stood at the blackboard armed with a cue. The pupils were hushed and attentive, in marked contrast to the young woman in a grubby print wrapper who sat on the plush-topped barrier of the ring idly filing her nails with an emery board. She yawned. She paid them no attention. The chimps put themselves through their own paces; the trainer's woman was no more than their keeper and Monsieur Lamarck, a feckless drunkard, left them to rehearse on their own.

Walser could make no sense of the diagram chalked on the black-board yet the chimps appeared to be occupied in transcribing it to their slates. The partings in the centres of their glossy heads were white as honeycomb. The Professor made a few swift passes with his left hand and pointed to the lower right-hand corner of the diagram; a female towards the back of the class raised her arm eagerly. When the Professor pointed his cue at her, she performed a sequence of gestures that reminded Walser of the movements of the hands of Balinese dancers. The Professor considered, nodded and chalked in another arabesque on the diagram. The neat, shining heads at once bent in unison and the air shrilled with the scratching of a dozen slate pencils, a sound like a flock of starlings coming in to roost.

Walser smiled under his matte white; how irresistibly comic, these hirsute studies! Yet his curiosity was piqued by this mysterious scholarship. He squinted again at the diagram but could not tease a meaning out of it. Yet there seemed to be . . . could it be? Was it possible? . . . was there *writing* on the blackboard? If he crept round towards the Tsar's box, he might be able to see better . . . Stealing softly across the tiered benches in the clown's long shoes he had not yet learned to master, the clumsy toe knocked against an empty vodka bottle left in the angle of a step. The bottle skipped down the rest of the tiers and banged against the barrier.

At this unexpected noise, the silent group all turned and fixed the intruder with thirteen pairs of quick, dark eyes. Walser slipped on to a bench and tried to make himself inconspicuous, but he knew he had stumbled on a secret when the lesson immediately stopped.

The Professor whipped out a yellow duster and wiped off the diagram in a trice. The girl who'd asked the question solemnly stood on her head on the lid of her desk. Her desk-mate took a catapult from his pocket and struck the Professor full in the face with a juicy ink-pellet, inducing in him a farcical and gibbering outrage.

Their bored keeper went on filing her nails. It was only the 'apes at school' number.

Faced with this insurrection in the classroom, the Professor happily discovered a cache of dunces' caps stacked behind the blackboard. He bounced round the ring, disposing a cap on each capering head; then, on impulse, leapt lightly across the barrier and Walser got a dunce's cap, too. The Professor's face, grinning like a Cheshire cat, was not six inches from Walser's own as he popped it on. Their eyes met.

Walser never forgot this first, intimate exchange with one of these beings whose life ran parallel to his, this inhabitant of the magic circle of difference, unreachable . . . but not unknowable; this exchange with the speaking eyes of the dumb. It was like the clearing of a haze. Then the Professor, as if acknowledging their meeting across the gulf of strangeness, pressed his tough forefinger down on Walser's painted smile, bidding him be silent.

The chimps, effortlessly recapitulating their entire routine, now raced round and round the ring upon the fleet, single wheels of monocycles. They had all flung off their sailor suits to reveal satin shorts beneath and they played all manner of tricks on one another. Some stuck their clever, five-fingered feet in one another's spokes to dislodge the rider while others clambered on to the saddles of their monocycles and balanced there on one leg until the force of gravity brought them low. But Walser noticed how the Professor glanced at these frolics with an air of grave melancholy while the chimps themselves seemed to take no pleasure from the sport, going through the motions with a desultory, mechanical air, longing, perhaps, to be back at their studies, whatever they were, for nothing is more boring than being forced to play.

In the distance, a vague roaring of the great cats.

The Professor, as if coming to a decision, took hold of Walser's hand. Though no more than three and a half feet tall to Walser's six plus, he was a remarkably strong and determined little fellow and forcibly persuaded Walser down the aisle to the ring. The spinning chimps came to a halt, dismounted, dropped their bikes and clustered round him in a gesticulating circle, so that he could have sworn they were discussing what to do with him, although the confabulation took place in noisy silence. Just then, Samson the Strong Man arrived, in his tigerskin loincloth, fresh from raising his weights, his thighs and biceps gleaming with oil, but the Strong Man paid as little heed to the chimps as they to him. The Ape-Man's woman put away her emery board, however.

The Professor pointed to Walser's dunce's cap. The chimps rocked back and forth on the palms of their feet as if in soundless laughter. Then the female who'd asked that salient question – Walser recognised her by the green bow in her hair – startled him badly, she jumped right up in his arms and, clutching his torso with her hairy thighs, reached up and behind, found the stud at the back of his neck that released his entire shirt-front. Off it snapped. Down she jumped.

The Strong Man's hand released a small, white breast from the overall of the Ape-Man's woman, while her own freshly manicured fingers set free from its tigerskin cache-sexe a tool of proportions commensurate with the owner's size, curved like a scimitar. Both were oblivious to Walser's plight.

Green Hair-Ribbon laid Walser's shirt-front carefully down on a nearby desk and gestured him to take off his patchwork jacket. Nervously, Walser looked to his new friend, the Professor, for advice. The Professor nodded: 'Yes.' What do they want of me? Walser asked himself, undressing obediently. When the Professor picked up his cue, again, the chimps returned to their desks to take up their pencils and Walser tentatively answered himself: 'Perhaps . . . an anatomy lesson . . . '

Clearly the apes had suffered a surfeit of practical biology demonstrations, for they had no eyes for their keeper, stretched out as she was full-length on a red plush banquette while the twin moons of the bum of the Strong Man rose and fell above her, although outside her field of vision.

Now Walser wore nothing but the dunce's cap, which they did not bother to remove, although they made him take his shoes off so that the Professor could check the number of his toes. It occurred to Walser they thought his white, red and black clown make-up was his real face and they were, perhaps, sympathetic to him because they thought he might be some relation to the baboon. Were they, he pondered, grappling with Darwin's theory – from the other end? Green Hair-Ribbon returned to her desk and the lesson started in earnest. Walser stood before them, nude and exemplary, and the Professor prodded him in the thorax with his cue, not urgently, making those swift passes of the hands with which they seemed to communicate. Walser wilted under the scrutiny of the eyes of his little cousins twice removed. Squeak, squeak, went the slate pencils. Prod, went the cue; Walser obediently turned round to present the class with his backside. The Professor expressed particular interest in the vestigial remains of his tail.

A profound and unusual, even disturbing, silence now filled the building, broken only by the rhythmic grunts of the copulators.

The Professor made a few brisk movements as if introducing a new theme. He turned Walser round to face his class, once more, and the eructation of the slate pencils broke out again when the Professor lightly touched Walser's mouth with his cue and persuaded his lips apart. Then the Professor went to fetch a bucket some careless hand had abandoned in the ring, upturned it and stood on it, the better to peer inside Walser's mouth. After that, he stared directly into Walser's eyes, producing afresh in Walser that dizzy uncertainty about what was human and what was not. How grave, how beseeching the Professor looked as he started to open and close his own mouth like a goldfish reciting a poem.

The grunts of the Strong Man began to accelerate.

Walser presently understood the Professor wanted him to speak to them, that his speech was of surpassing interest to them. The Professor continued to perch on the bucket, gazing ardently within Walser's mouth at play of tongue and uvula, as Walser hesitantly began:

'What a piece of work is man! How noble in reason! How infinite in faculty!'

The Strong Man accomplished his orgasm in a torrent of brutish shrieks, such a hullabaloo that Walser stumbled over his recitation but, in the midst of the Strong Man's ecstasy, Sybil burst into the ring as if shot from a gun, at a remarkable turn of speed for a pig. She sent the desks and scholars flying. Her white ruff was ripped and askew and she was screeching as though it were sticking time.

She cleared the barrier in a mighty bound and promptly went to earth in the royal box, never letting up her hellish racket even as she burrowed deep down under the velvet carpets for safety.

The Strong Man bellowed; Sybil shrieked; there rose up the desolate cry of the Colonel, whose pig was in danger; and, from the menagerie, suddenly, came an immense fugue of roaring, as if all the cats were stops on a gigantic organ that was being played flat out. Then, a fearful shout:

TIGER OUT! TIGER OUT!

The Professor kicked over the clanking bucket in his haste. His pupils leaped over the overturned desks and shinned up the poles to the orchestra platform, to crouch in a huddle among the music-stands, big-eyed and twittering with agitation, full of atavistic, jungle terror. The lovers on the plush banquette rose up, white-faced and shaking.

Walser, naked, abandoned by the apes, thought: 'I shall *not* meet Death in a dunce's cap!' And snatched it from his head.

He ran. He vaulted the barrier and was half-way up the amphitheatre towards the main exit when, Lot's wife-like, he could not resist a backward glance.

The tiger ran into the ring, hot on the scent of Sybil.

It came out of the corridor like orange quicksilver, or a rarer liquid metal, a quickgold. It did not so much run as flow, a questing sluice of brown and yellow, a hot and molten death. It prowled and growled around the remains of the chimps' classroom, snuffing up its immense, flaring nostrils the delicious air of freedom fragrant with the scent of meat on the hoof. How yellow its teeth were; the festering teeth of carnivores.

The Strong Man tore off the woman's clinging arms, clutched his loincloth round his privates and made for the auditorium door. He was a fine specimen, in prime condition; he swung from tier to tier of the seating, past Walser struck like a pillar of salt, up and away. The exit banged to behind him. Walser heard the sound of the shooting of the bolts.

Now the only way out of the ring was that by which the tiger had entered it.

I am in a perfect death trap, thought Walser.

The Ape-Man's woman, her ankles as securely trapped by her dropped knickers as if the garment had been a pair of bolas, let out a blood-curdling scream.

We are in a perfect death trap, thought Walser.

When the tiger heard the woman scream, it knew that something better than pork was on the menu. It arched its back. Its tail stood to attention. It raised its heavy head. Its yellow eyes went round and round the ring like searchlights, seeking the source of the scream.

The terrified woman scrambled out of her underwear and ran along the circular bank of seating.

The tiger's swivelling eyes caught sight of her. The tiger scratched with its hind paws, raising little puffs from the sawdust. It laid back its round, disingenuous ears. Her wrapper, flapping like a sail, caught on an ill-hammered, jutting nail and tripped her up. She fell forward on her face in the gangway.

Walser recovered the use of his limbs. Before he was aware he had made a decision, he hurled himself down the amphitheatre towards the amber-eyed brute just as it was about to spring. Involuntary as his heroics, Walser let rip a tremendous, wordless war-cry: here comes the Clown to kill the Tiger!

Kill it, how? Strangle it with his bare hands, perhaps?

THREE

Then there was a room hissing with greenish gaslight, in which Walser opened his eyes to see a looming figure dipping lint into a bowl of pink water powerfully redolent of carbolic acid. He lay on some kind of day-bed. It was his blood tinged the water pink. He closed his eyes again. Fevvers re-applied the damp lint to his shoulder without gentleness. Now he was conscious, he howled.

'Easy does it,' advised Lizzie, tilting the rim of a mug of hot, sweet tea to his lips. Tea with canned, condensed milk in it. English tea. Fevvers did not release her pressure on his dressing. She wore a stern, white shirt secured at the throat with an emphatic necktie but this did not render her in the least masculine. Upholstered in the snowy linen, her bosom looked as vast as its mother's does to a child as she bends over its bed in sickness. Her displeasure was palpable.

'So you've run away to join the circus, have you, love?' she asked, not quite pleasantly. Evidently she no longer felt the need to call him 'sir'.

Walser twitched between her ministrations, disturbing the shawl in which they'd wrapped him. This shawl was made from dozens of little squares of knitted wool sewn together to form a patchwork and its workmanship had the touching incompetence of that of children, first *real* evidence, he noted, of the existence of the tribe of Cockney nephews and nieces they were always talking about. His wig was gone and his hair was sopping wet.

'Tiger took one swipe at you and then the Princess turned on the hosepipe,' said Lizzie. 'Whoosh! Blast 'em with water, that's the trick. Knocks the breath out of the buggers. Knocks 'em backwards. Then you scoop 'em up with a net.'

There were comforting, familiar things in Fevvers' new dressing-room. A gilt clock topped with Father Time, stopped at twelve. A dog-eared poster on the wall. A puffing spirit kettle. Lizzie made him drink more tea.

'Course, it isn't a *tiger*, exactly!' Fevvers informed him. 'Didn't give you a chance to check out its privates, did it. Tigress. Female of the species. Deadlier than the male, and all that.'

'Charging a bleeding tigress!' exclaimed Lizzie. 'What the 'ell got into 'im?'

'He was having it off with the Ape-Man's missus, wasn't he,' said Fevvers in a flat tone. She pressed too firmly on the compress, so Walser howled, again.

'No use denying it.'

'Quick work,' said Lizzie.

'She's a pin-cushion,' said Fevvers.

'I take it,' said Lizzie to Walser, 'that you wish to remain incognito.'

'We're the only ones that *know*,' said Fevvers, in the tones of one pondering blackmail.

'But what the 'ell's his game?' Lizzie asked Fevvers, as if he were not there.

'I'm sure *I* don't know.'

'I'm here to write a story,' he said. 'Story about the circus. About you and the circus,' he added in as conciliatory manner as he knew how.

'That involve screwing the Ape-Man's missus, does it?'

She eyed the compress narrowly and let it alone, tipped the bowl of water into the slop pail under the wash-stand and wiped her hands on her pleated skirt with a dismissive air. Yet, as if obeying a scenario that predated their disappointment with him, the women treated him with rough compassion. A frock-coated doctor soon arrived to bandage his scratches, whom Fevvers paid.

'Settle up with me later,' she said in the accents of a tart with a twenty-four carat heart.

A female chimp (wearing a green hair-ribbon) delivered a pile of neatly folded clothes, and wig and school cap, too, and they dressed him up again before they sent him back to Clown Alley. Fevvers even slapped a hasty coat of wet white over his features, to preserve his disguise for him, since his right arm hurt far too much for him to do it for himself. All the same, he felt himself much diminished in their eyes and was glad to get out of the dressing-room.

As he closed the door behind him, Lizzie said thoughtfully to Fevvers: 'How do you think he gets his dispatches through the censor?'

In some pain, and painfully aware that, by the very 'heroicness' of his extravagant gesture, he had 'made a fool of himself' just as the Colonel had predicted he would, Walser made his shaky way through the courtyard, where the mittened and muffled children of the wire-walking Charivaris were now playfully teetering along the Princess's empty washing-line. It was already dark. From the monkey house, echoing on the night air, came a rhythmic thud as the Ape-Man beat his woman as though she were a carpet.

FOUR

---◦◉◦---

Clown Alley, the generic name of all lodgings of all clowns, temporarily located in this city in the rotten wooden tenement where damp fell from the walls like dew, was a place where reigned the lugubrious atmosphere of a prison or a mad-house; amongst themselves, the clowns distilled the same kind of mutilated patience one finds amongst inmates of closed institutions, a willed and terrible suspension of being. At dinner time, the white faces gathered round the table, bathed in the acrid steam of the baboushka's fish soup, possessed the formal lifelessness of death masks, as if, in some essential sense, they themselves were absent from the repast and left untenanted replicas behind.

Observe, in his behind-the-scenes repose, Buffo the Great, the Master Clown, who sits by rights not at the head but at the magisterial *middle* of the table, in the place where Leonardo seats the Christ, reserving to himself the sacramental task of breaking the black bread and dividing it between his disciples.

Buffo the Great, the terrible Buffo, hilarious, appalling, devastating Buffo with his round, white face and the inch-wide rings of rouge round his eyes, and his four-cornered mouth, like a bow tie, and, mockery of mockeries, under his roguishly cocked, white, conical cap, he wears a wig that does not simulate hair. It is, in fact, a bladder. Think of that. He wears his insides on his outside, and a portion of his most obscene and intimate insides, at that; so that you might think he is bald, he stores his brains in the organ which, conventionally, stores piss.

He is a big man, seven feet high and broad to suit, so that he makes you laugh when he trips over little things. His size is half the fun of it, that he should be so very, very big and yet incapable of coping with the simplest techniques of motion. This giant is the victim of material objects. Things are against him. They wage war on him. When he tries to open a door, the knob comes off in his hand.

At moments of consternation, his eyebrows, black and bushy with mascara, shoot up his forehead and his jaw drops as if brow and jaw were pulled by opposing magnets. Tsking his tongue against his yellow, gravestone teeth, he fits the knob back on again with exaggerated care. Steps back. Approaches the door, again, with a laughably unjustified self-confidence. Grasps the knob, firmly; *this* time, he knows it is secure . . . hasn't he just fixed it himself? But –

Things fall apart at the very shiver of his tread on the ground. He is himself the centre that does not hold.

He specialises in violent slapstick. He likes to burn clown policemen alive. As the mad priest, he will officiate at clown weddings where Grik or Grok in drag is subjected to the most extravagant humiliations. They do a favourite 'Clowns' Christmas Dinner', in which Buffo takes up his Christ's place at the table, carving knife in one hand, fork in the other, and some hapless august or other is borne on, with a cockscomb on his head, as the bird. (Much play with the links of sausages with which this bird's trousers are stuffed.) But *this* roast, such is the way of Buffo's world, gets up and tries to run away . . .

Buffo the Great, the Clown of Clowns.

He adores the old jokes, the collapsing chairs, the exploding puddings; he says, 'The beauty of clowning is, nothing ever changes.'

At the climax of his turn, everything having collapsed about him as if a grenade exploded it, he starts to deconstruct himself. His face becomes contorted by the most hideous grimaces, as if he were trying to shake off the very wet white with which it is coated: shake! shake! shake out his teeth, shake off his nose, shake away his eyeballs, let all go flying off in a convulsive self-dismemberment.

He begins to spin round and round where he stands.

Then, when you think, this time, Buffo the Great *must* whirl apart into his constituents, as if he had turned into his own centrifuge, the terrific drum roll which accompanies this extraordinary display concludes and Buffo leaps, shaking, into the air, to fall flat on his back.

Silence.

The lights dim.

Very, very slowly and mournfully, now strikes up the Dead March from *Saul,* led by Grik and Grok, the musical clowns, with bass drum and piccolo, with minuscule fiddle and enormous triangle struck with back-kick of foot, Grik and Grok, who contain within them an entire orchestra. This is the turn called 'The Clown's Funeral'. The rest of the clowns carry on an exceedingly large coffin draped with the Union Jack. They put the coffin down on the sawdust beside Buffo. They start to put him in it.

But will he fit? Of course he won't! His legs and arms can't be bent, won't be bent, won't be ordered about! Nobody can lay out *this* force of nature, even if it *is* dead! Pozzo or Bimbo runs off to get an axe to hack bits off him, to cut him down to coffin-size. It turns out the axe is made of rubber.

At long, hilarious last, somehow or other they finally contrive to load him into the box and get the coffin lid on top of him, although it keeps on jerking and tilting because dead Buffo can't and won't lie down. The clown attendants heave the coffin up on their shoulders; they have some difficulty co-ordinating themselves as pall-bearers. One falls to his knees and, when he rises, down goes another. But, sooner or later, the coffin is aloft upon their shoulders and they prepare to process out of the ring with him.

At which Buffo bursts through the coffin lid! Right through. With a great, rending crash, leaving behind a huge, ragged hole, the silhouette of himself, in the flimsy wood. Here he is, again, large as life and white and black and red all over! 'Thunder and lightning, did yuz think I was dead?'

Tumultuous resurrection of the clown. He leaps from his coffin even as his acolytes hold it high, performing a double somersault on his way to the ground. (He started out in life as an acrobat.) Roars of applause, cheers. He darts round and round the ring, shaking hands, kissing those babies who are not weeping with terror, tousling the heads of bug-eyed children teetering between tears and laughter. Buffo who was dead is now alive again.

And all bound out of the ring, lead by this demoniac, malign, enchanted reveller.

The other clowns called him the Old Man, as a mark of respect, although he was not yet quite fifty, hovering about the climacteric of his years.

His personal habits were dominated by his tremendous and perpetual thirst. His pockets always bulged with bottles; his drinking was prodigious yet always seemed somehow unsatisfactory to himself, as if alcohol were an inadequate substitute for some headier or more substantial intoxicant, as though he would have liked, if he could, to bottle the whole world, tip it down his throat, then piss it against the wall. Like Fevvers, he was Cockney bred and born; his *real* name was George Buffins, but he had long ago forgotten it, although he was a great patriot, British to the bone, even if as widely travelled as the British Empire in the service of fun.

'We kill ourselves,' said Buffo the Great. 'Often we hang ourselves with the gaudy braces from which we suspend those trousers loose as the skirts that Muslims wear lest the Messiah be born to a man. Or, sometimes, a pistol may be sneaked from the lion-tamer, his blanks replaced with live bullets. Bang! a bullet through the brain. If in Paris, you can chuck yourself under the Metro. Or, should you have been so lucky as to be able to afford mod. cons, you might gas yourself in your lonely garret, might you not. Despair is the constant companion of the Clown.

'For not infrequently there is no element of the *voluntary* in clowning. Often, d'you see, we take to clowning when all else fails. Under these impenetrable disguises of wet white, you might find, were you to look, the features of those who were once proud to be visible. You find there, per example, the *aerialiste* whose nerve has failed; the bare-back rider who took one tumble too many; the juggler whose hands shake so, from drink or sorrow, that he can no longer keep his balls in the air. And then what is left but the white mask of poor Pierrot, who invites the laughter that would otherwise come unbidden.

'The child's laughter is pure until he first laughs at a clown.'

The great white heads around the long table nodded slowly in acquiescence.

'The mirth the clown creates grows in proportion to the humiliation he is forced to endure,' Buffo continued, refilling his glass with vodka. 'And yet, too, you might say, might you not, that the clown is the very image of Christ.' With a nod towards the mildly shining icon in the corner of the stinking kitchen, where night crawled in the form of cockroaches in the corners. 'The despised and rejected, the scapegoat upon whose stooped shoulders is heaped the fury of the mob, the object and yet — yet! also he is the *subject* of laughter. For what we are, we have *chosen* to be.

'Yes, young lad, young Jack, young First-of-May, we *subject* ourselves to laughter from choice. We are the whores of mirth, for, like a whore, we know what we are; we know we are mere hirelings hard at work and yet those who hire us see us as beings perpetually at play. Our work is their pleasure and so they think our work must be our pleasure, too, so there is always an abyss between their notion of our work as play, and ours, of their leisure as our labour.

'And as for mirth itself, oh, yes, young Jack!' Turning to Walser and waving an admonitory glass at him. 'Don't think I haven't very often meditated on the subject of laughter, as, in my all too human rags, I grovel on the sawdust. And you want to know what I think? That they don't laugh in heaven, not even if it were ever so.

'Consider the saints as the acts in a great circus. Catherine juggling her wheel. St Lawrence on his grill, a spectacle from any freak-show. Saint Sebastian, best knife-throwing stunt you ever saw! And St Jerome, with his learned lion with the paw on the book, great little animal act, that, beats the darkie bitch and her joanna hollow!

'And the great ringmaster in the sky, with his white beard and his uplifted finger, for whom all these and many other less sanctified performers put on their turns in the endless ring of fire which surrounds the whirling globe. But never a giggle, never a titter up there. The archangels can call: "Bring on the clowns!" until they're blue in the face but the celestial band will never strike up the intro to "The March of the Gladiators" on its harps and trumps, never, no fear – for we are doomed to stay down below, nailed on the endless cross of the humiliations of this world!

'The sons of men. Don't you forget, me lad, we clowns are the sons of men.'

The others all droned after him, in unison: 'We are the sons of men,' as in some kind of clerical response.

'You must know,' continued Buffo to Walser in his graveyard intonation, 'you must know that the word "clown" derives from the Old Norse, "klunni", meaning "loutish". "Klunni", cognate with the Danish, "kluntet", clumsy, maladroit, and the Yorkshire dialect, "gormless". You must know what you have become, young man, how the word defines you, now you have opted to lose your wits in the profession of the clown.'

'A clown!' they murmured softly, dreamily amongst themselves. 'A clown! Welcome to Clown Alley!'

Meanwhile, to the accompaniment of Buffo's sermon, the meal went on. Spoons scraped the bottoms of the earthenware bowls of fish soup; the spatulate, white-gloved hands reached for the shanks of black bread, food sad and dark as the congregation of sorrow assembled at the ill-made table. Buffo, scorning a glass, now tipped vodka straight from the bottle down his throat.

'There is a story told of me, even of me, the Great Buffo, as it has been told of every Clown since the invention of the desolating profession,' intoned Buffo. 'Told, once, of the melancholy Domenico Biancolette, who had the seventeenth century in stitches; told of Grimaldi; told of the French Pierrot, Jean-Gaspard Deburau, whose inheritance was the moon. This story is not precisely true but has the poetic truth of myth and so attaches itself to each and every laughter-maker. It goeth thus:

'In Copenhagen, once, I had the news of the death of my adored mother, by telegram, the very morning on which I buried my dearly beloved wife who had passed away whilst bringing stillborn into the world the only son that ever sprang from my loins, if "spring" be not too sprightly a word for the way his reluctant meat came skulking out of her womb before she gave up the ghost. All those I loved wiped out at one fell swoop! And still at matinee time in the Tivoli, I tumble in the ring and how the punters bust a gut to see. Seized by inconsolable grief, I cry: "The sky is full of blood!" And they laughed all the more. How droll you are, with the tears on your cheeks! In mufti, in mourning, in some low bar between performances, the jolly barmaid says: "I say, old fellow, what a long face! I know what *you* need. Go along to the Tivoli and take a look at Buffo the Great. He'll soon bring your smiles back!"

'The clown may be the source of mirth, but – who shall make the clown laugh?'

'Who shall make the clown laugh?' they whispered together, rustling like hollow men.

Little Ivan, oblivious to the meaning of the foreign babbling issuing from the blanched, jack-o'-lantern faces that hung over the table, ran round collecting the clinking soup bowls, unnerved yet more and more fascinated by this invasion of glum, painted comedians. The meal, such as it was, was over. All produced pipes, baccy and fresh vodka while the baboushka, kneeling before the samovar, performed the endless, contentless, semi-prayerful gestures of those hands deformed by decades of common toil. Her daughter, the axe-murderess, was far away in Siberia, but, although the baboushka's life was composed of these gestures simulating praying, she no longer possessed sufficient energy to pray for her daughter's soul. The charcoal reddened, black-ened, reddened.

'And yet,' resumed Buffo, after a pull at a bottle, 'we possess one privilege, one rare privilege, that makes of our outcast and disregarded state something wonderful, something precious. We can invent our own faces! We *make* ourselves.'

He pointed at the white and red superimposed upon his own, never-visible features.

'The code of the circus permits of no copying, no change. However much the face of Buffo may appear identical to Grik's face, or to Grok's face, or to Coco's face, or Pozzo's, Pizzo's, Bimbo's faces, or to the face of any other joey, carpet clown or august, it is, all the same, a fingerprint of authentic dissimilarity, a genuine expression of my own autonomy. And so my face eclipses me. I have become this face which is not mine, and yet I chose it freely.

'It is given to few to shape themselves, as I have done, as we have done, as you have done, young man, and, in that moment of choice – lingering deliciously among the crayons; what eyes shall I have, what mouth . . . exists a perfect freedom. But, once the choice is made, I am condemned, therefore, to be "Buffo" in perpetuity. Buffo for ever; long live Buffo the Great! Who will live on as long as some child somewhere remembers him as a wonder, a marvel, a monster, a thing that, had he not been invented, should have been, to teach little children the *truth* about the filthy ways of the filthy world. As long as a child remembers . . . '

Buffo reached out a long arm and purposefully goosed Little Ivan as he passed by with glasses of tea.

' . . . some child like Little Ivan,' said Buffo, who did not know Little Ivan had watched from the top of the stove as his mother chopped up his father, and assumed the child was both innocent and naive.

'Yet,' he went on, 'am I this Buffo whom I have created? Or did I, when I made up my face to look like Buffo's, create, *ex nihilo*, another self who is not me? And what am I without my Buffo's face? Why, nobody at all. Take away my make-up and underneath is merely not-Buffo. An absence. A vacancy.'

Grik and Grok, the pair of musical clowns, old troupers, always together, the Darby and Joan of the clowns, turned their faces towards Walser, bending to catch the feeble lamp-light, and he saw those faces were mirror images of one another, alike in every detail save that Grik's face was left-handed and Grok's face was right-handed.

'Sometimes it seems,' said Grok, 'that the faces exist of themselves, in a disembodied somewhere, waiting for the clown who will wear them, who will bring them to life. Faces that wait in the mirrors of unknown dressing-rooms, unseen in the depths of the glass like fish in dusty pools, fish that will rise up out of the obscure profundity when they spot the one who anxiously scrutinises his own reflection for the face it lacks, *man-eating* fish waiting to gobble up your being and give you another instead . . . '

'But, as for us, old comrades that we are, old stagers that we are,' said Grik, 'why, do I need a mirror when I put my make-up on? No, sir!

All I need to do is look in my old pal's face, for, when we made our face together, we created out of nothing each other's Siamese twin, our nearest and dearest, bound by a tie as strong as shared liver and lights. Without Grik, Grok is a lost syllable, a typo on a programme, a sign-painter's hiccup on a billboard – '

' – and so is he *sans* me. Oh, young man, you First-of-May, we cannot tell you, how would we have sufficient words to tell you just how useless we used to be before Grik and Grok came together and pooled our two uselessnesses, abandoned our separate empty faces for the one face, *our* face, brought to bed the joint child of our impotences, turned into more than the sum of our parts according to the dialectics of uselessness, which is: nothing plus nothing equals something, *once –*'

' – you know the nature of plus.'

Having delivered themselves of the equation of the dialectic, they beamed with gratification beneath their impenetrable make-up. But Buffo wasn't having any.

'Bollocks,' he said, heavily, belching. 'Beg pardon, but balls, me old fruit. *Nothing* will come of nothing. That's the glory of it.'

And the entire company repeated after him soft as dead leaves rustling: 'That's the glory of it! Nothing will come of nothing!'

Yet the musical clowns, such was their ancient authority within the tribe, stubbornly at once set out to prove they could at least make a little something out of it, for Grik began to hum the softest, tiniest kind of melody, while Grok, his old lover, started to drum, softly, his gloved fingertips against the table top, hum of a drowsy bee and rhythm faint as a pulse but sufficient for the clowns, for the others now rose up from their benches and, in the dim gloom of the Petersburg kitchen, they began to dance.

It was the bergomask, or dance of the buffoons, and if it began with the same mockery of gracefulness as the dance of the rude mechanicals in *A Midsummer Night's Dream*, then soon their measures went sour, turned cruel, turned into a dreadful libel upon the whole notion of dancing.

As they danced, they began rhythmically to pelt one another with leftover crusts of black bread and emptied their vodka bottles over one another's heads, mugged pain, resentment, despair, agony, death, rose up and pelted, emptied, turn and turn about. The baboushka lay drowsing on the stove by now, her ample sorrows forgotten, but little Ivan, entranced, hid in the shadows and fearfully could not forebear to watch, his thumb stuck firmly in his mouth to give him comfort.

The guttering paraffin lamp cast awry shadows on the blackened walls, shadows that did not fall where the laws of light dictated that they should. One by one, each accompanied by his twisted shadow, the clowns climbed up on the table, where Grik and Grok remained seated one at each end, like gravestones, humming and drumming.

One lanky, carrot-haired fellow, whose suit was latticed in prismatic colours like a matador's suit of lights, took firm hold of the window-pane check baggy pants of a tiny creature in a red velvet waistcoat and poured the contents of an entire pint of vodka into the resultant aperture. The dwarf broke out in a storm of silent weeping, and, with a backward somersault, attached himself to his aggressor's neck to ride there like the old man of the sea although the harlequin now began to spin round in such a succession of cartwheels he soon disappeared in a radiant blur, to reappear in his turn on the back of the dwarf. At which point, Walser lost sight of this couple in the mêlée of the savage jig.

What beastly, obscene violence they mimed! A joey thrust the vodka bottle up the arsehole of an august; the august, in response, promptly dropped his tramp's trousers to reveal a virile member of priapic size, bright purple in colour and spotted with yellow stars, dangling two cerise balloons from the fly. At that, a second august, with an evil leer, took a great pair of shears out of his back pocket and sliced the horrid thing off but as soon as he was brandishing it in triumph above his head another lurid phallus appeared in the place of the first, this one bright blue with scarlet polkadots and cerise testicles, and so on, until the clown with the shears was juggling with a dozen of the things.

It seemed that they were dancing the room apart. As the baboushka slept, her too, too solid kitchen fell into pieces under the blows of their disorder as if it had been, all the time, an ingenious prop, and the purple Petersburg night inserted jagged wedges into the walls around the table on which these comedians cavorted with such little pleasure, in a dance which could have invoked the end of the world.

Then Buffo, who had been sitting in his Christ's place all this while with the impassivity of the masked, gestured to Little Ivan – to innocent Little Ivan – to bring to the table that black iron cauldron from which the fish soup had been served and place it before him. And so the tranced child stepped into the act.

Rising ceremoniously to his feet, the Master Clown fished within the cauldron and found there all manner of rude things – knickers, lavatory brushes, and yard upon yard of lavatory paper. (Anality, the one quality that indeed they shared with children.) Chamber-pots appeared from nowhere and soon several wore them on their heads, while Buffo served up more and yet more disgusting tidbits from the magic depths of his pot and dealt them with imperial prodigality about his retinue.

Dance of disintegration; and of regression; celebration of the primal slime.

Little Ivan gaped, near panic, near hysteria, yet all was silent as a summer day – only the drone and pulse of Grik and Grok and, like a sound from another world, the occasional snore and groan of the baboushka on the stove.

In spite of Fevvers' ministrations and the attentions of the doctor, Walser was still stiff and sore from the embrace of the tiger and, although he knew this display was, in some sense, put on for his benefit, was even a kind of initiation, he had no great taste for it and slipped through one of the fissures of the revelry into the freezing alley outside. At the touch of cold, his wound buzzed like a saw.

On a crumbling wall, reluctantly lit by a meagre streetlamp, was a freshly pasted poster. He could not read the legend, in Cyrillic, but he could see her – Fevvers, in all her opulence, in mid-air, in her new incarnation as circus star. The Colonel had taken the French dwarf's design but added to it, by some less skilful hand, representations of the Princess of Abyssinia, the cats, the apes, the clowns themselves, so that they all seemed sheltered by Fevvers' outspread wings in the same way that the poor people of the world are protected under the cloak of the Madonna of Misericordia.

As Walser eyed this poster sardonically, a shadow detached itself from those beneath the streetlamp, crossed the street like a gust of wind and threw itself, weeping, at Walser's feet, covering his hands with kisses.

FIVE

And that was how Walser came to inherit the Ape-Man's woman, although he did not understand one word she said, except her name, Mignon, and she continued to grovel in the street, clinging to his short pants with her poor, bony hands.

She was still dressed as she had been that morning, in the thin, faded, cotton wrapper, no coat or shawl, so her bare arms were dappled mauve with cold. The little white rabbit-bones of her ankles stuck out above the torn, felt carpet slippers on her bare feet. Her limp, light hair dangled from her small head in draggled rats'-tails. With his left hand, his good hand, he pulled her upright and she came easily, she was light as an empty basket. She leant against him whilst she finished off crying, knuckling her eyesockets like a child. The dark marks on her face could have been either tearstains or bruises.

Nothing else moved on the street of warped, shuttered houses. The fog closed down like the lid of a pot. A melancholy dog barked in the distance. In the lodging house behind him, the clown's malign fiesta. Nowhere to take this waif delivered to him by chance except – the Madonna of the Arena waggled her bum from the poster; his decision was made. He lirruped and chirruped to the girl in the way the equestrienne invokes docility in a shy horse and led her through the maze of hovels until they debouched abruptly upon a glittering street.

What thundering noise! what brilliant lights! Crowds of people, of horses, of carriages! Walser was touched to see how little Mignon, accustomed only to poor lodgings, and caravans, and the underside of spectacle, soon left off sobbing and gazed about her with wonder and excitement. She was adenoidal and breathed through her mouth but she had a pale, undernourished, unhealthy prettiness. When she stopped crying, she had breath enough to cough.

They made a strange pair. A painted streetwalker with a veil over her eyes and a good, fur-collared coat turned to watch them pass. She crossed herself, she thought she saw a pair of holy fools, but the doorman at the Hotel de l'Europe, in his maroon dress-uniform, less superstitious, advanced upon them with his hand outstretched, barring entry through the glass door with the gesture of the guardian of paradise.

Walser tried out his few words of Russian, repeated 'please' several times, but the doorman laughed and shook his head. He wore the epaulettes and braided cap of, at least, a general. Mignon, hanging on Walser's arm, gazed and gazed through the glass door at the fairyland inside, the dazzle of electricity, the furry carpets, the fine ladies, no prettier than herself, who showed their bosoms to bowing gentlemen in evening dress. She gazed with a joyous awe, almost a gratitude, that luxury should exist; she never expected the door-keeper might relent and let them in, why should he? She knew, better than the foolish clown, such treats were not for the likes of them, but, all the same, just the sight of that forbidden sweety-shop of a hotel foyer was sufficient in itself to compensate her for a day in which she had been abandoned to the mercies of a hungry tiger by her lover, then beaten to tatters and thrown half-naked on to the Russian winter streets by her husband. She made small guttural sounds of wistful admiration at the back of her throat. Her eyes were big and round as millstones.

Then Walser thought he might bribe the doorman but just as he funbled under his shirt for the 'grouch bag', as Grik called it, in which he'd been taught to hide his roubles, a firm hand in a bronze kid glove descended on his good shoulder, whilst another, similarly clad, flourished before the doorman's eyes two pink slips of paper which he recognised as complimentaries for the opening night of the Greatest Show on Earth. He and Mignon were swept at once into the warm, perfumed air inside in Fevvers' wake as the doorman bowed almost to the ground with servility and gratitude.

Her suite appeared to be furnished exclusively in flowers but, peering beneath a couple of bushels of white lilac, Fevvers located a red velvet armchair of the size of a sitz bath and plumped down in it, kicking away her high-heeled shoes and shrugging off a flowery Spanish shawl with gestures of furious exhaustion. Under her shawl, she wore an extravagant satin dress in that shade of red blondes are told to avoid because it 'drains' them; but it did not drain Fevvers, whose rouge was even brighter. Her dress was decorated with flounces of black lace and cut down at the front almost to her nipples, probably in an attempt to distract attention from her hump. All the same:

'Tomorrow,' she growled morosely, 'all the fine ladies in Petersburg will go hunchbacked. Another social triumph, Mr Walser.'

Misericordia was in a vile temper.

'What's this the cat's brought in?' she inquired, eyeing Mignon coldly. 'Quick, our Liz, run her a bath before we catch something off her.'

Lizzie, throwing Walser an old-fashioned look, stumped off into the bathroom to do as she was bid.

Blissfully unaware of their cool welcome, the girl, looking no older than thirteen in the remorseless light of the electric chandeliers, was quite overcome by the drawing-room and turned round and round in one spot on the carpet drinking everything in – the beautiful pictures on the walls; spindly-legged tables holding onyx ashtrays and chalcedony cigarette boxes; the merry log fire; plush, glitter and high-piled rugs. Ooooooh!

As she watched the starveling girl's delight, Fevvers' good nature fought with her resentment. She sighed, softened and addressed Mignon in a clatter of languages, Italian, French, German, all barbarously pronounced and grammatically askew but rapid as machine-gun fire. When she struck German, the girl smiled.

Fevvers poked about beneath a festering collation of orchids, retrieved a beribboned box the size of a kettle-drum, cast aside the lid and revealed layer upon layer of chocolates packed in frilly tutus of white paper. She thrust the box at Mignon.

'Go on. Stuff yourself. Essen. Gut.'

Mignon, gawky as a boy, clasped the box to her bosom, sniffing with half-closed eyes, almost swooning at the mingled odours of infantine voluptuousness, cocoa, vanilla, praline, violet, caramel, that rose up from the ruffled depths. She seemed hardly able to dare to touch them. Fevvers brusquely chose a fat choc with a lump of crystallised ginger pressed on top of it and popped it into the pale pink mouth that opened like a sea-anemone to engulf it. A glittering snail-track of the Strong Man's dried semen ran down Mignon's leg. She stank. Until she married the Ape-Man, she followed a strange profession; she used to pose for the dead.

She was the child of a young man who killed his wife, the mother of his children, for lying down with soldiers from a nearby barracks. This young man took the woman out to a pond on the edge of town, cut her throat, threw the knife into the pond and came back to their lodgings in good time to prepare supper for their children. Mignon and her little sister were playing in the square outside. Mignon skipped and her sister turned the rope. She was six, her sister was five.

They saw their father come back. 'Supper will be ready soon,' he said. He went into the house. There was blood on his shirt but didn't he work in the slaughterhouse? Wasn't his job that of washing down the slaughterhouse floor? So they took no notice of the blood on his shirt, or of his wet trousers.

But he came out of the house in a minute. 'The breadknife is lost,' he said. 'I must go and find the breadknife.' Later, people asked the children if he were acting strangely, but how can a six-year-old, a five-year-old, tell what is strange behaviour and what is not? The breadknife had never been lost before. That was strange. But father often got the supper because mother took in washing for the soldiers at the barracks and went out in the evenings to deliver the starched shirts so the officers could have them fresh in time for dinner.

'Bath's ready,' said Lizzie from an open door, in a billow of flower-scented steam.

Mignon tussled with her wrapper, but, since she would not let go of the box of chocolates, shifting it from beneath one arm to beneath the other as she struggled with her sleeves, it took her some time to emerge. She hugged the ribboned box so close you would have thought she had fallen in love with the chocolates.

Since he could not make their supper without cutting bread, her father went off to look for the breadknife in the pond and searched for it so industriously that he drowned himself in five feet of water. They found the breadknife when they dragged the pond. 'Is this your breadknife?' asked the judge, quite kindly. 'Yes,' said Mignon, and stretched out her hand for it, but they would not let her take it back. That was later.

The little girls went on skipping in the square until it got dark. Mignon took her turn at turning the rope. The other end of the rope was tied to the doorhandle. Now all the windows in the house had lights in them, but not their window. Then her sister was hungry, so they untied the rope and went upstairs. Mignon didn't know how to make a light but she found the loaf by touch on the table in the dark and broke pieces off it for her sister and herself, so they ate that.

'Gawd!' exclaimed Fevvers when she saw Mignon's nakedness. Mignon's skin was mauvish, greenish, yellowish from beatings. And, more than the marks of fresh bruises on fading bruises on faded bruises, it was as if she had been beaten flat, had all the pile, the shine banged off her adolescent skin, had been beaten threadbare, or as if she had been threshed, or beaten to the thinness of beaten metal; and the beatings had beaten her back, almost, into the appearance of childhood, for her little shoulderblades stuck up at acute angles, she had no breasts and was almost hairless but for a little flaxen tuft on her mound.

Unconscious of their startled looks, she dropped her wrapper on the floor and scampered to the bathroom, all legs and elbows. She did not forget to take her chocolates with her. Lizzie picked up the discarded garment with the firetongs and dropped it on the blaze, where it flared, crackled, turned into a black ghost of itself and disappeared up the chimney. Fevvers put a summoning finger on the room service bell.

The small girls cried and slept. In the morning, father did not come, only the neighbours came. Of the inquest, Mignon retained only the vaguest memory, vaguer than that of the bounce of offal in the frying pan when her father stole a handful of guts from the slaughterhouse, or of the pretty ribbon a soldier gave her that her mother took away again. (Why had she done that?)

And, now she was a grown girl, she could have recalled, of her father, only a smell of stale meat and a pair of blond moustaches that always dropped down at the tips, his moustaches, which had entirely submitted to despair long before he seized the breadknife, concealed it in his shirt, took his wife by the hand and led her out to look at sunset reflected in the water.

Of her mother, hands moist with soapsuds; hands that took things away from her. And tears, inscrutable in memory as they had been in life, those tears that came when the faithless woman clasped her daughters to her bosom as she sometimes, although infrequently, would do.

In the short space of time Fevvers had been in Petersburg, it seemed she had mastered sufficient bad Russian to order meals and she added, as an afterthought, a bottle of that international beverage, champagne. Clearly Mignon's condition had melted her heart, although, by the rasp of her blue eyes when she cast them at Walser, one would never have thought so.

Housed in the city orphanage, the children prayed, and, the rest of the time, busied themselves with household tasks. Then it was as if her sister went one way and Mignon the other; one morning, they woke in one another's arms in the same bed and, that night, Mignon went to sleep on a heap of rags in the corner of a kitchen full of dark shapes of spits and pots and jars and presses to flatten ducks.

She bore it for six months, because it was winter, and the house in which she skivvied was stuck in the middle of the country in the middle of the snow. But when it was spring, she ran away and a peasant taking a load of cabbages to the city gave her a lift in exchange for sucking his prick. She did not dare go back to the orphanage, although for a long time she used to hang around the outside on the off-chance her sister might still be there but she never saw her sister again so she supposed she got a good place, somewhere, too.

Throughout the summer, Mignon made a living picking up discarded flowers in the market and putting them together in crippled bunches. She learned to exercise some ingenuity in arranging these little nosegays and also soon learned to augment her *trouvailles* with blooms picked from public gardens, but it wasn't a good living, it was begging with paint on its face, and she stole other things, food, odd items of clothing, in order to get by.

She slept where she could, in passages, under bridges, in shop doorways, and it was all right as long as it was warm. She soon made a large acquaintance among the other street arabs, the accidental children of the city, and when the cold weather came she pooled resources with an entire gang of young creatures who made their headquarters in a disused warehouse.

From beggar to thief is one step, but a step in two directions at the same time, for what a beggar loses in morality when he becomes a thief he regains in self-respect.

Yet however accomplished in pickpocketing, these children of the lower depths remained – children. They made themselves big bonfires, at nights, partly to warm themselves, partly for the fun of the flames crackling, they would play games of tag, and hide-and-seek, and jump-across-the-embers, and fall to childish quarrelling and squabbling among themselves, and then the fire got too big for its boots, consumed their quarters, ate up some of them, too. The home and the family Mignon had invented for herself went up in smoke and she was on her own again.

So she thieved, a bit, and tossed off nervous boys in back alleys for a few coppers, and let them put it into her against dreary walls for a few coppers more. She would have been about fourteen then.

The waiter knocked; and rolled in a clinking trolley. A tureen, and champagne in a silver ice-bucket, deliciously misted with chill. The waiter spread a place on one of the gay little tables with a shining white cloth, all the while furtively peering at Fevvers' noble cleavage until Walser felt a strange desire rise within him to punch the young man's nose. If Fevvers had ordered food for only Mignon, there were four glasses, like saucers on stems. These she peremptorily signed to be changed for flutes, a scrupulosity of refinement that charmed Walser.

Fevvers raised the lid of the tureen – bread and milk for the abused child, a maternal touch. She scooped some up on her finger, tasted it, made a wry face, sprinkled sugar lavishly from the silver caster. She replaced the lid and tucked a napkin round the tureen, to keep its contents warm. In spite of these hospitable preparations, the Cockney Venus remained in a foul mood, darting Walser speaking glances of contempt and irritation from eyes that, tonight, were as dark a blue as sailors' trousers.

Ecstatic splashing and coos of delight came through the edges of the bathroom door, together with little puffs of steam. Then Mignon began to sing.

She possessed a sweet, artless soprano, so far so good; to that extent, her voice matched her immature body. But it was as though the scarcely-to-be-imagined tragedy of her life, the sea of misery and disaster in which she swam in her precarious state of innocent defilement, all found expression, beyond her consciousness of her intention, in her voice. She sang:

> So we'll go no more a-roving
> So late into the night
> Though the heart be still as loving
> And the moon shine still as bright.

All three who listened felt the hairs rise on the napes of their necks, as if that lovely voice were something uncanny, its possessor either herself a sorceress or under some spell.

'I thought she didn't speak English,' muttered Fevvers, ruffled, as if the child had been deceiving them.

'Don't you see?' whispered Lizzie. 'She knows the words but she doesn't understand them.'

One winter's night, as the snowflakes whirled around the chimneypots, Mignon, bold with hunger, strayed into the arcades of the commercial part of the city, where she rarely ventured. A gentleman in a snug greatcoat and a top hat rendered melancholy by the weight of snow upon its brim came hurrying down the pavement towards her, absorbed in his own affairs. She put herself in his path. She had not eaten for two days. She was so thin she did not cast a shadow. He made as if to brush her off, as though she were a fly who had settled on his arm, but then, glancing abstractedly at her face, an expression of low cunning and mean surmise crossed his own.

He was a medium and held office hours in his comfortable apartment above a grocer's shop on the next block. Delicious odours of cloves, dried apricots and ham sausage seeped up through the cracks in the floorboards and, for the first time in her life, Mignon got enough to eat; but she did not put on any weight, it was as though something inside her ate it all up before she could get to it but she didn't have worms.

This man, Herr M., had been returning home from a service at the spiritualist church where he occasionally officiated when he encountered the little streetwalker with the shawl over her head. He had indeed been preoccupied with a serious problem, to which her appearance provided the solution. For, only the previous week, his assistant, a buxom lass from Schleswig-Holstein, whom he trusted absolutely, ran off with a Brazilian gentleman, a travelling salesman who visited the grocer downstairs with samples of coffee. She having slipped downstairs one day to buy a snack of cheese and cookies, the pomaded and expansive Latin took time off from his little bags of green beans to bandy words with her in an irresistibly syncopated accent. She accepted his invitation to lunch in a fashionable restaurant one Sunday when Herr M., the medium, was visiting his aged aunt in a tree-shaded suburb. One thing led to another and, if the medium had keen eyes for the world beyond, he was blind as a bat to the developments taking place under his nose – until, under that nose, pinned, in fact, to the very pillow on which he was accustomed to wake to find her pig-tailed head, he discovered, instead, the note advising him she was already on the train that would take her to the port from whence she and her beau would embark for Rio. H'm!

The absconding assistant took a few bits and pieces of portable property such as Herr M.'s gold watch and a roll of banknotes he had deposited inside the grandfather clock for safekeeping, but he was a magnanimous man and felt he owed her *that* much. He also felt some relief that, far away in sunny Brazil, she would be in no position to spill another kind of beans than those in which her senhor dealt. But he was gravely inconvenienced to be without an assistant and regarded his meeting with Mignon as truly ordained by the spirits.

It was her great resemblance to a spectre that struck him most.

> For the sword outwears the sheath
> And the heart outwears the breast
> And love itself must cease
> And the heart itself take rest.

Mignon sang her foreign song without meaning, without feeling, as if the song shone through her, as though she were glass, without the knowledge she was heard; she sang her song, which contained the anguish of a continent.

Herr M., a once-a-night, on-and-off man, screwed Mignon with the absent-minded regularity with which he wound the grandfather clock, although never for quite so long. As for Mignon, she could hardly believe her luck: a bed, with sheets; an armchair; a warm stove; a table, with a cloth; mealtimes! He had her deloused, paid a doctor to ensure a clean bill of health – miraculously, she had escaped infection; and sent her to the dentist, who pulled her rotten molars, greatly increasing the resemblance of her face to a skull thereby. Because she possessed only the rags she stood up in, he bought her several sets of underwear, some dresses of thrifty wool and cotton mix for everyday and, for working hours, some pretty white nighties trimmed with broderie anglaise. She did not need a coat because he never let her out of the apartment. Mignon thought she was in heaven but it was a fool's paradise and, in literal terms, that is an exact description of Herr M.'s establishment.

Herr M. had early formulated the following maxim: why steal, when there is more intellectual satisfaction to be obtained from cheating?

Mignon's daily work henceforward consisted of personating the dead, and posing for their photographs.

Every morning, over breakfast, Herr M. studied the obituary columns in the newspaper, marking the deaths of young women with a mourning stripe of thick black pencil. Although young wives, preferably those who died in childbed, sometimes proved eminently satisfactory, marital relations could turn sticky, on occasions, and, best of all, he preferred the demises of only daughters of elderly parents. Epidemics of diphtheria and scarlet fever always put a smile on his lips and set him a-tapping at the top of his egg with an especially jaunty air. After he consumed his egg, his cheese, his salami, his toast and a couple of spoonsful of preserves – he enjoyed a hearty breakfast – he settled down with a second cup of coffee and entered the satisfactory results of his researches in his filing system.

Sometimes, solemn as an undertaker and garbed in similar fashion, he attended those funerals where he judged there would be so few mourners that his presence would be remembered, and sent, to others, exquisitely chosen flowers such as a bunch of white violets or a garland of scarcely opened rosebuds, accompanied by his black-edged card. But, on the whole, he did not believe in striking while the iron was hot. No. He let the first fierce grief pass before he closed in. He preferred to work on subjects who knew from experience they were inconsolable.

He prided himself on his knowledge of the human heart.

So, for the main part, he relied on word-of-mouth advertising and kept up excellent relations with wreath-makers, embalming parlours and monumental masons. Of all his clients, he liked best those who sought him out independently. Cheeks creased with the trace of tears, they would come to inquire tentatively, often in almost an embarrassed way, at the Spirit Church, where the verger, an aged Swedenborgian of impeccably lunatic integrity, would take the names and addresses and allow Herr M. to approach them at his leisure. He liked to make them wait a little, not too much, only enough to let them understand how difficult were the negotiations he must make.

'And shall we see her? Shall we truly see her?'

Oh, yes; she will cross from the abyss from beyond, she will leave her couch in beds of asphodel and materialise in this very apartment, when the curtains are drawn, in the dim light . . . she cannot stand the sunshine, now, you see, nor the artificial glare of the gas mantle, but she will bring with her her own radiant mist.

All young girls look the same after a long illness. Mignon wore a white nightgown, buttoned to the neck, and her hair loose. The bereaved sat at the round mahogany table with the red plush cover edged with a fringe of balls. They clasped hands. Herr M. was solid and reliable as a bank manager in his expansive waistcoat and his dark green velvet jacket and his oleaginous sentimentality. There was a little skullcap embroidered with arcane signs that he put on for his seances. His aunt sewed it for him.

He believed the best illusions were the simplest. However, as a hobby, he experimented with various optical toys and magic lanterns of the most sophisticated kind. Herr M. spent considerable sums on such devices, engaged in perfectly respectable research on systems of mechanical reproduction and, indeed, possessed many of the characteristics of a scientist *manqué*. He was sincerely fascinated by the art and craft of illusion and, during the entire time that Mignon worked for him, he was conducting a learned correspondence with a certain Mr

Robert Paul, in London, about an invention which Mr Paul had patented. Mr Paul claimed his invention would materialise the human desire to live in the past, the present and the future all at once. It consisted of a screen on which was projected at random a number of sequences of pictures showing simulated scenes from time past, time present and time to come whilst the audience, seated in comfortable *fauteuils*, were subjected to a soft breeze directed at them from a hand-cranked wind machine to simulate the wind of travel. Herr M. even began discussions, on behalf of his colleague, with a troupe of dancers who worked in a cabaret he knew of, that they would personate historical personages for his own camera. (He was, it goes without saying, an excellent photographer.) All above board and in perfect taste.

But, although he was passionately devoted to this hobby and spent most of his spare hours closeted in his study with his Praxinoscope, his Phasmatrope and his Zoopraxiscope, projecting on to a white screen photographs of plants and animals that often seemed to move, these studies remained no more than peripheral to his business, which consisted of fleecing the living by arranging interviews with their departed.

She will not speak; she will not smile.

Ah! how illness has changed her! how it has ravaged her little face! but, in the happy land where now she dwells, there is no sickness, no pain.

'Oh, my darling!'

'Hush! don't burden her with your grief, for pity's sake!'

So you can see there were still traces of common humanity in Herr M., and these he often applauded in himself; did he not comfort, did he not console? Did he not, out of the goodness of his compassionate heart, assuage the suffering souls who brought their pain into his parlour? Had he not hit upon that one compassionate innovation that set him apart from other mediums, could he not sell his unhappy clients authentic pictures of the loved and lost ones, that proved, in whatever world they now inhabited, they flourished still?

He busily interpreted unheard voices, with the best of intentions.

'She begs you: "Papa! Mama! don't cry!" ' Or: 'She's saying that she cannot rest in peace while you still grieve.' Herr M. tucked the banknotes into his grandfather clock with a satisfaction that was not purely fiscal, was at least partly that of a justified Samaritan.

'If they didn't pay, they wouldn't *believe*, and then they'd get no benefit at all, at all.'

His L-shaped drawing-room had lace curtains looped over the archway to the foot of the L, beside the green-glazed jardinière on which stood a Boston fern. Pointing towards this alcove was Herr M.'s mahogany camera, like a little wooden room itself. Behind the camera stood the round table at which Herr M. joined the hands of the parents as solemnly as if he were marrying them and begged them, in an urgent whisper, to stay stock-still. Although their line of vision was somewhat obscured by the camera, they always did as they were bid, never craned or peered, too much in awe. If the mourner came alone, Herr M. would clamp his or her hands down on the table with the assurance that, if contact with the plush were lost for one single moment, the ghost would vanish.

The alcove itself was always in darkness, and purple clouds of incense billowed out from Chinese pots. The bookcase against the further wall swung inwards on well-oiled hinges. Herr M. went round dimming the rest of the lights.

'It's only mummy and daddy, little one, come to visit you.' Or: 'Won't you come to Hubby? Won't you come back to Hubby?' Whatever suited the clients' condition. They sat at the table, held hands and hoped.

'Come when I knock on the table, little one.'

Mignon, in her nightgown, slipped into the alcove from behind the bookcase. She carried an electric torch under her nightgown so that her outline glowed. It was as simple as that. Lit from beneath, clouded with incense, half hidden by the lace curtains, the reticulated fronds of fern and the bulk of the camera, she could have been any young girl.

And when they saw their heart's desire their eyes were often blind with tears.

She smiled. Sometimes she held a lily in her hand and could hide behind it, if Herr M.'s tactful inquiries had discovered any facial peculiarity about the deceased, a squint, a harelip, something like that.

A breeze blew through the room, sweetly rattling the chimes of a glass harp behind her.

Herr M. ducked his head under the hood of the camera. In the unexpected thunder and lightning of the flash, Mignon's face looked to each one who saw it the perfect image of the lost.

When the smoke cleared, she was gone and Herr M. went about lighting up the gas mantles again.

Why was he proficient only at summoning female ghosts? Because, he implied, taking out his tobacco-scented handkerchief and blowing his nose as if concealing manly emotion in a manly fashion, he himself, once, long ago, in a kingdom by the sea . . . Her high-born kinsman arrived, in due course, and took her away, but Herr M. contrived a deal with the high-born kinsman, provided he invoked exclusively spirits in the same category, to whit, young girls.

In spite of this specification, Mignon got a nasty fright the very first time he took her photograph. She went into the dark room with him out of curiosity and excitedly watched the picture crystallise on the paper as if by magic in the trough of acid. But then she tucked her underlip under her rather prominent front teeth; she was troubled. For the face that swam out of the acid emerged to her out of her memory in the same way.

'Mother . . .'

Herr M. hugged her with genuine compassion.

'Accidents can happen,' he apologised.

In his undertaker's weeds, he delivered the photographs by hand, each wrapped in a crisp shroud of tissue paper. The spirits are shy, he would assure his patrons; she wishes only those she loves best to see her thus. Show these photographs to *nobody*, or else her face will disappear! The indistinct features melting into darkness surrounding them were those of whomever longing and imagination made them.

He tipped his gloomy topper and accepted gratitude as if it were his due.

Mignon impersonated the dead so successfully that Herr M. even briefly contemplated giving her a salary as well as her keep but decided that, if he did so, she might save up and run away. So they lived out an odd kind of illicit, respectable life together. He was pleased to find she could sing, a little, and often wondered if there was a way he could incorporate her fresh, untrained voice in the act; angelic voices, perhaps? But then he thought, it will make things too complicated; and left her alone a good deal, curled up in an over-stuffed armchair in the drawing-room, lost in incoherent daydreams, whilst in his study he probed the problems of persistence of vision.

He lasted so long because he was venal but not greedy and always behaved with tact, discretion and even kindness. Finally, a mother could not resist it, showed the photograph of a dead darling to an older sister whose nose had been put so far out of joint by the late arrival that she could not endure the thought of her sibling's posthumous rivalry, stole the portrait and took it to the police. Posing as a bereaved uncle, a burly detective knocked over the camera just as Herr M. fired off the flash and trapped Mignon by the tail of her nightgown as she made a hasty exit through the swinging bookcase. How she giggled! It had never been anything more than a game to her.

The jig was up. Herr M., rational as ever, made a full confession at once and produced Mignon in her nightgown in court as irrefutable proof. The scandal killed his aged aunt, unhappily, but Herr M. served only two years out of six in prison, maximum remission for good behaviour, making a number of valuable contacts amongst other upstanding embezzlers, frauds and confidence men whilst inside. On his release, he moved immediately to another city where, after a few difficult months, he set up in business, again, although, this time, he forswore spiritualism and set up a profitable line in exotic snapshots.

He reopened his correspondence with Mr Paul to such effect that, a year or two later, he was able to give up pornography altogether, and went into the motion-picture business. He prospered, although sometimes, in the teeth of his own scepticism, he felt almost tempted, now and then, to try to pierce the veil just once, this time for *real,* and have a word with auntie, whom he missed terribly.

Yet many of those who had been deceived by Herr M. did not believe in his confession. They took the cherished photographs out of those lavender-scented bureaux drawers in which they shared an old glove-box with, perhaps, a first curl in an envelope, or a rattle of cast milk teeth, and, however hard they scrutinised the glossy prints, they never saw Mignon's face but saw another face, and heard, in their mind's ear, the soft, familiar voice demanding the impossible: 'Mama! Papa! don't cry!' So you could say the evidence of Herr M.'s crime remained, in itself, perfectly innocent. Oh, dear delusion! And still Mama sleeps with the picture under her pillow.

Mignon got off scot-free, no charges were so much as pressed against her, secure as she was in the victim's defence of no responsibility. Now she had some nice clothes, she got herself a decent job serving in quite a good class of bar and she had a little room of her own and often thanked her lucky stars. She would sing, too, when the accordion player came round. She loved to sing. Sometimes she went home with the accordion player, sometimes not, she picked and chose. Those were her best days, although there was always something feckless about her, something slack and almost fearful in her too frequent smile, so that when you saw Mignon being happy, you always thought: 'It can't last.' She had the febrile gaiety of a being without a past, without a present, yet she existed thus, without memory or history, only because her past was too bleak to think of and her future too terrible to contemplate; she was the broken blossom of the present tense.

One Saturday night, a gentleman in evening dress under an elegant red-lined cape came into the bar hand in hand with a miniature edition of himself, all but for the feet, for this little person, squat in stature, somewhat long in the arm, could find no shoes to fit him in any shop in the world. They took a booth in a corner and Mignon, full of curiosity, trotted over to serve them. The small person's sleek, black hair was combed back from a centre parting. With grave ceremony, he took the carnation from his buttonhole and handed it to Mignon. She burst out laughing. 'Don't hurt his feelings,' said the Ape-Man in a charming French accent. So Mignon took the flower and fixed it in her hair.

The Ape-Man ordered a bottle of wine and Mignon begged a banana from the kitchen. 'My friend and colleague, the Professor. Give the pretty lady a kiss, Professor.' The Professor was already investigating the banana but he put it down carefully on his plate, stood up on his chair, leaned across the table, put his arms round Mignon's neck and gave her a smacking, tickling kiss on the cheek. You could say the Professor did the Ape-Man's courting for him. Yes; she'd be delighted to share their wine.

She was still only fifteen and he took her on solely in order to abuse her. He had such a fine nose for a victim it was a wonder he'd elected to spend his life among the astute chimps, who whisked out of the way of his boot and, if he got them no supper, would steal his wallet from the pocket of his jacket as he lay on his bunk in a drunken stupor and go out and buy supper for themselves. He was a dark man out of Lyons and his eyebrows met. She went back to his van – he was with a travelling circus, then, that put up its canvas in parks – and next morning gawped like a child at the wise monkeys washing their faces in a bucket and queueing up to comb their hair at the cracked square of mirror in their travelling cage.

She did not bother to go back to her own room to pick up her clothes. She ran away with the circus, although it turned out he was a drinking man, hard, taciturn, violent.

On the third day on the road, he beat her because she burned the cutlets. She was a lousy cook. On the fourth day, he beat her because she forgot to empty the chamber-pot and when he pissed in it, it overflowed. On the fifth day, he beat her because he had formed the habit of beating her. On the sixth day, a roustabout got her down on her back behind the freak-show. The beating was now an expectation that was always fulfilled. On the seventh day, three Moroccan acrobats took her back to their van, gave her some raki, which made her cough, some hashish, which made her eyes shine, and then had her, in a variety of ingenious ways, one after the other, among the shining brass and cut-glass ornaments of the teak interior. Word about Mignon passed round quickly.

She had an exceedingly short memory, which alone saved her from desolation.

There was a stable-boy from England, an odd type, who heard her singing as she swept out the chimps' cages and taught her a lot of new songs, some, though not all, of which had very rude words, not that Mignon understood them. He liked to hear the whey-faced orphan singing obscenities that were meaningless to her but he also liked to hear her sing other kinds of songs, for he was a musical boy, and she learned from him some German songs, about the quick trout and the rose in the heather, and more.

He spoke good German but kept himself to himself for he had a secret, he was running away from a scandal at his public school, he liked boys too much and left Mignon alone, for which she was grateful. She would go and sit with him in an odorous corner of the horse-box and they would sing in harmony: 'Jolly boating weather'; 'The lark now leaves his watery nest'.

One day, the Ape-Man knocked him insensible with a broom and beat her until the broom broke but the boy never recovered consciousness. They were on the road, camped outside a scrubbed conurbation of cuckoo-clocks in Switzerland, and the Ape-Man dragged the boy into some bushes and left him there.

The Ape-Man's evening suit and cape, the uniform in which he escorted his charges into the ring, swung from a wooden coat-hanger (stolen from a Paris hotel) on a peg in caravans, in lodging-houses, in dressing-rooms. She bore this dress suit no resentment, although it had deceived her, and if she soon lost interest in the chimps, too, she did not treat them badly. She did their laundry and mended their costumes. The Professor never gave her another flower but, then, she never gave him another banana.

What the chimps thought about all this is a problem. One who had made a profound study of those creatures as they went through their routines that mocked us, the cycle race, the tea party, the schoolroom, might have concluded that the apes, in turn, were putting their own studious observations of ourselves to use in routines of parody, of irony, of satire. The more the Ape-Man drank, the more they ignored him.

A knock at the door announced the arrival of the waiter with the flutes. Fevvers irritably gestured him to be silent.

> Though the night be made for loving
> And the day return too soon
> Yet we'll go no more a-roving
> By the light of the moon.

Then came the rushing roar of water let out of the bath.

'She doesn't understand the words,' repeated Fevvers. Her face was wet with tears. When he saw that, Walser felt an extraordinary sensation within his breast: his heart dissolved. He reached out his hand towards the woman and sparked off a sharp pain in his mauled shoulder; exclaimed; discovered he, too, was crying. She looked towards him, her night-dark eyes brimming, and for once, there was no irony, malice or suspicion within them. His molten heart spilled out of his bosom and flowed towards her, just as one drop of mercury flows towards another drop of mercury.

At that moment, Mignon came back through the bathroom door.

She was wrapped up in a spotless, fleecy, towelling robe and her freshly washed hair was bundled in a white towel. Now she was sparkling clean and wreathed in smiles, though greenish with bruises. She still clutched the drum of chocolates under her arm but all that was left of the top layer was a mass of chirruping papers. She looked a mite aggrieved when Fevvers, after blowing her nose rather disgustingly between her fingers, served her a nursery bowl of bread and milk, but she perked up when she saw the champagne, sat down at the table with lamb-like obedience and tucked in willingly enough.

Fevvers now held a rapid communication with the waiter, at the conclusion of which she reached in her reticule for another complimentary ticket to opening night and must have already learned enough Russian to make jokes for the man abruptly guffawed before he bowed out again. Lizzie was already ripping the foil on the bottle. Fevvers clinked glasses all round. Her eyes were quite dry now, and had turned strangely pale. There was a hard, bright, dangerous quality to her, suddenly.

'We'll make an honest whore of her yet!' she toasted her visitor in a voice that rasped like the tongue of a tiger and Walser, with nervous glee, perceived that she believed Mignon to be his mistress and was – heaven be praised! – consumed with jealousy. Fevvers drained her glass in a gulp, belched and tossed it into a corner, where it smashed. This gesture seemed more a display of temper than one in accordance with the custom of the country.

'Come 'ere,' she ordered Walser peremptorily. 'Liz – the cold cream.'

'Kneel, Mr Walser.'

Prepared for anything, Walser knelt at her feet, to find himself firmly grasped between thighs accustomed to gripping hold of the trapeze. He suffered a sudden access of erotic vertigo and attempted to engage her eyes in another exchange but she looked steadfastly away from him as she ripped off his wig and ruffled up his flattened blond hair with a large nurse's hand, competent, impersonal, tetchy. Then she smothered him in cold cream.

'Make you pretty,' she said. When he tried to speak, she stuffed a handful of cold cream in his mouth. She seized a napkin from the trolley and scrubbed his matte white off with such vigour he emerged brick red and polished like a floor. Mignon, already giggling with champagne, was helping herself to seconds of bread and milk. Lizzie, for some reason tense with disapproval, abstracted herself from this scene, drew some pamphlet or other from her bag and immersed herself in it. Fevvers straightened Walser's tie and eyed his costume with displeasure.

'Gawd, the poor girl! Out of the Monkey House into Clown Alley! Talk about the frying pan and the fire! Don't you know how I hate clowns, young man? I truly think they are a crime against humanity.'

The waiter now returned and stood expectantly by the door. Lizzie turned a page with a rustle of crisp disaffection. Mignon, having finished her supper, looked round with curiosity to see what would happen next.

'Well, get on with it,' said Fevvers. 'Up on your feet and sweep her off hers. I've booked you the bridal suite, haven't I.'

The tittering waiter bowed and opened the door. Walser rose to his feet with as much dignity as he could muster, cracked Fevvers his whitest grin and offered Mignon his good arm with a show of old-fashioned courtesy that made the giantess drum her fingers on the arm of her chair. Mignon ducked back to pick up the box of chocolates she had almost forgotten in this sudden turn of events; a dithering trail of paper wrappers scattered behind their exit. As they left the two women alone, Lizzie flung aside her paper and announced mirthlessly: 'Laugh! you'll be the death of me.'

In the bridal suite, a predictable nest of rosy satin and gilded mirrors, the waiter drew Mignon's attention with a lordly wave to a stiff, scentless bouquet of florist's red roses by the bed, obviously a special touch ordered by Fevvers, then, beaming, chortling even, he withdrew.

Walser's first, deplorable impulse was to throw himself on the poor child and force her, to teach somebody or other – he was not quite sure whom – a lesson. But he was a fair man and the fierce pain in his wounded arm when he seized Mignon by the shoulder reminded him it would be unjust, so he let her be.

If Mignon's day had started badly, it was ending well. It was ending like a girlish dream come true in fact, especially when Walser backed off. And she could not get over those roses! She cooed to them, caressed them, made soft, loving passes at them, hovered and purred around them with such heart-breaking, unknowing grace that Walser, by no means an insensitive man, let out an almost sob of touched perplexity.

'Oh, Mignon, what am I to do with you?'

To be addressed directly in the English language struck some chord in that peculiar and selective organ, her memory. She pulled the towel off her head and her Gretchen yellow hair sprayed out in all directions. She smiled. This smile contained her entire history and was scarcely to be borne.

'God save the Queen,' she said.

Walser could stand no more and rushed from the room.

SIX

Two things, so far, have conspired together to throw Walser off his equilibrium. One: his right arm is injured and, although healing well, he cannot write or type until it is better, so he is deprived of his profession. Therefore, for the moment, his disguise disguises – nothing. He is no longer a journalist masquerading as a clown; willy-nilly, force of circumstance has turned him into a *real* clown, for all practical purposes, and, what's more, a clown with his arm in a sling – type of the 'wounded warrior' clown.

Two: he has fallen in love, a condition that causes him anxiety because he has not experienced it before. Hitherto, conquests came easily and were disregarded. But no woman ever tried to humiliate him before, to his knowledge, and Fevvers has both tried and succeeded. This has set up a conflict between his own hitherto impregnable sense of self-esteem and the lack of esteem with which the woman treats him. He suffers a sense, not so much that she and her companion have duped him – he remains convinced they are confidence tricksters, so that would be no more than part of the story – but that he has been made their dupe.

In a state of mental tumult, conflict and disorientation, he wanders the freezing city night, now gazing at the ice thickening on the dark waters of the Neva, now peering at the great horseman on his plinth with a vague terror, as though the horseman were not the effigy of the city's founder but the herald of four yet more mythic horsemen who are, indeed, on their way to confound Petersburg forever, though they won't arrive yet, not quite yet.

SEVEN

Brisk, bright, wintry morning, under a sky that mimics a bell of blue glass so well it looks as if it would ring out glad tidings at the lightest blow of a fingernail. A thick rime of frost everywhere, giving things a festive, tinsel trim. The rare Northern sunlight makes up in brilliance for what it lacks in warmth, like certain nervous temperaments. Today the Stars and Stripes billow out bravely, as if they meant it, above the courtyard of the Imperial Circus, where the courtyard is as full of folk and bustle as a Breughel – all in motion, all hustle-bustle!

Amid laughter, horse-play and snatches of song, rosy-cheeked, whistling stable-boys stamp their feet, blow on their fingers, dash hither and thither with bales of hay and oats on their shoulders, sacks of vegetables for the elephants, hands of bananas for the apes, or heave stomach-churning pitchforkfuls of dung on to a stack of soiled straw. Well-mittened and mufflered, the little Charivaris practise their familial occupation along the Princess's washing-line, teetering along with much hilarity while the washing-line's owner, a sack over her habitual morning *deshabille* to keep out the cold, oversees the unloading of a hideous cargo of bleeding meat from a knackers' van drawn by a gaunt, restive hack an inch away from horseflesh itself.

Noisy vendors from the town invade the Colonel's peripatetic empire to hawk hot jam pies and kvass from wheeled barrels. A lugubrious gypsy strays into the courtyard to add the wailing of his fiddle to the clatter of boot-heels on cobbles, the babel of tongues, the perpetual, soft jangle as the elephants within the building agitate their chains, the sound that reminds the Colonel, always with a shock of pleasure, of the outrageous daring of his entire enterprise. ('Tuskers across the tundra!')

For Colonel Kearney, up betimes, presides over the carnival-like proceedings; how he loves hurry-scurry, loves it purely, loves it passionately, for its own sake! He feels about bustle like Russians feel about sloth. He sticks his fingers in either pocket of the starry waistcoat that swells as if his paunch were pregnant with profit as he struts about on his bandy little legs in their striped trousers, bright and twisty as candy sticks. He has just shone up his dollar sign belt-buckle. He is the living image of the entrepreneur.

He dodges back and forth amongst his employees as they fly about their business, fending off the native salespersons with quick flips of the elbow under which Sybil, squealing intelligently, has been stowed, a moving cloud of blue cigar-smoke round his head and an affable and optimistic smile on his well-satisfied visage as he tosses a cheery word to one and all.

That morning, the newspapers carry an anonymous letter which claims that Fevvers is not a woman at all but a cunningly constructed automaton made up of whalebone, india-rubber and springs. The Colonel beams with pleasure at the consternation this ploy will provoke, at the way the box-office tills will clang in the delicious rising tide of rumour: 'Is she fiction or is she fact?' His motto is: 'The bigger the humbug, the better the public likes it.' That's the way to play the Ludic Game! With no holds barred! Another motto, in one word: 'Bamboozlem.' Play the game to win!

Yessir!

He plots a news item, tomorrow, inserted in the foreign news by his contacts. This, contradicting the vicious 'clockwork' rumour, will proclaim that Fevvers, all woman as she is, is, back home in England, secretly engaged to *the Prince of Wales*.

Yessirree!

The apes had already emptied their chamber-pots on to the dung-heap and rinsed them out under the pump. Back in their quarters, they swept up, laid down fresh straw and made up their bunk beds. They composed themselves in silent groups, heads bent over books. Now and then, one would gesticulate in that measured, urgent fashion of theirs and another would nod or shake its well-brushed head or answer with a little dance of fingers. Monsieur Lamarck, the Ape-Man, was nowhere to be seen, slumped in drunken slumber on the sawdust of a low bar.

A casual observer might have thought the apes, dedicated little troupers or well-programmed organisms that they were, could not leave off their act for even one moment and now were rehearsing for the 'apes at school' routine. In fact, it was their dedication to self-improvement that was boundless. Even the absence of Mignon, for whom they felt disinterested pity, did not interfere with their studies. The female with the green ribbon spared a thought for the wounded clown, however.

If all was quiet on the monkey front, fearful sounds erupted from the cages of the cats as they prowled their confined space. The tigers roared, first one, then another, then all at once: Where is our breakfast? We never got delicious clown, yesterday! Now we want our beef, our horseflesh, our legs and ribs of goat!

When she heard their imperatives rise above the clamour, the Princess filled her arms with bleeding meat.

The Princess of Abyssinia had never visited, even on business, the country whose royal title she usurped, nor did she come from any other part of Africa. Her mother, a native of Guadeloupe in the Windward Islands, taught the piano for a living until she upped and ran away with a man who visited her sleepy town with a travelling fair. This man kept a mangy, toothless lion in a cage, for a sideshow, and called himself an Ethiopian, although he hailed, in fact, from Rio de Janeiro. The impetus of their elopement took them as far as Marseilles, where their daughter was born. Her parents were devoted to each other. Her mother sat in the cage and played Mozart sonatas. They prospered. Her father crowned himself King and went into tigers; if tigers are not native to the Horn of Africa, then neither was he. When her parents died, the Princess inherited piano and cats. She polished the act to its present splendour. So much for her history, which was only mysterious in that she told it to nobody because she never spoke.

In the ring, she looked like a member of the graduating class at a provincial conservatoire, in a white frock with starched flounces, white cotton stockings, flat, strapped shoes of the kind called Mary Janes, and a butterfly bow of white satin in the crisp hair that stuck out half-way down her back. In this garb, she played the piano and the tigers danced.

At the beginning of the act, the cats bounced into the ring, roaring to illustrate their own ferocity, while the grooms ran round the caged arena firing off blank shots from guns. She came after, in her good girl's dress, and sat down at the Bechstein grand.

This was the only time, as she seated herself with her back towards them, that she felt lonely. Uneasy. At the first chords, the cats, whom she could not see, leapt on to the semi-circle of pedestals placed ready for them and sat there on their haunches, panting, pleased with themselves for their obedience. And then it would come to them, always with a fresh surprise no matter how often they performed, that they did not obey in freedom but had exchanged one cage for a larger cage. Then, for just one unprotected minute, they pondered the mystery of their obedience and were astonished by it.

Just for that moment, while she knew they wondered what on earth they were doing there, when her vulnerable back was turned towards them and her speaking eyes away from them, the Princess felt a little scared, and, perhaps, more fully human than she was used to feeling. Sometimes, then, she thought how much she'd like an accomplice, somebody else in the ring with her, not a stable-boy, not a groom, but somebody she trusted, somebody who could keep an eye on the cats during that tense moment when she played the invitation to the waltz whilst she asked herself, if, today of all days, this might be the day when they decided they would not take up her invitation. Whether tonight, of all the nights of their mutual treaty, the cats would not, one by one, succumb to the music and come down to choose their partners, but would . . .

She always kept a gun on top of the piano, just in case, and *this* gun was not loaded with blanks.

Nevertheless, she lived in the closest intimacy with her cats, nesting beside their cages in a bale of clean straw. She washed their eyes with boric acid and Argyrol, to prevent infection. She rubbed their tender feet with ointment for them. But she never smiled at her cats, because theirs was not a friendly pact; it existed in order to prevent hostilities, not to promote amity. And: 'Cat got your tongue!' you might have said to the Princess. Because, early in her career, she discovered how they grumbled at the back of their throats and laid their ears flat when she used that medium of human speech which nature denied them.

It was rumoured she was herself a tigress's foster-child, abandoned in the jungle and suckled by wild bears. But there is no jungle near Marseilles. Since she said nothing, she never denied these stories. The Colonel spread them freely.

On the rare, random occasions when she took some other human back to her bed in the straw beside the sleeping tigers, she always made love in the dark because her body was, every inch, scarred with clawmarks, as if tattooed. That was the price they made her pay for taming them.

Now the crackling perfume of frying sausages and bacon mingles with heavy odours of dung, meat, pastry and wild beasts in the courtyard. The cookhouse – a stove, a counter – has opened up and is: heaven be praised! cry the stable-lads, serving honest English breakfasts.

When Samson, the Strong Man, brushing aside the Russian peddlers with a xenophobic oath, came to get his morning mug and doorstep, he suffered a deal of joshing from the roustabouts munching their bacon sandwiches, to have lost – according to the swiftly disseminated gossip of the circus – his inamorata to a clown. Samson never once let on he'd left Mignon to the mercies of the escaped tiger and *that* was when the clown stepped in; far from it! He boasted, flexing his gleaming pects, of what he'd do to that bastard clown when he got his hands on him and, indeed, his pride was genuinely piqued because Mignon had run off to Clown Alley after her saviour. In all this, Mignon assumed a woman's place – that of the cause of discord between men; how else, to these men, could she play any real part in their lives?

The Colonel doffs his billy-cock hat with delighted glee as Fevvers, looking not in the least like india-rubber but very much flesh for the Prince of Wales, that connoisseur, stumps past. She is as ugly a walker as an unhorsed Valkyrie but her amazing curves promise delights of which the Colonel often dreams.

Lizzie, humping her handbag, which could look like that of a midwife or of an abortionist, hurled the Colonel a black look from some unguessable depths of Sicilian malice. For himself, the Colonel regarded the chaperone as the stumbling block between himself and an intimate *diner à deux* with the *aerialiste* which might lead – who knows to what? Yessir!

He burst out with a veritable plume of smoke at the thought, crushing Sybil to him in his enthusiasm so vigorously that she shrieked.

Lizzie paused to toss the gypsy fiddler a kopek, receiving in return a burst of incomprehensible gratitude and, for some reason, a tract or ballad sheet of some kind, which she stowed away in her handbag without a glance. The Colonel thought no more of it, although the hot jam pie vendor, in reality a member of the secret police, would have been curious to see the transaction. But Fevvers chose just that moment to disencumber him of his entire stock and lavishly distribute them among the Charivari children, who came tumbling off the washing-line for the treat, jumping about the pieman with such Latin enthusiasm he could scarcely see to take the money.

The two women had some girl with them, or, rather, a young lady – fair-haired, slim, nattily turned out in red wool. She impressed the Colonel only with a vague familiarity: 'Ain't I seen that somewhere before?' And she made no impression at all on the Strong Man, so engrossed was he in describing to his friends the injuries Walser would suffer when they met again.

The Colonel chewed his cigar and sighed, because Fevvers gave him only the brusquest nod as the two females, with their guest, disappeared into the menagerie as if hot on the track of the bloody spoor the Princess had left behind her. The Colonel's admiration for Fevvers grew in direct ratio to her indifference and the advance bookings.

But: 'Hi, there! Hi, hi, hi!' His easily distracted attention fixed on the tumultuous entry of the clowns and their pack of yapping dogs. His own recruit, he noted happily, was present and correct, if looking a little worse for wear – arm in a sling, and all.

'Now's your chance!' said the guffawing stable-boys to Samson, but Samson took one look at Buffo, big as a house and already half seas over, shepherding his flock into the circus with his customary deranged majesty and the air of one about to commit grievous bodily harm. 'Not 'alf,' opined the Strong Man, judging discretion the better part. He shoved his mug back on the counter and buggered off. Catch 'im when 'e's on 'is tod.

Buffo, leading the clowns. The dozen clowns. Hold hard, what's this? A *baker's* dozen clowns! Where, yesterday, had been twelve, today there were thirteen, and the thirteenth distinctly on the small side.

The clowns. See them as a band of terrorists. No; that's not right. Not terrorists, but irregulars. A band of irregulars, permitted the most ferocious piracies as long as, just so long as, they maintain the bizarrerie of their appearance, so that their violent exposition of manners stays on the safe side of terror, even if we need to *learn* to laugh at them, and part, at least, of this laughter comes from the successful suppression of fear.

Little Ivan's relations with the clowns went thus: first, he was afraid of them; then, he was entranced by them; at last he wished to become as they, so that he, too, could terrify, enchant, vandalise, ravage, yet always stay on the safe side of being, licensed to commit licence and yet forbidden to act, so that the baboushka back at home could go on reddening and blackening the charcoal even if the clowns detonated the entire city around her and nothing would really change. Nothing. The exploded buildings would float up into the air insubstantial as bubbles, and gently waft to earth again on exactly the same places where they had stood before. The corpses would writhe, spring apart at the joints, dismember – then pick up their own dismembered limbs to juggle with them before slotting them back in their good old sockets, all present and correct, sir.

So then you'd know, you'd seen the proof, that things would always be as they had always been; that nothing came of catastrophe; that chaos invoked stasis.

It was as though a fairy godmother had given each clown an ambivalent blessing when he was born: you can do anything you like, as long as nobody takes you seriously.

Buffo sewed bells on a three-cornered cap for his newest apprentice, so that he 'won't hear the trickle as his brains run out.'

Little Ivan, in cap and bells, somersaulted round the ring as if emancipated altogether from the bipedal posture until he bumped into Buffo somersaulting round the ring in the other direction. Then he got a thrashing for getting in the way and for at least five minutes thought better of running away with the circus but, though he sat sulking in the front row with his thumb in his mouth, still he could not take his eyes off the comedians.

Buffo thought up a routine especially for Walser, since he could no longer stand on his hands.

'Crow like a cock.'

'Cock-a-doodle-do,' said Walser obediently.

'Cock-a-doodle-dooski!' amended Buffo as a little tribute to the Tsar of all the Russias. 'Flap your arms about a bit.'

'Cock-a-doodle-dooski!' Entering into the spirit of the thing, Walser rose up on his toes and kneaded the air with his arms as best he could with one in a sling.

'Ladies and gentlemen, boys and girls,' intoned Buffo, 'I give him – and you can take him! – the Human Chicken!'

Grik found an egg, not too fresh, inside his fiddle and tossed it between Walser's eyes. Buffo creaked approval. Grok found a couple of eggs in the belly of his tambourine. Amid ululations of glee, all the clowns followed suit, whipping eggs out of various parts of their clothing and anatomies, and pelted Walser until egg liquor streamed down his face, blinding him. Grik and Grok struck up 'A-hunting we will go!' on their various instruments. Little Ivan thought how many pancakes his granny could have made with all those eggs that now spattered the sawdust but he did not think so for long because he was laughing too much to think.

Walser's invisible tormentors whisked their satin coat-tails out of his reach as he lunged at them, tripped him up with their long shoes, shoved out their stilts to bring him down. When he heard Little Ivan's peals of merriment, his anger rose: 'What the hell's so funny about this?' And he lashed out, he knew not where.

They told him, afterwards, that his baulked gestures of fury were the funniest thing, as they drove him round the ring with blows and mocking cries; his baulked gestures of fury and his comic wound.

Henceforward, Walser will wear a cockscomb. And Buffo, after a little thought, massaging his great, white lantern jaw, decided that, with his cockscomb and his crowing, the Human Chicken should forthwith feature on the menu at the Clowns' Christmas dinner.

Walser's new profession was beginning to make demands on him.

Meanwhile, Fevvers, in the menagerie, maintained an animated if one-sided conversation with the Princess in raw French.

'*Quelle chantoqze!*' she said. '*Quelle spectacle!*'

The Princess, in her bloody apron, opened a panel in the cage and tossed in half a butcher's shop. The tigers fell on the feast, snarling and cuffing one another about the ears in their greed. As she watched them, the Princess's dark face was that of Kali and the perfume round her dense enough, rank and pervasive enough, to act as an invisible barrier between herself and all those who were not furred. Fevvers knew she was a tough customer. She was undaunted.

'*Elle s'apelle Mignon. C'est vachement chouette, ça.*'

Mignon leaned against Fevvers' shoulder, vaguely gazing at motes of dust in the light, unaware she was the subject of all this. If her new maroon dress with the quasi-military froggings reminded you a little of the uniform of the doormen at the Hotel de l'Europe, that was just what, until six o'clock that morning, it had been. ('Just a stitch here and there, and it'll fit her perfect. You don't mind, do you, old chum.') Lizzie had done her yellow hair in twisted braids round her head. She looked like a minister's daughter, not a murderer's whelp.

The Princess gave Fevvers a quizzical, interrogative look and tapped her own mouth. Fevvers understood.

'To sing is not to speak,' said Fevvers, her syntax subtler than her pronunciation. 'If they hate speech because it divides us from them, to sing is to rob speech of its function and render it divine. Singing is to speech what is dancing is to walking. You know they love to dance.'

('Cross fingers and hope for luck,' she added to herself.)

The Princess's charges yawned and stretched. She took off her apron. She looked Mignon up and down. They were just the same height, both little things, frail, one as fair as the other was dark, twinned opposites. And both possessed that quality of exile, of apartness from us, although the Princess had chosen her exile amongst the beasts, while Mignon's exile had been thrust upon her. Perhaps it was that homeless look of Mignon's that made up the Princess's mind for her. She nodded.

The replete cats lay with their heavy heads between their paws among the bloody bones, a beautiful still-life or *nature morte* of orange tawny shapes composed around the Princess's open Bechstein grand; they drowsed like unawakened desire, like unlit fire. A tangerine cub curled for a nap on the piano stool.

Mignon realised for the first time the plans the grown-ups had laid for her and, when the Princess stepped into the cage, she hung back, clinging to Fevvers' hand and mewing faintly with alarm but Fevvers, beaming encouragement, hugged her, scooped her up bodily and deposited her within, closing the door behind her sharply. The Princess motioned Mignon to a position beside the piano, from whence she could outstare the cats. But the cats, enjoying their postprandial snooze, registered Mignon's presence by only the faintest twitchings of nostrils and whisker. The Princess patted the rifle on the piano top. That consoled Mignon somewhat.

The Princess set the sleeping cub among the straw and took its place. She softly fingered the keys, as if the piano might suggest appropriate music of its own accord.

Mignon stuck close to the piano but soon grew so enchanted at the sight of the Princess's black fingers on the white keys that she forgot to be afraid. Fevvers, watching intently, absently stripped off her kid glove so that she could bite her nails. Lizzie, squatting on her handbag, muttered rapidly to herself in some language that was not quite Italian.

When the piano told the Princess what she should play, she pushed her hair back behind her ears with a bravura gesture and attacked the keyboard in earnest. Mignon started in recognition.

Do not think the English schoolboy whom her husband murdered omitted to teach Mignon the song that was written for her before she was born; how could he have resisted it, once he learned her name? He hesitated deliciously between Liszt's setting and Schubert's. However odd the accompaniment sounded on his wheezing harmonica, he made sure Mignon knew her own song although she did not understand the words, even though they were in her own language.

To speak is one thing. To sing is quite another.

Here and there among the cats, an eyelid flickered.

Almost as if she awed herself at her daring, Mignon's voice quavered as she asked them if they knew that land.

The cats stirred in the straw.

No. No, it's too early in the morning.

Do you know the land where the lemon trees grow?

Oh! let us sleep a little longer. We've only just eaten!

Do you know that land where the lemon trees grow, asked, implored Mignon, as she saw their eyes open, their eyes like precious fruit.

They stirred and rustled. For might not this land be the Eden of our first beginnings, where innocent beasts and wise children play together under the lovely lemon trees, the tiger abnegates its ferocity, the child her cunning? Is it, is it?

The cats all lifted their huge heads and their eyes dropped amber tears as if for their own dumb fates. Slowly, slowly, all the beasts dragged themselves towards the source of music, softly beating their tails against the straw. At the end of the first verse, a soft, ecstatic purring rose up from them all until the entire menagerie sounded like the interior of a huge hive of bees.

And then, there are the mountains . . .

As Mignon's voice, at first a little uncertain, gathered certainty and strength and floated through the menagerie, the apes looked up from their books with unanswerable questions in their eyes; even the clowns grew still and hushed; the elephants, for just as long as the song lasted, ceased to rattle their chains.

The Princess knew the problem of the pause of terror was solved.

When the song was over, the tranced cats sighed and shifted a little on their haunches but the cue for the dance never came; the Princess was kissing Mignon.

Fevvers and Lizzie let out great breaths of relief and likewise kissed each other.

'The cruel sex threw her away like a soiled glove,' said Fevvers.

' – but us girls 'ave gone and sent her to the cleaner's!' Lizzie concluded triumphantly.

That appeared to conclude the hiring. The Princess made Mignon curtsey to the cats. The girls came out of the cage hand in hand. The cats dropped back their noses on their paws. The Princess kissed Fevvers on both cheeks, in thanks.

'A real class act,' congratulated Fevvers. They left them commencing to rehearse the waltz.

And now the courtyard had emptied itself like an unplugged bath, its morning business done. The Colonel was gone to the box office to check the till; the cookhouse counter shuttered up; roustabouts and stable-boys off to the odorous warmth of the menagerie to play cards and imbibe vodka. The little Charivaris, seized with dreadful stomach pains from gobbling down the secret policeman's pies, were tucked up in their bunks with hot-water-bottles on their bellies. Mama blamed Fevvers. In the deserted silence, the birds returned, to peck at the refuse, and there was a young man in comedy suspenders stooping to sluice his face under the water-pump as well as he could with one arm.

'It's your beau,' said Lizzie without pleasure. 'It's Hank the Yank, the reporter Johnny.'

Fevvers advanced upon Walser from behind and, judging her moment, slapped her hands over his eyes as soon as his face emerged from the stream of water.

'Boo!'

Unaccustomed to love, he diagnosed the effects of a sleepless night when his heart banged at the sight of her. She eyed him with reluctant speculation, swaying back and forth on high heels that gave her a couple of inches advantage over him in height, an advantage she enjoyed.

'How's the wonky arm?' she enquired.

He showed his sling.

'You take care of it. Scratch of a tiger, can fester something rotten, that can.'

She dropped her voice a couple of decibels, until it sounded lubricious.

'I hear . . . ' she said, 'you walked out on Death-warmed-up, last night, after all that. Seems like I got it wrong, love. Seems like you weren't knocking her off, after all.'

Walser hid his face, polishing away the last of the egg-stains with his sleeve. Fevvers giggled and struck him lightly with her gloves, the moodiness of the previous night quite gone, replaced by a mysterious coquettishness.

'I must say, Mr Walser,' she added in a provocative tone, 'it's very flattering you should pursue me thus, to the ends of the earth, you might say. Eh?'

Before Walser could reply, Lizzie, as if she could wait no longer for this courtship ritual to reach its consummation, tugged impatiently at the sleeve of his good arm.

'Oh, Mr Walser, there's a question of some *letters home* . . . we, that is, Fevvers and me, was just wondering whether – oh? you're not despatching at the moment, due to your wound? Well, then, all the more room for *our* stuff!'

From her enormous handbag she withdrew a cornucopia of papers and thrust them at him.

EIGHT

Since the star had not worked circuses before, there was a good deal of animosity towards her in the company, especially amongst the Charivaris, high-wire dancers themselves for centuries, who were engaged in the same debate with gravity as she – except that she was cheating! They were sure of it: they knew it in their bones; they needed no proof. And the cheat had nudged them out of their customary place at the top of the bill with the aid of mechanical contrivances. They even held, a little, to the 'gutta-percha' theory concerning Fevvers' anatomy. That very morning, over breakfast coffee and milk, the children suggested perhaps there was some way she might be dropped from heaven – 'to see if she would bounce.' Mama remonstrated: 'Naughty, naughty!' but she and Papa exchanged thoughtful looks. When Fevvers turned the children's stomachs with her gift of poisoned pies, it was the last straw.

They resentfully arrived to witness Fevvers' band rehearsal, dozen upon dozen of them, Papa, Mama, brothers, sisters, cousins. They possessed in full measure that Italian knack of making a crowd, so the Charivaris *en masse* seemed far more than the sum of their parts, even without the little children who stayed home in their bunks, groaning. As if by right, the Charivaris occupied the Imperial Box, for the family had entertained every European emperor of note since Nero. Indeed, they felt themselves to be a vital part of circus history, and it was at such a rich tradition they thought that Fevvers thumbed her nose. All bore fixed expressions of hostility and contempt upon their faces. Little people, delicately made but wiry, in leotards. The women left curling rags in their hair in order to show contempt.

It is a phenomenon of the trapeze that its practitioners always look larger upon it than they are in life. Little and lithe is, therefore, the rule for the air (as it is, as the Charivaris well knew, for the wire); a big flyer looks a clumsy flyer, no matter how great the art. The ideal female flyer turns the scale at, say, a hundred pounds and stands no higher in her slippers than five feet two. Her male partner might give her, perhaps, ten more pounds and three more inches but still he will be a small man on the ground though he might look like a Greek god as he hurtles through the air at those speeds of theirs in excess of sixty miles an hour. Fevvers, remember, was six feet two in her stockinged feet and turned the scale at fourteen English stone.

God, she looked *huge*. Her crimson, purple wings, in flight, obscured the roof-tree of the Imperial Circus. Yet those marmoreal, immense arms and legs of hers, as they made leisurely, swimming movements through the air, looked palely unconvincing, as if arbitrarily tacked on to the bird attire.

Walser, drawn to the ring like a moth to a flame, thought, as he had before: 'She looks wonderful, but she doesn't look *right*.'

Yet he could not put his finger on what was wrong, could not identify in quite what way the proportions seemed distorted, since there existed no correct proportions to compare hers with; or, was the trouble this: there was an air about her that suggested, whilst convincing others, she herself remained unconvinced about the precise nature of her own illusion.

The slowness of her trajectory, her modest chug at twenty-five m.p.h. was the whole trick. It made the Charivaris huff.

With her right hand, she caught hold of the rung of the trapeze.

There was a clean, twanging snap.

A rope broke.

The Colonel, watching her, now, in besotted terror, as, a moment before, he'd gazed in besotted ecstasy, had judged it a publicity coup to use, not hack musicians, but the cream of the Petersburg Conservatoire for the pit band at this booking. The snag was, these longhairs did not know the first rule of the spectacle – that the show must go on. And now 'The Ride of the Valkyries' (superbly played) broke down on an aghast discord as the trapeze dropped Fevvers a dozen feet and left her swinging to and fro like a pendulum above the tiny eye of sawdust, the vortex of gravity, down there, down below.

Her wings quivered and the little feathers round the edges nervously whipped the air. But she showed no fear, even if she felt it. She twisted round and, with her free hand, waved, or, as they say in the circus, 'styled' at the Imperial Box in an ironic gesture. She even poked out her tongue. Musicians, horns and fiddles dangling from their hands, the Colonel, Walser, watched, helpless, hearts in mouths, for an endless minute; the Charivaris, on edge, watched.

Only in her own good time did she agitate her pendulum. She swung upon it, faster and faster, and, when she gained enough momentum, only then did she let go, and launched herself off, again, to arrive at the other side of the big top, where she landed upon her other trapeze, abruptly sat, briskly furled, folded her arms like a furious washerwoman and, vast, immobile, sulking, ignored the commotion that broke out below.

A confused murmur issued from the Imperial Box, in which sound it was possible to discern disappointment.

'Bastards!' cried Lizzie and repeated and augmented her abuse in several dialects of Italian. The Charivaris energetically fired back. The Colonel lit a fresh cigar and appeared to be imploring his pig for advice. Aloft, Fevvers hunched in a pet.

No. She won't come down. She's safer up here, isn't she. Why did nobody test the rope? What murderous fuckers have been tinkering with the rig?

High as she was, you could hear every word.

A roustabout discovered the rope which snapped had been neatly sawn half-through.

A plot!

Suspicion instantly falls upon the Charivaris. The Charivaris expostulate tumultuously, rising up and running back and forth along the ledges of the boxes. Lizzie hurls a torrent of quick, angry speech at the Colonel while the gesticulating Charivaris put forward whatever cases of their own they feel might hold water. The Colonel champs at his cigar and tickles his pig's ears and knows, in his heart, when Sybil squeals and nods, there will be nothing for it but to send the Charivaris packing. Give them a bonus on top of their unearned pay, strike them off the bill, send them back to Milan on the next train.

Either that, or he loses Fevvers. Which is not to be imagined. Especially since Fevvers has consented to dine with him that night, on condition he auditions Mignon.

Not, of course, that this *will* be the last of it, as far as the Charivaris are concerned. For the rest of their professional careers, the entire family will suffer from footrot, boils on the bum, headaches, indigestion . . . all the small, irritating, painful ailments that poison life for you but do you no lasting harm, that don't kill you but keep you permanently off-colour. Nothing in itself bad enough to keep any one of them from the high-wire; only, henceforth, upon it all will perform less well.

Off form. Their collective destiny is always to be off form. The children who wanted to see if Fevvers bounced will never quite recover from the secret policeman's pies. They will suffer the fate of never equalling their parents, even when those parents are off form. In the future, if ever Lizzie so much as thinks of the Charivaris, one or other of the clan will suffer an undiagnosable twinge. The historic tribe, who rope-danced before Nero, Charlemagne, the Borgias, Napoleon . . . the Charivaris will now enter a long, slow eclipse. Finally, forced to emigrate, two millennia of circus art will peter out in a pizza concession on Mott Street.

Good night.

When the Colonel reluctantly consented to sack the Charivaris, Fevvers came down to earth, again, although she did not jump, as she'd jumped down at the Alhambra, but, like any other trapeze artiste, used the rope ladder provided. Her grumblings grew louder as she approached terra firma.

Walser, half-laughing, half-wondering, almost, yet not quite, convinced himself the woman had been in no more danger than a parrot might be if you pushed it off its perch. And though he was altogether unwilling to believe this might be so, still he was enchanted by the paradox: if she were indeed a *lusus naturae*, a prodigy, then – she was no longer a wonder.

She would no longer be an extraordinary woman, no more the Greatest *Aerialiste* in the world but – a freak. Marvellous, indeed, but a marvellous monster, an exemplary being denied the human privilege of flesh and blood, always the object of the observer, never the subject of sympathy, an alien creature forever estranged.

She owes it to herself to remain a woman, he thought. It is her human duty. As a symbolic woman, she has a meaning, as an anomaly, none.

As an anomaly, she would become again, as she once had been, an exhibit in a museum of curiosities. But what would she become, if she continued to be a woman?

Then he saw she was pale under her rouge, as if recovering from real fear, and bundling herself in her feathery cape as if it would warm her. She gave him a thin smile.

'Nearly came unstuck, eh?' she said ambiguously.

Lizzie ran to her with half a bottle of brandy from the bar. The Colonel hovered, uttering flattering, sweet words, but Fevvers, subsiding into a ringside seat, shushed him silent as an iron clanking heralded the erection of the enormous cage in which the Princess and her cats performed.

'My protégée,' said Fevvers, gulping brandy. '*Now* you'll see something.'

Walser tried to sit down beside her but Lizzie firmly pushed him out of the way so he sat down beside the Colonel instead.

Preoccupied with Mignon's debut, the Princess had spared no thought for herself, forgotten to so much as pop on a frock, and both her petticoat and chemise could have done with a wash, hem of one stained with excrement of the cages and waist of the other with bloody prints from absent-minded wipings of her hands. But, as for Mignon — what fairy godmother had touched the little street-waif with her wand?

Her flaxen hair was piled up in soft curls and secured with a pink satin rose. A regular ballgown, white as icing, all romantic frills and lace, was cut in a way that showed how well her bruises were healing. She thrust out her meagre bosom as if to let a caged bird within it free.

Only, by the second verse, the Colonel began to rustle a little.

'Lieder in the tiger-cage!' he brooded aloud. 'Thassa real class act, yessir. But mightn't it be *too* high class? Get my meaning? Wasted on the hoi polloi? Mightn't — '

'Shush!' remonstrated Fevvers sharply.

Walser's eyes prickled and that vertiginous sensation he by now associated with the presence of the *aerialiste* overwhelmed him, although he knew, this time, the music was as much to blame as she.

A scatter of applause from the little audience, modified by an aggressive silence from Sybil that justified somewhat the Colonel's apprehensions, for he held great store by his pig's commercial acumen. No. Not for *this* show. Not *that* song. There was cash to be coined from the singer but not if she and her accompanist persisted in turning the ring into a concert hall. He strove to recall how his great predecessor, Barnum, marketed Jenny Lind, the Swedish nightingale, for the great American public . . . Sign up Mignon, yes; but sign her up with *this* cat act? H'm! Problems.

'What else,' he rasped, champing his butt, 'can you do?'

Mignon, manipulating her romantic skirts with marvellous dexterity, approached the biggest tiger on his pedestal and curtsied. The ladies' excuse-me!

The tiger's tail twitched and the tunnels of his nostrils tingled in response to the tasty civet in her perfume. The Princess gave out the preliminary chord. Down he jumped from his perch.

The Princess, out of respect for the city, chose to play the grand waltz from *Onegin*. One, two, three. Mignon waltzed with the tiger. *One*, two, three. The tall beast, a little stiff and grandfatherly, tenderly bent over the debutante, fully six feet tall on his hind legs and, it would seem, somewhat discommoded by the leather gauntlets secured to his forepaws with string lest, in the excitement of the moment, he let out his retracted claws with disastrous consequences to Mignon's bare shoulders, which had only the appearance of marble.

Round and round they went, Mignon humming along with the tune in an absent-minded, ensorcellating voice, as pleased with herself and the effect she made as any girl at her first ball. But the tiger's bride was sad to be cut out and, perhaps, even jealous at losing her partner to the pretty girl. Putting back her ears, she began to growl a sulphurous undermusic.

Hand in the tiger's paw, Mignon 'styled' to the crowd, as the Princess taught her, then curtsied to the tiger, to the other dancers, beaming with her customary lack of discrimination for it was all in the day's work to her, pretending to be dead or dancing with the fearful living.

More applause, far more than hitherto because every single one of the Educated Apes crept in to perch along the upper benches. Few of the non-simian habitués of the Imperial Circus could have behaved with more decorum as they clapped to see their former keeper in her new incarnation. One of them, with the green hair-ribbon, caught Walser's eye and winked at him. The Ape-Man was, as usual, elsewhere, nailed to some low bar by liquor, no doubt.

This time, Sybil could barely contain her enthusiasm and the Colonel's doubts vanished. He was quite consoled for the loss of the Charivaris.

'That beats all, don't it, Sybil! What nerve, what class! Whatta nattraction! If that little blondie ain't a wonder! And, as for the brown-skinned gal, why, she's just the amazing thing! Tell you what,' he confided to Sybil, 'what say we *drop* the song; just drop it. Forget it. Drop the song, go straight into the dance.'

Mignon led her partner back to his pedestal and dropped a kiss on his plush forehead before courteously handling him up. But a huge, amber tear dropped out of the tigress's eye, and then another. The Princess tapped her teeth with her fingernail when she saw those disappointed tears and beckoned impatiently at the observers. Walser felt a nudging at his bad arm and, looking down, saw that Sybil was poking him with her snout.

'Don't you see, man,' interpreted the Colonel, in a julep-haunted whisper, 'the Princess wants a volunteer. Sybil knows. Sybil can tell.

Off ye go, young feller, and do your duty! Do your duty by the Ludic Game and Colonel Kearney's Circus!'

''Ere, Mr Colonel,' said Fevvers. 'I say, ain't that a bit much?'

The Princess beckoned again; Sybil nudged again, this time ferociously.

'Ain't you an *Amurrican*?' implored the Colonel. 'Where's your spirit?'

'But that's the cat tried to eat me!' cried Walser, aghast.

'So you've been introduced, already? Fine!'

'But my arm –'

''E's a wounded soldier, poor sod –'

Walser looked from side to wide, seeking escape but saw, instead, the apparition of the Strong Man, come to gawp at Mignon. A vision of gleaming muscle, the Strong Man saw Walser at the same moment. His biceps rose, as if reflexively. Fevvers covered her eyes with one hand and raised the brandy bottle to her lips with the other.

'Walser by name I may be, ma'am, but I fear I'm no dancing man,' apologised Walser to his auburn partner but the lovely creature, with the relief of the reprieved wallflower, laid her head on his injured shoulder with a gentle, reassuring pressure and it was just as well she was in an appeasing mood since there was no time to procure her gloves. She led. She steered Walser round the ring with complete assurance and a wonderfully grave concern.

One, two, three. *One*, two, three.

Mignon whirled by, flashed the clown a brilliant smile and Walser, supported by the unforged steel of the tigress's forepaws, thought: There goes Beauty and the Beast. Then, looking into the tigress's depthless, jewelled eyes, he saw reflected there the entire alien essence of a world of fur, sinew and grace in which he was the clumsy interloper and, as the tigress steered his bedazzlement once more round the Princess's white piano, he allowed himself to think as the tigers would have done:

Here comes the Beast, and Beauty!

The breath of the tigress was wonderfully foul because of the putrid remains of breakfast still stuck between her teeth. That was the only thing that jarred.

All the tigers were on their hind legs, now, waltzing as in a magic ballroom in the country where the lemon trees grow.

The bars of the arena went past, first one by one, then, as the tempo quickened, resolving themselves into one single blurred bar, a confinement apprehended but no longer felt, until that single bar itself dissolved and all that remained was the limitless landscape of the music within which, while the dance lasted, they lived in perfect harmony.

This time, the applause was tumultuous and, if the Princess herself joined in, so did every single member of the circus (with the exception of the sulking Charivaris) for, as Walser took his bow, he saw all the stable-boys, roustabouts and grooms, besides elephants and equestrians he could not put a name to, unknown tumblers, jugglers, girls who were shot from guns, and every single clown, all drawn to the amazing spectacle, all succumbed to it. The Colonel sank right down in his seat and kicked his little legs in the air with delight. Fevvers toasted Walser with the empty brandy bottle.

Walser led the tigress back to her pedestal and bowed to her. She knocked him backwards with her rumbling, gratified, evil-smelling purr. Exquisitely formal, the Princess kissed him on both cheeks but Mignon she kissed on the mouth and the two girls clung together for a little longer, only a moment longer, than propriety allowed although, such was the vigour of the ovation, nobody noticed except those to whom it came as no surprise.

Then the Princess snapped shut the piano lid, took up her rifle and gestured imperiously with it. The cats leapt off their pedestals and disappeared down the chute. Abruptly discontinuous, the enchantment was over.

The Colonel was well pleased with the progress of the august he had himself selected, who was now both Human Chicken and tigress's gigolo. But, later that afternoon, the Strong Man beat Walser to a pulp and only the intervention of the *aerialiste* saved him.

The cuckolder cuckolded wears a double set of horns; the Strong Man's forehead buckled under the weight. He lurked in the gamy tranquillity of the menagerie, biding his time until Walser passed through the bowels of the building on his way to piss in the courtyard and jumped upon him from behind, knocking him down on the cobbles in front of the elemental indifference of the elephants. Walser's cockscomb and wig fell off.

The Strong Man knelt on Walser's back and kneed his kidneys again and again but you would have thought it hurt him more than it hurt Walser because he blubbered like a child. Walser, his right arm useless, could do nothing to defend himself and writhed under the great, grunting succubus until a drench of water descended on them both.

That put the Strong Man's fire out. He rolled off Walser, bawling and dripping, a sorry sight. This time it was Fevvers who flourished the hosepipe with which the Princess had already rescued Walser once before. She shook out a last few drops in a disturbingly masculine fashion and laid it aside. Mignon looked out of the cat-house at the sound of the commotion. When she saw Samson, the Strong Man, reduced to such pathetic, liquifying misery, her face took on an April hue of sympathetic showers. She had too short a memory to hold a grudge.

Walser, ignored, got up and looked for his head-coverings. Water ran out of his sleeves and down his trouser-legs. Fevvers shooed the excombatants towards the Princess's quarters, although, when the Strong Man saw the tigers perking up and looking inquisitive, he began to bellow again, this time out of fright. He was dressed, as usual, only in his tigerskin loincloth, to which the Princess pointed meaningfully.

'What she means is, off with that,' Fevvers said to him. 'They don't like the look of it.'

He knuckled his eyes and would not budge so she removed it for him, disclosing for a moment his enormous prick now crouched and shrunken, altogether the ghost of itself, before she wrapped him in a towel and chucked his loincloth to a safe distance. Walser made haste to take off his own trousers before, oh! agonising, oh! delirious notion, she could get her hands on *him*. Soon both were draped in towels and seated on bottles of straw. It was four o'clock and Mignon ran to the freshly opened cookhouse for warming mugs of tea.

Mignon's balldress hung from a bar on a wooden hanger marked *Hotel de l'Europe*. At home, the cat-tamers looked like a pair of schoolgirls surprised at a game in the dorm. Like the Princess, Mignon didn't bother to dress up in private, although *her* underthings were brand-new, exquisite batiste and broderie anglaise. A price tag still hung from the petticoat hem.

The Strong Man took a swallow of tea and then his tears burst forth afresh. Fevvers, with impersonal motherliness, took his curly head in her arms and pillowed it on her bosom. Walser was aggrieved, for he was the battered one and nobody paid him any attention except Mignon who, discovering hitherto untapped areas of competence within herself, snatched up a beefsteak and slapped it on his face to quell the beginnings of a monstrous black eye. But hers was not the attention he craved and, the more the Strong Man sobbed and snuggled, the more Walser felt put in the wrong and ill-used.

'I never laid a finger on her!' he declared to the Strong Man, only to spark off a fresh storm. The Strong Man mumbled something between Fevvers' breasts, where only she could hear.

'He says he loves you,' she told Mignon. Mignon presented a blank face. Fevvers hastily translated herself. Mignon laughed. The Strong Man wept and mumbled some more.

'He says he loves you but he's a coward.'

This time, Mignon did not laugh but kicked at the straw with her bare toe.

Mumble, mumble, mumble.

'He says he loves you; he's a coward; and he can't bear to think of you in the arms of a clown.'

It was the Princess who burst out laughing, this time, while Mignon shook her head: 'No! Never a clown!'

The Strong Man brightened up at that, and managed to get his tea down.

The word 'iron' was crudely inscribed on the knuckles of his right hand, and 'steel' on his left: the tattoos had a miserably self-inflicted look, as if carved with a penknife then filled in with ink during a deprived, self-mutilatory childhood. All of his bulk was muscle and simplicity, there was no flesh nor flab nor wit on him. He had a good, snub nose and, as he left off snivelling, his face once again took on its habitual expression of baffled innocence, of perpetual wonder at the ways of the world.

The Strong Man was naive and knew no tricks. During the gaps between the acts, while the cage or the trapeze went up, as the clowns mugged, Samson would strut round the ring holding a horse above his head.

Yes; he was very strong, and, as he knew deep down, a spiritual weakling. But, and this is what he did *not* know about himself, he was a great sentimentalist, so that, all the time he was poking the Ape-Man's woman, he never thought much about her, except that she was easy, but, as soon as she went off with the clown – or so he thought – and took a bath, had her hair done, put on a pretty dress, turned into a star, his heart turned over like a pancake whenever he thought how he'd get his huge tool in her no more. But don't think great loves haven't sprung from less likely sources than that in the history of the world. If, when the Strong Man watched the tiger waltz Mignon out of his reach for ever, he thought his heart was breaking, sentimental he might have been but break it did. Out of the fracture, sensibility might poke a moist, new-born head.

As all sat inconclusively around the cat-house, came a dragging, bumping sound; the Professor entered, backwards, through the open door to the courtyard, pulling the insensible Ape-Man along by his feet. The Professor was making heavy weather of it, panting, blowing and wheezing, clearly painfully conscious of the indignity of his task. The Ape-Man's head thudded against the cobbles at each tug the Professor gave his boots but the smile on his insensible features did not lift.

'Mein husband!' said Mignon.

'Here, Samson, me old duck, you go and give that poor hairy fellow a hand before he has a heart attack,' said Fevvers. The Strong Man rose obediently, tucking the ends of his towel round his waist. He carted the Ape-Man off to his bunk, the Professor trotting along beside him chattering to himself with annoyance.

Fevvers dropped some remark in German that made Mignon smile, another in French that made the Princess smile, too, but they did not smile at Fevvers, they smiled at one another and one white hand and one brown one reached out and clasped together.

'That's that, then.' At last she addressed Walser. 'You cop hold of your duds and come along with me, me old China. Leave the love-birds together.'

Love-birds, was it? Of course it was!

Hand in hand, the girls now went back into the cage, where the tigers slept the afternoon away, for the Princess was teaching Mignon more lieder. So she would not sing in the ring; well and good. So much the better, in fact! They would cherish in loving privacy the music that was their language, in which they'd found the way to one another.

When the Strong Man came running back from the apes, he, love locked out, shook the bars that kept him from his beloved but the musical lovers did not hear, so wrapt were they.

Left alone, the Professor went through the pockets of the Ape-Man. He withdrew his flat wallet, found what he was looking for – Monsieur Lamarck's contract with the Colonel – read it through and tore it up. He pierced the unconscious Ape-Man with a regard of pure simian contempt. He seized the Ape-Man's greatcoat from the foot of his bunk in order to pass unnoticed in the crowd and sped off.

In the courtyard he discovered Walser sluicing his face for the second time that day, getting rid of blood and muddied make-up. The Professor caught his bad arm, making him jump and, after a tetchy display of contrition, drew Walser with him into the alley; although Walser, wearing only a towel, protested fiercely, he made it apparent he wished the clown to hail a cab for him.

Since the Colonel proposed to entertain his star to dinner that night, a date of which he nourished great hopes, he returned to his hotel early, in order to treat his blue jowls to a shave. In his rolled shirt-sleeves, humming 'Casey Jones' to himself around his clenched cigar, he was attacking his cheeks with a cut-throat razor in the bathroom of his suite when the Professor, in too much of a hurry to fuss with the front desk, shinned up a drain-pipe and knocked peremptorily at the frosted glass window. The Colonel, after a few exclamations of Kentuckian astonishment, let the Professor in and ushered him to the drawing-room, to wait while he wiped the suds from his cheeks. When he returned, the Professor was seated at the writing desk, penning rapidly on hotel notepaper.

'Nature did not give me vocal cords but left the brain out of Monsieur Lamarck. He is a hopeless drunk with no business sense. I therefore propose to take over all the business management of the "Educated Apes" and demand the salary and expenses formerly payable to Monsieur Lamarck now be paid to me.'

'Well, here's a do, Sybil.' Colonel Kearney addressed his pig. 'The madmen take over the lunatic asylum.'

Undeterred, the chimp jotted down the sum he considered appropriate for the services of himself and his colleagues, which caused the Colonel's eyebrows to rise when he saw it and offer the Professor a friendly glass, hardly the most tactful hospitality, in the circumstances, which the Professor angrily refused. Uncorking a fresh bottle of bourbon with his teeth, the Colonel stroked a chin still stiff with soap and observed amusedly:

'Aw, shoot, Professor! If there ain't a man in the ring with you, people'll think you're just a bunch of high-school kids in monkey suits!'

The Professor uttered an indescribable noise that did not need vocal cords to express its meaning.

'I'll thank you to keep a civil tongue in your head, Professor! Well, sir, you know what I always say – let us consult the oracle.'

With a grunt, Sybil launched herself to the carpet as he spilled out the alphabet cards.

'"Cheap at the price",' pondered the Colonel. 'Well, I hate to disagree with you, Sybil, but this gentleman certainly strikes a mighty hard bargain. Are you *convinced* he's irreplaceable? You are? I'll be darned . . . '

He squinted at Sybil ruminatively, assailed by the first doubts of her integrity: that there might be some solidarity amongst the dumb beasts, that they could form a pact of some kind against him, was a disturbing possibility that, hitherto, never entered his mind. Finally he grudgingly extended his hand to the Professor.

'Gentleman's handshake is his bond where I come from. Oh. I see. Not where you come from. Well – '

Reluctantly he sat down at the desk and wrote out a new contract, but, even so, he was forced to strike out a brace of clauses and allow the Professor to attach a codicil before the chimp would sign. Refusing so much as a bite of one of Sybil's apples to clinch the deal, the Professor roared off, by the door this time, leaving the Colonel much vexed.

'Pork and beans,' he threatened Sybil. 'Spare-ribs. Hickory-smoked ham.'

But she jumped back upon her cushion and closed her eyes purposefully, brooking no further discussion, although the Colonel might have concluded his shave with even less equanimity had he known that, in the foyer, on his way out, the Professor had enlisted the aid of a passing Lizzie in obtaining from the desk clerk a copy of Cook's International Rail Timetable.

NINE

To wash down the caviare-stuffed pancakes and sour cream, the jellied carp, marinated mushrooms and smoked salmon, the Colonel preferred bourbon to vodka. After that, he found bourbon made the borsht go down better. Fevvers had some white burgundy with the first course, red burgundy with the soup, and plied her silverware with a will. An old hand at seduction dinners, she believed in making a hearty meal and the Colonel spared no expense. Roast goose with red cabbage and apples? She passed on that, however, choosing venison, instead, and changed to a château-bottled claret. The Colonel stuck to bourbon, and now confined his eating to crumbs from the bread rolls which he agitated with nervous fingers. Fevvers, however, found room for ice-cream, to finish up, plus a glass of Chateau d'Yquem, belched companionably and nodded when he, red-faced and already over-primed for the occasion, offered her a goodnight night-cap in his suite.

She enjoyed well-chilled champagne while the impresario lapsed into slumber on the couch beside her. Removing the bourbon bottle from his fist, she poked curiously into the aperture of his fly, which he'd just fumbled open before he passed out, and withdrew a string of little silk American flags. Sybil gave a reproachful grunt.

'How did it go?' inquired Lizzie in their own drawing-room, thick with the scent of hot-house flowers and the smell of the melted wax which the old woman was carefully dripping from a candle. She looked as if she were performing a witchcraft ritual but such was far from the case.

'Couldn't get 'is star-spangled banner up,' replied Fevvers. 'Britannia's revenge for the War of 1812. I say, our Liz, ain't you done with your invisible writing yet?'

'It'll be ready for his next consignment,' said Lizzie equably.

Fevvers drew back the brocade curtain and looked out at a frozen little crescent moon that lay on its back in the vast sky. She sighed.

'Seems a shame to play a trick like that on such a nice young man . . .'

'Not hatched out, yet,' Lizzie summed him up. 'The clowns may pelt him with eggs as if eggs cost nothing but his own shell don't break, yet.

He is too *young* for you, my girl. He's living proof that travel don't broaden the mind; instead, it renders a man *banal*.'

'Not his mind as interests me,' said Fevvers.

'Oh, Sophie, you're a devil for a pretty face.'

'Not his *face* as interests me – '

A rap on the door interrupted her. A yawning bell-boy delivered a fragrant, precious mound of out-of-season Parma violets; her lucky flower! She exclaimed with surprise; how did the unknown sender know that? Lizzie snatched the card that came with them, read it, compressed the corners of her mouth and tossed it into the fire but Fevvers greedily investigated the moist, ribbon-wrapped stalks of the flowers with her capable nurse's hands and discovered a shagreen box. Inside the box, to Lizzie's further displeasure, glittered a diamond bracelet, like a cold bandage.

'A pretty face is one thing, our Liz,' opined Fevvers, trying on the bracelet at once, 'but diamonds is another. 'ere's a punter good for a touch.'

Her pupils narrowed down to the shape of £ signs.

TEN

After the dizzy triumph of the Grand Gala Opening, Fevvers grew sick of flowers, even violets, and told the doorman of the Hotel de l'Europe to redirect her floral tributes to the lying-in hospital. Deluged with invitations, she permitted herself to accept only one single supper, and that for the final night of the engagement. This invitation came accompanied by a shagreen box, twin of the one that brought the diamond bracelet, containing a pair of diamond earrings the size of hazelnuts and a note promising a necklace to match on the evening in question. Therefore she concluded this punter was prepared to put his money where his mouth was – or, rather, where his mouth hoped to be.

On the final night, as it happened, Buffo the Great, having harkened to the voice of drunken Russia, went out to celebrate his departure from the Capital of Vodka together with the Ape-Man. The saturnine Frenchman, the first casualty of the party, succumbed in a low dram-shop, was piled to one side like so much lumber and there abandoned. Little Ivan it was, anxiously searching the back-alley bars, who found Buffo still on his feet, though wavering, and led him back to Clown Alley, there to settle him on an upturned stool before a rectangle of cracked mirrors, where Buffo flailed about, wriggled, moaned and struggled to prevent Grik and Grok repairing the ravages his debauch had made upon his make-up.

For he presented a deplorable sight. His natural skin showed through his matte white in ghastly streaks and runnels and, in the course of his peripatetic carousing, he had mislaid his bald piece so that a mean fringe of coarse, greying hair, spiked with sweat, surmounted a piebald face that seemed, rather than its customary mask-like inhumanity, now hideously partly human. Grik and Grok clucked, gibbered and wrung their hands at the state into which the master clown had got himself but Buffo was well away and bellowed like a bull:

'Tonight shall be my Cavalry! God, we'll make 'em split their sides!'

He had the air of a revenant back from the grave in flapping cerements stained with dung, mire and vomit, but he was stubbornly, indeed, dementedly, still bent upon a spree. He drained a bottle from his pocket as he swayed before the mirror. Grik and Grok ferreted out another bald piece for him and cocked a fresh conical hat at a rakish angle. That pleased him, for some reason, and he puckered up his rouged lips at himself in the mirror, pouted like a young girl, and then, all at once, his bowels opened and Grik and Grok ran squeaking off for water and scrubbing brush and a fresh pair of drawers but, at the great clown's request, Little Ivan trotted away in the other direction to fetch another pint of vodka.

The Colonel, in the box office, counting out the takings, poohpoohed Walser's account of Buffo's obscene and perilous condition. 'Drunker he is, the funnier he is.' He stuffed a last handful of rainbow-coloured banknotes in the cash-box and locked it up with a pleased expression on his face, for it was 'house full' and 'standing room only' tonight, once again, and there were more grand-dukes, archduchesses, princes and princesses in the audience that night of nights than the Colonel himself had consumed fried chicken dinners in his entire life.

As the band started in on 'The March of the Gladiators', the Colonel's heart filled with a kind of holy awe, to have provided for such an illustrious gathering so rich a banquet of astonishment, and to have coined so much profit from it. He felt himself both to be glorified and also the entrepreneur of glory; above his scrubby head floated an invisible halo composed of dollar bills.

The circus parade passed off without any untoward occurrence. Buffo's lurching gait and uncoordinated gesticulations of arms and legs went unnoticed among the antics of the other clowns, who were so concerned to 'cover' for him that each excelled himself in outlandish capers, leaps and pratfalls. When Buffo tripped over a poodle, it was the work of a moment for Grik and Grok to seize either end of his disarticulated carcass and go into an improvised version of the 'Clown's Funeral', wiping imaginary tears from their eyes with lavish gestures of their flowing sleeves. Buffo kept rearing and bucking away between his pallbearer's shoulders as if he were having so much fun in his death throes that he simply couldn't bear to stop, while his shrill, ear-splitting voice stuttered out imprecations that, so long as you did not understand them, were funnier than you could have believed possible: such thwarted fury, such incomprehensible rage! The clowns carried Buffo round the ring and off, behind a section of high-stepping and contemptuous horses, who could spot a Yahoo when they saw one, while Buffo cursed the world and all who dwelled therein, to the uncomprehending delight of all observers.

They dumped him down in the menagerie, to await the clowns' last cue. He sent Little Ivan running for another pint of vodka and, when it was time for the Feast of Fools, the Clowns' Christmas Dinner, the Lord of Misrule himself, possessed as he was by the spirits in the bottle, went out of his mind.

They bore the trestle table into the ring and, with their customary wealth of by-play, spread it with its white dust-sheet and laid it with the rubber knives and forks and plates, prodding, stabbing and poking at each other the while sufficient to procure gales of mirth. They took their places round the table, tucking their napkins into their neck-bands, and the audience took time out to catch its breath.

Buffo, in the wings, emptied the fresh bottle and tossed it aside. When he saw the glare of the arc lights, he covered his eyes with his hands and screamed. 'Oh, don't you see!' he cried to Little Ivan. 'The moon has turned to blood!' But Little Ivan spoke no English and understood only Buffo's scream. Into the ring he staggered, the child tagging anxiously at his heels.

His fresh make-up was already flaking and his bald piece wrinkling up until it threatened to dislodge his cap. He picked up the carving knife and flourished it most horribly; from the tip floated an ominous knot of red ribbons. Little Ivan had the job of getting the blue butcher's apron on him and skipped round and round the teetering colossus, now on one side, now the other, in order to push him back on his unstable balance each time he threatened to lose it. The audience burst its lungs when it saw him, as if not to laugh would have provoked the most savage punishment. Buffo the Great! Nobody like Buffo the Great!

Little Ivan steered and tugged him to the head of the table, and Buffo collapsed on his collapsing chair. If his ensuing wrestling bout with the chair had all the defiance and bravado of Jacob's with the angel, only the clowns suspected that, tonight, the harmless chair had indeed assumed in Buffo's imagination the shape and form of some far from angelic adversary and, as he and the chair grappled with one another, the company around the table grew a little closer together, their tatterdemalion garments rustling as a wind of consternation blew through them, and then they, too, along with every child in the house, broke out in a great shout of pleasure and relief when Buffo finally, miraculously, got the chair down unprotesting on its four feet, smashed the seat flat with a crashing thwack on his palm, and, at long last, planted his bum thereon.

Backstage, Walser, the Human Chicken, his pants' seat crammed with sausage links, crouched in a Japanese obeisance upon a silver platter amid a circle of papier-mâché roast potatoes. Grik tucked a sprig of parsley into his cockscomb.

'Grab for the carvers,' said Grik. 'Grab the carvers off him, if you get the chance.'

'Why's that?' demanded Walser uneasily.

'In 'is cups, 'e *can* be homicidal.'

Then the domed silver dish-cover descended upon Walser, plunging him into a metal-smelling, resonant darkness, around which shushed and hissed, like the sound of waves inside a shell, the echoes of the old clown's whisper: 'Homicidal . . . homicidal . . . '

'Here goes,' said Grik to Grok. They picked up the roast between them and tottered with it into the ring.

Buffo peered at the great silver dish set down before him with mild surprise. For a moment, just one moment, the heaving, writhing horrors around him settled down in a kind of turbulent tranquillity. The roar of the crowd, the stench of greasepaint and naphtha, the weird company of acolytes who surrounded him, raising their faces towards him, comforted him and warned him and though, at any moment, a cock might crow, thrice, he was, for just this last space of a few heartbeats – ten; or, fifteen – again the loving father about to divide meat between his children. A last touch of grace passed over him; indeed, was he not the very Christ, presiding at the white board, at supper, with his disciples?

But, where was the bread? And, above all, where were they hiding the wine? He looked round for loaf and bottle but could see none. An immense suspicion wakened in his red-rimmed eyes. He recalled the carvers in his hands and lightly clashed the fork against the knife, agitating the bloody streamers in the air.

The elastic moment stretched, and stretched further, and stretched too far to sustain its comic tension. The laughter died away. A querulous ripple ran through the crowd. Although Walser, in the dish, could see and hear nothing, he had already acquired enough of the instinct of the trouper to know that, if Buffo were too far gone to unveil the entrée, the entrée must unveil itself.

Walser flexed his muscles with pleasure since his position was exceedingly cramped and uncomfortable and let out a rousing 'Cock-a-doodle-do!' The dish-cover went bounding and rebounding down the table, sending the rubber settings bouncing this way and that way. Up Walser rose out of his garnish like Venus from the foam, spraying parsley and roast potatoes around him, spewing sausages from his trouser vent, and, flapping his arms, he sang out again:

'Cock-a-doodle-dooski!'

Buffo screamed most horribly and brought the carving knife smashing down.

'Oh, my *gahd*!' said the Colonel, at the back of the auditorium, clutching Sybil so tight she squealed, champing down so hard on his cigar he bit it in two. 'My gahd!' He saw his glory depart, his halo fly away.

But Walser, his reflexes exquisitely refined by fear, took a gigantic leap into the air the very moment when, reflected in the dreadful mirror of the eye, he saw the great clown's reason snap.

Buffo brought down the carving knife upon only the debris in the silver dish; the bird had flown.

Howls of delight!

The halo fluttered back to hover over the Colonel's head, again, although now it had an uncertain, impermanent look. Troubled, he spat out the destroyed cigar, fumbled for another and, prompted by a furious convulsion from Sybil, scuttled out to the foyer to summon a doctor.

No sooner was the Human Chicken on its feet again than it took to its heels and sprinted the length of the board. Buffo was detained, for a moment, as he tugged the carving knife out of the table – for such was the force of his blow the blade had pierced the dish to the wood beneath – and then, with a high, whinnying scream, he was after him.

All present agreed it was a fitting climax to the great clown's career, that chase after the Human Chicken, round and round the great ring, round as the apple of an eye, of the Imperial Circus in the Imperial City of St Petersburg. How the little dogs enjoyed the fun, snapping and nipping the ankles of hunter and prey, running away with links of sausages, playing football with the roast potatoes, getting under everybody's feet while the other clowns dashed hither and thither, at a loss as to what to do, concerned only to give the illusion of *intentional* Bedlam, for the show must go on. And, even if Buffo at last *had* contrived to plunge his carving knife into the viscera of the Human Chicken, nobody in that vast gathering of merry folk would ever have been permitted to believe it was *real* manslaughter; it would have seemed, instead, the cream of the jest.

And now Buffo, in his delirium, began to shake, to shake and shiver most horribly, to most horribly grimace and to convulse himself in such a way that his immense form seemed to be everywhere at once, dissolving into a dozen Buffos, armed with a dozen murderous knives all streaming rags of blood, and leap and tumble as he might, Walser could find no place in the ring where Buffo was not and gave up hope for himself.

Why didn't Walser run out of the ring the way he'd been carried into it? Because the exit was blocked already by the iron paraphernalia of the Princess's cage and the cats, sniffing blood and madness on the air, were growling uneasily, pacing to and fro swishing their tails while the two girls stared from between the bars, distraught, until the Princess took matters into her own hands and stepped out of the cage, with the nozzle of the hose-pipe in her hand.

The shock of water blasted Buffo back into one single form, blasted him off his feet, blasted him up into the air in the final somersault of his career, and then flattened him on his back. A few moments later, as the crowd held its aching sides and mopped its eyes, Samson the Strong Man hauled prone, soaked, semi-conscious, fearfully hallucinating Buffo off up the gangway that led to the foyer as little children gave him one last tittering poke for luck before he vanished as from the face of the earth, while the clowns ran round and round the tiers of seats, kissing babies, distributing bonbons and laughing, laughing, laughing to hide their broken hearts.

The frock-coated doctor waited in the champagne bar accompanied by two stern-faced Mongolian giants who held a strait-jacket invitingly open between them. As the Princess lifted the lid of her white piano in the ring while Mignon flounced her lacy skirts, Buffo, babbling obscenities, was loaded into a waiting cab, leaving the circus for the last time, as he had never done before, in the way that gentlemen did, by the front entrance.

Farewell, old man. And from the coffin of your madness there is no escape.

Walser, pale, shaking and, once again, drenched to the skin, ducked his own dance with the tigress and sought refuge in Fevvers' dressing-room, only to find the place festering with discord. Lizzie bent over some missive home, leaving the *aerialiste* to don her costume unaided. Fevvers gave Walser brandy and a towel kindly enough but only 'tut-tutted' at the terrible story of Buffo's Last Supper in the most perfunc-tory manner and it was apparent something quite other than the show was on her mind. Her red satin evening dress swung behind the door, ready, evidently, to take her off to secret delights after the performance was over. The French dwarf's poster, somewhat dog-eared with travelling, flapped on the wall, as if to remind you she was capable of anything.

Looking febrile and somehow illicit with excitement, she sat in her dressing-gown in front of the mirror. There was a vast diamond bracelet on her right wrist and she fixed in her ears a pair of earrings each composed of a stone fit to make the Kohinoor blink.

'Like 'em?' she said, scintillating at Walser. 'They're a girl's best friend.'

Lizzie spluttered derisively at that and might have spoken, but then such a roar of passionate but unidentifiable emotion came from the distant audience that they could hear it even in their little eyrie above the courtyard. Such a sound as the Roman audience must have made when a lion ate a Christian.

Then the crack of a shot.

As the band broke into furious music, came a frantic banging and rattling at the dressing-room door.

It was the Colonel, clutching Sybil like a drowning man, sucking as on a teat on the black stub of an extinguished cigar, tears standing in his veiny eyes. If he had shied away from Fevvers for a while, after the débâcle of their date, now he came to throw himself on her favour.

'Fevvers, my dear, you're on next! Daren't wait for the interval. Unexpected turn of events. Sudden catastrophe –'

He broke down and blubbered like a baby. Fevvers rose up impassively, surveying the Colonel from the majestic balcony of her bust.

'I say,' she said. 'Be a *man* and pull yourself together.'

From the courtyard below rose up the sound of a great weight being dragged across the cobbles, accompanied by a woman's sobbing. Clustering at the window, they witnessed, in the dismal light of the moon, a dreary procession. First, Samson, called on for his strength a second time that night, hauling by a rope tied round her middle the body of Walser's former dancing partner, the tigress, which left a bloody trail behind it, and, following on, the tigress's chief mourners, with their shoulders carelessly bare to the freezing night in their white dresses, but both those dresses smeared with blood and Mignon's hanging from her back in ripped shreds.

The Princess carried the rifle with which she had shot the tigress, a peerless bullet straight between the eyes, the moment after, just one moment after the jealous tigress, deprived of her escort, could bear the sight of Mignon dancing with her mate no longer. The Princess shot the tigress the moment after the tigress whirled from her pedestal down amongst the circling cats and got her claws in Mignon's frills; the Princess shot the tigress just before she got her claws in Mignon's flesh. All the same, it was Mignon who cried.

Fevvers shut the window with a clang. The longhairs from the Conservatoire had learned their lesson well; the show indeed went on but the relentless jollity of the circus orchestra did not drown the baying of the crowd.

'Cheer up, Colonel,' she said. 'I'll make them forget. They ain't seen nothing like *me* before.'

When she dropped her wrap and donned her plumed topknot, it was as though a huge, not altogether friendly bird appeared among them. She cast a glance at the opulence reflected in the mirror, admired her own bosoms. In the auditorium, they demanded her. She cocked an ear.

'Suckers,' she said.

Lizzie morosely flung the feather cloak over her young friend's shoulders and the *aerialiste* stumped out, slamming the door behind her to open it again for a parting shaft.

'I'll expect a bonus for this.'

This time, the slam made the gas-jets tremble.

'She's in a filthy mood,' said Lizzie. 'She must and will have supper with this Grand Duke. She won't take a word of advice. Headstrong. And mercenary. Headstrong and mercenary. A real tartar, she is. Here, my love –' suddenly crooning to the pig '– does it want a bit of choccy, then?'

While she was rummaging in her handbag, the Colonel recovered himself sufficiently to pitch headlong out of the door after Fevvers. Having lost two of his star turns already that night, he dared not let his eyes off the Cockney Venus for a second. Sybil, thwarted of her chocolate, protested shrilly from his arms. The plangent strains of 'A Bird in a Gilded Cage' drifted over from the auditorium as if all were going exactly to plan, as if the circus could absorb madness and slaughter into itself with the enthusiasm of a boa constrictor and so, continue.

Walser cast his quick, reporter's eye over the room, caught sight of a note tucked into a mirror, picked out two words – 'alone', and 'unaccompanied' – before Lizzie pressed her bundle of papers into his hand, adjuring him to make all haste to catch the diplomatic bag with them, to run and see to it this minute.

Had it not been for the sudden sting of jealousy that struck him when he thought of Fevvers, 'alone', 'unaccompanied', in her gaudy dress in the Grand Duke's arms, he would, out of sheer curiosity, have stopped to check out Lizzie's letters, that she was so anxious to despatch to London before the circus train pulled out of Petersburg. Might even have spotted the code; the secret writing. Have found a story, there, that would have turned him back into a journalist, again. As it was, he was too full of misery to care, and let Lizzie, careless of his hurt, push him irritably from the room.

As she stowed the bottles and boxes of eyeblack, rouge and powder away in straw hampers, packed rug and hairpins, rolled up the autographed poster, she bubbled with ill humour like a boiling pot and, when Fevvers blew back, incandescent with applause, she opened her mouth –

'No, no, no!' snapped the enormous girl. 'Once and for all, you're *not* to come with me, hobbling along like a rotten old procuress the way you do, you old cow.'

'Well, you just watch yourself,' said Lizzie darkly. 'Fucking aristos. Can't trust fucking aristos.'

Make-up off unaided, evening dress on, Fevvers leaned forward to greet her real face in the mirror with a brilliant smile.

'Here, today; gone, tomorrow. In actual fact, our Lizzie, we're not even gone tomorrow, but gone to-bloody-night. Train leaves at midnight, doesn't it. Can't miss that, can I, not if it were ever so.'

She cast a meaningful glance at the stopped clock and giggled.

'Pshaw!' said Lizzie. 'If you think I'd lift a finger to help you, you've got another think coming, my girl. Sheer *greed,* that's what it is.'

'What harm can a touch of sham with a grand duke do, our Liz? Not when the carriage awaits without, me old duck! Hasn't he said he'll give me the diamond rivière to match, tonight? Just so long as I go by myself. Don't want you along to cramp my style, you rancid old bawd. Can you just fasten up my hair?'

Lizzie grouched towards the mirror but could not help herself depositing a kiss on her foster-daughter's defenceless nape as she pinned up her curls.

'Well, you just watch it.'

'You'd chuck a hand grenade at the poor old fellow, if you got half a chance. For myself, I prefer finesse.'

With a conjurer's flourish, she drew out a toy gilt sword from her corset and made some fencer's passes with it.

'Remember I go *armed* into combat, Lizzie! Call it, the Nelson touch. D'you think I'd leave my weapon off, tonight, of all nights?'

Lizzie reached out to test the blade with her thumb.

'Go for the ballocks, if needs must,' she advised, satisfied.

In her red and black lace, it hurt the eyes to look at Fevvers and she was, besides, flushed and resplendent with the way she'd just snatched victory from disaster, erased the memory of the madman and the carnivore by the winged miracle of her presence. She was feeling supernatural tonight. She wanted to *eat* diamonds.

At the courtyard gate, a glamorous droshky stood ready to receive her, behind the melancholy van from the knacker's yard. As a befurred footman handed Fevvers into the one, the Strong Man pitched the carcass into the other.

Amid all the bustle and hurry of the dismantling, roustabouts and stable-lads dashing this way and that, horses neighing, the refreshed jingling of the elephants' chains as the bull-hands slid the great feet into leather boots against the cold, the Professor now made an appearance. He carried a bulging carpetbag in one hand and a shiny new briefcase in the other. His colleagues came marching behind. All wore sturdy greatcoats and one or two had donned the wide sheepskin hats or *chapkas* of the peasants, bought in the markets to keep their ears warm. All were loaded up with bags, cardboard suitcases and hat-boxes, or carried small trunks on their shoulders. One bore a folded-up blackboard. They were hotly pursued by the agitated Colonel; Sybil, under her own steam for once, accompanied him, showing a fair turn of porcine speed.

The Colonel caught up with the Professor, grasped him by the shoulders and shook him so that he dropped his briefcase. That made the Professor terribly angry, he shrieked and gibbered, and the Colonel thereupon adopted a conciliatory tone, evidently begging and pleading with him. Sybil got up on her hind legs, at one point, and laid a beseeching trotter on the Professor's forearm. The Professor absent-mindedly patted her but did not stop shaking his head emphatically at the Colonel and produced a piece of paper clotted with sealing wax stamps from his inner pocket. He jabbed a stubby finger at a clause in the contract outlined in red ink and marked in the margin with several exclamation marks. One by one, the stable-lads knocked off work to enjoy the argument.

The Colonel attempted to reason with the Professor. The stable-lads watched with interest. The ·Professor lost his temper completely, crumpled his paper into a ball and thrust it down the Colonel's throat. The stable-lads greeted this action with a burst of ironic cheering and scattered applause. The Professor, newly aware of his audience, granted it a jerky little bow. He stroked Sybil's ears, apparently in farewell; then he and his entire troupe precipitated themselves outdoors, leaving the Colonel choking. Though one chimp, a green hair-ribbon peeking from beneath her smart tam, looked behind her, even wistfully, perhaps for a last glimpse of Walser, but Walser was off running Lizzie's messages.

When he spat out the contract, the Colonel said: 'They're booked in on the night train to Helsinki. "No Siberia for us," he says. Or, rather, scribbles. Come up to me, bold as brass, after the show – informs me – scrawls a note, dreadful handwriting, dreadful! – informs me they've earned a bonus on account of the applause at the end of their act lasted longer'n five minutes. Wrote the clause in 'isself. I signed it, to my shame. *My* watch put the applause at four minutes ninety-nine seconds precisely. Darned ape won't listen to reason. Darned ape.'

The Colonel opened his arms to Sybil and pressed his disconsolate face into the pig's neck, for comfort, although Sybil, loyalties somewhat torn, snorted thoughtfully to herself.

And the apes were by no means the only defectors that night. Many a stable-lad, already sufficiently glutted with adventure, went under the net, using his earnings to purchase a ticket at the Finland Station and roll off through the pine forests, on the way home. Buffo the Great was incarcerated in a Russian madhouse. The tigress lay in a Petersburg knackers' yard. It was a depleted company the Colonel would take across the tundra, towards the islands where the sun was already rising.

And, that night, he almost lost his star as well.

ELEVEN

Amidst a fine, masculine smell of leather upholstery, lapped to the eyes in a rug of sables, Fevvers rolled through the beautiful city as the snow came whirling down in huge, soft flakes. The old woman, the big baboushka in the sky, was shaking her mattress overhead, shaking it with great abandon as if preparing a feather bed for a gargantuan coupling. Snow whirled down on to the Neva, there to dissolve upon the ice-thickened water; some snow clung to the crowns and folded forearms of the civic monuments, to the carved cornices of pediment and portico, to the mane and tail of the mount of the stone horseman, a white, transforming fall – the first touch of winter, a visitation that arrives with such a magical caress you can scarcely believe, at first, how the winter of these latitudes will kill you at its vast leisure – if it gets the chance.

But Fevvers saw no death in the snow. All she saw was that festive sparkle of the frosty lights that made her think of diamonds.

She hugged the sable rug about her as she climbed the skidding steps to his front door under an umbrella the coachmen held above her head. A couple of capripede caryatids looked after the door and there was a coat of arms above it, a unicorn goring a knight. The street was deserted. Yellow streetlamps sifted the inexorable snow. The coachman bowed and vanished, leaving Fevvers to tug on the melodious doorbell by herself. The Grand Duke did her the honour of letting her in. (So all the servants had been sent away for the night, had they? H'm.)

'I want the carriage back at eleven thirty p.m. precisely,' she informed him crisply, dropping his sables on the floor. Let him pick them up hisself, if he wanted.

His house was the realm of minerals, of metals of vitrification – of gold, marble and crystal; pale halls and endless mirrors and glittering chandeliers that clanged like wind-bells in the draught from the front door . . . and a sense of frigidity, of sterility, almost palpable, almost tangible in the hard, chill surfaces and empty spaces.

Always the same! thought Fevvers censoriously. Money is wasted on the rich. For herself, if she'd been as Croesus-wealthy as her host, she'd have fancied something like the Brighton Pavilion to call home, something to make each passer-by smile, a reciprocal gift to those from whom the wealth had come.

And, conversely, she went on to herself, sneering at the Grand Duke's palace, poverty is wasted on the poor, who never know how to make the best of things, are only the rich without money, are just as useless at looking after themselves, can't handle their cash just like the rich can't, always squandering it on bright, pretty, useless things in just the same way.

Let me tell you something about Fevvers, if you haven't noticed it for yourself already; she is a girl of philosophical bent.

Since *money* it is that makes us rich or poor, why, then: abolish money! she sometimes said to Lizzie. For all that money is, is a symbolic means of facilitating exchanges that should, by rights, be freely made or not at all.

But Lizzie would whistle through her moustache at Fevvers' naivety and reply: the baker can't make a loaf out of your privates, duckie, and that's all you'd have to offer him in exchange for a crust if nature hadn't made you the kind of spectacle people pay good money to see. All you can do to earn your living is to make a show of yourself. You're doomed to that. You must give pleasure of the eye, or else you're good for nothing. For you, it's always a symbolic exchange in the market-place; you couldn't say you were engaged in productive labour, now, could you, girl?

But neither does *this* one toil nor spin, thought Fevvers in the Grand Duke's palace. Yet he is so rich that money hasn't any *meaning* for him. The sums he is about to squander on this bright, pretty, useless thing, myself, have nothing to do with my value as such. If all the women in the world had wings, he'd keep his jewels to himself, to play at ducks and drakes on the icy waters of the Neva. My value to him is as a *rara avis*.

In his marble halls, she smiled like a predator. Here comes Property Redistribution Inc. to take away your diamonds, Grand Duke!

She stalked up an outflung arc of marble staircase, the Grand Duke attentively behind her, his eyes fixed on the throbbing bulges at the base of her shoulders, and, as she proceeded, she priced the candle-holders, the mirrors, the oriental jars – even the hot-house blooms within them. She made the progress of an auctioneer and, with every step, added a further sum to the price she'd already put upon whatever entertainment she might be asked to provide.

His study was more ruminative, a steep-sided, oval room with a mezzanine gallery wreathed in shadow. Busts of Dante, Shakespeare and Pushkin atop the bookcases looked down upon a table laid for an intimate supper. Little glasses for vodka, funnels for champagne and, in the middle, something to make her gasp: herself, in ice. And life size! At full spread, 'styling' and smiling, a cold masterpiece that would have turned into a puddle of ice by the time that dawn would find her chugging across the taiga, as she again promised herself it would.

The ice-sculpture stood on the tip of one foot in a black gravel of caviare and round its neck there blazed away the thousand, thousand rainbow facets of the most magnificent parure she'd ever seen. Oh, the incendiary stones! Her fingers itched to snatch it. But she could scarcely burst out of her bodice, flutter up and make off with it before so much as the soup was served, could she! She was a well-bred girl, after all; wasn't she? She choked on baulked greed. She felt a sulk might be coming on.

'Well,' she said and sank down on a sofa, drawing off her long, black gloves for the sake of something to do. The Grand Duke seized hold of one hand as soon as it was bare and pressed his bearded mouth to the palm, giving her a sensation of hot, wet, turbulent, unpleasant hairiness.

'May you melt in the warmth of my house just as *she* melts,' he murmured, with a nod to the ice-sculpture. Fat chance, thought Fevvers, retrieving her hand and wiping on to her napkin the trace of saliva he left behind. She did not like his greeting; she cast an uneasy glance at the ice-sculpture, to make sure it had not started to melt already.

He was a man of medium height in a green velvet smoking-jacket of exquisite cut. His French matched his style. He possessed an infinite number of versts of black earth, pine forest and barren tundra beneath which bubbled oil. Fevvers kept her Spanish shawl wrapped tight. She refrained from catching his eye. He thought she was overawed by everything. She priced with astonishment the worn old Persian carpet underfoot and added another nought to the price in sterling of tossing him off.

He offered her vodka. She was glad of a drink but wary of the pile of glasses beside the bottle: did he intend to ask his friends in? But now, smiling, he arranged the glasses into a series of Roman letters. She watched what he was at with slitted, suspicious eyes until it dawned on her that he was writing the letters of her name with the vodka glasses.

Her christened name. S-O-P-H-I-A. But – how does he know that?

Ooo-er, she thought. The familiar, goose-walking-over-a-grave feeling that Tom-Tit-Tot suffers in the old story. She hated to be called, by strangers, Sophia.

'An old Russian custom,' he said, giving her a stiff little bow. 'In your honour.'

Then he filled up all the glasses to the brim with vodka.

He's never –

One by one, he knocked each back. She counted, mesmerised. Thirty-five.

And still on his feet!

At this point, she formed the opinion the Grand Duke was not as other men and could have wished, after all, that she *had* let Lizzie come along.

'A little caviare?' he offered.

She enjoyed caviare, which she preferred to eat with a soup spoon, and judged it best to fortify herself against whatever might happen next. While she tucked in, the Grand Duke said: 'You shall have music with your supper. You must know I am a great collector of all kinds of *objets d'art* and marvels. Of all things, I love best toys – marvellous and unnatural artefacts.'

He winked at her in a manner she found lewd and offensive. It occurred to her: has he believed the Colonel's story? does he think I'm really made of rubber? If so – where does he imagine the caviare is going to?

He pressed a button at the side of the stove and a section of the bookcase with which the walls were lined flew up. The gilded leather spines were only so much painted *trompe l'oeil* all the time! A musical trio, all together on a round, wheeled podium, rolled forward out of the dark cavity within the wall. The wall fell back into place with a soft thud.

These musicians were almost full-grown, about the size of Sicilian puppets, only a little less large than we are and constructed of precious metals, semi-precious stones and the plumage of birds, which last made Fevvers shudder as a cowboy does when he sees a blond scalp on an Indian's belt.

And, indeed, one was in the very shape of a bird, of a thrush or a nightingale, but a very big bird, and the skilled artisan who made it had given it a Joseph's coat of feathers of all kinds of soft, dark, winy, topazy colours and sharp little eyes of red gemstones. It stood on two sturdy legs scaled in overlapping shingles of beaten gold. Instead of a beak it bore a flute, an intricately carved flute, of ivory.

There was a stringed instrument, too; a harp or lyre in the form of a hollow woman, or, rather, a woman with no torso. For there was a head, and shoulders, and breasts, and there was a pelvis, but there was nothing in between the breasts and the pelvis except a set of strings attached to pegs on either side. She had arms, too, arms extended in a supplicatory gesture that had come about quite accidentally for they were stuck where they were when the mechanism that operated her last wound down. Her arms terminated in beautiful, cunningly articulated hands, with fingers and fingernails, all complete, and she was made of gold, with mother-of-pearl for the fingernails, and a mass of hair made of golden wires, and fine eyes of lapis lazuli on white enamel. At the impulse of a random current of air, she emitted a single, ghostly twang of her own accord.

The percussion section was the least unnerving. It was just a bronze gong, set in an ebony frame, but there was no sign of a gong-stick.

The Grand Duke surveyed his clockwork orchestra with a satisfied air. A bored Emperor commissioned them long ago, in China. A mandarin murdered the Emperor to obtain them. A bored ancestor of the Grand Duke's murdered the mandarin to get them for himself. They had the authentically priceless glamour of objects intended only for pleasure, the impure allure of the absolutely functionless. The Grand Duke pressed another button.

The gong agitated itself and gave out a sweet thunder. The golden shoulder of the female harp moved, and, in moving, set in motion a complex, hidden mechanism of wheels and pulleys that drew up her elbows and brought the hands against the heart-strings. Her golden fingers, her pearly fingernails, flexed and stretched. She plucked a chord from herself, while the big bird whistled down its nose a strange, tritonic, almost-melody that meandered through its mathematical possibilities in a time that did not seem to be that of this planet but of some remote and freezing elsewhere.

Fevvers thought: there's a musical box inside the bird. And, anyone who could make a grandfather clock could put that harpy together. And, the gong is sounded by electrical impulses. All the same, the hairs on her nape rose and the Grand Duke turned to her a satisfied smile, as if, all along, he intended her to be afraid of him.

For the first time in her life, she refused champagne.

Adding another percussive note to the uncanny harmonies, a drip fell from the nose of the ice Fevvers and struck the glass rim of the caviare dish with a plink. For an aghast moment, she thought a diamond had melted.

The Grand Duke gave her his arm: come to the gallery and inspect the rest of my collection! His breath, fiery with vodka, singed her cheek that, moment by moment, grew more chilly as the weird geometry of the haunting, circular, not-quite-random, fully inhuman music deformed the angles of the room.

The gallery was lined with glass cases lit up in such an ingeniously subdued way that each one glowed like a distinct little world.

'My eggs,' said the Grand Duke, 'are full of surprises.'

I bet, thought Fevvers.

Yet each glass case contained an egg, truly an egg, a wonderful egg that never came from a chicken but out of a jeweller's shop and he told her she could have whichever egg she chose just as soon as she took off her shawl and let him see her wings.

'Egg first.'

'After.'

'No.'

'Yes.'

'No.'

The Grand Duke shrugged and turned his back on her. All at once, every light in the place went out, leaving her in the dark with only the hooting, plucking and rattling of the artificial musicians down below for company and the faint plash as the ice dripped off her own effigy, down below. When she heard her nose melt, she felt faint.

'Very well,' she said sulkily. When the lights came on, her shawl was off and the Grand Duke went behind her to take a good look at the twin swellings in her bodice.

'But you can't touch!' she said. Even in this extremity, some steely edge in her fishwife's voice made him keep his hands to himself.

What inwards things his eggs were! And, indeed, full of surprises. For this one is made of pink enamel and opens up lengthwise to reveal an inner carapace of mother-of-pearl which, in turn, opens to reveal a spherical yolk of hollow gold. Inside the yolk, a golden hen. Inside the hen, a golden egg. Now we have diminished to the scale of Lilliput but we have not done yet; inside the egg there is the tiniest of picture-frames, set with minute brilliants. And what should the frame contain but a miniature of the *aerialiste* herself, in full spread as on the trapeze and yellow of hair, blue of eye as in life.

In spite of the increasing sense of diminishment she felt, and the odd shapes the music made of the corners of the room, Fevvers was flattered by this tiny tribute and her crude sense of justice told her it was only fair to give the Grand Duke permission to run his hands over her breasts and round beneath her armpits. After he ascertained she was not made of rubber, he sighed, perhaps with pleasure, and started to agitate the plumage rustling under the red satin.

Squeak, twang, bang and splash from below; squeak, twang, bang and splash.

A simple egg of jade sat in a gem-encrusted egg-cup in the next case, as if waiting for a spoon to tap it. Fevvers gazed expectantly at the Grand Duke, eager as a child, in spite of her apprehension. She guessed there was more to the egg than that. He left off his fumbling for a moment.

'Let me turn the little key . . . '

Noticing how his virile member now briskly outlined itself under the whipcord of his riding breeches, she bethought herself that, in some respect, he *must* be the same as other men and gave it a brisk, conciliatory pat, as if telling it to bide its time.

The egg-shell fell apart in two hollow halves, revealing a little tree in a tub of white agate overlaid with gold trelliswork. The tree was covered with leaves individually carved from dark green semi-precious stones. Its golden boughs were studded with flowers made out of pearls split four ways round a diamond centre and fruits made of citrine. The Duke reluctantly released his right hand from its business under her shoulder-blades and touched one of these fruits. It, too, split open and out flew the smallest of all possible birds, made of red gold. It moved its head from side to side, flapped its wings and opened its beak and a shrill sweet warbling came out: 'Only a bird in a gilded cage'. Fevvers gave a start. It finished the chorus, folded its wings and the hollow jade closed over again.

For all the delight she felt to see this beautiful toy, Fevvers found this tree and its bird exceedingly troubling and turned away from it with a sense of imminent and deadly danger.

Oooo-er, she said to herself, again.

Squeak, twang, bang and splash; squeak, twang, bang and splash. And she felt more and more vague, less and less her own mistress. Walser would have recognised the sensation which gripped her; he had felt much the same in her dressing-room at the Alhambra, when midnight struck the third time.

I *may* be getting out of my depth, she thought. Oh, Lizzie, Lizzie, my darling! Where are you now that I need you!

All the same, since fair is fair and he deserved *something* for going to so much trouble, she reached round behind her and unfastened the hooks and eyes at the back of her dress. There was a swishing rush of released plumage and the Grand Duke exclaimed softly under his breath. Nuzzling away, he begged her to spread a little more and she did, whilst, although he did not ask her to, a deep instinct of self-preservation made her let his rooster out of the hen-coop for him and ruffle up its feathers, as he was ruffling hers.

Yet it was then, as her eyes went round the shadowy, two-tiered room, that she saw there were no windows anywhere and, when the Grand Duke's arms tightened around her, she realised he was a man of quite exceptional physical strength, sufficient to pin even her to the ground.

Then the worst she could, at that moment, imagine happened. His investigation of her torso flushed out Nelson's sword from its hiding place in her corset.

'Give me that back – '

But he held the lethal toy out of her reach, examining it curiously, chuckling under his moustache before he bent his knee to snap the sword in two across it. He sent the pieces flying to either end of the gallery, where they disappeared in the darkness that was seeping in through the walls like water. Now she was defenceless. She could have wept.

Down below, the mechanical musicians continued to play and the ice continued to melt.

She gathered together her scattered wits as well as she could and moved resolutely on to the next case, continuing to manipulate him as she did so, as if her life depended on it. He dragged his feet, growing so blissful he scarcely noticed her open the case with her free hand.

And, here, inside a silver egg criss-crossed by a lattice of amethyst chips, she found, to her incredulous delight, nothing less than a model train – an engine, in black enamel, and one, two, three, four first-class carriages in tortoiseshell and ebony, all coiled round one another like a snake, with, engraved on the side of each in Cyrillic, the legend *The Trans-Siberian Express.*

'I'll have that one!' she cried, reaching in greedily. Her exclamation and sudden movement roused the Grand Duke from the trance she had induced, although she never stopped caressing him; she'd not served her apprenticeship at Ma Nelson's academy for nothing.

'No, no, no,' he forbade her, although his voice was glutinous with tumescence. He weakly slapped the hand that held the train but she did not let go. 'Not that one. The *next* one's for you. I ordered it especially. They delivered it this morning.'

It was white gold and topped with a lovely little swan, a tribute, perhaps, to her putative paternity. And, as she suspected, it contained a cage made out of gold wires with, inside, a little perch of rubies and of sapphires and of diamonds, the good old red, white and blue. The cage was empty. No bird stood on that perch, yet.

Fevvers did not shrink; but was at once aware of the hideous possibility she might do so. She said goodbye to the diamond necklace down below and contemplated life as a toy. With oriental inscrutability, the automatic orchestra laid down the geometrics of the implausible and, by the thickening of his member, the movements that now came of their own accord, by his panting breath and glazed eye, Fevvers judged the Grand Duke's time was nigh.

Then came a wet crash and clatter as the ice-carving of herself collapsed into the remains of the caviare in the room below, casting the necklace which had tempted her amongst the dirty supper things. The bitter knowledge she'd been fooled spurred Fevvers into action. She dropped the toy train on the Isfahan runner – mercifully, it landed on its wheels – as, with a grunt and whistle of expelled breath, the Grand Duke ejaculated.

In those few seconds of his lapse of consciousness, Fevvers ran helter-skelter down the platform, opened the door of the first-class compartment and clambered aboard.

'Look what a mess he's made of your dress, the pig,' said Lizzie.

The weeping girl threw herself into the woman's arms. It was the dark abyss of the night, into which moon plunges. In this abyss she had lost her magic sword. The station master blew his whistle and waved the flag. The train, slowly, slowly, began to pull its great length out of the station, dragging with it its freight of dreams.

'I've learned my lesson' said Fevvers and, sitting up, ripped off her bracelet and earrings.

There was a sudden flurry and a burst of outraged boyish protest in the corridor. The door of their stateroom burst open and in came Walser, clutching in his arms a kicking, vehemently protesting little bundle dressed up in a clown's clothing.

'Sorry to disturb you, ma'am,' he said to Fevvers. 'But *this* young gazooney ain't gonna run away with the circus, not for a few years yet!'

The train slid slowly past a platform thickly piled with freshly fallen snow. Lizzie let down the window, letting in a gust of cold air, and Walser dropped the howling child outside, inside a snowdrift.

'Now pick yourself up and run straight home to granny!'

'And give her *these*!' cried Fevvers.

Little Ivan rolled in the snow, pelted with diamonds. Through our children we might be saved, perhaps.

The train picked up a little speed. Walser hung out of the stateroom window until he was quite sure that Little Ivan had not jumped back on board further down the train, then hauled the window up again on its thick leather strap. When all was secure, he turned back to the occupants of the carriage and was struck dumb to see Fevvers, raddled with tears, hair coming down, again, gypsy dress ripped and clotted with semen, trying as best she could to cover her bare breasts with a filthy but incontrovertible tangle of pin feathers.

SIBERIA

ONE

How do they live, here? How do they cope with it? Or aren't I the right one to pop the question, I'm basically out of sympathy with landscape, I get the shivers on Hampstead bloody Heath. As soon as I'm out of sight of the abodes of humanity, my heart gives way beneath me like rotten floorboards, my courage fails. Now parks, I love, and gardens. And small fields with hedges and ditches round 'em and useful cows in 'em. But if you *must* have a wild hillside, let there be at least a sheep or two posed picturesquely on an outcrop of rock, ready to have its wool wound off, something like that . . . I hate to be where the hand of Man has badly wrought and, here, we are on that broad forehead of the world that had the mark of Cain branded on it when the world began, just as the old man at the station who came selling us the bears he'd carved had 'convict' branded on his cheek.

I bought all the bears he had, to send home to the children when we reach Vladivostok and a post-office. You couldn't call it a 'cheap' gesture, he charged enough for the things, I'm sorry to say. *And* I got an earful along with it, for Lizzie swore I 'did it for posterity', meaning, for the young American to take note of.

'Since he made himself known to us in Petersburg, you've been acting more and more *like* yourself,' she says.

Outside the window, there slides past that unimaginable and deserted vastness where night is coming on, the sun declining in ghastly blood-streaked splendour like a public execution across, it would seem, half a continent, where live only bears and shooting stars and the wolves who lap congealing ice from water that holds within it the entire sky. All white with snow as if under dustsheets, as if laid away eternally as soon as brought back from the shop, never to be used or touched. Horrors! And, as on a cyclorama, this unnatural spectacle rolls past at twenty-odd miles an hour in a tidy frame of lace curtains only a little the worse for soot and drapes of a heavy velvet of dark, dusty blue.

The rasp of charcoal in the corridor means they're stoking up the samovar for tea. How cosy we are.

Brass monkey weather, outside, but, in our carriage, snug and warm – there's a little stove. And a round table with a velvet cover, blue to match the curtains, and an easy chair upholstered likewise in which our Lizzie sits, dealing out a game of patience for herself.

Patience. Give me patience.

'What I mean is, you grow more and more like your own publicity,' says Lizzie. 'Ever the golden-hearted Cockney who don't stand on ceremony. Huh.'

'Well, who *am* I supposed to be like, then, if not meself,' I snap bad-temperedly, lying on my belly like Miss O'Malley as needs must, on the seat they make up into my bed at nights.

'That's another question, innit,' she replies, unperturbed as ever. 'You never existed before. There's nobody to say what you should do or how to do it. You are Year One. You haven't any history and there are no expectations of you except the ones you yourself create. But when you come a cropper, Gawd – you *really* come a cropper, don't you. You *flirt* with the adversary, as if he'll put by his wiles if you pretend to be an ordinary gal. I'm afraid for you. That's why I don't like leaving you alone. Remember that bloody Grand Duke. Broke your mascot you set such store by, didn't he!'

She knows how to hurt. Find the sore point, then probe it – that's Liz's style.

'Broke your mascot and could have broken *you*. He nearly did for you once and for all, and then, no future, no Year Two nor any more years. Nix, nought, nothing.'

Nothing.

The train now ground to a halt with an exhausted sigh. The engine wailed softly, the locking wheels clicked and groaned but nothing in sight, not even one of those frilly little wooden stations like gingerbread houses they put up in these parts, mocking the wilderness with their suggestion of the fairy tale. Nothing but streaks of snow standing out unnaturally white against the purple horizon, miles away. We are in the middle of nowhere.

'Nowhere', one of those words, like 'nothing', that opens itself inside you like a void. And were we not progressing through the vastness of nothing to the extremities of nowhere?

Sometimes the lengths to which I'll go for money appal me.

In the sudden, almost supernatural silence, we could hear the rumble of a tiger's roar and the ting-a-ling of the chains of the elephants, which never ceases.

Tuskers through Siberia! The hubris of the little fat Colonel!

Often the train made these incomprehensible halts. Out of the taiga like imps conjured from air children would spring up and run along the side of the track holding out little offerings – a baked potato; a paper cone of frost-bitten berries; sour milk in a bottle too precious to be sold, so you fill up your own cut-glass water-flask with its contents. But, by tonight, we've rolled far too far away from any peasant homestead or settlement. The tow-headed, filthy hawkers never venture here, where wild things are.

A cold wind began to get up a bit, and whine.

'I say, our Liz, can't we . . . hurry things up a bit?'

Lizzie, at her cards, shook her old grizzled head. No tricks. Why not? For the things my foster-mother can pull off when she sets her mind to it, you'd not believe! Shrinkings and swellings and clocks running ahead or behind you like frisky dogs; but there's a logic to it, some logic of scale and dimension that won't be meddled with, which she alone keeps the key of, like she keeps the key of Nelson's timepiece stowed away in her handbag and won't let me touch.

Her 'household' magic, she calls it. What would you think, when you saw the bread rise, if you didn't know what yeast was? Think old Liz was a witch, wouldn't you! And, then, again, consider matches! Lucifers; the little wooden soldiers of the angel of light, with whom you'd think she was in complicity if you'd never heard of phosphorus.

And when I think I once sucked milk from those flat old, dry old dugs under your black silk bodice, Lizzie, oh, yes! I know what you mean by 'magic'.

Now, down the train, in the 'wagon salon', there's the Princess trying out the parlour organ there. Grunt, grunt, grunt. Oh, such ecstasies of boredom I experienced on the Great Siberian Railway!

Not that the 'wagon salon' isn't very pleasant, if it don't give you the willies to travel through this wilderness as of the pre-Adamite world in a repro Empire drawing-room done up in white lacquer and enough plate-glass mirrors for a mobile bordello.

I hate it.

We have no right to be here, in all this *gemütlich* comfort, stuck on our fat bums down this straight track from which we never deviate, like tightrope walkers in a dream traversing an unacknowledged abyss in five-star comfort, through the deep core of winter and this inimical terrain.

'Feel like a bird in a gilded cage, do you?' inquired Lizzie, noting her foster-daughter's fidgeting. 'Then how would you prefer to travel?'

Fevvers, thus pushed, could think of no reply. The springs twanged beneath her as she rearranged herself in order to squat on her haunches with her sulky chin on her knees and her muscular hands clenched round her femurs. How long have we been grinding through Limbo? One week? Two weeks? A month? A year?

The Princess at last had her way with the parlour organ and produced from it a Bach fugue that hushed the tigers while the world tilted away from the sun towards night, winter and the new century.

'Think of your bank account, dearie,' Lizzie ironically advised her sullen foster-child. 'You know it always cheers you up.'

Fevvers, in her petticoat, stockingless, corsetless, dug in Lizzie's handbag for a pair of little scissors and began to clip her toenails for want of anything better to do. She presented a squalid spectacle, a dark half-inch at the roots of her uncombed hair which tangled with the dishevelled plumage that had already assumed a dusty look. Confinement did not suit her.

Then, as she clipped away at her toenails, just as the train had stopped for no reason, so, for no reason, she began to grizzle.

How can I tell why I began to blubber away like that? Who hasn't cried since Ma Nelson died. But to think of Ma Nelson's funeral only made me bellow more, as if the enormous anguish that I felt, this anguish of the solitude of our abandoned state in this world that is perfectly sufficient to itself without us – as if my sudden and irrational despair hooked itself on to a rational grief and clung there for dear life.

'Cry away!' said Lizzie, and, by the echoes in her voice, her foster-daughter knew a prescient fit had seized her. 'Cry all you like! We don't know if you'll get enough time to cry later on.'

Inexplicably as it had halted, the train now moved off again. In the hard class, the clowns played cards under a mauve canopy of cigarette smoke, or slept. A heavy somnolence was upon them; they seemed in a state of suspended animation, here and yet not here. Now and then, one or another of them would remark they'd have to work out a whole set of new routines now that Buffo was gone. 'Time enough for that,' came the reply. Yet the days passed and they did no more than shuffle and reshuffle the cards. The rocking-horse rhythm of the train lulled them into a state of passive acquiescence in which they waited, though none would admit it, for their Christ to rise again. So there was no need of new routines, no need. Pass the bottle, deal out the pack again. He will come back. Or else . . . we shall return to Him.

The Colonel, however, trotted up and down the corridors a-bubble with the excitement of the pathfinder, a striking figure in his striped leotards and starry vest – 'showing the flag', he called it. He'd brought ample supplies of bourbon with him and soon taught the steward in the restaurant car to fix a passable julep using sprigs from a pot of mint he'd had the forethought to pick up from a Petersburg horticulturalist.

He soon acquired the reputation of a 'character'. He and his pig often rode in the cabin with the engineer. The engineer leant back with the papirosse glued to his nether lip and let the Colonel frolic at the controls. But, most of all, the Colonel enjoyed visiting the elephants, feeding them buns he bought by the hamperful from kerchiefed peasant women at the wayside halts and contemplating the dazzling occurrence; that he, this good old boy from Kentucky, had bested Hannibal, the Carthaginian, classical hero of antiquity, for, if Hannibal had taken his jumbos over the Alps, had he not himself taken his bulls over the Urals?

Yet, even to his always optimistic eye, it was apparent the bulls were taking the trip badly. They were housed comfortably enough, lapped in straw in a cattle truck that usually took immigrants across the steppes, and, a special measure for the pachyderms' comfort, this truck had been equipped with a stove. But the elephants no longer resembled the pillars of the world, capable of supporting the sky on their broad foreheads. Their little eyes were filled with rheum and sometimes they coughed. The train took them further and further into bitter weather that would penetrate their leather boots and freeze their feet, invade and devastate their lungs. Far north, much further north, in the extreme, unimaginable north of which this terrain was the, comparatively speaking, temperate margin, their cousins, the mammoths, lay locked in ice; so it seemed that ice was already overcoming these caryatids of the world and the Colonel, for all the Polyanna in his soul, was yet seized by isolated and wounding moments of doubt when he saw the bulls were weakening, succumbing. Then he would urge the conductor to feed more charcoal to the stove; surely they suffered just a chill . . . and, as to their depression, why, a few buns would cheer them up!

He bit down upon his doubts as upon an aching tooth and refused to believe his eyes.

These days, the tigers watched the Princess in the same way their little cousins who live amongst us watch a bird in a tree too high to climb. The Princess petitioned the Colonel, via the medium of Mignon, who now spoke for her and was roughly translated by Fevvers, to let her commandeer the 'wagon salon', and the Colonel, after much cigar mastication, permitted her to do so on the advice of Sybil, who thought a change of scene would distract them all. None of the conductors dared enter the 'wagon salon' thereafter but the tigers appreciated their new quarters in their own way. They ripped open the pale brocade with which the armchairs were upholstered, made nests of the stuffing and cuffed at their reflections in the mirrors that took up their stripes and multiplied them while Mignon leant against the Princess's shoulder and they tried out a whole new repertoire to suit the organ, sentimental parlour songs, Bach chorales, the Methodist hymn-book, anything that might calm the tigers' spirits. But the Princess knew the cats no longer trusted her and, worst of all, nor did she trust them. She was consumed with guilt and despair because she had used her gun.

The Colonel did not like to hear the parlour organ since, when he thought of the corpse of the tigress, the fatal last night at Petersburg came back to him in a fugue of failure. Indeed, his constant excitement had something febrile and desperate about it, for the apes had left him in the lurch, his master clown had somersaulted out of the ring into the madhouse – the Princess's loss wasn't the half of it. And, in his heart, although his head hotly denied it, he knew the elephants grew each day more feeble. It was a singularly depleted Grand Circus he would present before the God Emperor of Japan unless he could acquire, on the way, a performing bear or two, perhaps. Siberia could afford no other kind of recruit.

He knew full well that those who play the Ludic Game sometimes win but sometimes . . . lose. (Oh, those humiliating headlines in *Variety*!) His heart missed a beat when Mignon sang: 'Oh, sacred head, sore wounded', and he imagined his own scrubby pate buffeted by fortune.

Outside the 'wagon salon', the Strong Man stood with folded arms. He was the watchdog.

If Samson's heart still knocked in his chest like a bird in a box when he saw the frail shape of Mignon, he'd learned to subdue himself sufficiently to fetch and carry humbly for the girls, to muck out for them, assist them with all the tasks to which his muscles condemned him.

Unrequited love was performing a peculiar alchemy within the Strong Man and yet the object of his love was changing its nature. Stark lust for lost Mignon slowly resolved itself, out of sheer propinquity, into an awed veneration for these beings who seemed, as a pair, to transcend their individualities. He knew he could not love the one without the other as he could not love the singer without her song, and must love both without touching either, so, by degrees, he grew less physical. He'd taken to wearing clothes, a visible sign of his changing sense of himself, had bought himself a stout, belted Russian shirt and in it looked already less of a hulk. He nourished his sensibility, which was still at the stripling stage, by standing guard over them.

He let the Colonel pass with a curt nod.

The Colonel counted his blessings over fish soup in the dining car: thank God! he retained exclusive use of the Cockney Venus!

The mellow pink shade of the table lamp soothed the hysterical brilliance of the rouge with which she had concealed the traces of her fit of tears. Although a corset was too much to contemplate, tonight, she had made a token effort to dress up to first class standards, put on a tea-gown of cream lace and pinned up her hair so that you did not notice her dark parting, but the tea-gown, cut to drape over her bosom, was unbecoming, giving her a middle-aged, thickening look, and her pinned-up curls were drooping, already. The 'lucky' violets bravely pinned on her shoulder were unconvincing imitations, cheap, tatty things, a child's birthday present, perhaps.

The waiter watched with fascination as the Colonel tied a napkin round Sybil's neck.

'Pigs eat everything a man eats,' he informed the table. 'That's why a man tastes same as a pig. That's why cannibals called roasted *homo sapiens* "long pig", yessir! Omnivores, see; mixed feedin'! Gives us both that gamey taste.'

As if the notion of cannibalism refreshed his appetite, he attacked a veal cutlet with gusto, although, by its texture, the cutlet had been cooked in the station buffet at Irkutsk several days before, loaded on the train and reheated in a gravy far too bright a brown for authenticity.

As for me, I slipped the nasty thing on my own plate across to Sybil, who speedily despatched it just as the Colonel said she would. I'd a great affection for the clever little pig, I must say, and she looked well on travel, far better than I did. Her ruff was as pristine as the day we left Petersburg, more so; who did the Colonel get to goffer it for him? The girl who looked after the samovar? The steward? And she shone with the oilings the Colonel was never too far gone in his cups to give her and I thought, I could do with a massage meself, if it was young Jack-me-lad give it to me.

Here he comes.

What *is* it this young man reminds me of? A piece of music composed for one instrument and played on another. An oil sketch for a great canvas. Oh, yes; he's unfinished, just as Lizzie says, but all the same — his sun-burned bones! His sun-bleached hair! Underneath his make-up, that face like a beloved face known long ago, and lost, and now returned, although I never knew him before, although he is a stranger, still that face which I have always loved before I ever saw it so that to see him is to remember, although I do not know who it is I then remember, except it might be the vague, imaginary face of desire.

Absentmindedly she bit into a chunk of bread that had the colour and texture of devil's food cake. As the Colonel took Sybil on his lap to make hospitable room for Walser, the young man felt the hungry eyes upon him and it seemed to him her teeth closed on his flesh with the most voluptuous lack of harm.

All she had done was to define the necessary innocence of the adventurer and to take advantage of it.

Spoon chinked upon soup-plate; knife ground against cutlet; the fringed pink lamps swayed this way and that, reflected in the dark windows as if they might be blooms upon the branches of the enfilades of trees through which they now were passing; the waiters rolled suavely to and fro as if on invisible wheels with dishes lined along their arms; from the invisible kitchen came the clatter of pans. There was a macedonia of fruit for dessert.

Then, just as the Princess and Mignon arrived in the restaurant car in bloody aprons, Samson dogging their footsteps, on the way to the kitchen to collect the tigers' dinners, there came a thunderous boom. And, as if at the command of the biggest drum-roll in the entire history of the circus, the dining-car rose up in the air.

For a split second, everything levitated — lamps, tables, tablecloths. The waiters rose, and the plates rose from their arms. Sybil was lifted up, as was the chunk of canned pineapple on which her jaws were just about to close. The feet of the dark girl and the fair girl in the doorway were propelled upwards from the rising floor. Then, before shock or consternation could cross their faces, the whole lot fell down again and, with a rending crash, flew apart in a multitude of fragments.

The train immediately ceased to be a train and turned into so many splinters of wood, so much twisted metal, so many screams and cries, while the forest on either side of the devastated track burst aflame, ignited by the burning logs cast far and wide from the fire-box of the now demolished engine.

The giantess found herself trapped under the collapsed table at which she'd been engaged in picking pale maraschino cherries from her macedonia and spooning them into the dish of the pet pig. Her first emotions were surprise and indignation. Nearby in the dark, her foster-mother expostulated eloquently in her native dialect but none of Lizzie's tricks could get them out of *this* hole. Only the strength of the muscles Fevvers now stretched to their fullest extent would shift the wreckage and let them and their bruises scramble out into the open air which in itself was hazardous, filled with flame and flying debris. The wind, now risen to a gale, scorched them.

I have broken my right wing. As the first shock passes, I feel the pain. It hurts. Hurts as much as a clean fracture in the forearm. But no more. A lot to be thankful for. I can still keep the use of my right arm, even though the wing is broken. God, it hurts. Could be worse. Keep a stiff upper lip, girl; keep on telling yourself how it could be worse!

Indeed, it seems all we in the restaurant car were fortunate. Here's Mignon surfaced! Having sustained a black eye from the blow of a flying brandy bottle but otherwise unhurt, she's dragging the Princess out from under a cascade of crockery and silverware that has cut and scratched and concussed her. Lizzie gives a quick check, no bones broken, but she can't wake up the Princess, who has passed out . . . As for the Colonel, it must be *he* who's made of india-rubber, not I, for here he comes bouncing out of the rubble with his pig safe in the bosom of his jacket. Did Sybil foresee *this* fix, for all her talent as a seer? Did she, hell! Her ruff is a casualty, though; flat as a pancake. The Colonel strips her off, from now on this little pig will go naked.

Of my young man, no sign.

Then, amongst the ruins of the 'wagon salon', I beheld a great wonder. For the tigers were all gone into the mirrors. How to describe it. The 'wagon salon' lay on its side, ripped open like the wrappings of a Christmas toy by an impatient child, and, of those lovely creatures, not a trace of blood or sinew, nothing. Only pile upon pile of broken shards of mirror, that segmented the blazing night around us in a thousand jagged dissociations so you might think, if you had time or patience to fit them back together, then, suddenly, all would be as it had been before, the forest, the plain, the twin tracks of the railway lines bearing forwards towards the infinity of the horizon the pretty little carriages and the puffing train which now seemed to me to have been a kind of gauntlet flung down in the face of Nature – a grand gesture of defiance which Nature had picked up, then tossed disdainfully back upon the heaving earth, shattering it into fragments.

And, as for the tigers, as if Nature disapproved of them for their unnatural dancing, they had frozen into their own reflections and been shattered, too, when the mirrors broke. As if that burning energy you glimpsed between the bars of their pelts had convulsed in a great response to the energy released in fire around us and, in exploding, they scattered their appearances upon that glass in which they had been breeding sterile reduplications. On one broken fragment of mirror, a paw with the claws out; on another, a snarl. When I picked up a section of flank, the glass burned my fingers and I dropped it.

Mignon was cuddling the Princess in her arms. Now and then, tiger-fashion herself, she licked the forehead next to her shoulder. But what shall the tamer do when the beasts are gone? Or Orpheus without his lute, for that matter? For I could not guess where her own piano might have got to and the parlour organ from the 'wagon salon' lay higgledy piggledy in bits on the melting snow, a random collection of pipes as if there had been a cataclysm in a plumber's.

It was a frosty night yet the snow melted in the heat. Up above, you never saw such stars.

And of my clown, no trace.

But the rest of Clown Alley began to heave and bubble up from the smithereens of the hard class, wiping the rubble out of its eyes. Accustomed as they were to catastrophe, it was no more to them than any other incendiary vehicle, I dare say, and their dogs shook themselves and ran around and snapped and whined and got under everybody's feet and still I couldn't find him.

Retain the use of my hands as I may, I'm in some discomfort. Imagine you've got an extra arm, hinged on at the back, and it's dangling down, it's broken.

I got down on my knees in the dining-car, excavating a cache of veal cutlets that had broken out of the ice-box and were littering up a place where my bewildered eyes thought they'd glimpsed a movement, and the conductors and the engineers and every single one of the waiters, all in one piece more or less, or so it seemed, came to jostle me and impede my search as they quested for the train's supply of vodka, but, of the young fellow who was *my* quest, not so much as a great toe or a little finger I could keep in a locket as a souvenir.

Then a soft, moist, questing thing attacked me in the back of the neck, causing me to jump. It was, for God's sake, the tip of the trunk of an elephant.

For, poor things, it turns out this very moment should be the fated moment, the moment of destiny, when indeed their chains all parted and they were free! Yet free for what? They achieve their longed-for liberty at just the moment when it won't do them any good!

They'd smashed their way easily out of the remains of their confinement and, formed up in a line good as gold, some passed bits of wreckage along to one another while others filled their trunks with melted snow and squirted upon the fires in an attempt to put them out. All this as though they'd never heard tell of pneumonia. The jumbos were a lesson to us all and, had we the chance to join them in their sterling work, no doubt we'd have left the wreck neat as a new pin by morning but we were forced to leave them to it because, while I was digging away for some relic of the young American, all we survivors of Colonel Kearney's circus were kidnapped, every one.

Liz said it was as though our abductors materialised out of a copse of birches, like guardian spirits of the woods – a band of rough-looking coves in sheepskins, armed to their teeth. Evidently they lacked ponies or draught beasts for one or two of these men were dragging odd contraptions behind them – long poles of larchwood with leather strips criss-crossing them, the kind of cart you might invent if you hadn't thought of the wheel. They'd come as if prepared to ferry away the injured, although only the Princess lies in need of a stretcher. They barked out a few orders of which my friends understood not one word, being reluctant linguists, but the language of the gun is picked up very quickly and our captors soon nudged them into a column with their rifle butts.

But I've no proper recollection of all this; I only know what Liz told me. That I am screeching like one possessed as I scratch and scrabble in the wreckage and push them pettishly away when they come prodding me with their guns. At which I'm picked up bodily and dropped on my face in one of the carts. Lizzie thinks to throw over me a blanket which she's salvaged as I am too far gone to think of covering meself up.

So off we go at gun-point, and the rest of the survivors, why, they don't give a monkey's! They've just found the liquor cupboard and don't so much as turn their heads to look though Liz says I'm making an awful racket. But I remember nothing.

They say the Angel Tubiel watches over *small* birds but I'm a little on the large side for such protection; big birds must look after themselves, so I'd better snap out of it sharpish, hadn't I!

TWO

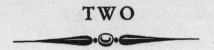

Walser was buried alive in a profound sleep. Knocked out by a blow on the head when a cupboard door in the bulkhead above him flew open, he immediately submerged beneath an avalanche of stowed-away tablecloths and napkins, some clean, some soiled. The busy elephants piled various other items from the demolished dining-car, cruets, corkscrews, boxes of biscuits, on top of the soft tomb in which his adventures would have ended except, after a lapse of time and consciousness, a murderess came and dug him up.

THREE

Although no signpost points the way there and even the track made by the shackled feet of its inhabitants in the course of the dolorous journey to the place is soon obscured by the rapid summer growth of mosses and small plants or erased by winter's snow so that no trace remains of their arrivals, we are in the vicinity of the settlement of R., near which, in the year, 18—, the Countess P., having successfully poisoned her husband over a period of years with an arsenical compound and got away with it, and finding herself, in her widowhood, much possessed by the idea that other women had committed the same crime as she with less success, set up, with the permission of the government, a private asylum for female criminals of the same stripe as herself.

Do not run away with the idea it was a sense of sisterhood that moved her. If, though the years passed, she herself never forgot the precise nature of the seasonings she'd added to her late husband's borsht and piroshkis, she assuaged the conscience that pricked her by becoming, or so she claimed, a kind of conduit for the means of the repentance of the other murderesses.

With the aid of a French criminologist who dabbled in phrenology, she selected from the prisons of the great Russian cities women who had been found guilty of killing their husbands and whose bumps indicated the possibility of salvation. She established a community on the most scientific lines available and had the female convicts build it for themselves out of the same kind of logic that persuaded the Mexican *federales* to have those they were about to shoot dig their own graves.

It was a *panopticon* she forced them to build, a hollow circle of cells shaped like a doughnut, the inward-facing wall of which was composed of grids of steel and, in the middle of the roofed, central courtyard, there was a round room surrounded by windows. In that room she'd sit all day and stare and stare and stare at her murderesses and they, in turn, sat all day and stared at her.

There are many reasons, most of them good ones, why a woman should want to murder her husband; homicide might be the only way for her to preserve a shred of dignity at a time, in a place, where women were deemed chattels, or, in the famous analogy of Tolstoy, like wine bottles that might conveniently be smashed when their contents were consumed. No reasonable female would hold it against their Countess P. that she poisoned her obese, oafish count, although the blend of boredom and avarice that prompted her to do so was in itself the product of privilege – she suffered sufficient leisure to be bored; her husband's wealth provoked her greed. But, as for Olga Alexandrovna, who took a hatchet to the drunken carpenter who hit her around once too often, Olga Alexandrovna acted out of a conviction that His eye was on the sparrow and therefore on even such a weak, timorous and unworthy creature as herself, so that the life being beaten out of her was surely worth as much, in the general scheme of things, as the life of the man with the fists – perhaps, since she was a loving mother, more. But it turned out the court thought otherwise than she and so, for a time, she suffered atrocious pangs to find the court believed she was a wicked woman.

'You're in luck,' the turnkey told the convicted woman after the French phrenologist measured her head and asked the court that she should be transferred to the Countess's 'scientific establishment for the study of female criminals'. Good luck, indeed! No hard labour, no flogging for Olga Alexandrovna, bound as she was for the Countess's seminary. And the turnkey laughed, raped her and chained her. Next day, she set out for Siberia.

During the hours of darkness, the cells were lit up like so many small theatres in which each actor sat by herself in the trap of her visibility in those cells shaped like servings of *baba au rhum*. The Countess, in the observatory, sat in a swivelling chair whose speed she could regulate at will. Round and round she went, sometimes at a great rate, sometimes slowly, raking with her ice-blue eyes – she was of Prussian extraction – the tier of unfortunate women surrounding her. She varied her speeds so that the inmates were never able to guess beforehand at just what moment they would come under her surveillance.

As for the inmates, indeed they toiled not, neither did they spin, just as Olga Alexandrovna's turnkey had foretold. Not even the lash disturbed the even tenor of their days. They were fed morning and evening; the food, black bread, millet porridge, broth, was delivered through a grille and it was certainly as good, if not better than Olga Alexandrovna was accustomed to. A bucket of water arrived in the mornings, when the previous day's toilet-pail was taken away and a fresh one delivered. The bedding was changed once a month. No mail was permitted and the isolation of the place itself, far off in the taiga, would alone have precluded the possibility of visitors, even if they had not been strictly forbidden.

By the standards of the time and place, the Countess conducted her regime along humanitarian, if autocratic lines. Her private prison with its unorthodox selectivity was not primarily intended as the domain of punishment but, in the purest sense, a penitentiary – it was a machine designed to promote penitence.

For the Countess P. had conceived the idea of a therapy of meditation. The women in the bare cells, in which was neither privacy nor distraction, cells formulated on the principle of those in a nunnery where all was visible to the eye of God, would live alone with the memory of their crime until they acknowledged, not their guilt – most of them had done that, already – but their *responsibility*. And she was sure that with responsibility would come remorse.

Then she would let them go for, by their salvation, strenuously achieved through meditation on the crime they had committed, they would have procured hers.

But, so far, the gate had never opened to allow one single departure.

You could think of this wheel-shaped House of Correction as a kind of prayer-wheel, intended to rescue the Countess who was its hub from perdition, although the only thing in it which rotated like a wheel was herself, on her revolving chair.

Olga Alexandrovna was no great reader, although, unlike many of her neighbours, she knew her letters well enough, hard and pointless as the task of learning them had seemed when imposed on her in her childhood. All the same, she'd have liked the scriptures with her, to help her out in some of the ethical discussions she conducted with herself, but books were forbidden because they helped time pass.

So she sat and pondered, inside the House of Correction in which there was no hint of the wide world outside, for there were no windows to let in daylight, ventilation being provided by a system of ducts. Above the arched gateway that let in a glimpse of daylight only when it opened to admit another inmate, there was a clock that told the Moscow time that was not the time of these latitudes and this clock regulated their risings, their feedings, registered every slow minute of incarceration and sometimes the face of this clock seemed indistinguishable from the livid face of the Countess.

The Countess intended to look at them until they repented. But sometimes the women died, it would seem for no reason, or as if life, in that perverse honeycomb, was such a faint and faded thing that anything would be an improvement. When one died, a guard humped the corpse out of the cell and buried it under the paving stones of the circular passage in which they took their morning exercise. Even death was no escape from the House of Correction. As soon as a cell was empty, another murderess was delivered up to the gate which closed upon her with a definitive clang.

So the ordeal of penitence began; an ordeal constructed from a perfected variety of the bitterest loneliness, for you were never alone, here, where her gaze was continually upon you, and yet you were always alone.

But, so far, although the Countess lived in hope, not a single one of the objects of her gaze had shown the slightest quiver of remorse.

By the end of the third year of her incarceration, Olga Alexandrovna would never have said she was innocent; she'd always admitted her crime freely. But every day she offered extenuating circumstances to the lenient and merciful judge in her mind and every day they made more and more impression on the judge. Each night, before she stretched out on her straw mattress and slept, he brought in another verdict of self-defence, so that Olga Alexandrovna was more and more startled to wake up again in her cold cell to discover the eyes of the Countess raking over her as if they were raking over the ashes of the crime, always finding there more significance than mere manslaughter. Then the devil's advocate in Olga Alexandrovna's mind found it necessary to order a retrial and she had to start all over again. So her days passed.

The floors of the cells were lined with felt and, as well as a similar lining of felt on the walls, there was, at a distance of five inches from the surface of both walls and ceilings, a wire mesh covered with paper, an arrangement intended to prevent the inmates communicating with one another by means of knockings and tappings. So there was perfect silence within this place, except for the muffled footfalls of the wardresses, who were forbidden to speak. Silence, but for their footfalls; and the sound of the metallic slidings of the grilles; and the shrill insistence of the bell that rang in the morning, to wake you, and the bell that rang in the evening, to tell you to lie down, the bell that told you dinner was ready, the bell that ordered you to have your dirty bowls and plates ready for collection, the bell that ordered you to stand by the door ready for the exercise hour, round and round the yard, the

Countess turning slowly in her chair to pace you. The bell that said the exercise hour was at an end. Silence, but for these sounds; and that of the ticking of the clock.

Snow piled against the outer walls of the House of Correction; spring came and the snow melted but the inmates saw neither the fall nor the vanishing, and neither did the Countess, either, for the price she paid for her hypothetical proxy repentance was her own incarceration, trapped as securely in her watchtower by the exercise of her power as its objects were in their cells.

This merciless woman nevertheless believed herself to be the embodiment of mercy, which she conceived of as the opposite of justice, for had she not removed her women from the sphere in which justice, which is necessarily merciless, operates – the court, the prison – and placed them in this laboratory for the manufacture of souls?

With so much looking, her eyes had grown quite white.

How did she sleep and were her sleeps troubled? No; not troubled, but random and infrequent, for she never liked to close her eyes although even she, deficient as she was in common humanity, needs must recharge her batteries in the good old human way. But when she snatched a wink, she drew Venetian blinds down on her windows and left lights burning so her prisoners could not tell if indeed she slept or was only pretending to do so, because sometimes she would draw the blinds when she was *not* asleep in order to demonstrate that she could escape from the tyranny of their eyes any time she chose though they were never free of hers. This was the only area in which she was able to exercise freedom although she was the inventor and the perpetrator of this wholesale incarceration.

The wardresses were also trapped, women – for the House of Correction was manned exclusively by women – who lived barrack-style amongst those they policed, and were imprisoned by the terms of their contract just as securely as the murderesses. So all within were gaoled, but only the murderesses knew this was the case.

The longer that Olga Alexandrovna rehearsed in her mind the circumstances of her husband's death in her ample, and, it sometimes seemed, posthumous leisure – for in that place she felt as good as dead – the less she felt she was to blame. She went over and over everything, again and again, starting from the beginning, childhood in the tenement. Her weary mother stooped with toil, marriage, birth of the son she would never see again, the way her husband repeated with relish old Russian proverbs in praise of wife-beating, how she pawned her wedding ring to buy the food only to have him rob her of the cash for drink – blame it on vodka! Blame the priest who married them! Blame the stick that beat her and the old saws that helped to shape it!

But, don't blame me. And, having exonerated herself, let the judge think what he would – she at last slept easy, the first untroubled night she'd passed in that place.

She was a woman of considerable intelligence, which the phrenologist had classified as 'low peasant cunning'. She had quickly learned to mark the passage of the days by making a scratch with her fingernail on the plaster surrounding the bars through which she and the Countess did their reciprocal observing; this was the only area of her cell which could not be seen from outside. Though never, until pressed by circumstances, any great shakes at arithmetic, she'd made considerable strides in simple addition since she'd been here and, the secret inner surface was fairly pock-marked with the scars of empty days when, the morning after that good night's sleep, she did her sums and discovered her third year in the place was over and the fourth year just begun.

Having survived all those who had been in the place when she was shipped there, she now qualified as a 'long-stay' prisoner. She decided the time had come to make herself at home and began to sit up and take notice.

Now, according to regulations, the silent wardresses wore hoods when they delivered meals, hoods which concealed all the features of their faces except their eyes, for even the Countess was forced to concede they must be able to see where they were going. But she wanted them to remain anonymous instruments, to exhibit no personal qualities that might obtrude upon the isolation of each inmate, so they never lifted their eyes from the ground, not when they served breakfast, or when they served supper, or when they unfastened the cages to let the women out for exercise.

But their gloved hands were at risk, as they slid the trays through the grilles. Olga Alexandrovna, who, in a former life, had followed the profession of a seamstress, possessed fine, slim fingers and, besides, was of a sociable temperament. Though speech and looking were denied her, still she thought she might be able to touch one of these fellow-prisoners – because Olga Alexandrovna, sitting and thinking, thinking and sitting as the clock ticked the days that turned to weeks to months to years, had come to the obvious conclusion that the guards were as much the victims of the place as she.

That morning, she sat waiting at the grille for breakfast, one eye cocked on the revolving Countess, the other on the clock, and, when the minute hand hit the hour, the bell rang and the grille slid open with a metallic rasp, she slipped one lovely hand (for lovely hand it was) into the gap and clasped the hand in the leather glove that pushed in the tray from the other end.

At the touch of Olga Alexandrovna's white fingers, the hand under the black glove quivered. Emboldened, Olga Alexandrovna clasped the leather glove more warmly. With a courage far beyond Olga Alexandrovna's imaginings, the woman in the hood raised her eyes to meet those eyes that Olga Alexandrovna now fixed on her.

Then the bell rang and the grille clanged down and Olga Alexandrovna lost her breakfast because the tray fell to the floor outside the cell and the porridge spilled, but she did not care about that.

Though the light was burning behind the Venetian blinds, the Countess must have nodded off for a moment for she did not see this mute exchange, although they saw one another clearly. And that was the moment, even before the gate opened and let them all out, as it was bound, sooner or later, after that touch, to do – at that moment, Olga Alexandrovna knew whoever it was who might truly sit in judgment on her had elected to dismiss the charge.

That evening, after a free if surreptitious exchange of looks as supper was served, Olga Alexandrovna found a note tucked into the hollowed-out centre of her bread roll. She devoured the love-words more eagerly than she would have done the bread they replaced and obtained more nourishment therefrom. There was not a pencil nor pen in the cell, of course, but, as it happened, her courses were upon her and – ingenious stratagem only a woman could execute – she dipped her finger in the flow, wrote a brief answer on the back of the note she had received and delivered it up to those brown eyes that now she could have identified amongst a thousand, thousand pairs of brown eyes, in the immutable privacy of her toilet pail.

In her womb's blood, on the secret place inside her cell, she drew a heart.

Desire, that electricity transmitted by the charged touch of Olga Alexandrovna and Vera Andreyevna, leapt across the great divide between the guards and the guarded. Or, it was as if a wild seed took root in the cold soil of the prison and, when it bloomed, it scattered seeds around in its turn. The stale air of the House of Correction lifted and stirred, was moved by currents of anticipation, of expectation, that blew the ripened seeds of love from cell to cell. The slow hour's walk around the covered inner courtyard, where the guards kept pace with the inmates, when, for just that single hour, the bars did not divide them, took on something of a bridal, a celebratory quality, as the flowers that sprang from those seeds grew in silence, as flowers do.

Contact was effected, first, by illicit touch and glance, and then by illicit notes, or, if either guard or inmate turned out to be illiterate, by drawings made in and on all manner of substances, on rags of clothing if paper was not available, in blood, both menstrual and veinous, even in excrement, for none of the juices of the bodies that had been so long denied were alien to them, in their extremity – drawings, as it turned out, crude as graffiti, yet with the effect of clarion calls. And if the guards were all subverted to the inmates' humanity through look, caress, word, image, then so did the inmates wake up to the knowledge that, on either side of their own wedge-shaped cubes of space, lived other women just as vividly alive as themselves.

Silently, surreptitiously, as the unacknowledged autumn changed to winter outside, a warmth and glow suffused the House of Correction, a glow so inappropriate to the season that the Countess herself felt the effects of the palpable change of temperature within, so she would sweat, yet she could not, no matter how hard she looked, detect a single visible change in the mechanical order she had laid down and, even though she gave up sleeping altogether and introduced a hysterical randomness into her revolvings, so that she sometimes made herself quite giddy and sometimes stuck stock-still for almost an entire minute by the authority of the clock, she never saw one suspicious thing.

She never thought the guards might turn against her; did she not keep their contracts in a locked iron box in her watch-room? Had she not bought them? Were they not forbidden discourse with the inmates? Did not the forbidden thing itself forbid?

Her white eyes were now veined and rimmed with red. As she went round and round, she drummed nervous tattoos on the arm of her chair.

The notes, the drawings, the caresses, the glances – all said, in various ways, 'if only', and 'I long . . . ' And the clock ticked the time of another lifetime, another place, above the gateway that grew each day larger in their imaginations until the clock and the gateway that had signified the end of hope now spoke to them of nothing but hope.

So it was an army of lovers who finally rose up against the Countess on the morning when the cages opened for the final exercise hour, opened – and never closed. At one accord, the guards threw off their hoods, the prisoners came forth and all turned towards the Countess in one great, united look of accusation.

She took out the pistol she kept in her pocket and fired off shot after shot that banged but did not reverberate as they ricocheted off the bricks and bars of that echoless chamber. Her firing scored one bull; she stopped the clock, shot the time right out of it, broke the face and stilled the tick forever, so, henceforth, when she looked at it, it would remind her only of the time that *her* time ended, the hour of their deliverance. But that was an accident. She was too stricken with surprise to aim straight, she wounded nobody and was easily disarmed, chattering away with outrage.

They locked up her door, took away the key and threw it into the first snowdrift they encountered when they opened the gate. They left the Countess secured in her observatory with nothing to observe any longer but the spectre of her own crime, which came in at once through the open gate to haunt her as she continued to turn round and round in her chair.

Kisses, embraces and the first sight of unseen, beloved faces. After the first joy was over, the women formed a plan – to make their way to the railhead, since they lacked maps or even compasses, and orient themselves by the railway track. Once they were sure they knew where they were, then they would decide on where they should go, whether, as some of them, even in the first throes of their new loves, still wanted, to trek back four or five thousand miles to the village or the town where their mothers still tended children orphaned by the law, no matter what befell after, or to strike off by themselves and found a primitive Utopia in the vastness round them, where none might find them.

Vera Andreyevna knew the place Olga Alexandrovna kept in her heart for the small son she'd last seen when he had milk teeth, and kept her peace.

They were armed and all clad in good stout greatcoats and felt boots stuffed with straw taken from the guardroom. They had food with them. The white world around them looked newly made, a blank sheet of fresh paper on which they could inscribe whatever future they wished.

So, taking bearings by the pale sun, they set off hand in hand, and soon started to sing, for joy.

FOUR

When darkness came, they found themselves in the shelter of the forest and decided to bivouac in brushwood shelters for fear of losing themselves in the night. Once they were settled down, they noticed a red glow in the sky above the trees, in the direction of the railway. Olga Alexandrovna and Vera Andreyevna were chosen by common consent as advance party and crept forward, concealing themselves amongst what bushes they could find, until, from a bluff, they saw a remarkable sight: an entire train, disarticulated like a broken toy, the carriages scattered by the explosion that had twisted the tracks until they resembled knitting got at by kittens. Many of the carriages still blazed with the same fire that had set light to the trees nearest the railway track, although some ineffectual efforts seemed to have been made at putting the fire out.

And, lying among the debris, toppled like giant ninepins, something untoward, something extraordinary – beings such as Olga Alexandrovna, in her childhood, once saw in the Tsar's menagerie in her native St Petersburg. Elephants! Enough dead elephants to fill a fair-sized graveyard; and then a movement amongst the wreckage showed them that one huge beast was still living and was engaged, even in extremis, in lifting from here to there beams and twisted wheels with its trunk.

Then, most strange, the sound of music, of fiddle and tambourine, and Vera Andreyevna drew Olga Alexandrovna back behind a tree to let a peculiar procession pass. And pass it did, without the outlaws who policed it spying the women, for which they were grateful. Outlaws, bristling with weapons. Outlaws, with hostages – a fair girl, crying; and a huge brute, dressed like a peasant, comforting her in a language that was not Russian. And a little man in striped trousers who was shouting out, could the women have understood him, 'I demand to see the U.S. consul.' And there were a couple of primitive, wheelless carts, dragged by more outlaws, in which lay blanket-covered mounds, one silent but one bawling fit to bust. And a little grizzled, dark woman muttering to herself in a language different to the one the others spoke but which was not Russian, either. All most unexpected. And then more outlaws.

But it was the motley band who brought up the procession that made the women cross themselves, for these were men of all shapes and sizes, some small as dwarves, some long and lanky as clothespoles, less than a dozen of them, in the ragged remains of what had once been bright clothing in the strangest styles. Some had huge red noses, others big black rings round their eyes, but the paint was peeling from all the faces, so they looked piebald. Two of these men, wizened and old and inclined more to the stature of dwarves than of giants, provided the music for the party – but the fiddle was small, as if shrunken, and the other augmented his tambourine with a metal triangle hanging behind his back, at which he kicked up with every step he took. And they were playing, with a bravado that might have touched the hearts of Vera Andreyevna and Olga Alexandrovna, if they'd known the tune: 'Rule Britannia!'

A few yapping dogs of breeds as various as this human zoo of odd types ran back and forth around, often coming in for a kick from an outlaw's foot.

The escaped women looked askance at these representative examples of the world from which they had been exiled in the House of Correction.

As soon as the outlaws and their foreign captives were out of sight, the women returned to their comrades and debated what was to be done. They soon reached a decision: they did not feel they could take on the outlaws so would leave their captives in the hands of fate, which would make suitable provision, but they could and would go down to the wrecked train, even if a rescue party were to arrive and arrest them as escapees and deserters while they tendered what assistance they could to the injured and the dying.

Under the stars, the snow shone a nightmarish, glaring, luminous blue, as if the snow itself gave off a kind of corpse light. But, though the fires were dying down, still there was light enough for the women to see that, in fact, little was left for them to do.

As they approached, the last living elephant gathered its final reserves of strength together to lift a broken cupboard in its trunk and fling it towards the woods, where it scattered a hail of salt-cellars, pepper-shakers and vinegar bottles. Then, with a heart-rending bellow that, for a moment, filled all the great solitude, the elephant fell upon its side, fell not slowly, in stages, but in one crashing motion, down upon the melting snow. After that, a dreadful quiet, except for the crackling of the underbush that burned as if it might not be consumed.

Then Olga Alexandrovna stumbled over a body and thought at first it was a corpse but when she saw the bottle in its fist she knew it was still living though, kick and pinch it as she might, it would not budge. The entire train crew, as it turned out, conductors, waiters, cooks, were prone about the wreck, as at the conclusion of a peasant wedding. The warmth of the fires kept them from freezing. These appeared to be the only survivors and all seemed in perfect health. The women judged it wisest to let them lie, since it was clear they would come to no harm.

Olga Alexandrovna, attracted by the bright colours – she'd been starved of colours – picked out a quilt from a snowdrift, a quilt made of knitted squares sewn together such as children make.

'Here's a treasure-trove of useful things left in the wilderness as if by some miracle, especially for us!' she said. She was a practical woman.

After a heartening meal of bread and sausage they had brought with them, taken in the welcome heat of the forest fire, they set to to salvage what equipment they could.

First, Olga Alexandrovna found the gilded figure of an old man with a scythe that had evidently snapped off a broken box of springs and small brass wheels. Vera Andreyevna tentatively identified the figure of that of Father Time.

'But, wherever we go, we'll need no more fathers,' she pronounced. So they threw it away.

Following on from this notion, Vera implored her friend to forbear from the use of the patronymic when she addressed her, which Olga promised to do, and asked her friend to do the same as regards herself.

Under a mass of broken chandeliers and torn upholstery, Olga next found a shard of mirror strangely painted with umber stripes on orange. When she touched it, it burned her fingers. She dropped it. It broke into a thousand lesser fragments, leaving, to her horror, a trace of smoking liquid in the snow. A superstitious fear overcame her.

'Let's get out of here,' she said to Vera.

'Where shall we go, my darling?'

Under the glazing stars, the railway track ran from its fiery terminus back, back, back, the thousand, thousand miles to St Petersburg, to the narrow tenement in which Olga's aged mother crouched before the charcoal under the samovar in the continuous repetition of her daily toil, while the little boy who no longer remembered her played outside in the alley at games at which she could no longer guess. Vera kept her eyes down, as she had done before their fingers touched. She knew that to look is to coerce and, whatever else might lie in store for them, at this moment, they were free to choose.

Olga, in inner turmoil, sat down on the pile of table-linen that had been disclosed when the last elephant cleared the last cupboard. By the shattered remains of tables, vases, bottles and silverware around them, this must have been the restaurant car. Other women, decisions made, picked over the detritus of the kitchen near at hand, putting on one side all manner of things that would come in useful – saucepans, kettles, cauldrons, knives, all of such large sizes as would suit communal kitchens.

They carried out stocks of food, sacks of flour and sugar and beans, although they left behind the gravy browning with which the kitchen was so plentifully stocked. There were even a great many eggs, in wire baskets, that, on a whim of the explosion, had escaped destruction.

Above the clatterings and the exclamations: 'Here's strawberry jam!' 'I say, chocolate!' 'Would you believe, my dear, a patent *ice-bucket*!', Olga's prison-quickened ears now believed they detected a moan such as a sick or frightened child might make, coming from inside the place where she sat. She leapt to her feet and hurled aside the cloths and napkins.

So she uncovered him, a ruddy, flaxen-haired young man in a child's short, white trousers, sleeping sound as if between white sheets on a feather bed. His breath did not smell of liquor. There was a contusion on his forehead.

'How shall we wake him?'

'The old tales diagnose a kiss as the cure for sleeping beauties,' said Vera, with some irony.

Olga's maternal heart did not heed that irony. She pressed her lips to his forehead and his eyelids slowly fluttered, slowly opened and he lifted up his arms and slowly put them round her neck.

'Mama,' he said. That universal word.

Smiling, she shook her head. She saw that Walser no longer knew enough to ask: 'Where am I?' Like the landscape, he was a perfect blank.

They lifted him to his feet, to see if he could walk. After a few tries and demonstrations, he got the hang of it and laughed out loud with delight and pride as he toddled with increasing confidence back and forth from Olga's arms to Vera's less welcoming ones, until he could manage by himself. Shortly after that, he discovered in himself sensation. He rubbed his hand on his belly in a circular motion and searched the absence that had been his memory but he could find nothing there to tell him what to say. So he kept on rubbing.

Olga Alexandrovna found a can of milk in the kitchen, crumbled bread in it and got him to take some of that from her fingers because he no longer knew how to use a spoon. He was pleased with everything and cooed, gazing round him with eyes the size of saucers. When he finished his bread and milk, he rubbed his belly again, to see what might be forthcoming *this* time.

Olga Alexandrovna picked up the wire basket of eggs.

'Does he want a nice eggy, then?'

The sight of the eggs set the jumble behind his eyes in motion. All manner of connections took place. Up he rose on tiptoe and flapped his arms.

'Cock-a-doodle-dooski!'

'Poor thing,' said Olga Alexandrovna. 'Lost his wits, may the Good Lord protect him.'

Then a shrill whistle pierced the night and, far off, they saw the sparks and glowing tender of a railway engine, arriving from the direction of the railhead at R., and they made out the shapes of men with torches, lanterns, ropes and axes, walking alongside the slowly moving engine. The white apron of a nurse flashed as she leant out of the cabin to catch a glimpse of the work that lay before her. So Olga Alexandrovna's decision was made for her; and all now hastened to gather together bundles of useful tools and utensils, and to make off into the woods, towards the radiant uncertainties of love and freedom.

Olga, in a hurry, stuck a pin into an egg and gave it to Walser to suck, which he did eagerly.

'Cock-a-doodle-do!'

'I hate to leave the poor thing,' she said to Vera.

'He is a man, even if he has lost his wits,' replied Vera. 'We can do without him.'

Still Olga lingered, as if she thought there *must* be something useful this young man could do for them, if only she could think of it . . . but time was running out. When she kissed Walser goodbye, she kissed goodbye to her own son and all the past. The women vanished.

Walser crouched over the basket of eggs but found they were easily crushed. Disgruntled, he kicked the basket over and had some fun watching the eggs that remained whole roll around. The rescue party drew nearer, at a stately pace, for, however great the emergency, the antique stock would only chuff along at the most geriatric rate. Walser had some more fun jumping on the rolling eggs and smashing them, but not as much fun as all that. Bored, he flapped his arms, again.

'Cock-a-doodle-do! Cock-a-doodle-dooski!'

When he realised the kind ladies were all gone, tears ran unhindered from his eyes. Crowing like a cock, flapping his arms up and down, he sprinted off among the trees in search of them but soon forgot his quest in his enchantment at the sight of dappled starlight on the snow.

FIVE

As soon as we turned our backs on the train, it ceased to exist; we were translated into another world, thrust into the hearts of limbo to which we had no map.

They took us further and yet further into the margins of the forest, which, no hasty gulper, swallowed us up at its primeval leisure. It took me a long while to somewhat recover my composure and by then we were inside it as securely as Jonah in the belly of the whale and in almost as profound a darkness, for the close boughs of the evergreens blotted out the sky except when a lump of the snow with which they were lined fell on our heads like the dropping of a big, cold-blooded bird, and then a few scraps of red light from the fire we left behind us showed through the gap, bloodying the night-time clouds.

Our hosts, of whose intentions I grew moment by moment more apprehensive, appeared, through long custom and the most intimate knowledge of the woods, to need no light to guide them along the path they had hewn among the close-grown trunks, and they did not speak to us or one another. Now and then I caught a whiff of the ones who dragged me along and they smelled like hell, I must say.

Once I'd come to myself, prone on that jolting litter, I pummelled their backsides until they let me off and there was our Liz, again, so I gave her a kiss on what bit of her anatomy I could get at, which turned out to be her nose.

'Satisfied, now you're on foot?' she greeted me, the old witch. 'Find this method of progress more appropriate to the scenery, do you?'

Now, when I call Liz a 'witch', you must take it with a pinch of salt because I am a rational being and, what's more, took in my rationality with her milk, and you could say it's too much rationality as procured her not altogether undeserved reputation, for when she puts two and two together sometimes she comes up with five, because she thinks quicker than most. How does she reconcile her politics with her hanky-panky? Don't ask me! Ask that family of anarchist bomb-makers of hers! Who put the bomb in the *bombe surprise* at Jenny's wedding? Work of a moment for our Gianni, for all his weak lungs; and who would ever think to look for dynamitards in an ice-cream parlour, amongst those bonny babies, to boot?

And, at this very moment, back home in Battersea, our babies may be asking: 'Where's our Auntie Liz, now? Where's Fevvers?' But, as for Fevvers and Liz, why, they can't answer that question themselves! When I think of the babies, I feel on my front for the lucky violets my Violetta gave me last Christmas, and, of course, there they aren't, they've dropped off somewhere in Siberia.

Hearing me give out a little sob, Liz says under her breath: 'How's the broken pinion?'

'Bad enough.'

She gives my hand a squeeze.

'*And* I've lost my lucky violets,' I add. She drops my hand sharpish; she hates sentiment.

'Bugger your lucky violets, wherever they are,' she says. 'Prepare yourself for the worst, gel; we've lost the bloody clock, haven't we. Burnt to a crisp in the wreck, most likely. First your sword, now my clock. We'll soon lose all track of time, and then what will become of us. Nelson's clock. Gone. And that's not all. My handbag. That's gone too.'

This was a disaster so great I scarcely dare think of the distress it would cause us.

Forward, we went, deeper and deeper into an unknown terrain that was, at the same time, claustrophobic, due to the trees shutting us in, and agoraphobic, because of the enormous space which the trees filled. We dragged one increasingly weary foot before the other weary foot, all dreary and incomprehensible as a wet Sunday, until we got to a clearing full of dirty snow with, behind a spiked stockade, all manner of haphazard dwellings in it, some like wigwams made of skins, some like tents put up by soldiers, and a few sheds of raw, split logs with all the signs of the hastiest construction, cracks stuffed with earth. I could see everything by the light of sputtery torches of pinewood our captors now ignited and my suspicions there were no women amongst them were amply confirmed. I would not say this discovery gave me more confidence in my hosts.

They all crowded round especially me, stared at only me, and muttered and exclaimed to themselves, but for the Princess or Mignon they never spared a glance. It seemed I formed a special item on the menu, although I kept that blanket tight around me, I can tell you.

But they treated us quite kindly. They gave us hot tea and ardent spirits and offered us cold roast, I think, moose, but I could eat nothing, I was overcome by silly weeping at the sight of food, which Liz said, then, was the effect of shock, but afterwards assured me that to see me off my feed was the first cause of real concern I'd given her since I was a baby.

They showed us even more consideration that night; they forbore to subject us to interrogation or stuff of that order, since we were so distraught and travel-weary, but put us all in a largish shed, where, to sleep on, was a wood platform with piles of furs, principally bearskins, not too well cured, by the smell. They left us huddled up all together, the poor remains of the Colonel's circus, and he chattering with indignation as, apart from the indignities we'd suffered, he'd no great liking for the vodka they had hospitably provided for us, craving his lost bourbon like a baby snatched too early from the nipple and forlornly demanding an American consul be summoned 'toot sweet', he said. 'Toot damn sweet.'

There was a clang and a bang outside – the buggers have slid the bolt on us, amidst much disputation in the Russian language. For these men are not the natives of the place. The native woodsmen are low in stature, yellow of skin; sometimes we've seen 'em at the stations, loading skins from high-piled sleds into the baggage vans, and they wear curious hats, of a triangular shape, and chink with ornaments made of tin. But our men are big, sturdy fellows, although we're far too far away from farmland for them to come of that peasant stock imported into Siberia centuries ago to till the soil. And I do think they're strangers here as much as we.

There was a fire in the lodging and some of the smoke went up through a hole in the roof. A small boy was left with us, whose task was to sit by the fire all night and feed it with sticks, for they did not trust us with the means of combustion. The clown-dogs bounced around to see the little fellow, thinking they'd have a game with him, but when one black poodle bitch with its red satin bow still in its curls jumped up at him, beseeching friendship, this jolly little chap seized hold of her and broke her neck with one clean snap of his long-fingered hands, which put all the clowns in a terrible humour and didn't reassure me as to the good hearts of our hosts in the least.

And the looks the fire-boy gave poor Sybil the pig were exactly those the ragged urchins that hopscotch on the Queenstown Road give Gianni when he calls out 'Icey, icey, ice-cream!' So I didn't give Sybil much longer in this world, I can tell you, and she is clearly apprehensive herself and climbs right down inside the Colonel's waistcoat and buries her snout in his breast, whimpering occasionally.

Nevertheless, I persuaded the fire-boy to split a log so Liz can make splits for my broken wing, binding the splints with strips she tore off our underlinen, and then I felt easier. But we couldn't conceal what we were up to from the fire-boy and his eyes went big as cart-wheels when he saw what I'd got to show. God, he stared. And, would you believe, he crossed himself.

The Princess woke up at last and broke that life-long silence of hers with a vengeance but to no purpose, since she babbled away hysterically and her words made no sense. Even Mignon could not console her for it was plain to see the Princess knew Othello's occupation was gone. She kept her hands stuck out straight in front of her as if they no longer belonged to her, as if, henceforward, she would have no use for them *as* hands. Her poor fingers were stiff as chapel hat-pegs already.

She made such a hullabaloo, lamenting, presumably, the passing of her keyboard and her tigers, that the clowns grew restive and were all for getting the fire-boy to open the door and shove her out in the snow but Lizzie found a pack of cards in her handbag and they settled down, resentfully but quietly, while the Princess's passion wore itself out until she lay still in Mignon's arms, racked only by exhausted sobs.

Liz hugged me and kissed me and, no matter what state she might have been in under her surface calm, she was fast asleep under the stinking bearskins in two shakes but my nerves were so ravaged by the shocking tragedy we had undergone I could not close my eyes although at last the clowns slept, cards and glasses in their hands, the Colonel slept, Mignon and the Princess both drifted into sleep.

The silence of the forest was interrupted only by the howling of the wolves, a sound that chills to the bone by virtue of its distance from humanity, and told me only how lonely I was and how the night around us contained nothing to assuage the infinite melancholy of these empty spaces.

There I lay, my face buried in my arms, and then I heard the softest step on the earthen floor, and then a touch, the smallest, tenderest touch you might imagine, on my back. Quickly as I sprang up, I didn't catch him at it but now the fire-boy crouched cross-legged by the hearth, again, with, in his hand, a purple feather.

I had no heart to reprimand him.

My movement disturbed the Colonel; he rolled on his back and soon was snoring away in concert with his pig. Perhaps their duet lullabied me for slept I must have, although my young man was burned to a crisp, because the next thing I remember is the unbolting of the door.

Turns out the leader of the outlaws wants to see me all by myself and they've come to take me to his hut. They set me at a rough trestle in front of a goodish breakfast of sour milk, black bread and tea. Sleep had refreshed me, and I thought: While there's life, there's hope. So, in spite of my sorrow, I dipped my bread into the buttermilk and got a little something down. Meanwhile, he tugged his moustaches, which depended in two thin plaits from his upper lip to his Adam's apple, and subjected me to a piercing scrutiny from his close-set but not inherently malevolent eyes.

I must have cut a farcical figure, guyed up in what remained of that lace tea-gown, which never suited me even when new, bought it from Swan and Edgar's for the joke. Minus a petticoat. Plus a blanket around me, toga-fashion. His manners, however, had all the stately courtesy of the poor; he never asked me once to show my feathers, though you could tell he wanted, ever so, but knew it would be rude.

'Now you are in Transbaikalia, where the rivers freeze solid to the bottom and trap the fish like flies in amber,' he announced. You know I have knack with foreign languages, pick 'em up like fleas, and though his Russian was not that of Petersburg, I could follow it well enough and pitch in my own three ha'pence, too.

'Charmed, I'm sure,' I said.

'Welcome to the brotherhood of free men.'

'Brotherhood', is it? I'm not a man, nor your brother, either! His fraternal greetings don't go down half so well as his victuals and I give him a sneer, of which he takes no notice, but surges on:

'We are neither prisoners, nor exiles, nor settlers, madame, though our ranks, on occasion, have been swelled by all three conditions of men; we exist outside a law that shows us no pity and we demonstrate by our lives and deeds, how the wild life in the woods can bring liberty, equality and fraternity to those who pay the price of homelessness, danger and death. Swords are our only sisters, now: our wives are those rifles with whom faithfully each night we share our mattresses and jealously never let out of our sight. We go towards our deaths as joyously as we would towards a marriage.'

Don't think I'm unsympathetic to the spirit of his peroration, although the letter wants attending to here and there, to my mind.

'Swords for sisters, rifles for wives', indeed! What kind of intercourse is that? And anyone with any sense would go towards their *marriage* as if towards the noose, rather than the other way around. This fellow mixes his metaphors the way a toper does his drinks and, I daresay, gets just as tipsy on them. Furthermore, it seems to me his speech would sound well set to music, scored for brass and tympani, and a male voice chorus wouldn't come amiss, at points. Nevertheless, although he's kidnapped us, at this moment, I'm more for him than against him.

'Only catastrophe,' he goes on, 'can lead a man to this remote territory.'

But ain't I living proof that women don't come here of their own accord, either? To cover up my irritation, I ask him for another glass of tea. With this request, he courteously complies, amidst a clank and bang of armaments, for, besides the rifle propped against the trestle in easy reach of his hand, he'd a pair of pistols at his belt and his peasant caftan was criss-crossed by bandoliers. He'd a wide-bladed sword of a somewhat Turkish design to complete the ensemble. It was the outfit of a conspicuously untamed man, well set-off by the extraordinary ferocity of his moustaches. If this get-up smacked a bit of the comic-opera bandit, it must have been because they copied his get-up, not he theirs, and there was nothing of the wooden prop about his gun, although it looked old enough to have seen service in the Crimea.

'Each man of us, even including the first fire-boy, is here in flight from a law which would extract punishment from us for the vengeance we took upon those minor officials, army officers, landlords and such like petty tyrants, who forcibly dishonoured the sisters, wives and sweethearts of flesh and blood we all once had, who are now left far behind us.'

So that's where women come into the libretto! Absent friends!

'What do you mean, "dishonour"?' I says, hooking with distaste a dead fly out of my tea but, too cold for flies here, as it turns out, it's nothing but a tea-leaf, to my relief. I probe him further on the 'dishonour' question.

'Wherein does a woman's honour reside, old chap? In her vagina or in her spirit?'

Which pithy quibble wouldn't sound badly set to music, either. Nevertheless, it troubled him, although it might have been I spoke a dirty word that momentarily stemmed his flow. He sucked in his moustache braids and chewed them vehemently, unused to having his opinions questioned.

'I do think, myself,' I added, 'that a girl should shoot her own rapists.'

And I gave his rifle such a proprietorial glance that, if he'd anything of that nature in the back of his mind, then he'd got another think coming.

'It was my lads,' he said, evidently not wanting to debate the point with me, 'that blew up the railway track.'

'Well done!' I says ironically. 'Smart move! Dynamite a circus train! What kind of strategy is that?'

And then, oh! then, great, innocent, big-hearted stupid that he was, his eyes spilled over with fat tears and he cast aside the trestle, knocking over the remains of my scarcely finished breakfast in his enthusiasm, so he could fall on his knees before me and go into his big aria.

'Remarkable lady from beyond the mountains and the distant sea! It is well known that the Tsar, the Little Father of All the Russians, would, if he but knew of it, never permit that honest peasants such as we should be driven from the plough to live like beasts far away from home outside the law because we did no more than he himself would do if dishonour threatened the Little Mother or his precious girls.

'The last time we robbed the railhead at R., we took away the newspapers to see whether they carried any stories about us and there we read how you, the famous *aerialiste*, the winged wonder, the Britannic angel, the intimate of the English royal family –'

Curse the Colonel and his publicity stunts!

' – would pass through Transbaikalia on your way to the Great Ocean, where you will cross to the Land of the Dragonfly to hobnob with another Emperor. We blew up the track, dear lady, solely in order to take you hostage so that we can beg with you, plead with you, plead on my knees beating my forehead on the ground before you –' suiting his actions to his words ' – to intercede with your mother-in-law-to-be, the Queen of England.'

Whatever has the Colonel been up to now? What fresh lies has he been spreading? I'll pay him back for this!

'To intercede with the great Queen Victoria, the well-beloved baboushka who sits on the throne of England and with her royal bellows keeps alight the charcoal under the bubbling samovar of the Empire on which the sun never sets. I beg you, gracious and amazing creature, to intercede with this Queen Empress to ask her granddaughter's husband, the Tsar – see! it is a family matter! – to ask the

Tsar to forgive us all, so that we might return free men to our native villages, take up the plough we left lying in the fields, milk the cows that have long been lowing untended with swollen udders since we were forced to leave, to harvest the corn we left uncut.

'For the Tsar is the friend of simple truth and doesn't know the half of what his officials get up to on the side.'

I could have laughed, if I wasn't near tears, myself, by that time, at the pitiful simplicity of the man, at his truly appalling greatness of heart, that he believed, in his misfortune, there was some higher authority which was infallible and must always know and love the truth when it saw it, as in *Fidelio*, by Beethoven; nobility of spirit hand in hand with absence of analysis, that's what's always buggered up the working class. Though I tried to stop the brigand chief, he covered the hem of my tea-gown with wet kisses.

'Wonderful lady, you shall – you must! write to her a letter, a letter to Queen Victoria, and we will take it to a train and the train will chug away with it far, very, very far, even so far as unto the city of London. And there, one foggy morning, a liveried butler will bear our letter, with its invisible cargo of hope and faith of honest men, even unto the Queen Empress as she sits tapping away with her golden egg-spoon at her breakfast egg in its golden egg-cup, propped up on the pillows in her bed in Buckingham Palace. When she sees your well-known and beloved writing on the envelope, how gladly she'll cry out: "A letter! A letter from my dear almost daughter-in-law!" And then – '

By now my knees were sopping wet with tears and kisses and I could bear it no longer.

'Oh, my old duck, you shouldn't believe everything you read in the papers! I'm never engaged to the Prince of Wales! Hasn't he got a perfectly good wife of his own, already! I'm not even *intimate* with him, love, and such an intimacy he'd offer the likes of me wouldn't go down well with the Widow of Windsor at all, at all! What idle folly is this, that you fancy these great ones care a single jot about the injustice you suffer? Don't the great ones themselves weave the giant web of injustice that circumscribes the globe?'

First, he didn't believe me; then, when my arguments convinced him, he broke out in a furious tempest of rage, grief and despair, well-nigh Wagnerian in its intensity, berating the world, the newspapers, the duplicity of princes and his own gullibility and I must say I heartily sympathised with him but then he took to breaking every single object in his tent, even kicked the trestle and the chairs apart, such was the fury of his disappointment. All the other bandits rushed in but could do nothing to curb his excesses, so I said: 'Send for Samson,' and good old Samson the Strong Man got him in a half-nelson and hit him over the head and in the ensuing hush we adjourned to our hut, which, such is the human heart's capacity for fixing on whatever security offers itself even in the most extreme circumstances, already feels like 'home'.

'Bastards,' said Liz when I told her all and she did not mean the bandits. Even the Colonel looked abashed, as well he might, although he would take no responsibility for our plight, muttering it was a case of 'caveat emptor' and fools should take responsibility for themselves.

But – what will the brigand chief do with us, when he wakes up? Will he vent his rage upon ourselves? No use commandeering his weapons, since all the bandits are armed to the teeth and have their muzzles trained upon us. We're in a pretty pickle, I must say.

The Princess is pacing up and down, bereft, her useless hands outstretched, looking ghastly as Lady Macbeth in the sleep-walking scene, Mignon one step behind to make sure she does no harm to herself, but the clowns have perked up sufficiently to entertain the fire-boy with a few simple card-tricks, episode of the poodle either forgotten or forgiven, but I foresee storms ahead when they run out of cigarettes. The Colonel, possibly from unacknowledged guilt, now overcomes his resistance to vodka to such an extent he is soon well away and sings songs of Old Kentucky over and over to himself in a high baritone. So all those still willing and able to form a council of war settle down together on that wooden platform and they are: yours truly; Lizzie; and – the Strong Man.

I am aware that strange changes are going on in Samson's frontal lobes. His eyes that used to be so brightly vacant are darkening and growing more introspective hour by hour and though the time is not yet ripe for him to leap into discourse, I begin to have great hopes of him in that department, should we all live so long. If he does not partake in our discussion, he follows with a lively comprehension and, as we are, is torn between genuine compassion for the deceived outlaws and concern as to our own predicament.

'The sun shines bright,' warbles the Colonel, 'on my old Kentucky home.'

Sybil appeared to have given up on him now he was in his cups and was nesting down in the bearskins as far away from the fire-boy as she could burrow but we thought we might as well 'consult the oracle' and Lizzie extracted the letter cards from the Colonel's pocket without him taking a blind bit of notice. But all the advice Sybil will give is: 'W-A-I-T A-N-D S-E-E', while, outside, the snow started to come down again, which spurred the fire-boy into action, I'm glad to say.

Then we heard the unmistakable sounds of the bandits drowning their sorrows and, comic operetta brigands as they were, they now indulged in a bass baritone chorus of laments, in parts, although, as time wears on, the part-singing becomes increasingly ragged. And it was sad music fit to make you cut your throat.

'Here we are,' opined Liz, 'lodged up the arsehole of the universe with a bunch of scabby bandits so sunk in false consciousness they thought the Queen of England would shed a tear for them if only she knew their misery and your wing is broken so we can't fly away. And our clock is gone for good. *And* no means of knowing if that last lot of mail got home or not.'

Which seems the least of our problems, whether the comrades in London got hot news of the struggle. When I say that, we fell out, first time in our lives! Hard words pass between us. We withdraw to separate corners of the shed, to sulk, and, what with our bad feeling, and the Princess moping and mowing, and Mignon carrying on, and the Colonel running through the Stephen Foster songbook in ever a more discordant manner, as if vying with the lamentations of the outlaws outdoors as by the water of Babylon they sit down and weep, add to that the ululations of the wolves and the raucous laughter which accompanies the increasingly indecent games in which the clowns engage the fire-boy, I'm beginning to think I must have done something wicked in a former life to land in such a mess in this one.

And, silly superstitious little tremor as it is, childish and whimsical . . . all the same, the little sword that always armed me, and Father Time, who was once on our side – both these are gone, quite gone.

Besides, I suspect that not only my wing but also my heart has been a little broken.

No dinner brought us, because the bandits are too preoccupied with their dirges. But Lizzie, whose doings I keep watch on out of the corner of my eye, begs a knife off the fire-boy and starts in on cutting up the bearskins, so I see she's a plan to make us all some good new clothes of a kind to withstand the weather outside and I can't help but wonder if she's cooking up some scheme of her own in her wily old head. But I don't care to ask, since we're not on speakers.

Then comes a knocking at the door and a strange, new voice in educated tones demands: 'Anyone at home?'

'Bolt's on the other side!' I sings out. 'Open up and walk in!'

Which is how we made the acquaintance of the escaped convict.

SIX

———◦◉◦———

Early morning. The dark blue sky stains the snow dark blue. The moon appears and disappears teasingly behind a scarf of blue gauze. Everything looks transparent. A volatile figure with its jaw now lightly clad in silvery beard flits through the thickets, evidently impervious to cold, for it exhibits no discomfort although it is half naked since it has lost its trousers, its comedy suspenders and its wig. There are feathers of the snowy owl, the goldeneye, the raven, stuck in its hair, along with burrs, thorns, twigs, mushrooms and mosses. This man looks as if both born in and born of the forest.

He mistakes the stars for birds and chirrups at them as if he knew no other language. Perhaps that angel who keeps the small birds under his wing has, in spite of his size, adopted him, for, apart from scratched shins, no harm has befallen him, and the odds and ends of cast-offs knocking about inside the box that used to hold his wits sometimes come together, kaleidoscope-wise, in the image of a feathered, tender thing that might, once upon a time, have sat upon his egg.

Although his cockscomb is long gone, he still cries: 'Cock-a-doodle-do!'

The empty centre of an empty horizon, Walser flutters across the snowy wastes. He is a sentient being, still, but no longer a rational one; indeed, now he is all sensibility, without a grain of sense, and sense impressions alone have the power to shock and to ravish him. In his elevated state, he harkens to the rhythm of the drum.

Strange phenomenon of the landscape! as if it might have been sounds from the earth under the snow, or the heavens above it. A hollow, insistent drumming, soft at first, then increasing in intensity . . . a pitter-pat, a rat-tat-tap, and then a bim-bam-bom. Ruddeby-dub-bedy-dub and rat-a-tat-a-tat, tattoos and riffs of more than Afro-Caribbean complexity.

Not that he can identify the drumming *as* drumming. It might, might it not, be nothing but the product of his disordered brains. He pauses on one leg, like a stork, sniffing the air as if to smell out from which direction, if any, this invocation comes but the cold snaps at his testicles when he stands still and, with a brief scream, he leaps off, again, coming to rest before the antlers of a reindeer bull sticking up out of the snow and looking for all the world like an abandoned hat-rack.

When Walser sniffed the air *this* time, his nostrils dilated at a whiff of something savoury, something aromatic on the cold-scoured air. The drumming grew louder and louder, more and more rhythmically innovative, as he pursued the delicious scent; until, among the trees, he found a brazier containing a small fire from which fragrant smoke issued. Beside the fire stood a being composed, or so it would seem, of fringed leather, gaudy rags and tinkling metal ornaments, applying the wooden stick he held in one hand to a skin drum the size of a dustbin lid, of the kind Irish musicians call a 'bodrum', brightly painted with all manner of strange devices, stretched on a wooden frame. This drum was talking to the wilderness in its own language.

The Shaman was not in the least surprised to see Walser, for he had drummed himself into that state of transcendental ecstasy demanded by his profession and his spirit was now disporting itself with a company of horned ancestors, of birds with fins and fish on stilts and many other physiologically anomalous apparitions, amongst which Walser cut rather an everyday figure. Walser squatted by the fire, enjoying the smoke and reacquainting himself with the sensuality of warmth until the Shaman's eyes popped, his lips frothed and he fell down, dropping the drum, which rolled a little way on the snow and then toppled over.

Walser reached out for it but found he could coax only a few little muffled rumbles out of it. He did not know how to make the drum speak and, if he found out by accident, he could not have understood it.

Time passed. The Shaman sighed, got up, shook the snow off the skirts of his leather dress and saw that Walser was still there. The Shaman was prepared for anything when he took a spirit journey and greeted Walser affectionately, assuming he was an emanation of the wild which had elected to stick around a while after the drumming that summoned him stopped and would, in its own good time, softly and silently vanish away. But when Walser, recalling how nice things happened after he had done so once before, began to rub his belly with a circular motion, the Shaman had second thoughts.

He addressed Walser in his native tongue, an obscure Finno-Ugrian dialect just about to perplex three generations of philologists.

'Whence cometh thou? Whither goeth thou?'

Walser giggled, went nowhere, went on rubbing his belly. From the satchel in which he transported his fetishes, the Shaman unpacked the tumbler in which he'd proposed to serve himself tea (prepared on the brazier with the aid of a tea-brick) to restore himself after his exertions. He modestly turned his back, raised his skirt and pissed into this tumbler. Then, with smiling formality, he offered the steaming glass of amber fluid to his unexpected guest.

'No sugar,' complained Walser. 'No lemons.'

But he was thirsty and he drank.

Then his eyes began to spin round and round in his head and to send off sparks, like Catherine wheels. Even the Shaman, well used to the effects of fly agaric distilled through the kidneys, was startled. Walser entered an immediate fugue of hallucinations, in which birds, witches, mothers and elephants mixed up with sights and smells of Fisherman's Wharf, the Alhambra Theatre, London, the Imperial Circus, Petersburg, and many other places.

All his past life coursed through his head in concrete but discrete fragments and he could not make head nor tail of any of it. He began to babble helplessly in a language unknown to the Shaman, which excited the Shaman's curiosity all the more.

The Shaman packed up his belongings and slung his drum over his shoulder. He emptied the fire out of the brazier and stamped on it to put it out. He packed up the brazier. Himself, he was pretty sure, by now, that Walser, whatever he was, was *not* one of his own hallucinations, and might, he conjectured, be an apprentice shaman from another tribe, of, he noted, a markedly different physical type, who had wandered off-course during the ill-planned trip. He picked Walser up in a fireman's lift – he was a small man, but tough – and started off back to his own village with him.

Upside-down Walser continued to upbraid the embroidered back of the Shaman's ceremonial frock. The hallucinogenic urine put the sluggish motor in his skull into overdrive.

'Oh!' he declaimed to the oncoming Siberian dawn. 'What a piece of work is man!'

SEVEN

The Escapee opened up, came inside, had a good toast at the fire and was tickled pink to discover such a motley crew held hostage in the outlaws' camp. He was a well-educated man – boy, I should say, for he wasn't above twenty and didn't look his age, a fresh-faced, bright-eyed, eager little cherub who spoke very fair French and enough English to get by. And he was a breath of fresh air in this miserable place, I can tell you, for he never mentioned 'yesterday'. All *he* could talk of was 'tomorrow', a shining morrow of peace and love and justice in which the human soul, ever through history striving for harmony and perfection, would at last achieve it. And to the coming century he looked for the delivery of the concentrated essence of all the good things of that ideal 'tomorrow'.

He'd been sent off to exile for trying to bring Utopia one step nearer by blowing up a copper-shop, which made our Liz look kindly on him at first. But when he embarrassedly confessed there'd been no bang nor damage because the dynamite was damp, Liz 'tut-tutted' his ineffi-ciency, her brow darkened with displeasure at him and with his 'soul', with his 'tomorrow', she ferociously took issue.

'First place, what is this *soul* of which you speak? Show me its location in the human anatomy and then I might believe in it. But, I tell you straight, dissect away how much you like, you won't find it. And you can't make perfect a thing that don't exist. So, scrub the "soul" from out of your discourse. Second place, as we say in our country: "tomorrow never comes", which is why you're promised jam tomor-row. We live, always, in the here and now, the present. To pin your hopes upon the future is to consign those hopes to a hypothesis, which is to say, a nothingness. Here and now is what we must contend with. Third place, how will you recognise "perfection" when you see it? You can only define the *future perfect* by the *present imperfect,* and the present, in which, inevitably, we all live, always seems imperfect to *somebody*. This present time seems quite sufficiently perfect to such as that Grand Duke that wanted my foster-daughter, here, to add to his collection of toys. For the wretched peasants whose rents pay for his extravagances, the present is merry hell.

'If we abandon the grammatical metaphor, I'd certainly agree with you that this present which we contemporaneously inhabit is *imperfect* to a degree. But this grievous condition has nothing to do with the soul, or, as you might also call it, removing the theological connotation, "human nature". It isn't in that Grand Duke's nature to be a bastard, hard though it may be to believe; nor does it lie in those of his employees to be slaves. What we have to contend with, here, my boy, is the long shadow of the *past historic* (reverting back to the grammatical analogy, for a moment), that forged the institutions which create the human nature of the present in the first place.

'It's not the human "soul" that must be forged on the anvil of history but the anvil itself must be changed in order to change humanity. Then we might see, if not "perfection", then something a little better, or, not to raise too many false hopes, a little less bad.'

So I could tell she was feeling more chipper and the Escapee was getting more than he bargained for when he took shelter in the outlaw camp, but before he and Liz came to blows on how humanity might be most efficaciously rendered more virtuous, I steps in quick, asks him what's going on, outside.

Seems the outlaws are so sunk in gloom to find I'm *not* the Princess of Wales, nor ever shall be, they are drowning their sorrows but it doesn't cheer them up. The more they drink, the more they weep, as if what goes in must come out, and, if we don't console them, somehow, the Escapee thinks it's very likely that they'll have a little shooting party and so, goodnight. God bless. Finito.

But he has more news. For it seems he fell in with a band of women, trekking towards the interior, all of whom had broken out of an institution for the criminally insane nearby, leaving the governess locked up inside behind them as, for what he said they said, she thoroughly deserved to be. These women planned to found a female Utopia in the taiga and asked a favour of the Escapee; that he should deliver 'em up a pint or two of sperm, which, speedily freezing at the inhospitable temperature of the region, could be stored away in a patent ice-bucket like an enormous thermos flask they carried with them, so they could use it, when they got settled, to impregnate such of them as were of child-bearing age and so ensure the survival of this little republic of free women. With this request, he had complied. I could see he was a perfect gentleman.

'What'll they do with the boy babies? Feed 'em to the polar bears? To the *female* polar bears?' demanded Liz, who was in truculent mood and clearly thought herself back in Whitechapel at a meeting of the Godwin and Wollstonecraft Debating Society. I hushed her up. Mention of the patent ice-bucket piqued my curiosity.

'I asked them where they got it from,' said the Escapee. 'And they told me, from the dining-room of a wrecked train on the Great Siberian Railway.'

The Colonel broke down when he heard about the elephants, how these women saw the lifeless bodies lying around the track like so many overturned pantechnicons, and only forestalled tears by blowing his nose forcefully again and again on a succession of the small silk American flags of which he kept a seemingly inexhaustible supply upon his person. But I pressed the Escapee for news of human survivors and – bless me! – it turned out the woman found a *blond foreigner* tucked up among some tablecloths with not a scratch on him but left him behind when they saw a rescue party on the way and, by the time the Escapee met them, were already regretting having abandoned such a fine repository of semen. I was overcome with emotion when I heard all this. I forgot myself so far as to cry out:

'My young man will come and save us!'

'Hold hard, you sentimental booby, sounds like he's in no fit state to save himself,' said Lizzie. 'I like the sound of the rescue party better!'

But it turns out the Escapee is primarily on the run from the rescue party, which would 'rescue' him right back to the penal colony. And the outlaws, too, had best shift themselves sharpish or they'll have a lot to answer for when the fire, ambulance and police arrive.

The Colonel is as pleased as punch, however. I can see he is already plotting the tall headlines in all the newspapers – just wait until he gets to a telegraph! He reckons this catastrophe will end up making a mint for him, one way or another. His optimism is of the remorseless kind, that can't see the cloud for the silver lining, and his sudden burst of renewed high spirits – he lets out a series of American Indian war-whoops and commences to jig – his exuberance brings me down to earth for, whatever happens next, we're at this moment stuck in the outback in a snowdrift amongst a crowd of trigger-happy brigands far gone in liquor and armed to the teeth, whom we needs must persuade, for their own good, to leave us behind and run away.

'Now, lads,' says Lizzie to the clowns. 'The time has come to shake off your lethargy. You must put on such a show for our hosts as will wake 'em up so they'll listen to reason. Make 'em smile, make 'em laugh – then we can talk to them. Bring them back to life, my lads.'

Perhaps hers was an unfortunate choice of words, recalling as it did their old routine of the Clown's Funeral, which they would never undertake again. They were leery of the idea at first because, with Buffo gone and all their gear, only got left the rags they stood up in, and the fiddle, the tambourine, the triangle, no more, they couldn't see their way to doing their best, although their card tricks went down so well with the fire-boy.

'Think of it,' pleads Lizzie, 'as a requiem for Buffo.'

At that, they all exchange a look, a strange, dark, sad look that, had it been sound, would have reverberated round and round amongst them like the notes of a solemn organ in a great cathedral. When the last echoes of that look, that unspoken message, that mute avowal of some intent unknown to us, died away, old Grok picks up his triangle, gives it a kick, and Grik removes the little fiddle from his hat. I won't say they give me much joy when they start up the Dead March from *Saul*; I get that goose-walking-over-my-grave feeling that tells me something is up, but it's a start. One red-headed fellow, after a bit, picks up a log of wood and hits a dwarf with it. The fire-boy is convulsed with mirth. I unbar the door and out they troop.

The outlaws had summoned up enough spirit to light a fire in the middle of the camp and were all sitting round on tree stumps in the attitude of Rodin's Thinker. A light snow falling, snow settled on their heads. The clowns had lost their leader so it took a little while for them to work out what to do. One performed a cartwheel in a desultory manner until another tripped him over and then, for these were simple folk, the outlaw chief's cheeks crumpled under the flicker of a smile. That seemed to give the clowns heart, or some more complex motivation, for they all snapped to and, Grik and Grok striking a more rhythmic note, they all began to dance.

But what was the tune they played? Damned if I can put a name to it; eldritch music from a witches' sabbath. And, as for their dancing – was 'dance' the right word for it? Nothing about that dance to cheer the heart. God, I thought, we're *fools;* did you ever, yourself, Fevvers, laugh at a clown, not even if it were ever so? Didn't the clowns always summon to your mind disintegration, disaster, chaos?

This dance was the dance of death, and they danced it for George Buffins, that they might be as him. They danced it for the wretched of the earth, that they might witness their own wretchedness. They danced the dance of the outcasts for the outcasts who watched them, amid the louring trees, with a blizzard coming on. And, one by one, the outcast outlaws raised their heads to watch and all indeed broke out in laughter but it was a laughter without joy. It was the bitter laugh one gives when one sees there is no triumph over fate. When we saw those cheerless arabesques as of the damned, and heard that laughter of those trapped in the circles of hell, Liz and I held hands, for comfort.

They danced the night into the clearing, and the outlaws welcomed it with cheers. They danced the perturbed spirit of their master, who came with a great wind and blew cold as death into the marrow of the bones. They danced the whirling apart of everything, the end of love, the end of hope; they danced tomorrows into yesterdays; they danced the exhaustion of the implacable present; they danced the deadly dance of the *past* perfect which fixes everything fast so it can't move again; they danced the dance of Old Adam who destroys the world because we believe he lives forever.

The outlaws entered into the spirit of the thing with a will. With 'huzzahs' and 'bravos', all sprang up and flung themselves into the wild gavotte, firing off their guns. The snow hurled wet, white sheets in our faces, and the wind took up the ghastly music of the old clowns and amplified it fit to drive you crazy. Then the snow blinded us and Samson picked us up one by one and slung us back in that shed and leaned up hard against the door, forcing it closed against the tempest with his mighty shoulders.

Though bullets crashed into the walls and the wind came whistling through the knotholes and picked up burning embers from the fire, hurling them about until we thought we might burn to death in the middle of the snow and ice, the shed held firm. It rocked this way and that way and it seemed at any moment the roof might be snatched away, but this little group of us who, however incoherently, placed our faiths in reason, were not exposed to the worst of the storm. The Escapee, however, faced with this insurrection of militant pessimism, turned pale and wan and murmured to himself comforting phrases of Kropotkin, etc., as others might, in such straits, recite the rosary.

When the storm passed, as pass it did, at last, the freshly fallen snow made all as new and put the camp fire out. Here, there was a shred of scarlet satin and, there, Grik's little violin with the strings broken but, of the tents, shacks, muskets and cuirasses of the outlaws, the clowns and the clowns themselves, not one sight, as if all together had been blown off the face of the earth.

But one poor dog is left behind. The whirlwind must have dropped him off, poor thing. A little mongrel pup with a pom-pom on his tail, running round in circles, whining.

And I hope that outlaw chief was blown clear back to his own village, to find the plough waiting for his hand, the swollen udders of the cow anticipating his fingers, the brown hen clucking for him to collect neglected eggs, and all as it had been – the dear home of nostalgia enriched by absence. But, where the clowns had got to, I do not know. Gone to join George Buffins in the great madhouse in the sky, no doubt.

Lizzie offers no apology for having unwittingly precipitated this denouement. She shrugs; observes: 'Good riddance to bad rubbish'; strips off and puts on a set of the bearskins which she's stitched into coats and trousers for us all. With her moustache and brown face and the shako she's made herself to keep her ears warm, she looks like a little bear, herself.

'Shanks's pony,' she says. 'Let's be off.'

Although the battered shed still stands, none of us survivors have any inclination to stay in that ill-omened place. We shall set boldly forth and rescue ourselves. We don the products of Lizzie's improvised tailoring to keep us warm en route and strike off in what the Escapee thinks is the direction of the railway track. After some thought, he consents to come with us as guide; the Colonel had made extravagant promises about American passports and this young man has the face of one who will believe the beautiful promise of the Statue of Liberty.

The others are amazed at what has come to pass but all that Liz and I know is, the clowns made an invocation to chaos and chaos, always immanent in human affairs, came in on cue. But the Escapee remains most troubled in his mind over the occurrence and tries to engage me in debate on its significance.

'Look, love,' I says to him, eventually, because I'm not in the mood for literary criticism. 'If I hadn't bust a wing in the train-wreck, I could *fly* us all to Vladivostok in two shakes, so I'm not the right one to ask questions of when it comes to what is real and what is not, because, like the duck-billed platypus, half the people who clap eyes on me don't believe what they see and the other half thinks they're seeing things.'

That shut him up.

I'm glad to see the Colonel takes the loss of the clowns in his stride, no doubt rehearsing in his mind the interviews he'll give the press: 'Clowns blown away in blizzard! Eye-witness account of famous circus proprietor.' But some of us are less resilient. Mignon clings tight to the Princess's hand but the Princess's eyes are vacant.

'If we don't get that girl to a keyboard, soon, it will go the worse for her,' I says to Liz.

Samson wraps her in furs and carries her, Mignon trotting behind. And so we leave the outlaw camp, or what remains of it, and the last little clown dog comes with us, not wanting to be left by himself. And, what makes me sad, I find, upon the wind-blown snow, a little way on, just the one feather, the purple feather the fire-boy stole from me, that must have fallen from his jacket as the wind swept him off.

And so our journeyings commenced again, as if they were second nature. Young as I am, it's been a picaresque life; will there be no end to it? Is my fate to be a female Quixote, with Liz my Sancho Panza? If so, what of the young American? Will he turn out to be the beautiful illusion, the Dulcinea of that sentimentality for which Liz upbraids me, telling me it's but the obverse to my enthusiasm for hard cash?

Trudge on, trudge on, girl, and let events dictate themselves.

But, although we trudged long and far, we stayed in the forest, seemed to get no nearer to the railway track than when we'd started out, and the Escapee adopts a worried look. Has he taken a wrong turning, out here, where there *are* no turnings? Or, rather, in this trackless waste, at any single point one stands at an imaginary crossroads, at the confluence of all directions, none of which might be the right direction. And on we go, for fear of freezing to the spot if we stand still.

Then the trees thin out and stop and the Escapee is mightily discomforted, for we've come to the bank of a wide, frozen river, which he hadn't taken into account at all. But, on the other side of the river, there is a little house of that most unsuitable, frilled and goffered kind the Russians elect to build out here and the Escapee guesses, by its loneliness, it is the home of an exile such as he was, who will give us a welcome. So we slip and slide across the river, with little spectral eddies and scurries of wind-blown snow starting up around us like agents of foul weather, and walk up to the front door nice as you please, as if making a formal call in Belgravia, London.

Nailed to the wall beside the door is a shingle on which, in the Cyrillic script, is the inscription: 'Conservatoire of Transbaikalia'. And then a name, with a string of letters after. But this shingle is so stained with moss and age the name is indecipherable; the shingle looks as though it has been uselessly advertising for pupils for some decades.

The Escapee knocked at the door. No reply. No light shone inside, no smoke came out the chimney. He knocked once more and then we pushed the door open to find the stink of humanity inside, certainly, but, in the first room we came to, no other sign of it. The building itself was built of pine, the only flooring being a deep layer of fishbones that shone like ivory and told us that the tenant of this dolorous place ate mostly fish from the river.

In the next room, a stove, with the cold remains of fire in it, and an unlit lamp. The Colonel dipped his finger in the lamp, discovered it was filled with fishoil and at once applied for a dose in order to give a polish to Sybil, whose skin was losing its gloss and suppleness without her daily going-over, so she was looking more and more like a wallet. Liz let him dab a bit on one of his little flags. He squatted down at once, rubbing away as if she were not a pig but Aladdin's lamp. What an aroma – pooh!

I should say the place was furnished – roughly, even exiguously, with a few chairs and a table whose red plush covers, mildewed though they were, hinted touchingly at former pretensions. On the wall, a daguerrotype of a young man standing between a potted palm and a grand piano. And, what's more, a print, as it might have been antique, of a boy in a perruque that Liz swore was Mozart. So whoever lived here, or what *had* lived here, but, by the smell, might recently have dropped off his perch, had been of a musical bent. I immediately drew the Princess's attention to these relics but they were not sufficient, by themselves, to cheer her up.

We lit the lamp and fixed up a fire in the stove with some wood Samson found in an outhouse to fumigate the old mortality from the place before we opened the door to the third room.

To find, of all things, as if in answer to a prayer, not the photograph of a grand piano but the very thing itself! With the lid open, like a big, black butterfly just come to rest, and, upon it, a metronome. The Princess said nothing but the glaze lifted from her eyes and she flexed her fingers and clapped her hands like a delighted child. Coming back to herself in an instant, she sprang forward to the instrument but, just then, a tall, gaunt something, hitherto hidden from us by the ebony wings, starts up from an unseen stool at the keyboard and gives out with a wail.

The shadows cast by the lamp Liz held turned him into something frightful, ghoulish, even. Hair down to his bum and mixed in with the beard that reached his navel, and his fingernails were as long as those of

Struwwelpeter in the picture book, you could see he hadn't had the heart to touch his piano in a month of Sundays for all he threw himself protectively across the keys, letting forth such a clatter of discordant notes you could tell it hadn't been tuned in years, either.

No doubt, when he first caught sight of us, he thought a pack of bears had come visiting. He whinnied with terror, jerking his grasshopper limbs in all directions, producing a cornucopia of atonal effects, and then he scrambled up on top of the thing, waving his arms as if either he'd protect it with his life or else dive into its innards to hide – he seemed undecided as to which course to follow. He dislodged the metronome, which fell to the floor on its side on the carpet of fish-bones, and commenced to tick like a clock.

'Mad as a hatter,' said our Liz. 'Fit to be tied.'

The Princess made faint, mewing sounds, stretching her hands towards the piano beseechingly in a manner fit to melt a heart of stone but the mad old man no longer knew he had a heart. Mignon it was who, restraining Lizzie with a brusque gesture, kicked the ticking metronome to death, cleared her throat, expectorated neatly, and began to sing.

When we first heard her sing, in my room in the Hotel de l'Europe, it sounded as if the song sang itself, as if the song had nothing to do with Mignon and she was only a kind of fleshy phonograph, made to transmit music of which she had no consciousness. That was before she became a woman. Now she seized hold of the song in the supple lassoo of her voice and mated it with her new-found soul, so the song was utterly transformed and yet its essence did not change, in the same way a familiar face changes yet stays the same when it is freshly visited by love. If she sang *a capella* and so only gave us half the song, still it was almost too much for me because she chose the last song of the 'Winter Journey', where the mad young man drifts off into the snow, following the organ-grinder. And will the winter journey of the young man wandering so far away from me turn out so badly? And what of my own journey, what of that? Bereft of my sword, as I am; crippled, as I am . . . yesterday's sensation, a worn-out wonder – pull yourself together, girl.

The hairy old man went on scratching himself during the first verse but slowed down somewhat during the second and, during the third, he stretched out first one leg, then the other, you could hear the bones creak, and flopped back down on the piano stool. I never heard an instrument so out of tune and harsh as he picked out the little phrase in the accompaniment that mimics the hurdy-gurdy. Very slowly, with a perceptible clicking of the finger-joints, he picked out that phrase, again, then again, and the discords made no difference because it was supposed to sound out of tune, like a hurdy-gurdy.

'Course, a baritone should sing it, really.'

I'd never heard the Princess say so much as 'good morning', before, so it came as a shock, the real, rough French of Marseilles and, as one might have expected, a low voice, like a growl.

'Fuck and shit,' she said. 'That piano needs a screwdriver.'

Happily the old man, after some thought, discovered a bit of rusty French and tried it out and we left the three of them quarrelling happily about how best to strip the piano down and so on. You could not make out any change in the old man's facial expression, due to his abundance of facial hair, but he seemed to be taking everything in his stride.

All there was in his larder was a tiny portion of smoked, at a guess, elk, and a semi-refrigerated rat, the latter – I should have thought – the accidental victim of a private misfortune rather than a regular item of diet. When we found the larder so bare, there fell out an ugly disagreement between the Colonel and the Escapee over Sybil, who looked like a good dinner to the one but, for the other, lay under the protection of the taboo against the slaughter of beasts whom we love. In spite of that taboo, Sybil might have escaped the gluttony of the fire-boy only to succumb to the democratic appetite of her friends because at last the Escapee said: 'Let's vote on it.'

Fond as I was of the little pig, not a bite had passed my lips since my interrupted breakfast and greater love hath no pig, that it should lay down its life . . . Sybil knew something was in the wind, although her clairvoyant talents did not stretch far enough to tell her what it was. She burrowed for cover down into the Colonel's waistcoat, where she quivered like a disturbed paunch.

'Eat me before you eat her!' cried the Colonel. 'Make a supper of *long pig* before you tuck into *my* pig, you cannibal!' But the Escapee ignored emotional blackmail.

'All those in favour of roast pork, raise your hands!'

Just as he, Liz, me and Samson formed a reluctant majority, the clown-dog, who'd tagged along with us thus far, now foolishly drew attention to himself by whining at the door to be let out, perhaps thinking to make a getaway, but we forestalled that, we ate him instead of Sybil, boiling him in melted snow because he was too tough to roast, so there was a bit of broth as well. Fido or Bonzo or whatever he was called didn't go far amongst seven but he staved off the pangs so this last relic of the gigantic uselessness of the clowns served some function, in the end. And, next morning, or nearly noon, I should say, for day breaks in a sluggish fashion in the winter of these latitudes, the mad old man dragged himself away from the music room long enough to take those non-musicians amongst us to the river and show us how he did his fishing. So, as regards grub, things were looking up.

The old man's clothes, if perfectly acceptable on the concert-hall rostrum, were a mite out of place in the middle of nowhere especially since, for outdoor wear, he donned a stovepipe hat somewhat concertina'd in the crown. But he knew what he was doing. He left behind the rod and lines and took a big knife with him, and what he did was this: he knelt on the solid ice, cut out a block and held it up to see if there was a fish in it. Third time, lucky; he'd cut in half a frozen carp. Then we all set to and carried home enough for breakfast, though the ice weighed very heavy.

Long before we reached the front door, we heard them. Sound travels far on that vacant air and it is possible the wooden halls of the little house, acting as a sounding-box, improved the tone of the piano whilst magnifying its sound. Anyway, clear as a bell. She'd fixed it so it was as good as new, the marvellous girl, and if I might prophesy squabbles in the future as to who should solo, the old man was too moved to hear them, at that moment, to complain.

Mignon's song is *not* a sad song, not poignant, not a plea. There is a grandeur about her questioning. She does not ask you if you know that land of which she sings because she herself is uncertain it exists – she knows, oh! how well she knows it lies somewhere, elsewhere, beyond the absence of the flowers. She states the existence of that land and all she wants to know is, whether you know it, too.

Just as, drawn by the magnet of the song and insensible to all else, we reached the garden gate, humping the lumps of ice whose dripping weight we had forgotten in our pleasure, Sybil, tucked into the Colonel's waistcoat, whimpered and her nose began to twitch.

We saw the house was roofed with tigers. Authentic, fearfully symmetric tigers burning as brightly as those who had been lost. These were the native tigers of the place, who had never known either confinement or coercion; they had not come to the Princess for any taming, as far as I could see, although they stretched out across the tiles like abandoned greatcoats, laid low by pleasure, and you could see how the tails that dropped down over the eaves like icicles of fur were throbbing with marvellous sympathy. Their eyes, gold as the background to a holy picture, had summoned up the sun that glazed their pelts until they looked unutterably precious.

Under that unseasonable sun, or under the influence of the voice and the piano, all the wilderness was stirring as if with new life. Came a faint shimmer of bird-song, and a whirring as of wings. Soft growls, and mews, and squeaks of paw on snow. And a distant crack or two, as if the ice in the river had broken up in ecstasy.

I thought to myself: when those tigers get up on their hind legs, they will make up their own dances – they wouldn't be content with the ones she'd teach them. And the girls will have to invent new, unprecedented tunes for them to dance to. There will be an altogether new kind of music to which they will dance of their own free will.

The cats were not our only visitors. A little way off, towards the margins of the forest, I made out a group of living creatures who at first seemed almost indistinguishable from the undergrowth, for they were dressed in skins and furs of the same tawny, brownish colour. But one of them was hung with little talismans of carved tin that glittered with an artificial brilliance now that the sun came out and struck him. First one, then another of them moved cautiously forward; although their Mongolian features were characteristically inscrutable, it seemed to me most of them wore a puzzled look. They were the native woodsmen; I could tell at a glance.

I did not see the big one riding the reindeer until the beast, until the attraction of the music, shifted out of the screening branches of the pines. A big one, a huge one, twice the size of the others. And, ooh! didn't he shine; he was so hung with baubles he looked all lit up like Piccadilly and, though he was too far away for his face to be clearly visible, I could see that face was white as milk. The sunlight struck silver off his hair, and off his jaw, which at first seemed silver-plated, but it was a beard.

The beard, at first, deceived me; and his long, shaggy skirts, with the red ribbons on them. And the big drum he held in his hand, like a shield, so he looked wild. What a sea-change! Or, rather, forest-change, for we were as far from the sea as you can get on this planet Earth. I thought he was become a wild, wild woman and then I saw his jaws glint, as if silver-plated, but all it was, was – a beard. He has been gone from me long enough to grow a beard! Oh, my heart . . .

My heart went pit-a-pat, I can tell you, as I watched him listen as if he, too, like the savage beasts (though unlike his savage adopted brethren) were entranced, although he knew the singer and the song so well. My heart went pit-a-pat, and turned right over.

'Jack! Jack!' I cried, interrupting the last verse, I'm sorry to say, such was my impetuous haste, and breaking, alas! the entire spell.

'Jack Walser!'

The tigers raised their heads and roared in a troubled, irritated way, as if wondering how they'd got themselves into such a state in the first place. The people who'd come out of the wood all shook themselves, too, took a good look at the tigers as if they hadn't noticed them before and didn't much like what they saw, now. Were they going to run away? Would *he* run away without seeing me?

I spread. In the emotion of the moment, I spread. I spread hard enough, fast enough to bust the stitching of my bearskin jacket. I spread; bust my jacket; and out shot my you-know-whats.

The Escapee's mouth dropped open, which is a risky thing to happen in this climate, your lungs can freeze. The old man fell on his knees and crossed himself curiously. The woodsmen all looked in my direction. From the woodsmen, a great shout went up. In the gap left by the broken music, came a drumming; the other fellow with tin spangles on started to batter away on his drum for dear life.

My enthusiasm carried me a few yards through the air; truly, I forgot my wing was broken. With the aid of the other, I fluttered lopsidedly a few yards more, until I could no longer sustain myself aloft upon it and crash-landed on my face in a snowdrift as the woodsmen kicked up their mounts and fled, the drummer still drumming away, and the tigers, as startled as anybody else, all streaked off, too, and we were alone again.

EIGHT

The one-eyed man will be King in the country of the blind only if he arrives there in full possession of his partial faculties – that is, providing he is perfectly aware of the precise nature of sight and does not confuse it with second sight, nor with the mind's eye's visions, nor with madness. As Walser slowly began to recover his wits among the forest dwellers, those wits proved of as little use to him as one crazy eye would have been in a company of the sightless. When he was visited by memories of the world outside the village, as sometimes happened, he thought that he was raving. All his previous experiences were rendered null and void. If those experiences had never, heretofore, modified his personality to any degree, now they lost all potential they might have had for re-establishing Walser's existential credibility – except, that is, his credibility as a dement.

Happily for Walser, his hosts thought none the worse of him for ranting away in strange tongues. Far from it. They did not treat him like a king but they *did* behave quite kindly to him – to exactly the extent that they believed him to be hallucinated, since, traditionally, the natives of those remote parts of Siberia regarded hallucination as a job of work.

Not, of course, that theirs was, in any sense, the country of the blind. As far as seeing went, they made good use of their eyes. Tracks of bird and beast upon the snow were legends they descried like writing. They read the sky to know from which direction wind, snow and the thaw would come. Stars were their compasses. The wilderness that seemed a bundle of blank paper to the ignorant, urban eye was the encyclopedia, packed with information, they consulted every day for every need, conning the landscape as if it were an instruction manual of universal knowledge of the 'Inquire within' type. They were illiterate only in the literal sense and, as far as the theory and the accumulation of knowledge were concerned, they were pedants.

The Shaman was the pedant of pedants. There was nothing vague about his system of belief. His type of mystification necessitated hard, if illusory, fact, and his mind was stocked with concrete specifics. With what passionate academicism he devoted himself to assigning phenomena their rightful places in his subtle and intricate theology! If he was always in demand for exorcisms and prophecies, and often asked to use his necromantic powers to hunt out minor domestic items which had been mislaid, these were frivolous distractions from the main, pressing, urgent, arduous task in hand, which was the interpretation of the visible world about him via the information he acquired through dreaming. When he slept, which he did much of the time, he would, could he have written it, have put a sign on his door: 'Man at work'.

And even when his eyes were open, you might have said the Shaman 'lived in a dream'. But so did they all. They shared a common dream, which was their world, and it should rather be called an 'idea' than a 'dream', since it constituted their entire sense of lived reality, which impinged on *real* reality only inadvertently.

This world, dream, dreamed idea or settled conviction extended upwards, to the heavens, and downwards, into the bowels of the earth and the depths of the lakes and rivers, with all whose tenants they lived on intimate terms. But it did not extend laterally. It did not, could not, take into account any other interpretation of the world, or dream, which was not their own one. Their dream was foolproof. An engine-turned fabrication. A closed system. Foolproof because it *was* a closed system. The Shaman's cosmogony, for all its complexity of forms, impulses and states of being perpetually in flux, was finite just because it was a human invention and possessed none of the implausibility of authentic history. And 'history' was a concept with which they were perfectly unfamiliar, as, indeed, they were with any kind of geography except the mystically four-dimensional one they invented for themselves.

They knew the space they saw. They believed in a space they apprehended. Between knowledge and belief, there was no room for surmise or doubt. They were, at the same time, pragmatic as all hell and, intellectually speaking, permanently three sheets in the wind.

Until they met the Russian fur-trader who, half a century previously, had introduced into the tribe the strain of gonorrhoea which accounted for their historically low birth-rate at this time, they had never encountered a foreigner – that is, one whose terms of reference were not their own terms. Since they did not have a word for 'foreigner', they used the word for 'devil' to designate the fur-trader and, later on, decided it had been such an apt choice they continued to use the word 'devil', as the generic term for those round-eyed ones who soon began to pop up everywhere.

Because, before you could blink, an entire alien township was clustering round that first wooden hut; and, now that the railway passed so close to them on its way to R. that their little children trotted alongside the great, lumbering, puffing engines, cheering them on, how much longer would this community of dreamers be able to maintain the primitive integrity of its collective unconsciousness against the brutal technological actuality of the Age of Steam?

For just so long, perhaps, as they conspired to ignore it. As long as none of those applauding children decided it wanted to be an engine driver when it grew up. Until such a time as one of them wondered where the trains really came from and where they were really going instead of looking at them with indifferent wonder. And it was indifference, a cultivated indifference, with which the tribespeople defended themselves against all the significance of the township of R. and its residents.

This indifference masked fear. They did not fear the strangers themselves; he who introduced sterility amongst them also introduced firearms, and aborigines and settlers quickly learned an armed neutrality was best. Nor did they fear the gonococci; it was another kind of infection that they feared – a spiritual infection of discontent, contracted from exposure to the unfamiliar, whose symptoms were questions. Therefore they visited the settlement of R. in order to trade and to scavenge. No more. For them, R. was just as much a town of dream as their own village, and they intended to keep it that way.

Although Walser was twice their average size, white as stripped birchwood, and his round eyes were minus the Mongolian fold, they knew he was not a 'devil' in the sense of a 'foreign devil', more a 'devil' in the sense of 'demonic visitant', or 'wood demon', or 'representative of the spirit world', because of the extraordinary rapture with which he was seized during most of his waking hours. The Shaman introduced his foundling to the rest of the tribe: 'Behold, this dreamer!' They listened respectfully to Walser's babblings and, when they did not understand him, took it as proof he was in a holy trance.

So, as Walser recovered from the amnesia that followed the blow on his head, he found himself condemned to a permanent state of sanctified delirium – or, would have found himself condemned, if he had been presented with any other identity but that of the crazed. As it was, his self remained in a state of limbo.

Walser lived with the Shaman. Even the father of the grandfather of the Shaman had been a shaman. When a sickly boy, he suffered from fainting fits, just as they had done before him. During one of these fainting fits, all his marvellous forefathers visited the boy. Some wore horns, others bore udders. They stood him up like a block of wood and fired arrows at him from their bows until he went off into another fainting fit within the fainting fit – put it another way: during his faint, he dreamed he fainted. Then his ancestors cut him up in pieces and ate him raw. They counted the bones that were left. There was one more than the regular number. That was how the ancestors knew the lad was made of the right stuff to follow the family profession.

This ritual lasted an entire summer and, while the ancestors were busy with it, the little boy was not allowed to eat or drink anything and so grew very pale. Now he was grown up, the Shaman looked at Walser's pale skin and thought that the counting of *his* bones must have taken much longer than a summer. Had there been some problem? Too many bones? Too few? And what might too many, or too few bones, mean in the great scheme of things? Just the sort of puzzle the Shaman enjoyed!

After the ancestors counted the bones, they put them back together again and restored the boy with a strengthening drink of reindeer blood. As he lay in his hut, his tongue began to sing of its own accord. His mother and father, both of whom were shamans, came to listen. The singing tongue told them what kind of drum their son should carry when he went to summon up the spirits. They went out to kill a reindeer and set to work at once to flay and cure the skin.

The Shaman gave Walser another tumblerful of piss and Walser started to sing. The Shaman listened very carefully. Walser sang:

> So we'll go no more a-roving
> So late into the night
> Though the heart be still as loving
> And the moon shine still as bright.

Such tender concern as the Shaman felt, to see the tears splash down his young charge's cheeks! But the sound of his singing seemed passing strange to the Shaman, unaccustomed as he was to European music. However, he was sure he interpreted the sounds correctly, so he killed a reindeer and stretched the skin out between two poles to dry. Due to the inclemency of the weather, he was forced to do this inside the hut, which soon smelled ripe. He stoked up the fire with dried branches of thyme and juniper, not so that the fragrant smoke would disguise the stink of rotting reindeer-hide – himself, he rather savoured that, though Walser gagged a bit – but because the incense of the burning herbs procured visions. Walser's eyes rolled round and round in their sockets, again; splendid!

Normally, Walser shared the Shaman's suppers, but, today, as an experiment, the Shaman decided to feed Walser the same diet he offered to the idols in the austere and windowless village god-hut, the quasi-anthropomorphs in front of whom he practised the mysteries of his religion. They thrived on a porridge made of crushed barley mixed with pine nuts and broth from boiled capercailzie. Walser supped up suspiciously, then pushed the porridge round and round the wooden bowl with his horn spoon. The dried herbs crackled above the stove. Walser's eyes fused.

'Hamburgers,' he ruminated aloud. The Shaman pricked up his ears. Walser rambled off down a gastronomic memory lane; who can tell what litany the Shaman thought he was reciting?

'Fish soup.' Walser's face was the mirror of his memory; he grimaced. He tried again. 'Christmas dinner . . . '

His face convulsed and he whimpered. The words, 'Christmas dinner', reminded him of something most fearful, of some hideous danger; they reminded him of the main course, they reminded him of . . . 'Cock-a-doodle-do!'

He cried aloud, assailed by dreadful if incomprehensible memories, then fell into a haunted silence until another happier thought came to him:

'Eel pie and mash.'

At that, he beamed and rubbed his stomach with his hand. Raptly attentive, the Shaman, the reader of signs, poured him more broth, and waited for further revelations.

'Eel pie and mash, me old cock,' said Walser appreciatively.

The Shaman decided Walser must mean the time had come to make him his shamanising drum. Next morning, he blindfolded Walser with a strip of reindeer hide, wrapped him up warmly, took him outdoors, spun him round three times on the spot to disorient him, and gave him a hearty push. Walser lurched off, the Shaman following after with an axe on his shoulder, listening intently to the soft voices of larch and birch and fir murmuring sweet nothings to him.

Walser wandered uncertainly forward, teased by increasingly unpleasant voyages his imagination took eyeless behind the blindfold until he could have sworn he heard, in the swish of the wind in the undergrowth, the hiss of a single word: 'Homicide!'

At that, Walser snatched off his blindfold and punched the Shaman on the nose. But the Shaman was confidently anticipating irrational behaviour and punched Walser right back, although he had to jump up in the air to do so since Walser was much taller than he. However, after that, he let Walser tramp on without the blindfold.

After a while, the Shaman heard a soft, persistent knocking. Walser, who could hear nothing – and, indeed, there was really nothing to be heard – watched the Shaman suspiciously from the corner of his eye as he went up to a tree whose name Walser did not know and put his ear to the trunk. After a moment, the Shaman shook his head irritably and motioned Walser to walk on.

That is what the drumming tree said to the Shaman: 'Yah! Fooled you!'

Soon another tree began to drum but it turned out this one, too, was enjoying a joke at the Shaman's expense. He began to mutter under his breath. But the third drumming tree announced disconsolately: 'I am the one.' The Shaman immediately cut it down and made Walser carry the trunk home. He cut the hoop of the drum out of the wood from this tree as he sat in front of the stove in his odorous house.

The Shaman's quarters were a neat, snug, square, one-storey house built of pine logs. Over the samovar hung a leather bag decorated with eagle feathers, tails of squirrels and rabbits, tin discs and little plaits of leather; this bag contained his amulet, which he let nobody see, not even Walser, even though he soon came to love Walser dearly. In his amulet resided the whole source of his extraordinary powers. His father, from whom he had inherited it, assured him he must never, ever reveal the contents. He was so secretive about the contents of his amulet-bag it might well have contained nothing at all.

The Shaman and Walser did not live alone. There was a bear, a black one, not yet a year old, still almost a cub. This bear was part pet, part familiar; he was both a real, furry and beloved bear and, at the same time, a transcendental kind of meta-bear, a minor deity and also a partial ancestor because the forest-dwellers extended considerable procreational generosity towards the other species of the woods and there were bears in plenty on the male side of the tribal line.

The Shaman believed the bear, as a baby, had been let down from the sky in a silver cradle. He saw the cradle drop down into a thicket from a silver cord but cradle and cord had both vanished by the time he reached the baby bear. He brought it home in his fetish satchel and gave it a rag dipped in reindeer milk to suck. When the cub progressed to solids, he ate what the Shaman ate – fresh-water fish; porridge; game. He would be offered bear-steaks only after he was dead.

The Shaman pierced the cub's ear and gave it copper earbobs, to make it pretty, and also gave it a copper collar, and put a copper bracelet on the left paw. On its first birthday, it would be taken to the god-hut and its throat would be slit in front of an ursine idol sitting above a heaping mound of skulls of bears who had met their fate in a similar fashion.

The Shaman himself did not do the deed. The bear's executioner was elected from amongst the villagers by the spirits, who manifested their choice in dreams or by other extra-terrestrial means, and the Shaman was glad of that because he always established such close relationships with the bears that it would have broken his heart to dispatch them, even though he knew it was all for the best. The entire village crowded into the god-hut to watch the ceremony, lamenting vigorously and apologising profusely: 'Poor bruin! We're so sorry, bruin! How we love you, poor little bruin! How bad we feel because we must do away with you!' Then the bear's head would be cut off and the rest of it roasted over an open fire. The severed head, still with the copper bobs in its ears, was set in the middle of a common table and the choicest titbits, the liver, the sweetbreads, the tender meat of loin and buttock, were laid in front of the bleeding relic whilst everyone else feasted on the remainder of the bear's anatomy. The celebrants of this Siberian sacrament pretended not to notice the provider of the banquet never touched a morsel himself.

Bruin, now free of his fleshy envelope, would carry messages to the dead; those who ate him would partake of the strength and valour of the bear; and, besides, since death was not precisely mortal in this theology, bruin would soon be up and about again, to be born again, captured again, reared again, killed again in a perpetually recurring cycle of return.

And, golly! didn't he taste good!

After the flesh was boiled away, his skull would be tossed on the heap in the god-hut that, were it to have been counted out, would have announced the extreme antiquity of these customs. But nobody ever counted the heap because none of them knew in what way the past differed from the present. They weren't too sure of what was different about the future, either. Meanwhile, the bear lived on in happy ignorance.

Walser shared with the Shaman and the bear a large brass bedstead which the Shaman, waste not, want not, had retrieved from the garbage heap at the railhead of R. Soon Walser shared the bear's vermin, too.

The Shaman believed that bears could talk to all other animals in the forest and so, sooner or later, his bear would strike up a meaningful conversation with Walser but time passed and, though the young man and the bear got on well enough together, they showed no signs of conversing. However, for want of anything better to do, time lying heavy on his hands during the long evenings, Walser taught the bear to dance. Following a deep, almost instinctual prompting, Walser led, although the bear was male too.

The first time the bear got the hang of it, another piece of the jigsaw of Walser's past fell into the incoherence of his present, although the jigsaw was not only incomplete but not yet recognised *as* a jigsaw. He and the bear circled the hut. His feet knew better than his brain what he was up to and obeyed the dictates of a certain otherwise forgotten rhythm: *one*, two, three, *one*, two three . . . He and the grunting bear circled the floor in front of the stove on which the dried juniper cracked and smoked, as once he had danced on a floor of sawdust with another clawed predator. As once he had danced a –

'Waltz!' he cried. And then, with glad recognition: 'Walser! Me, Walser!'

And let go the bear in order to beat himself on the chest.

'Walser is me!'

The Shaman understood perfectly and, for once, correctly. He was very pleased when his apprentice, in his ecstasy, executed a barbarous dance and, in an ecstasy, gave himself his professional name. Walser would be able to make his debut as a sorcerer very, very soon. The Shaman stretched the reindeer hide he had prepared over the hoop of the drum and left it to cure. The Shaman carved a drumstick from alder wood, trapped a variable hare, skinned it and covered the drumstick with the pelt that, at this season, was as white as the snow that lay all around. Now all that remained was the patient wait until such time as Walser exhibited the signs, the frothings at the mouth, the fallings, the shrieks, that would show he was ready to begin drumming.

Walser, by this time, was willy-nilly picking up a few words of the

Shaman's language, hard and lumpy as it was, spiked with k's and t's, clogged with glottal stops, all the clicking, gulping noises of axe on wood and boots in snow. In the haphazardly functional manner of a child learning to speak, he first acquired nouns: 'Hunger'; 'Thirst'; 'Sleep'. Then he acquired a rapidly increasing number of the seventy-four words in their language expressing different varieties of cold. Before long, he began to adventure with their rococo grammar.

His gradual acquisition of the Shaman's language set up a conflict within him, for his memories, or his dreamings, or whatever they were, were dramatised in quite another language. When he spoke out loud in that language, the Shaman paid him far more attention than he did when he asked for another glass of tea in proto-Finno-Ugric, because the Shaman assumed Walser's remembered English was the astral discourse that must be interpreted according to his own grand hypothesis, a set of conundrums that became perfectly scrutable with the aid of meditation and that distillate with which he continued to dose Walser.

The Shaman listened the most attentively to what Walser said after a dream because it dissolved the slender margin the Shaman apprehended between real and unreal, although the Shaman himself would not have put it that way since he noticed only the margin, shallow as a step, between one level of reality and another. He made no categorical distinction between seeing and believing. It could be said that, for all the peoples of this region, there existed no difference between fact and fiction; instead, a sort of magic realism. Strange fate for a journalist, to find himself in a place where no facts, as such, existed! Not that Walser would have known what a journalist was, any more. He was increasingly visited by memories; had he but known it, his head was clearing more and more day by day – he no longer crowed like a cock – but his memories were incomprehensible to him until the Shaman interpreted them.

The Shaman effortlessly reconciled the facility with which Walser spoke in tongues with the tenets of his own complex metaphysics. But, if Walser came to accept the notion he was unusually gifted with the power of dreaming, for this was the only theory of his difference available to him, sometimes, as with the rediscovery of his name, he brought himself up short:

'Is there, as I sometimes imagine, a world beyond this place?'

Then he would sink into troubled introspection. So Walser acquired an 'inner life', a realm of speculation and surmise within himself that was entirely his own. If, before he set out with the circus in pursuit of the bird-woman, he had been like a house to let, furnished, now he was tenanted at last, even if that interior tenant was insubstantial as a phantom and sometimes disappeared for days at a time.

But, in the circumstances, it was useless to ask if there was a world beyond – because the Shaman knew quite well there was! Didn't he visit it constantly? During the trances for which he possessed a hereditary disposition, he often travelled there. The Shaman was not alone in his familiarity with the world beyond; whenever he took a trip, he found the air above Transbaikalia thick with flying shamans! That world was as familiar to him as the one in which he had temporarily dropped anchor in order to discuss the proposition of another world with Walser, and that world and this world must surely be the same as the world Walser visited in *his* trances, because all worlds were unique and indivisible.

And that was that. End of discussion. The Shaman fell to caressing his bear.

But Walser, one day, wandered down by the railway track and found there a little tribal boy squatting on a stump in the snow, his eyes fixed on the middle distance upon whose whiteness a smudge of smoke from a departing train gradually erased itself. And on the face of this child Walser saw an expression of yearning that moved him, and, more than that, stirred his memory, for he recognised that expression, not with his eyes but with his heart; for just one moment he became again the tow-haired urchin who, a quarter-century ago, had gazed at the swelling sails, the belching smokestacks, of the ships that set out from San Francisco Bay towards the four corners of the world.

And so he remembered the sea. When he remembered the landless wastes, the infinite freedom of the eternally shifting waters, the fugal music of the deep, he knew the Shaman could never believe all that; the Shaman lived so far inland he would have taken an oar, had he ever seen one, to be a winnowing fan. And he could not interpret *this* vision; he could not decide what the sea *meant* – although, as his grasp of the Shaman's language grew, he was able to make a few stabs at interpreting the dream material as he went along.

'I see a man carrying a' – he fumbled for the word – 'a pig. You don't know what a pig is? A little animal, good to eat. The upper part of this man's apparel mimics the starry heavens. The lower part, by a system of parallel bars, represents, perhaps . . . felled trees . . . He brings light, and he brings food, but he also seems to bring . . . destruction . . . '

Walser had learned to speak in images in order to recount his visions so that the Shaman would understand them but the Shaman understood them in his own way. He identified the 'little, delicious animal' as the bear, of which Walser was almost as fond as he, and therefore interpreted this dream as the one in which the spirits named Walser as the bear's executioner, for the bear's time was drawing nigh. The spirits must also be using the dream to place an order for Walser's shamanising costume.

The Shaman therefore carved a dress out of elk-hide and cut some stars out of the remains of an old bully-beef tin he'd picked up in R. He went to a female first cousin of his who worked in a minor pastoral capacity as village midwife and wise woman and asked her to sew up the elk-hide dress and appliqué the tin stars to the bosom. She consented to do this in the spare time left over from the complex rituals surrounding the birth of her eldest daughter's first child. These rituals were especially complex because births were relatively rare in the community, these days, and it was necessary to deceive the spirits – to convince them no birth had, in fact, taken place, lest they come and steal away the little newcomer in order to increase the population of the other world, rather than this one.

Walser sat in front of the stove and thought of the stars and the stripes, and sang:

> Oh, say can you see
> By the dawn's early light . . .

He tried to translate the song for the Shaman but words failed him and he carried on in American. The Shaman enjoyed hearing Walser sing, although to his ears, the noise was raucous and discordant in the extreme, further proof of the extraordinary things the spirits kept up their sleeves for such as he. He liked to sing along with Walser, especially after a tot of piss, modifying the alien melodies with a quarter-tone or two of his own.

> But the rockets' red glare,
> Bombs bursting in air –

But no! the flag was *not* there; no star-spangl'd banner unfurled in the perfumed, hazy smoke of the Shaman's hut, with its brass bedstead, samovar, amulet bag and the bear with earrings scratching its armpits in front of the fire. The Shaman was busy fixing the drum. A stew of dried fish bubbled away for supper, adding to the rich odours of man and beast already present a reek as of a whore's drawers.

'A whore's drawers,' said Walser to himself, reflectively. 'A whore's drawers . . . '

The more of the past Walser put together in a crazy quilt out of the rag-bag of the memory he did not know *was* a memory, the more unlikely it seemed. He sat in the corner and puzzled away at it all until the Shaman shook him out of reverie in order to give him some lessons.

These lessons consisted of:

a) prestidigitation, or sleight of hand – the ability to conceal pebbles, sticks, spiders and, if any were obtainable, baby mice about his person and produce them in the course of a diagnosis or an operation;

b) ventriloquism – the assumption of a high, squeaky voice of the special kind associated with the voices of the spirits, and to 'throw' it, so it might seem as if it came from within the patient himself, or out of the fire, or from the muzzle of the earringed bear-cub, or from the carved mouth of an idol in the god-hut.

c) last but not least – the power of looking preternaturally solemn, as if he were the possessor of knowledge hidden from ordinary mortals.

Do not run away with the idea, from all this, that the Shaman was a humbug who would have been a prize addition to that series of Walser's 'Great Humbugs of the World', if he'd still been looking for candidates. The Shaman most certainly was *not* a humbug. His was the supreme form of the confidence trick – others had confidence in him because of his own utter confidence in his own integrity. He was the doctor and the midwife of the village, the dream-reader and the fortune-teller, the intellectual and the philosopher, to boot; he also conducted weddings and burials. Furthermore, he negotiated with and interpreted the significance of those natural forces to which the circumstances of their lives made them especially vulnerable.

But, though the Shaman might know full well how it was an evil spirit in the form of, for example, a mouse that was causing his patient's, say, diarrhoea, the patient would be convinced only by oracular proof and would continue to shit freely until the hypothetical mouse had been removed from his anus. The spirits took forms visible, unfortunately, only to the Shaman himself so that, to keep his customers satisfied, he must equip himself with corporeal imitations of these malevolent forms and then he could be seen to have cast them out. ('Seeing is believing.')

Hearing was believing too. The Shaman heard the idols in the god-hut speak quite clearly and listened avidly to the voices of the wind, but it was necessary to persuade those whose ears were not as sharp as his to harken also.

The solemn look was the prerequisite for the whole performance; who would believe a giggling Shaman?

And once the tribe stopped believing in the Shaman's powers, then – Othello's occupation gone. They might even have started thinking he was unbalanced. Or worse; for some of his habits, had they not been sanctified by tradition, would have seemed distinctly perverse. Worst of all, if they stopped believing in him, the Shaman might even have been expected to engage in – the spirits forbid! – productive labour, in the drudgery of hunting, shooting, fishing and the sporadic cultivation of late barley to which his neighbours were bound, of which labour, at the moment, he lived comfortably on the surplus, paid in kind by grateful patients or those whose dreams he had interpreted with a happy degree of accuracy.

He fully intended that Walser, the stray to whom the spirits directed him in the woods, the little bird hatched from an egg whose shell had disappeared in just the same way as the bear-cub's celestial cradle did – he intended that Walser, his adoptive son, should one day inherit all his power, all his authority, all his special skills, even unto his reindeer and his samovar. Day by day, he grew fonder of Walser. At night, he fondled and cuddled Walser affectionately before they went to sleep. He was even fonder of Walser than he was of his bear. Now that Walser was here, he would not miss the bear when the time came to immolate him.

The tribe counted the passing of time by blocks of light and darkness, of snow and summer; since their almanac was that of the seasons and their exposure to the foreign devils who put fire in the bladder had not tempted them to adopt any other calendar, they observed the winter solstice with a great deal of ceremony. A large larch tree, leafless at this season, stood outside the god-hut, and, as the slit of light at noon grew daily less and less, the Shaman and his female lieutenant, his first cousin, opened up a number of boxes inside the god-hut and took out enormous quantities of red ribbons, and also of pendants of tin in various shapes of stars, crescent moon and moons and men and women stylised as gingerbread people. The Shaman encouraged Walser to help the other two clamber up the tree and hang these decorations from its boughs. Walser thought the tree would look even nicer if they stuck lighted candles to the boughs, too, but there were no candles to be had. Walser thought that Christmas must be coming, but he could not remember what Christmas was, and, of course, Christmas had nothing to do with it. The village would also remain in ignorance of that moment, now approaching with great speed, when the nineteenth century would transform itself into the twentieth.

You could not even say they were exiles from history; rather, they inhabited a temporal dimension which did not take history into account. They were a-historic. Time meant nothing to them.

At this time, the cusp of the modern age, the hinge of the nineteenth century, had a plebiscite been taken amongst all the inhabitants of the world, by far the great number of them, occupied as they were throughout the planet with daily business of agriculture of the slash and burn variety, warfare, metaphysics and procreation, would have heartily concurred with these indigenous Siberians that the whole idea of the twentieth century, or any other century at all, for that matter, was a rum notion. Had this global plebiscite been acted upon in a democratic manner, the twentieth century would have forthwith ceased to exist, the entire system of dividing up years by one hundred would have been abandoned and time, by popular consent, would have stood still.

Yet, even then, even in these remote regions, in those days, those last, bewildering days before history, that is, history as we know it, that is, white history, that is, European history, that is, Yanqui history – in that final little breathing space before history *as such* extended its tentacles to grasp the entire globe, the tribespeople were already addicted to tea and handy with imported firearms and axes which they could not make themselves, being essentially Stone Age people. They knew more than they said. The future was more present to them than they were prepared to admit; every day they drank it and they handled it.

So they were not quite in the same position as those American Indians who, that day in fourteen hundred and ninety-two, woke up happy in the belief they were the lone inhabitants of the planet, smug in treacherous security of the conviction that, because nothing had ever changed in their world, nothing ever *would* change, and so, in their innocence, were doomed. These Siberian tribespeople knew they were not alone and their lives had changed already, although, at this point in time, it still seemed possible their flexible and resilient mythology would be able to incorporate the future into itself and so prevent its believers from disappearing into the past.

The Shaman's cousin finished making Walser's shamanising gown.

As requested, there were stars across the bosom and stripes athwart the skirt, although the Colonel would not have recognised the Old Glory in this incarnation, so thoroughly had the Shaman's cousin assimilated the design motifs with the traditional iconography of the tribe. She ran out of tin before she finished the ornaments so she went on reindeer-back to the settlement of R. and bartered a dose for a new kettle. When she got home, she cut up the kettle and made lots of little bells out of the metal. She sewed the bells on to the gown at the shoulderblades, under the arms and at the elbow joints.

'You must listen to the tinkling of the bells to find out . . .' and here the Shaman looked amazingly solemn '. . . certain things.'

But the tinkling suggested to Walser that he prance and caper. She sewed a little tuft of feathers on either shoulder, too. Although they were supposed to help him levitate, Walser broke down and cried like a baby when he saw the feathers. Why was that?

The Shaman mixed pigments extracted from various earths, mosses, lichens and berries and began to paint the surface of the drum. On the upper part, he painted sun, moon, birch trees, willow trees and horned mammals of indeterminate species. On the lower part, he painted frogs, fish, snails, worms and men. In the middle, feet in the lower part and head in the upper part, he painted an anthropomorphic figure designed to travel easily between the two zones; this figure was human, or, at least, bipedal, with nothing about it to hint at whether it was supposed to be male or female, and of impressive size. In order to facilitate its journeyings, the Shaman painted wings on the figure, big wings, outspread wings, and painted in the wings with pigment of a dull yet vibrant red he obtained by grinding dried lice with a pestle and mortar.

This figure troubled and delighted Walser even more than the bells and feathers on his garment. He gazed at the drum for hours at a time, cooing and chuckling, as if exercising his new-born sensibility. He knocked and tapped at the drum with the furry drumstick, trying to persuade it to speak to him. Nothing doing. He smiled at the figure and danced for it, both with the bear and without him. Finally, extending his arms towards the painted being in a supplicatory gesture, he came out with, in English:

'Only a bird in a gilded cage!'

Then a door slammed shut in his memory and, for the time being, he lived on as a tribal child, privileged only in that he was an unusually gifted one.

Next came the question of his cap, without which his shamanising outfit was not complete. The design of this cap must come from visionary inspiration, too, just as that for the rest of his outfit had done. The Shaman thought the best thing was to put Walser on a reindeer and let the reindeer itself judge where best to find the inspiration for the cap. When to do it, though – why, when else but the necromantic day of the winter solstice itself! when the sun temporarily laid low and strange beasts of night came out to frolic in the dusky air.

Since the winter had gone on for two or three months already, most of the villagers were ready for some fun when the late dawn of the winter solstice dawned; and, though the sun did not manage to heave itself above the horizon until well past the hour when, in a civilised country, they would have had their elevenses, it finally arrived in splendour. In almost too much splendour; so unseasonal was the weather that the Shaman, who'd been anticipating murk, felt oddly ill at ease, as if some kind of magic outside his control might be going on. However, the sunshine brought the villagers out, and when the Shaman and Walser were dressed up ready to go, a fair number of trippers gathered round them well supplied with odds and ends of picnic things. But the Shaman's cousin stayed home, in order to fix her daughter up in the shelter some distance from the village where mother and baby must stay in seclusion for ten days after the birth, so that the evil spirits would never know anything had happened.

Walser's reindeer, left to seek its own way, took them off in the direction of the sanctuary of the foreign devils and their accursed iron road. The Shaman was secretly disquieted yet, all the same, anything was possible, even a vision which would mean a shaman's cap made up after the style of those of the conductors of the Great Siberian Railway, so needs must all troop along behind. Walser dutifully applied his lessons in looking solemn so successfully that the Shaman, for all his inner perturbation, felt a sentimental pride.

It was as fine a day as the region could contrive at the time of year – a sky as blue as a baby's eyeball; pale, reticent sunshine that offered the bitter-sweet, Slavonic pleasure of evanescence, for it would be gone so very soon; and, today, the snow did not look a killing blanket but like a tender coverlet designed to keep the cold away from germinating seeds. The children scooped up snowballs and pelted one another. A snowball hit the back of the Shaman's hat, procuring a jingle from his bells and a subdued titter amongst the small fry. The Shaman noted this token of disrespect glumly. Proud as he was of Walser, some sixth sense still told him the day might not go well. He was delighted when Walser's reindeer veered away from the track to R. and started to plot a course in the general direction of the river; he perked up at once. All slithered and capered on in cheerful mood.

And then the radiant shadow of the implausible cast its transforming spell across the morning.

Out of nowhere, or out of the pale blue sky, or else issuing from the cool heart of the white, fragile sun, there came a voice raised in song—a human voice, a woman's voice, a lovely voice. Such a voice you might believe would bring on springtime prematurely. A voice to quicken all the little flowers so that they came out of the snow to dry their petals. A voice to make the larches shiver with pleasure and stretch their branches like children eager to dance. All of revivification, all of renewal was promised by that voice.

A soprano voice and a pianoforte accompaniment.

Birds rattled and soared out of the branches through the brightening air towards the source of the music. The undergrowth rustled with the movements of small mammals and rodents as they, too, made their way to drink thirstily from the miraculous fountain of song. Even the reindeer, on their feet like snowshoes, quickened their flapping pace.

But, if the fauna and flora of the Siberian forest responded as those of the Thracian forest once did to the music of Orpheus, the human forest-dwellers were deaf to the mythic resonances, since these awoke no echoes in their own mythology. This music had no charms for them, nor did it soothe their savage breasts at all, at all; they scarcely recognised the Schubert *lied as* music, for it had little in common with the scales and modes of the music they themselves, at the infrequent request of the spirits, made on skin drums, flutes fashioned from the femur of the elk and xylophones of stone. As far as singing was concerned, they preferred an edge like sandpaper on a voice; the honeyed tones of the girl soprano did not strike *their* palates like honey. The magic of her song was alien magic and did not enchant them. However, it intrigued them, even excited them; they, too, drew towards its source, pondering on how it might be the cacophony of uninvited gods who'd slipped across the border between the visible and the invisible on this unseasonably bright solstice. Each brow was furrowed, all lips pursed in query.

But Walser found he was shaking like the larch trees, for the music had the familiarity of a remembered dream. When he saw the dwelling in the clearing with its thatch of swooning tigers, it was so complex a vision he could not, at first, decode it, but kept his reindeer back a little as the eager and curious tribespeople swept forward.

The Shaman smelled a rat, however. He was accustomed to seeing, or seering, and then persuading others that they saw the same things as he; but now all those around him were seeing the same thing as he did, spontaneously. He thought that was odd. The piano, whose well-tempered scale set his teeth on edge, came out of somebody else's dream, not his own dream, not any dream with which he was familiar. If it came out of Walser's dream, then Walser was much further along the high road to full shamanship than the Shaman had realised. The homestead before them, the song that welled up from within it, the somnolent tigers on top of it and the odd-looking group of round-eyed individuals who now appeared from the direction of the river carrying blocks of ice containing fish, all this combined to unsettle the Shaman. He felt he was getting out of his depth.

When the round-eyes made their appearance, Walser felt as though an early thaw were softening his brain; uncertain what to think, uncertain even how to think any more, he urged his reindeer forward for a closer look.

'Jack! Jack!'

She might have been mimicking wood-chopping, so little sense did it make to him. The music ceased on a discord; loud and clear in the sudden silence now rang out:

'Jack Walser!'

His name, in the mouth of the winged creature. A sign! But it was not enough to make the Shaman happy. Accustomed as he was to negotiating with all manner of anomalous imaginary things, winged or otherwise, with heads of bears and feet of elk, torsos of fish and loins of the eagle, she, with her yellow hair, furred legs and plumage of bright, artificial colours only seen before on trade blankets, might or might not be inimical. Even if she knew his apprentice's name, she was still making an, on his terms, unearthly racket. Besides all that, her ostentatious wings were not even functional; now they let her down unceremoniously in a drift, with a wet thud. Incompetence of the apparition! And now she was letting loose the angry tigers upon them!

Hastily the Shaman began to beat out a magical defence upon his drum as the tribals scattered this way and that, in disarray, emitting sharp cries of disappointment and outrage. Walser, who appeared seized by an ecstatic fit fully the equal of any the Shaman could throw, attempted to stay the headlong flight of his mount but to no avail; it did not stop running until it got back to the village, where it shrugged him off its back, heaved a great sigh of relief and went off to nibble moss. Walser rolled about on the snowy ground, giggling and sputtering. He took hold of his rabbit-covered drumstick and with its aid released a hymn of joy from his drum.

'I have seen her before!' he told the Shaman eagerly when the Shaman caught up with him. 'I know her very well!'

The Shaman thought it very likely, but not that it necessarily boded well, for his apprentice was well on the way to overtaking him and could already drum out the secrets of the spirits.

'Woman, bird, star,' babbled Walser. 'Her name is – '

NINE

Although, from a distance, she could still pass for a blonde, there was a good inch of brown at the roots of Fevvers' hair and brown was showing in her feathers, too, because she was moulting. Lizzie's handbag might have contained peroxide to assist with the one growth and, perhaps, a bottle of red ink to aid the other – elementary household magic! – but the handbag was gone, irretrievably lost in the wreck of the train, and, every day, the tropic bird looked more and more like the London sparrow as which it had started out in life, as if a spell were unravelling. Fevvers felt glum and irritable when she sneaked a peek at herself in the old man's bit of flyblown mirror with the aid of which Lizzie trimmed his white mane to maestro-length, just brushing his collar.

'There! Doesn't he look a treat!'

His was a simple story. When already in his middle years, he was lured away from a secure post as music instructor of a girl's school in Novgorod by the promises of the corrupt Mayor of R., who pocketed a fat sum from the government for his project of a Transbaikalian Conservatory. What? asked the musician cautiously; teach the bears their scales and sol-fa to the ravens and the golden-eyes? No, no, no! the Mayor assured him, pouring more vodka. The little daughters of the fur-traders, the government officials, the station masters, wheeltappers and platelayers will flock to the conservatory, and, besides, what untold talent might not be discovered amongst the children of the native Siberian peasants themselves? The vodka helped him paint irresistible pictures of the untapped musical talent of the region. In front of the warm stove in faraway Novgorod, the Maestro's idealism was fired.

But the Maestro did not have the experience to know he was not the stuff of which pioneers are made, nor did he realise that the Mayor, as soon as he'd made his ill-gotten gains, would forget him completely. Lacking so much as the fare home, the Maestro was soon destitute in the house, miles out of town, assigned him for his musical academy, with only his piano, his top-hat and his shingle to remind him of who he once had been. He was deeply sunk in despair when, like a miracle, they came.

'It's as though he's found his long-lost daughter,' said Lizzie. 'As at the end of one of Shakespeare's late comedies. Only he's found *two* daughters. A happy ending, squared. Hark at 'em.'

The Maestro and the Princess were trying four hands in harmony, whilst Mignon, brow furrowed, studied the elements of counterpoint. Under the Maestro's eager tuition, she was showing an unusual flair for composition.

Fevvers, watching the fish boil, grunted she was glad *somebody* was happy. Her fractured wing, broken again in her last attempt to fly, was now strapped securely up with the Maestro's fishing-lines, and Lizzie firmly prescribed, for the moment, rest, nourishment and more rest. She was utterly indifferent to her foster-daughter's protestations that they must set off forthwith to rescue the young American from the clutches of the tribespeople.

'He looked as though he'd made himself at home. Gone native in his garments, I noticed.'

'But it's not a week since we all parted company! You can't go native in a *week*!'

'I don't know if it *is* only a week since we lost him,' said Lizzie. 'Did you see the long beard he had?'

'I saw his beard,' assented Fevvers uncertainly. 'What do you mean, you don't know if it *is* only a week . . .'

Lizzie turned on the other woman a face solemn enough to have impressed even the Shaman.

'Something's going on. Something we *wot not of*, my dear. Remember we have lost our clock; remember Father Time has many children and I think it was his bastard offspring inherited this region for, by the length of Mr Walser's beard and the skill with which he rode his reindeer, time has passed – or else is passing – marvellous swiftly for these woodland folk.

'Perhaps,' she mused, 'their time is running out.'

Fevvers was not impressed by these speculations. She spooned fish broth, tasted, grimaced, poked in the Maestro's cupboard and found no salt. The last straw. Lots of grub, but nothing fit to eat. Had she not been so proud, she would have broken down.

Her misery was exacerbated by the knowledge that the young American to whom she'd taken such a fancy was so near to her and yet so far away. Exacerbated, but not caused. Her gloom had other causes.

Did the speed with which she was losing her looks dismay her? Was it that? She was ashamed to admit it; all the same, she felt as though her heart was breaking when she looked in the mirror and saw her brilliant colours withering away. But there was more to it than that. She knew she had truly mislaid some vital something of herself along the road that brought her to this place. When she lost her weapon to the Grand Duke in his frozen palace, she had lost some of that sense of her own magnificence which had previously sustained her trajectory. As soon as her feeling of invulnerability was gone, what happened? Why, she broke her wing. Now she was a crippled wonder. Put on as brave a face as she might, that was the long and short of it.

The Cockney Venus! she thought bitterly. Now she looks more like one of the ruins that Cromwell knocked about a bit. Helen, formerly of the High-wire, now permanently grounded. Pity the New Woman if she turns out to be as easily demolished as me.

Day by day she felt herself diminishing, as if the Grand Duke had ordered up another sculpture of ice and now, as his exquisite revenge on her flight, was engaged in melting it very, very slowly, perhaps by the judicious application of lighted cigarette ends. The young American it was who kept the whole story of the old Fevvers in his notebooks; she longed for him to tell her she was true. She longed to see herself reflected in all her remembered splendour in his grey eyes. She longed; she yearned. To no avail. Time passed. She rested.

The Colonel's hands were shaking because the liquor was all gone and he was on his last box of cigars but he was in exalted mood because he had found a captive audience in the Escapee, who gazed at him with the beginnings of a wild surmise.

'These minor setbacks are but sent to try us, young man. I conceived the amazing feat – tuskers across the tundra! and, yes, I failed. Very well. Failure. I failed *prodigiously*. Have you ever stared stark failure in the face, young man? The trick is, to *outstare* it! Failure is the hazard of every great enterprise. That's the way the dice fall in the Ludic Game; some you win, some you lose, and to lose as I have done, to lose with such magnificence, such enormity, to lose every single little last thing, every bit, bob and button . . . yessir! that, in itself, is a kind of triumph.'

He rose up on his hind legs and flourished the stub of his last cigar.

'Transbaikalia be warned! I shall return! Out of the ashes of my enterprise I shall arise renewed! Colonel Kearney throws down his challenge to the icy wastes, the bears, the shooting stars – he will return again, with more and bigger elephants; larger and more ferocious tigers; an en-tire army of infinitely more hilarious clowns! Yes! The Old Glory will wave once again across the tundra!

'Colonel Kearney, the once and future impresario! Colonel Kearney salutes the New Age! Look out, Twentieth Century, here I come!'

Outside, under a sky the colour and texture of an army blanket, wild beasts, hunters, midwives, merchants, fur-traders and birds of prey went about their business in ignorance of the Colonel's challenge. Had they heard it, they would not have understood it; had they understood it, they would have mocked. Samson let in the ironic silence of the night when he brought an armful of logs from the woodpile but the Colonel, whose pale eyes grew ever more prominent as fresh bursts of excitement gripped him, chased the night right out again.

'Young man, make the acquaintance of ma *hawg*.'

Sybil thought of apple sauce every time she looked at the Escapee and attempted to withhold her trotter but the Colonel gave her a sharp blow at the back of the neck so she let him shake it.

'Sybil, the mystic pig, my partner in the Ludic Game. Yessir, we're old hands, Sybil and me. Years ago, years, down on my daddy's farm in Lexington, Kentucky – you ever heard tell of Kentucky, the "Blue Grass State"? God's own country, my boy; yessir, God's own country . . . down on my daddy's farm, I was jest a kid, then, knee-high to a ham hock when I first made the acquaintance, present company excepted, of the grandest little lady that ever drank pigswill . . .'

The Escapee was struck dumb by the Colonel's eloquence. He had never met anybody like the Colonel. Although the Colonel looked nothing like a siren, the song he sang was just as sweet as theirs. By the time the fish was cooked and eaten, the Escapee agreed to conduct the Colonel as far as the railhead at R. and thence:

'If necessary, I'll ride mah hawg!'

by whatever means were available to wherever the newspaper might be alerted to the stunning fate of Colonel Kearney's Circus and credit could be obtained to start the whole thing up again.

The resilience of the little fat Colonel! He was like one of those round-bottomed dolls that you cannot knock over, no matter how hard you push. With what missionary zeal did he confront the Escapee's puzzled virtue! The Escapee, who believed in man's inborn innocence and innate goodwill, had no defences whatsoever against the Colonel because, of course, the Colonel believed in both those self-same things, although the Colonel had quite a different angle on them.

'And this little lady, here, her great-grandma, the first of that long line of patriotic pigs, she stood up on her hind legs and taught me a lesson I never learned in school. And, young fellow-me-lad, that lesson was: "Never give a sucker an even break!"

'Ho, ho ho!' he chortled, having speedily assessed the Escapee as a sucker. His little eyes roved restlessly round the ascetic cabin, which the geometry of the music rapidly transformed into a high, white palace of transcendental thought. He did not like the look of it at all. He knew that Mozart had died penniless, on straw.

'Bamboozle 'em!' he confided to the Escapee, whose life, hitherto, had been dedicated to the project of the perfecting of mankind, whether it willed it or no. The Escapee took a little while to work out 'bamboozlem' and then blamed his poor English for failing to grasp what the Colonel meant, for that, surely, couldn't be what he'd said! But the Colonel chuckled when he looked at the fresh-faced, bright-eyed Escapee and thought: if the boy proved a useful recruit to the great project of the Ludic Game, he would give him the name, Bamboozlem, to use in America. He asked Sybil as to how he might best employ the Escapee when they returned to Civilisation. She cocked her head and pondered. The oracle delivered thus:

'B-U-S-I-N-E-S-S M-A-N-A-G-E-R.'

For a pure heart becomes a cashbox best. The Escapee contemplated the prospect of a new life in the New World. It exhilarated him immensely. He wanted to be up and off at once but then it turned out that Mignon and the Princess would not budge. Not one inch! When the Colonel tried to persuade them to return with him to the bright lights, they shook their heads. The Maestro, who showed every sign of soon expiring out of pure joy at having inadvertently founded that Musical Academy of Transbaikalia of which he'd given up hope, clasped its unique pupils to his breast. Through the measureless wilderness around them roamed the savage audience for which the women must make a music never before heard on earth although it was not the music of the spheres but of blood, of flesh, of sinew, of the heart.

This music, proclaimed Mignon, they had been born to make. Had been brought together, here, as women and as lovers, solely to make — music that was at the same time a taming and a not-taming; music that sealed the pact of tranquillity between humankind and their wild brethren, their wild sistren, yet left them free.

Mignon delivered her speech with such vigour and force all were moved.

'Can this truly be the same ragged child who came to me for charity those few short weeks ago?' pondered Fevvers. 'Love, true love has utterly transformed her.' When she thought how it was the presence of the other that made Mignon so beautiful, little tears pricked the backs of her eyes for she, Fevvers, was growing uglier every day.

The Colonel hummed and hawed but did not press. Their act was progressing along lines in which he saw small profit. 'Pearls before swine,' he would have said, had he not such a great regard for Sybil.

What of the Strong Man? The Colonel, remembering his feats, tempted him with fame and money, reminded him that all he could expect from these women, here, was friendship. Samson cleared his throat and moved from foot to foot in an embarrassed fashion before he spoke up.

'All my life I have been strong and simple and – a coward, concealing the frailty of my spirit behind the strength of my body. I abused women and spoke ill of them, thinking myself superior to the entire sex on account of my muscle, although in reality I was too weak to bear the burden of any woman's love. I am not vain enough to think that, one day, either Mignon or the Princess might learn to love me as a man; perhaps, some day, they will cherish me as a brother. This hope casts out fear from my heart and I will learn to live among the tigers. I grow stronger in spirit the more I serve.'

The Princess and Mignon reached out to shake his hands when he'd finished his little speech but a look of faint embarrassment crossed his face and he ducked outside, again, for more wood.

'"Out of the strong comes forth sweetness," as it says on the Golden Syrup tins,' said Lizzie. 'Samson turns up trumps. Well, I never.'

Fevvers was kicking the fishbones on the floor the while, looking mutinous. In reply to the Colonel's unspoken query, she announced in a raucous, angry voice:

'As for me, I'm going in the opposite direction to you, you rotten bastard; I'm going to look for the young American you lured into the circus and now propose to abandon to his fate amongst the heathen!'

The Colonel ground out that last stub of the last cigar on the sole of his shoe, cast a look of infinite regret at the shredded remains and, for want of a fresh cigar, rolled a strip of manuscript paper into a tube and chewed on that. He eyed his former star askance. The Feathered Frump.

Freed from the confines of her corset, her once-startling shape sagged, as if the sand were seeping out of the hour-glass and *that* was why time, in these parts, could not control itself. She lacked the heart to wash her face and so there were still curds of rouge lodged in her pores and she was breaking out in spots and rashes. She had screwed up her mostly mousy hair on top of her head all anyhow and pinned it securely in place with the backbone of a carp. Since she had stopped bothering to hide her wings, the others had grown so accustomed to the sight it no longer seemed remarkable. Besides, one wing had lost all its glamorous colours and the other was bandaged and useless. How long would it be before she flew again? Where was that silent demand to be *looked* at that had once made her stand out? Vanished; and, under the circumstances, it was a good thing she'd lost it – these days, she would do better to plead to be ignored. She was so shabby that she looked like a fraud and, so it seemed to the Colonel, a cheap fraud. Nevertheless, he gleefully exclaimed:

'Breaking your contract?'

Fevvers' head snapped up.

'Wot, no cash?'

'No cash,' stated the Colonel with spiteful joy. 'And, according to the small print, if you break your contract now, before we get to Yokohama, let alone Seattle, you forfeit the en-tire sum due for your performances in Petersburg.

'Ho, ho, ho!' he boomed, his spirits quite restored. He removed a string of flags from Sybil's ear, ignoring the pig's eyes, which reproached him for sharp practice.

'You've got to get up early in the mornin' to put one over on Colonel Kearney!' he cried, waving his streamers.

'You'll hear from my solicitors!' said Fevvers with a pathetic attempt at defiance.

'Send me the writ by *elk*.'

Upon this friendly exchange, the Colonel set off towards the railway with his guide bouncing enthusiastically ahead of him. Lizzie went as far as the gate to despatch them with as much bad feeling as she could muster. Her eyes spoke volumes but she was mute with fury because she could no longer avenge herself with anything concrete, such as piles or athlete's foot. Fevvers might have mislaid her magnificence along the road from London but Lizzie had fared much worse – she'd lost her knack of wreaking small-scale, domestic havoc; she'd kept it (where else?) in her handbag.

She consoled herself; she would not have needed to inflict baldness on the Colonel, because he was bald already.

She felt no malice towards Sybil, however, and was touched to see how the little pig hid her face behind her ears, embarrassed by her protector, snuffling with displeasure, tempted to jump right out of his arms and throw in her lot with those whom the Colonel left behind. But Sybil knew which side her bed was buttered and, disgruntled as she might be, she thought it best to stay with the Colonel, who always knew where the best butter might be obtained. The Colonel advertised his already buoyant spirits with a rendition of 'Yankee-doodle-dandy', and the Escapee added his heavy accent to the chorus, hesitantly at first, then with more and more conviction.

'There's a little soldier lost to free enterprise,' grieved Lizzie. Then shouted back to Fevvers, inside the house: 'See what a fine mess you've got us into now!'

TEN

The two women, heavily furred, committed themselves to the land-scape. Soon they lost sight of the Maestro's house and then they were quite alone.

'Don't you remember what a motley crew we were when we first set out from England?' said Lizzie, formal as if addressing a public meeting, so that Fevvers tensed in the expectation of a reprimand that had, as yet, been delayed.

'A motley crew, indeed – a gaggle of strangers drawn from many diverse countries. Why, you might have said we constituted a micro-cosm of humanity, that we were an emblematic company, each signifying a different proposition in the great syllogism of life. The hazards of the journey reduced us to a little band of pilgrims abandoned in the wilderness upon whom the wilderness acted like a moral magnifying glass, exaggerating the blemishes of some and bringing out the finer points in those whom we thought had none. Those of us who learned the lessons of experience have ended their journeys already. Some who'll never learn are tumbling back to civilisation as fast as they can as blissfully unenlightened as they ever were. But, as for you, Sophie, you seem to have adopted the motto: to travel hopefully is better than to arrive.'

'How?' asked Fevvers, carefully, 'have you reached this conclusion?'

'It's a fool's errand, Sophie. From that fleeting glimpse we caught of your fancy boy mounted on a reindeer and wearing a frock, it would seem he is not the man he was. Nothing left, Sophia! Nothing there . . . But it's me who is the bigger fool than you, because at least you're going off after him of your own free will while I tag along behind you through the middle of nowhere only because of the bonds of old affection.

'I am,' she added sourly, 'the slave of your freedom.'

Fevvers had listened to all this in increasingly angry silence and now burst forth.

'I never asked you to adopt me in the first place, you miserable old witch! There I was, unique and parentless, unshackled, unfettered by the past, and the minute you clapped eyes on me you turned *me* into a contingent being, enslaved me as your daughter who was born nobody's daughter – '

But there she stopped short, for the notion that nobody's daughter walked across nowhere in the direction of nothing produced in her such vertigo she was forced to pause and take a few deep breaths, which coldly seared her lungs. Seized with such anguish of the void that surrounds us, she could have wept and only restrained herself from doing so because of the satisfaction tears would give her foster-mother.

'There, there,' said Lizzie more gently, noting the girl's distress from the corner of her eye. 'I don't begrudge you my company, my darling. We must all make do with what rags of love we find flapping on the scarecrow of humanity.'

But this notion filled Fevvers with further gloom. She wanted more from life than that! Besides, she felt like a scarecrow herself, at the moment. She hunched up her shoulders miserably.

'But, oh, my dear,' Lzzie went on, oblivious of Fevvers' cavernous silence. 'Love is one thing and fancy another. Haven't you noticed here is bad feeling come between us since Mr Walser made his appearance? Misfortune has dogged our steps since you first set eyes on him. You're half the girl you were – look at you! Lost your weapon in the Grand Duke's house. Then you broke your pinion. Accidents? Too many accidents in a row to be altogether accidental. Every little accident has taken you one step down the road away from singularity. You're fading away, as if it was only always nothing but the discipline of the audience that kept you in trim. You're hardly even a blonde any more.

'And, when you *do* find the young American, what the 'ell will you do, then? Don't you know the customary endings of the old comedies of separated lovers, misfortune overcome, adventures among outlaws and savage tribes? True lovers' reunions always end in a marriage.'

Fevvers came to a halt.

'What?' she said.

'Orlando takes his Rosalind. She says: "To you I give myself, for I am yours." And that,' she added, a low thrust, 'goes for a girl's bank account, too.'

'But it is not possible that I should give myself,' said Fevvers. Her diction was exceedingly precise. 'My being, my me-ness, is unique and indivisible. To sell the use of myself for the enjoyment of another is one thing; I might even offer freely, out of gratitude or in the expectation of pleasure – and pleasure alone is my expectation from the young American. But the essence of myself may not be given or taken, or what would there be left of me?'

'Precisely,' said Lizzie, with mournful satisfaction.

'Besides,' added Fevvers urgently, 'here we are far away from churches and priests, who'll speak of marriage – '

'Oh, I daresay you'll find these woodsmen amongst whom your young man has found refuge uphold the institution of marriage as enthusiastically as other men do, although they may celebrate it differently. The harder the bargain men must strike with nature to survive, the more rules they're likely to have amongst themselves to keep them all in order. They'll have churches, here; and vicars, too, even if the vicars have weird cassocks and perform outrageous sacraments.'

'I'll snatch him away. We'll elope!'

'What if he doesn't want to come?'

'You're jealous!'

'I never thought,' said Lizzie stiffly, 'I'd live to hear my girl say such a thing.'

Ashamed, Fevvers strode more slowly. She turned Lizzie's words over and over in her mind.

'Marriage!' she exclaimed.

'The Prince who rescues the Princess from the dragon's lair is always forced to marry her, whether they've taken a liking to one another or not. That's the custom. And I don't doubt that custom will apply to the trapeze artiste who rescues the clown. The name of this custom is a "happy ending".'

'Marriage,' repeated Fevvers, in a murmur of awed distaste. But, after a moment, she perked up.

'Oh, but Liz – think of his malleable look. As if a girl could mould him any way she wanted. Surely he'll have the decency to give himself to me, when we meet again, not expect the vice versa! Let him hand himself over into my safekeeping, and I will transform him. You said yourself he was unhatched, Lizzie; very well – I'll *sit* on him, I'll hatch him out, I'll make a new man of him. I'll make him into the New Man, in fact, fitting mate for the New Woman, and onward we'll march hand in hand into the New Century – '

Lizzie detected a note of rising hysteria in the girl's voice.

'Perhaps so, perhaps not,' she said, putting a damper on things. 'Perhaps safer not to plan ahead.'

Fevvers thought her foster-mother's conversation was as dour as the empty landscape around them. She whistled, to keep her spirits up: 'The Ride of the Valkyries'. Something pathetic about her little whistle piping away in the middle of Siberia, but she persevered. After a short pause, Lizzie took another tack.

'However, I will say this for you; unless you propose to sell your story to the newspaper, my dear, and steal a march on Colonel Kearney —'

— Fevvers, hoping to change the subject, stopped whistling to interject:

' — whom, Liz, we could pillory in the press for his business practice and his treatment of employees —'

'Unless you plan to sell yourself in print, I can't see any profit in all this, try as I might. And perhaps it is a sign of moral growth in you, my girl —'

Fevvers began whistling again, but Lizzie pressed on :

' — that you pursue this fellow only for his body, not for what he'll pay you. Inconvenient as your acute attack of morality might prove in the long term, should it become chronic, as far as the financing of the struggle is concerned.'

'Have you finished? Have you quite finished? Why d'you come with me, if all you can do is carp?'

'You don't know the first thing about the human heart,' said Liz dolefully. 'The heart is a treacherous organ and you're nothing if not impetuous. I fear for you, Sophie. Selling yourself is one thing and giving yourself away is quite another but, oh, Sophie! what if you rashly *throw yourself* away? Then what happens to that unique "me-ness" of yours? On the scrap-heap, that's what happens to it! I raised you up to fly to the heavens, not to brood over a clutch of eggs!'

'Eggs? What have eggs got to do with it?'

And they would have immediately started to quarrel again, if, just at that moment, they had not seen, first sign of humanity for miles, a frail little shelter built of branches propped against a pine of grandfatherly dimensions. At first, you might not have noticed the shelter, for there were no doors, no windows nor apertures of any kind in it, so that it looked more like a wood-pile than a primitive hut, but, in the wilderness, a wood-pile was as out of place as an ocean-going yacht and, besides, as they drew nearer, they heard from within some muffled groans and sobs.

Liz motioned to Fevvers to remain behind, for the little woman was lighter on her feet by far than the heavy-treading *aerialiste*, and crept up to the shelter softly enough to surprise whatever lurked within. But the woman who lay there on a pile of filthy straw was in no condition to be surprised.

Removing a log, Lizzie peered in at her. It was the grey light of the end of the short day, outside, and there was no light or fire inside, so Lizzie made haste to find matches she'd stolen from the Maestro. By the little light, she saw the prone woman, in spite of the bitter chill of the approaching night, wore nothing but an old, fringed, buckskin dress, which had been slit up the middle to expose her still-bulging belly. Perhaps she had thrown off the bedclothes, for she seemed feverish, even delirious; at any rate, no bedclothes covered her, although there were a few cured skins lying here and there. A crude wooden container beside her proved itself to be a cradle when the baby inside it woke up and began to cry.

Lizzie carefully removed a couple more logs and stepped through the hole. She found a stub of candle in her bag and lit that. At first she thought the baby, with its rosy cheeks, looked very healthy; then, when she picked it up to soothe it, she saw that what disguised its waxen look was blood, smeared on like rouge, an old practice of the tribe. The mother opened her eyes. If she thought a bear had invaded the privacy of her postpartural ritual, she took it in her stride. Another bear dismantled yet more of the wall of her shelter and lumbered in. The mother's expression did not change. Lizzie felt her forehead with the back of her hand. It was very hot.

'Tuck her up,' said Liz to Fevvers, taking charge of the baby.

'What the 'ell is going on?' demanded Fevvers as she did as she was bid.

'I'm sure I don't know,' said Lizzie. 'Unless this tableau of a woman in bondage to her reproductive system, a woman tied hand and foot to that Nature which your physiology denies, Sophie, has been set here on purpose to make you think twice about turning from a freak into a woman.'

Lizzie held the baby to the young mother's breast but either the young mother's milk had not yet come or she had none, for the baby grasped the nipple in its mouth and sucked furiously, then, with a sharp cry of disappointment, let go, and, face crumpling, began to bellow and shake its fists. At that, the mother wept as much as her exhaustion and fever permitted her. Fevvers rubbed the cold hands in her warm ones while Lizzie tucked the baby snugly inside her fur.

'I'm not leaving this little babe out here and that's flat,' she announced. 'Poor little scrap'll catch its death as well as starve.'

'You always was partial to a foundling,' said Fevvers with an acid edge but also with renewed affection. 'What about its poor old mum, though? Ain't she a foundling, too?'

'You can manage her, ducks.'

'She's not much of a weight,' acknowledged Fevvers, heaving. The woman came to herself, briefly, and smiled. If she had realised Fevvers was not a bear but a woman, she would have complained bitterly because the taboos surrounding childbirth had been broken. As it was, she let herself be carried off with a good grace to, as she thought, the land of the dead. She was pleased to hear the babble of little cries as her baby set off in the same direction.

They kicked aside the walls of the shelter, the easiest way of returning to the open air. As Fevvers stepped over the scattered branches with the well-wrapped young mother in her arms, she glimpsed something in the disturbed snow that made her cry out.

'Oh, Liz!'

A miracle of frail violets, frost-nipped and pale, the colour of tired eyelids, yet big with perfume and optimism, were in full bloom among the sheltered roots of the big pine. Violets!

'Violets,' said Lizzie, 'on New Year's Eve.'

'Look at 'em, the little darlings,' bubbled Fevvers. 'Like a message from little Violetta, to say we're not forgotten. Here, did you say it's New Year's Eve?'

Liz nodded. 'I've been keeping count. By *my* count, it's New Year's Eve; we're on the cusp, my dear, tomorrow is another time-scheme.'

Fevvers hoisted the young mother over her shoulder and stooped but Liz adjured:

'Don't pick 'em, leave 'em to seed theirselves. Snow violets. Must be rare as rare.'

Beneath her apparent indifference, she, too, was moved, and the two women smiled at one another, knowing a truce, or even peace, had been declared again.

'I spy.' And Lizzie pointed. There was a footprint in the snow beside the violets; they had not been the first to stop and admire them. Print of a soft-soled boot. One footprint only, like Man Friday's, just as mysterious, just as ominous.

'Over there!' Fevvers turned to point. A rag of red ribbon was caught on the twig of a tree. The magic midwife took care to hide the tracks she made when she came to tend her hidden patient; but not sufficient care. Had not the bears come and kidnapped mother and child? A few yards beyond the red ribbon they came across a little tin bell lying at the side of a dissolving track of beaten snow. Now they were on the high road to somewhere, and strode along in better spirits than they'd known for days.

Soon they saw before them lights, faintly gleaming through thick windows paned with horn, and the roof of long, low, wooden houses, and smoke rising from chimneys, and a rich, strange smell of unfamiliar suppers cooking on unfamiliar hearths, and it was evening.

Fevvers' heart, already stirred by the surprise of the violets, warmed still further at these homely sights and odours. A village! Homes! The signs of the human hand keeping the wilderness at bay! Life seemed to her to have been held in suspension during their wanderings in the solitude; now the solitude existed no longer and things were about to pick up again. She might even find bleach or dye in this village, might she not, and start to put herself back together again.

And surely he was here; one of the wooden houses must shelter the young American. And she would see, once again, the wonder in the eyes of the beloved and become whole. Already she felt more blonde.

'Think of him, not as a lover, but as a scribe, as an amanuensis,' she said to Lizzie. 'And not of my trajectory, alone, but of yours, too, Lizzie; of your long history of exile and cunning which you've scarcely hinted to him, which will fill up ten times more of his notebooks than *my* story ever did. Think of him as the amanuensis of all those whose tales we've yet to tell him, the histories of those woman who would otherwise go down nameless and forgotten, erased from history as if they had never been, so that he, too, will put his poor shoulder to the wheel and help to give the world a little turn into the new era that begins tomorrow.

'And once the old world has turned on its axle so that the new dawn can dawn, then, ah, then! all the women will have wings, the same as I. This young woman in my arms, whom we found tied hand and foot with the grisly bonds of ritual, will suffer no more of it; she will tear off her mind forg'd manacles, will rise up and fly away. The dolls' house doors will open, the brothels will spill forth their prisoners, the cages, gilded or otherwise, all over the world, in every land, will let forth their inmates singing together the dawn chorus of the new, the transformed – '

'It's going to be more complicated than that,' interpolated Lizzie. 'This old witch sees storms ahead, my girl. When I look to the future, I see through a glass, darkly. You improve your analysis, girl, and *then* we'll discuss it.'

But her daughter swept on, regardless, as if intoxicated with vision.

'On that bright day, when I am no more a singular being but, warts and all the female paradigm, no longer an imagined fiction but a plain fact – then he will slap down his notebooks, bear witness to me and my prophetic role. Think of him, Lizzie, as one who carries the evidence –'

'Cushie-cushie-coo,' said Lizzie to the restless baby.

There were no streets or squares or alleys in this village; the houses were set sometimes close to, sometimes far apart, as if the arrangement had been copied from the random way cows lie down in fields. No sign of any inhabitants, all indoors at this hour, but a reindeer or two raised its antlered head to peer at the newcomers, then settled back to scratching for moss. Bells and ribbons were attached to a larch tree outside the longest, lowest, somehow most official-looking building in the village, giving it a festive air. Lizzie knocked on the door, noting how the frame was decorated with more red ribbons, feathers and (h'm) bones. When she knocked, came a muffled growl from inside, a flurry and a thump and a man's voice raised in an unfamiliar tongue.

'Does that mean "come in"?'

Fevvers shrugged.

'Open up. I'm perishing.'

They pushed the creaking door. No sign of life, inside, as far as could be seen – which wasn't much, for the draughty interior was lit only fitfully by a primitive lamp consisting of a tinware-saucer filled with melted beargrease in which the wick floated in imminent danger of shipwreck. This lamp hung by cords from the cross-beam and moved in the draughts, so that the shadows came and went with eerie unpredictability, offering unprepossessing glimpses of strange-shaped, oddly coloured objects against the walls and in the corners, hinting at lumpish, silent occupants crouched hither and thither, but covering up everything with darkness again almost immediately.

Below the lamp stood a long table marked with one or two odd-looking stains, on which lay a big wooden platter, hollowed out not with a chisel but by the application of fire, and a stone knife of antique shape but very finely honed as to the blade. Spattered on the beaten earth floor around the table were traces of old blood, of fur and of feathers, trodden into the ground by, presumably, the feet of priests and worshippers. The smell was hideous, as of incense mingled with death, and it was very cold.

'What did I tell you?' said Lizzie. 'One of their churches. Typical church atmosphere.'

Something – the wind in the rafters; a rat; a concealed priest – rustled when she spoke. And the place was so ill-lit the entire population of the village might have been concealed in the thick, haunted dark. There was a nightmarish sense of claustrophobia about the place, that was yet tense with expectancy, as if something hideous had been prevented from happening by their arrival, but the actors in the interrupted rite were patient, and could wait, were waiting and seeing what these beings who'd brought the mother and child back to the village were up to. Custom-built for holy, arcane, archaic practices, for revelations, for consultations with the dead, for sacrifices, the wild church was intended to impress, and was impressive.

But Lizzie and Fevvers owed their capacity for survival to a refusal to be impressed by their surroundings. Fevvers gently laid the young mother down on the table with a relieved grunt and stretched her weary arms. The young mother opened her eyes and took note of her surroundings. The god-hut of her native village! And why had the baby stopped crying? She found she felt a little less unwell and started to gather her strength in order to get up and investigate the preparations for her own funeral she was sure were under way.

'Look out!' hissed Lizzie.

There was a *man* in the corner.

No; not a man. The women breathed again. There in the corner, now lit, now dark again according to the swaying of the lamp, stood a wooden image, somewhat larger than the little life-size of the woodsmen, wrapped in furs, shawls and girdles, and there was one white shirt on him the front of which was stiff with dried egg-liquor. Fevvers' heart went pit-a-pat when she saw that. The idol's head bore several three-pointed caps made of black, blue and red cloth but it was hard to see much of its face because of the furs, shawls and bits of lace and tin and ribbon that covered it. Its maw appeared to be ravening, however, and its eyes, made of discs of beaten tin, flashed when visited by the wavering flame of the lamp.

The idol spoke.

'Whence cometh thou? Whither goeth thou?'

The startled baby bawled to hear the idol speak in good American. The young mother leapt from the table – *that* yell was never posthumous! – and grappled with Lizzie for possession of the baby, adding her own shrieks to the din. Lizzie delivered up the baby so she could catch hold of a growling something as it came out from under the table where the Shaman had kicked it when the sacrifice was interrupted before it began. The bear, affronted, cuffed Lizzie about the head and they scuffled together, knocking over the table as they did so. The dish and knife fell clattering to the floor. They banged against the idol in their wrestling. The idol toppled against another one, similarly clad, with more of a stag-like look. Toppling in its turn, the staggy deity knocked the next in line of the row of idols from its perch and so on, in a domino effect of comprehensive desecration. A number of skulls rolled round the floor, released from their stash under the ursine idol. It was not at first apparent these were the skulls of bears. The disturbed lamp swished back and forth, faster and faster, splashing hot grease over everything. Fevvers kept her head sufficiently to dance backwards from the mêlée, singing out:

'Come out, come out, wherever you are!'

The lamp dipped and swung with such energy the lit wick flew off, hit the wall and was extinguished, leaving the god-hut black as pitch, in which unseen presences made themselves felt with a vengeance, pinching, punching, sometimes made of fur, sometimes of leather, emitting weird screeches and jingle-jangling away their little bells; had the women been attacked by the ghosts of a team of morris dancers? Fevvers wrestled with an invisible until she smelt flesh and bit hard. She bit bone and tasted blood. It was alive. There was an ugly but unmistakably human squawk. She made a grab; another squawk, as she ascertained she wrestled with a male.

Once Lizzie got an arm-lock on the bear, she located the dropped stone knife with her foot and kept her foot firmly down on it, in spite of the blows with which some leathery, gibbering, tinkling thing belaboured her. Fevvers did not let go of the hand between her teeth as she tumbled the rest of the faceless anatomy to the ground, where she plumped herself down on his chest, breathing heavily. It shouted in a language that sounded not as if spoken but as if knitted on steel needles. It must have asked for some light on the business, for, a moment later, came an odd cadaverous glow from somewhere in a corner, accompanied by a peculiar smell.

The fuss died down, as if the light calmed them; a last whimper from the baby, a snuffle from the bear and, in the ensuing hush, Fevvers saw whom she straddled.

Walser wore his ceremonial dress and a triangular cap with a fur trim and a piece of tin cut in the shape of a dollar sign at the front. He was a little thinner in the face. To a European eye, the pale gold beard, which now reached half-way down his chest, ill-matched his leather petticoats and he could have done with soap and water; he stank. And that was not the half of it, for there was a vatic glare in his grey eyes, his eyes of a glossy brilliance, his eyes with the pin-point pupils. A vatic glare and no trace of scepticism at all. Furthermore, they seemed to have lost their power to reflect.

Fevvers felt the hairs on her nape rise when she saw that he was looking at her as if, horror of horrors, she was perfectly natural — natural, but abominable. He fixed her with his phosphorescent eye and, after a moment, his voice rose in song:

'Only a bird in a gilded cage — '

'Oh, my *Gawd*!' said Fevvers. For he had translated the familiar tune into some kind of chant, some kind of dirge, some kind of Siberian invocation of the spectral inhabitants of the other world which co-exists with this one, and Fevvers knew in her bones his song was meant to do her harm.

The Shaman identified her fur, her hair, her broken wing and was a little consoled to see how quickly she was fading. He eyed the young mother and her baby assessingly; did the bear-spirits intend them as a substitute for the cub? It would seem so. The smaller one still stood firmly on the sacrificial knife, however. Perhaps they intended to do the job themselves. The thing to do, obviously, was to assist the bear-spirits to fade away as quickly as possible, before they stretched mother and baby out on the altar, again. He snatched up his drum, which was propped against the wall, and banged away at an exorcism with the energy of the desperate. Walser's voice swooped and quavered with a sound, to Fevvers, like the very essence of madness.

Fevvers felt that shivering sensation which always visited her when mages, wizards, impresarios came to take away her singularity as though it were their own invention, as though they believed she depended on their imaginations in order to be herself. She felt herself turning, willy-nilly, from a woman into an idea. The Shaman re-doubled the vigour of his drumming and began to sing a song with strange yippings and yowlings in it. From an unseen censer, a purple, disorienting incense filled the god-hut, so the Shaman seemed to multiply himself until there were dozens of him, banging dozens of drums in the same appeal to this thing that was and was not Fevvers. In Walser's eyes, she saw herself, at last, swimming into definition, like the image on photographic paper; but, instead of Fevvers, she saw two perfect miniatures of a dream.

She felt her outlines waver; she felt herself trapped forever in the reflection in Walser's eyes. For one moment, just one moment, Fevvers suffered the worst crisis of her life: 'Am I fact? Or am I fiction? Am I what I know I am? Or am I what he thinks I am?'

'Show 'em your feathers, quick!' urged Lizzie.

Fevvers, with a strange sense of desperation, a miserable awareness of her broken wing and her discoloured plumage, could think of nothing else to do but to obey. She shrugged off her furs and, though she could not spread two wings, she spread one – lopsided angel, partial and shabby splendour! No Venus, or Helen, or Angel of the Apocalypse, not Izrael or Isfahel . . . only a poor freak down on her luck, and an object of the most dubious kind of reality to her beholders, since both the men in the god-hut were accustomed to hallucinations and she who looks like a hallucination but is not had no place in their view of things.

The door creaked, and creaked again, and Fevvers knew, without turning round, that some of Walser's new friends had arrived to see what the fuss was about. All manner of yellow faces now showed up at the door, looking like risen moons in the light of the lamps they carried. She felt their eyes on her back and tentatively fluttered the one whole wing at them. She was hesitant, uncertain, at first; but then her plumage – yes! it did! – her plumage rippled in the wind of wonder, their expelled breaths. Oooooooh!

As ever, that wind refreshed her spirits. It blew and blew through the god-hut, blowing away the drugged perfumes and smells of old blood.

She cocked her head to relish the shine of the lamps, like footlights, like stage-lights; it was as good as a stiff brandy, to see those footlights, and, beyond them, the eyes fixed upon her with astonishment, with awe, the eyes that told her who she was.

She would be the blonde of blondes, again, just as soon as she found peroxide; it was as easy as that, and, meanwhile, who cared! And of course her wing would mend – it would mend when the snow melted to reveal the whole taiga covered with violets; and that was when she would soar up on her mended wing above the village, above the forest, above the mountains and the frozen seas, her loved ones in her arms. Home! Yes! she would see Trafalgar Square, again; and

Nelson on his plinth; and Chelsea Bridge as it dissolved into the Thames at twilight . . . and St Paul's, the single Amazon breast of her beloved native city.

Hubris, imagination, desire! The blood sang in her veins. Their eyes restored her soul. She rose up from her kneeling position on Walser's chest. She put on a brilliant, artificial smile, extending her arms as if to enfold all present in a vast embrace. She sank down in a curtsey towards the door, offering herself to the company as if she were a gigantic sheaf of gladioli. Then she sank down in a curtsey towards Walser, now scrambling to his feet with an expression on his face as of the clearing of a haze. And then she saw he was not the man he had been or would ever be again; some other hen had hatched him out. For a moment, she was anxious as to whom this reconstructed Walser might turn out to be.

'What is your name? Have you a soul? Can you love?' he demanded of her in a great, rhapsodic rush as she rose up out of her curtsey. When she heard that, her heart lifted and sang. She batted her lashes at him, beaming, exuberant, newly armed. Now she looked big enough to crack the roof of the god-hut, all wild hair and feathers and triumphant breasts and blue eyes the size of dinner plates.

'That's the way to start the interview!' she cried. 'Get out your pencil and we'll begin!'

ENVOI

'For you must know that Liz just lost a child when she found me and so she took me to her breast and suckled me. And it was, of course, never *religion* that made her such an inconvenient harlot, but her habit of lecturing the clients on the white slave trade, the rights and wrongs of women, universal suffrage, as well as the Irish question, the Indian question, republicanism, anti-clericism, syndicalism and the abolition of the House of Lords. With all of which Nelson was in full sympathy but, as she said, the world won't change overnight and we must eat.

'Those letters we sent home by you in the diplomatic bag were news of the struggle in Russia to comrades in exile, written in invisible ink, so we made most grievous use of you, I'm sorry to say, for if the secret police had found out about it, you'd have been sent to Siberia somewhere we couldn't find you. But Liz *would* do it, having made a promise to a spry little gent with a 'tache she met in the reading-room of the British Museum.

'Furthermore, we played a trick on you with the aid of Nelson's clock the first night we met, in the Alhambra, London; but the clock is gone and I'll play tricks on you no more.

'We told you no other lies nor in any way strayed from the honest truth. Believe it or not, all that I told you as real happenings were so, in fact; and as to questions of whether I am fact or fiction, you must answer that for yourself!'

Without her clothes on, she looked the size of a house. She was engaged in washing herself piece by piece in a pot of water drawn from the samovar while Walser, naked but for his beard, waited on the Shaman's brass bed. He saw, without surprise, she indeed appeared to possess no navel but he was no longer in the mood to draw any definite conclusions from this fact. Her released feathers brushed against the walls; he recalled how nature had equipped her only for the 'woman on top' position and rustled on his straw mattress. He was as much himself again as he ever would be, and yet that 'self' would never be the same again for now he knew the meaning of fear as it defines itself in its most violent form, that is, fear of the death of the beloved, of the loss of the beloved, of the loss of love. It was the beginning of an anxiety that would never end, except with the deaths of either or both; and anxiety is the beginning of conscience, which is the parent of the soul but is not compatible with innocence.

Lizzie might sniff: 'Look at him, Sophie, all for mumbo-jumbo and ladies' dresses now!' But, apart from this shaft, had looked on him almost kindly for, in the light of his grey eyes, her foster-daughter was transformed back into her old self again, without an application of peroxide, even. After a deal of nodding and winking from Fevvers, Lizzie had adjourned with the Shaman, his cousin, her eldest daughter and the new baby, to the cousin's house, in which improvised maternity ward she embarked on the elaboration of an extensive ritual of mother-and-baby care, which, religiously implemented over the next decade, more than made up for the low birth rate by the reduction in perinatal mortality it procured.

The Shaman's cousin, the magic midwife, kept an amulet bag next to the samovar, just as he did. Lizzie cocked an interested eye; might she, perhaps, find herself a new handbag amongst these friendly and intelligent, if somewhat backward and superstitious, folk? The Shaman, entranced by her moustache, addressed her reverently as 'little mother of all the bears'; the bear-cub tagged along behind her like the victim of a teenage crush. Lizzie sternly repressed the temptation to take – just this once, just for the night – a little holiday from rationality and play at being a minor deity.

'Is there some place we can be alone?' Fevvers had suggested, batting her eyelashes in an unequivocal fashion. Walser, whose head was clearing minute by minute, seized her hand and ran her to the Shaman's house but lost the initiative immediately as she pinned him cheerfully to the bed and told him to wait while she freshened up. She seemed to be washing the colour back into her cheeks. She sang as she washed; what else but the 'Habanera' from *Carmen*. Am I biting off more than I can chew? pondered Walser.

He contemplated, as in a mirror, the self he was so busily reconstructing.

'I am Jack Walser, an American citizen. I joined the circus of Colonel Kearney in order to delight my reading public with accounts of a few nights at the circus and, as a clown, performed before the Tsar of All the Russians, to great applause. (What a story!) I was derailed by brigands in Transbaikalia and lived as a wizard among the natives for a while. (God, what a story!) Let me introduce my wife, Mrs Sophie

Walser, who formerly had a successful career on the music-hall stage under the name of –

'Oh!'

Unbeknownst to the lovers, midnight, that moveable feast, rolled over the taiga at that moment, disturbing nothing in its passage in spite of the era it was dragging in its wake. Precipitated in ignorance and bliss into the next century, there, after it was over, Walser took himself apart and put himself together again.

'Jack, ever an adventurous boy, ran away with the circus for the sake of a bottle blonde in whose hands he was putty since the first moment he saw her. He got himself into scrape upon scrape, danced with a tigress, posed as a roast chicken, finally got himself an apprenticeship in the higher form of the confidence trick, initiated by a wily old pederast who bamboozled him completely. All that seemed to happen to me in the third person as though, most of my life, I watched it but did not live it. And now, hatched out of the shell of unknowing by a combination of a blow on the head and a sharp spasm of erotic ecstasy, I shall have to start all over again.'

Smothered in feathers and pleasure as he was, there was still one question teased him.

'Fevvers . . . ' he said. Some sixth sense kept him from calling her Sophie. They were not yet sufficiently intimate.

'Fevvers, only the one question . . . why did you go to such lengths, once upon a time, to convince me you were the "only fully-feathered intacta in the history of the world"?'

She began to laugh.

'I fooled you, then!' she said. 'Gawd, I fooled you!'

She laughed so much the bed shook.

'You mustn't believe what you write in the papers!' she assured him, stuttering and hiccupping with mirth. 'To think I fooled you!'

Her laughter spilled out of the window and made the tin ornaments on the tree outside the god-hut shake and tinkle. She laughed so loud that the baby in the Shaman's cousin's house heard her, waved its little fists in the air and laughed delightedly too. Although he did not understand the joke that convulsed the baby, the Shaman caught the infection and started to giggle. The bear panted sympathetically; he would have laughed if he could have. The Shaman's cousin caught Lizzie's eye and they both doubled up. Even the young mother in her peaceful bed of reindeerskins smiled in her sleep.

Fevvers' laughter seeped through the gaps in the window-frames and cracks in the door-frames of all the houses in the village; the villagers stirred in their beds, chuckling at the enormous joke that invaded their dreams, of which they would remember nothing in the morning except the mirth it caused. She laughed, she laughed, she laughed.

It seemed this laughter of the happy young woman rose up from the wilderness in a spiral and began to twist and shudder across Siberia. It tickled the sleeping sides of the inhabitants of the railhead at R.; it penetrated the counterpoint of the music in the Maestro's house; the members of the republic of free women experienced it as a refreshing breeze. The Colonel and the Escapee, snug in a smoking compartment on the way to Khabarovsk, caught the echoes and found abashed smiles creeping across their faces.

The spiralling tornado of Fevvers' laughter began to twist and shudder across the entire globe, as if a spontaneous response to the giant comedy that endlessly unfolded beneath it, until everything that lived and breathed, everywhere, was laughing. Or so it seemed to the deceived husband, who found himself laughing too, even if he was not quite sure whether or not he might be the butt of the joke. Fevvers, sputtering to a stop at last, crouched above him, covering his face with kisses. Oh, how pleased with him she was!

'To think I really fooled you!' she marvelled. 'It just goes to show there's nothing like confidence.'

VINTAGE

VINTAGE

Also available in Vintage

Angela Carter

BLACK VENUS

'*Black Venus* displays the superbly witchy Angela Carter at
her best'
Sunday Telegraph

'Earthy, bawdy and bizarre in turn, there is a fine intelligence at work here'
Daily Telegraph

'She was one of the century's best writers, and her stories are
among her finest works'
Lucy Hughes-Hallett, *Sunday Times*

'Angela Carter has language at her fingertips'
New Statesman

VINTAGE